Debts of Honor

Maurus Jókai

Translated by Arthur B. Yolland

Esprios.com

WORKS OF MAURUS JÓKAI

HUNGARIAN EDITION

DEBTS OF HONOR

Translated from the Hungarian

By

ARTHUR B. YOLLAND

NEW YORK

DOUBLEDAY, PAGE & COMPANY

1900

by DOUBLEDAY & MCCLURE CO.

TRANSLATOR'S NOTE

In rendering into English this novel of Dr. Jókai's, which many of his countrymen consider his masterpiece, I have been fortunate enough to secure the collaboration of my friend, Mr. Zoltán Dunay, a former colleague, whose excellent knowledge of the English language and literature marked him out as the most competent and desirable collaborator.

ARTHUR B. YOLLAND.

BUDAPEST, 1898.

CONTENTS

CHAPTER
I. The Journal of Desiderius
II. The Girl Substitute
III. My Right Honorable Uncle
IV. The Atheist and the Hypocrite
V. The Wild-Creature's Haunt
VI. Fruits Prematurely Ripe
VII. The Secret Writings
VIII. The End of the Beginning
IX. Aged at Seventeen
X. I and the Demon
XI. "Parole d'Honneur"
XII. A Glance into a Pistol Barrel
XIII. Which Will Convert the Other
XIV. Two Girls
XV. If He Loves, then Let Him Love
XVI. That Ring
XVII. The Yellow-robed Woman in the Cards
XVIII. The Finger-post of Death
XIX. Fanny
XX. The Fatal Day!
XXI. That Letter
XXII. The Unconscious Phantom
XXIII. The Day of Gladness
XXIV. The Mad Jest
XXV. While the Music Sounds
XXVI. The Enchantment of Love
XXVII. When the Nightingale Sings
XXVIII. The Night Struggle
XXIX. The Spider in the Corner
XXX. I Believe...!
XXXI. The Bridal Feast
XXXII. When We Had Grown Old

CHAPTER I

THE JOURNAL OF DESIDERIUS

At that time I was but ten years old, my brother Lorand sixteen; our dear mother was still young, and father, I well remember, no more than thirty-six. Our grandmother, on my father's side, was also of our party, and at that time was some sixty years of age; she had lovely thick hair, of the pure whiteness of snow. In my childhood I had often thought how dearly the angels must love those who keep their hair so beautiful and white; and used to have the childish belief that one's hair grows white from abundance of joy.

It is true, we never had any sorrow; it seemed as if our whole family had contracted some secret bond of unity, whereby each member thereof bound himself to cause as much joy and as little sorrow as possible to the others.

I never heard any quarrelling in our family. I never saw a passionate face, never an anger that lasted till the morrow, never a look at all reproachful. My mother, grandmother, father, my brother and I, lived like those who understand each other's thoughts, and only strive to excel one another in the expression of their love.

To confess the truth, I loved none of our family so much as I did my brother. Nevertheless I should have been thrown into some little doubt, if some one had asked me which of them I should choose, if I must part from three of the four and keep only one for myself. But could we only have remained together, without death to separate us or disturb our sweet contentment, until ineffable eternity, in such a case I had chosen for my constant companion only my brother. He was so good to me. For he was terribly strong. I thought there could not be a stronger fellow in the whole town. His school-fellows feared his fists, and never dared to cross his path; yet he did not look so powerful; he was rather slender, with a tender girl-like countenance.

Even now I can hardly stop speaking of him.

Debts of Honor

As I was saying, our family was very happy. We never suffered from want, living in a fine house with every comfort. Even the very servants had plenty. Torn clothes were always replaced by new ones and as to friends—why the jolly crowds that would make the house fairly ring with merry-making on name-days[1] and on similar festive occasions proved that there was no lack of them. That every one had a feeling of high esteem for us I could tell by the respectful greetings addressed to us from every direction.

> [1] In Hungary persons celebrate the name-day of the saint after whom they are called with perhaps more ceremony than their birthday.

My father was a very serious man; quiet and not talkative. He had a pale face, a long black beard, and thick eyebrows. Sometimes he contracted his eyebrows, and then we might have been afraid of him; but his idea always was, that nobody should fear him; not more than once a year did it happen that he cast an angry look at some one. However, I never saw him in a good humor. On the occasion of our most festive banquets, when our guests were bursting into peals of laughter at sprightly jests, he would sit there at the end of the table as one who heard naught. If dear mother leaned affectionately on his shoulder, or Lorand kissed his face, or if I nestled to his breast and plied him, in child-guise, with queries on unanswerable topics, at such a time his beautiful, melancholy eyes would beam with such inexpressible love, such enchanting sweetness would well out from them! But a smile came there never at any time, nor did any one cause him to laugh.

He was not one of those men who, when wine or good humor unloosens their tongue, become loquacious, and tell all that lies hidden in their heart, speak of the past and future, chatter and boast. No, he never used gratuitous words. There was some one else in our family just as serious, our grandmother; she was just as taciturn, just as careful about contracting her thick eyebrows, which were already white at that time; just as careful about uttering words of anger; just as incapable of laughing or even smiling. I often remarked that her eyes were fixed unremittingly on his face; and sometimes I found myself possessed of the childish idea that my father was always so grave in his behavior because he knew that his mother was gazing at him. If afterward their eyes met by chance, it seemed as if they had discovered each other's thoughts—some old, long-buried thoughts, of which they were the guardians; and I often saw how my old grandmother would rise from her everlasting knitting, and come to father as he sat among us thus abstracted, scarce remarking that mother, Lorand, and I were beside him, caressing and pestering him; she would kiss his forehead, and his countenance would seem to change in a moment: he would become more affectionate, and begin to converse with us; thereupon grandmother would kiss him afresh and return to her knitting.

It is only now that I recall all these incidents. At that time I found nothing remarkable in them.

One evening our whole family circle was surprised by the unusually good humor that had come over father. To each one of us he was very tender, very affectionate; entered into a long conversation with Lorand, asked him of his school-work, imparted to him information on subjects of which as yet he had but a faulty knowledge; took me on his knee and smoothed my head; addressed questions to me in Latin, and praised me for answering them correctly; kissed our dear mother more than once, and after supper was over related merry tales of the old days. When we began to laugh at them, he laughed too. It was such a pleasure to me to have seen my father laugh once. It was such a novel sensation that I almost trembled with joy.

Only our old grandmother remained serious. The brighter father's face became, the more closely did those white eyebrows contract. Not for a single moment did she take her eyes off father's face; and, as often as he looked at her with his merry, smiling countenance, a cold shudder ran through her ancient frame. Nor could she let father's unusual gayety pass without comment.

"How good-humored you are to-day, my son!"

"To-morrow I shall take the children to the country," he answered; "the prospect of that has always been a source of great joy to me."

We were to go to the country! The words had a pleasant sound for us also. We ran to father, to kiss him for his kindness; how happy he had made us by this promise! His face showed that he knew it well.

"Now you must go to bed early, so as not to oversleep in the morning; the carriage will be here at daybreak."

To go to bed is only too easy, but to fall asleep is difficult when one is still a child, and has received a promise of being taken to the country. We had a beautiful and pleasant country property, not far from town; my brother was as fond as I was of being there. Mother and grandmother never came with us. Why, we knew not; they said they did not like the country. We were indeed surprised at this. Not to like the country—to wander in the fields, on flowery meadows; to breathe the precious perfumed air; to gather round one the beautiful, sagacious, and useful domestic animals? Can there be any one in the world who does not love that? Child, I know there is none.

My brother was all excitement for the chase. How he would enter forest and reeds! what beautiful green-necked wild duck he would shoot. How many multi-colored birds' eggs he would bring home to me.

"I will go with you, too," I said.

"No; some ill might befall you. You can remain at home in the garden to angle in the brook, and catch tiny little fishes."

"And we shall cook them for dinner." What a splendid idea! Long, long we remained awake; first Lorand, then I, was struck by some idea which had to be mentioned; and so each prevented the other from sleeping. Oh! how great the gladness that awaited us on the morrow!

Late in the night a noise as of fire arms awoke me. It is true that I always dreamed of guns. I had seen Lorand at the chase, and feared he would shoot himself.

"What have you shot, Lorand?" I asked half asleep.

"Remain quite still," said my brother, who was lying in the bed near me, and had risen at the noise. "I shall see what has happened outside." With these words he went out.

Several rooms divided our bedroom from that of our parents. I heard no sound except the opening of doors here and there.

Soon Lorand returned. He told me merely to sleep on peacefully—a high wind had risen and had slammed to a window that had remained open; the glass was all broken into fragments; that had caused the great noise.

And therewith he proceeded to dress.

"Why are you dressing?"

"Well, the broken window must be mended with something to prevent the draught coming in; it is in mother's bedroom. You can sleep on peacefully."

Then he placed his hand on my head, and that hand was like ice.

"Is it cold outside, Lorand?"

"No."

"Then why does your hand tremble so?"

"True; it is very cold. Sleep on, little Desi."

As he went out he left an intermediate door open for a moment; and in that moment the sound of mother's laughter reached my ears. That well-known ringing sweet voice, that indicates those *naïve* women who among their children are themselves the greatest children.

What could cause mother to laugh so loudly at this late hour of the night? Because the window was broken? At that time I did not yet know that there is a horrible affliction which attacks women with agonies of hell, and amidst these heart-rending agonies forces them to laugh incessantly.

Debts of Honor

I comforted myself with what my brother had said, and forcibly buried my head in my pillow that I might compel myself to fall asleep.

It was already late in the morning when I awoke again. This time also my brother had awakened me. He was already quite dressed.

My first thought was of our visit to the country.

"Is the carriage already here? Why did you not wake me earlier? Why, you are actually dressed!"

I also immediately hastened to get up, and began to dress; my brother helped me, and answered not a word to my constant childish prattling. He was very serious, and often gazed in directions where there was nothing to be seen.

"Some one has annoyed you, Lorand?"

My brother did not reply, only drew me to his side and combed my hair. He gazed at me incessantly with a sad expression.

"Has some evil befallen you, Lorand?"

No sign, even of the head, of assent or denial; he merely tied my neckerchief quietly into a bow.

We disputed over the coat I should wear; I wished to put on a blue one. Lorand, on the contrary, wished me to wear a dark green one.

I resisted him.

"Why, we are going to the country! There the blue doublet will be just the thing. Why don't you give it to me? Because you have none like it!"

Lorand said nothing; he merely looked at me with those great reproachful eyes of his. It was enough for me. I allowed him to dress me in the dark green coat. And yet I would continually grumble about it.

"Why, you are dressing me as if we were to go to an examination or to a funeral."

At these words Lorand suddenly pressed me to him, folding me in his embrace, then knelt down before me and began to weep, and sob so that his tears bedewed my hair.

"Lorand, what is the matter?" I asked in terror; but he could not speak for weeping. "Don't weep, Lorand. Did I annoy you? Don't be angry."

Long did he weep, all the time holding me in his arms. Then suddenly he heaved a deep and terrifying sigh, and in a low voice stammered in my ear:

"Father—is—dead."

I was one of those children who could not weep; who learn that only with manhood. At such a time when I should have wept, I only felt as if some worm were gnawing into my heart, as if some languor had seized me, which deprived me of all feeling expressed by the five senses—my brother wept for me. Finally, he kissed me and begged me to recover myself. But I was not beside myself. I saw and heard everything. I was like a log of wood, incapable of any movement.

It was unfortunate that I was not gifted with the power of showing how I suffered.

But my mind could not fathom the depths of that thought. Our father was dead!

Yesterday evening he was still talking with us; embracing and kissing us; he had promised to take us to the country, and to-day he was not: he was dead. Quite incomprehensible! In my childhood I had often racked my brains with the question, "What is there beyond the world?" Void. Well, and what surrounds that void? Many times this distracting thought drove me almost to madness. Now this same maddening dilemma seized upon me. How could it be that my father was dead?

"Let us go to mother!" was my next thought.

"We shall go soon after her. She has already departed."

"Whither?"

"To the country."

"But, why?"

"Because she is ill."

"Then why did she laugh so in the night?"

"Because she is ill."

This was still more incomprehensible to my poor intellect.

A thought then occurred to me. My face became suddenly brighter.

"Lorand, of course you are joking; you are fooling me. You merely wished to alarm me. We are all going away to the country to enjoy ourselves! and you only wished to take the drowsiness from my eyes when you told me father was dead."

At these words Lorand clasped his hands, and, with motionless, agonized face, groaned out:

"Desi, don't torture me; don't torture me with your smiling face."

This caused me to be still more alarmed. I began to tremble, seized one of his arms, and implored him not to be angry. Of course, I believed what he said.

He could see that I believed, for all my limbs were trembling.

"Let us go to him, Lorand."

My brother merely gazed at me as if he were horrified at what I had said.

"To father?"

"Yes. What if I speak to him, and he awakes?"

At this suggestion Lorand's two eyes became like fire. It seems as if he were forcibly holding back the rush of a great flood of tears. Then between his teeth he murmured:

"He will never awake again."

"Yet I would like to kiss him."

"His hand?"

"His hand and his face."

"You may kiss only his hand," said my brother firmly.

"Why?"

"Because I say so," was his stern reply. The unaccustomed ring of his voice was quite alarming. I told him I would obey him; only let him take me to father.

"Well, come along. Give me your hand."

Then taking my hand, he led me through two rooms.[2] In the third, grandmother met us.

> [2] In Hungary the houses are built so that one room always leads into the other; the whole house can often be traversed without the necessity of going into a corridor or passage.

I saw no change in her countenance; only her thick white eyebrows were deeply contracted.

Lorand went to her and softly whispered something to her which I did not hear; but I saw plainly that he indicated me with his eyes. Grandmother quietly indicated her consent or refusal with her head; then she came to me, took my head in her two hands, and looked long into my face, moving her head gently. Then she murmured softly:

"Just the way *he* looked as a child."

Then she threw herself face foremost upon the floor, sobbing bitterly.

Lorand seized my hand and drew me with him into the fourth room.

There lay the coffin. It was still open; only the winding-sheet covered the whole.

Debts of Honor

Even to-day I have no power to describe the coffin in which I saw my father. Many know what that is; and no one would wish to learn from me. Only an old serving-maid was in the chamber; no one else was watching. My brother pressed my head to his bosom. And so we stood there a long time.

Suddenly my brother told me to kiss my father's hand, and then we must go. I obeyed him; he raised the edge of the winding-sheet; I saw two wax-like hands put together; two hands in which I could not have recognized those strong muscular hands, upon the shapely fingers of which in my younger days I had so often played with the wonderful signet-rings, drawing them off one after the other.

I kissed both hands. It was such a pleasure! Then I looked at my brother with agonized pleading. I longed so to kiss the face. He understood my look and drew me away.

"Come with me. Don't let us remain longer." And that was such terrible agony to me! My brother told me to wait in my room, and not to move from it until he had ordered the carriage which was to take us away.

"Whither?" I asked.

"Away to the country. Remain here and don't go anywhere else." And to keep me secure he locked the door upon me.

Then I fell a-thinking. Why should we go to the country now that our father was lying dead? Why must I remain meanwhile in that room? Why do none of our acquaintances come to see us? Why do those who go about the house whisper so quietly? Why do they not toll the bell when so great a one lies dead in the house?

All this distracted my brain entirely. To nothing could I give myself an answer, and no one came to me from whom I could have demanded the truth.

Once, not long after (to me it seemed an age, though, if the truth be known, it was probably only a half-hour or so), I heard the old serving-maid, who had been watching in yonder chamber, tripping past the corridor window. Evidently some one else had taken her place.

Her face was now as indifferent as it always was. Her eyes were cried out; but I am sure I had seen her weep every day, whether in good or in bad humor; it was all one with her. I addressed her through the window:

"Aunt Susie, come here."

"What do you want, dear little Desi?"

"Susie, tell me truly, why am I not allowed to kiss my father's face?"

The old servant shrugged her shoulders, and with cynical indifference replied:

"Poor little fool. Why, because—because he has no head, poor fellow."

I did not dare to tell my brother on his return what I had heard from old Susie.

I told him it was the cold air, when he asked why I trembled so.

Thereupon he merely put my overcoat on, and said, "Let us go to the carriage."

I asked him if our grandmother was not coming with us. He replied that she would remain behind. We two took our seats in one carriage; a second was waiting before the door.

To me the whole incident seemed as a dream. The rainy, gloomy weather, the houses that flew past us, the people who looked wonderingly out of the windows, the one or two familiar faces that passed us by, and in their astonished gaze upon us forgot to greet us. It was as if each one of them asked himself: "Why has the father of these boys no head?" Then the long poplar-trees at the end of the town, so bent by the wind as if they were bowing their heads under the weight of some heavy thought; and the murmuring waves under the bridge, across which we went, murmuring as if they too were taking counsel over some deep secret, which had so oft been intrusted to them, and which as yet no one had discovered—why was it that some dead people had no heads? Something prompted me so, to turn with this awful question to my brother. I overcame the demon, and did not ask him. Often children, who hold pointed knives before their eyes, or look down from a high bridge into the water, are told, "Beware, or the devil will push you." Such was my feeling in relation to this question. In my hand was the handle, the point was in my heart. I was sitting upon the brim, and gazing down into the whirlpool. Something called upon me to thrust myself into the living reality, to lose my head in it. And yet I was able to restrain myself. During the whole journey neither my brother nor I spoke a word.

When we arrived at our country-house our physician met us, and told us that mother was even worse than she had been; the sight of us would only aggravate her illness; so it would be good for us to remain in our room.

Our grandmother arrived two hours after us. Her arrival was the signal for a universal whispering among the domestics, as if they would make ready for something extraordinary which the whole world must not know. Then we sat down to dinner quite unexpectedly, far earlier than usual. No one could eat; we only gazed at each course in turn. After dinner my brother in his turn began to hold a whispered conference with grandmother. As far as I could gather from the few words I caught, they were discussing whether he should take his gun with him or not. Lorand wished to take it, but grandmother objected. Finally, however, they agreed that he should take gun and cartridges, but should not load the weapon until he saw a necessity for it.

In the mean while I staggered about from room to room. It seemed as if everybody had considerations of more importance than that of looking after me.

In the afternoon, however, when I saw my brother making him ready for a journey, despair seized hold of me:

"Take me with you."

"Why, you don't even know where I am going."

"I don't mind; I will go anywhere, only take me with you; for I cannot remain all by myself."

"Well, I will ask grandmother."

My brother exchanged a few words with my grandmother, and then came back to me.

"You may come with me. Take your stick and coat."

He slung his gun on his shoulder and took his dog with him.

Once again this thought agonized me afresh: "Father is dead, and we go for an afternoon's shooting, with grandmother's consent as if nothing had happened."

We went down through the gardens, all along the loam-pits; my brother seemed to be choosing a route where we should meet with no one. He kept the dog on the leash to prevent its wandering away. We went a long way, roaming among maize-fields and shrubs, without the idea once occurring to Lorand to take the gun down from his shoulder. He kept his eyes continually on the ground, and would always silence the dog, when the animal scented game.

Meantime we had left the village far behind us. I was already quite tired out, and yet I did not utter a syllable to suggest our returning. I would rather have gone to the end of the world than return home.

It was already twilight when we reached a small poplar wood. Here my brother suggested a little rest. We sat down side by side on the trunk of a felled tree. Lorand offered me some cakes he had brought in his wallet for me. How it pained me that he thought I wanted anything to eat. Then he threw the cake to the hound. The hound picked it up and, disappearing behind the bushes, we heard him scratch on the ground as he buried it. Not even he wanted to eat. Next we watched the sunset. Our village church-tower was already invisible, so far had we wandered, and yet I did not ask whether we should return.

Debts of Honor

The weather became suddenly gloomy; only after sunset did the clouds open, that the dying sun might radiate the heavens with its storm-burdened red fire. The wind suddenly rose. I remarked to my brother that an ugly wind was blowing, and he answered that it was good for us. How this great wind could be good for us, I was unable to discover.

When later the heavens gradually changed from fire red to purple, from purple to gray, from gray to black, Lorand loaded his gun, and let the hound loose. He took my hand. I must now say not a single word, but remain motionless. In this way we waited long that boisterous night.

I racked my brain to discover the reason why we were there.

On a sudden our hound began to whine in the distance—such a whine as I had never yet heard.

Some minutes later he came reeling back to us; whimpering and whining, he leaped up at us, licked our hands, and then raced off again.

"Now let us go," said Lorand, shouldering his gun.

Hurriedly we followed the hound's track, and soon came out upon the high-road.

In the gloom a hay-cart drawn by four oxen, was quietly making its way to its destination.

"God be praised!" said the old farm-laborer, as he recognized my brother.

"For ever and ever."

After a slight pause my brother asked him if there was anything wrong?

"You needn't fear, it will be all right."

Thereupon we quietly sauntered along behind the hay-wagon.

My brother uncovered his head, and so proceeded on his way bareheaded; he said he was very warm. We walked silently for a distance until the old laborer came back to us.

"Not tired, Master Desi?" he asked; "you might take a seat on the cart."

"What are you thinking of, John?" said Lorand; "on this cart?"

"True; true, indeed," said the aged servant. Then he quietly crossed himself, and went forward to the oxen.

When we came near the village, old John again came toward us.

"It will be better now if the young gentlemen go home through the gardens; it will be much easier for me to get through the village alone."

"Do you think they are still on guard?" asked Lorand.

"Of course they know already. One cannot take it amiss; the poor fellows have twice in ten years had their hedges broken down by the hail."

"Stupidity!" answered my brother.

"May be," sighed the old serving-man. "Still the poor man thinks so."

Lorand nudged the old retainer so that he would not speak before me.

My brain became only more confused thereat.

Lorand told him that we would soon pass through the gardens; however, after John had advanced a good distance with the cart we followed in his tracks again, keeping steadily on until we came to the first row of houses beginning the village. Here my brother began to thread his way more cautiously, and in the dark I heard distinctly the click of the trigger as he cocked his gun.

The cart proceeded quietly before us to the end of the long village street.

Above the workhouse about six men armed with pitchforks met us.

My brother said we must make our way behind a hedge, and bade me hold our dog's mouth lest he should bark when the others passed.

The pitchforked guards passed near the cart, and advanced before us too. I heard how the one said to the other:

"Faith, *that* is the reason this cursed wind is blowing so furiously!"

"*That*" was the reason! What was the reason?

As they passed, my brother took my hand and said: "Now let us hasten, that we may be home before the wagon."

Therewith he ran with me across a long cottage-court, lifted me over a hedge, climbing after me himself; then through two or three more strange gardens, everywhere stepping over the hedges; and at last we reached our own garden.

But, in Heaven's name, had we committed some sin, that we ran thus, skulking from hiding-place to hiding-place?

As we reached the courtyard, the wagon was just entering. Three retainers waited for it in the yard, and immediately closed the gate after it.

Grandmother stood outside on the terrace and kissed us when we arrived.

Again there followed a short whispering between my brother and the domestics; whereupon the latter seized pitchforks and began to toss down the hay from the wain.

Could they not do so by daylight?

Grandmother sat down on a bench on the terrace, and drew my head to her bosom. Lorand leaned his elbows upon the rail of the terrace and watched the work.

The hay was tossed into a heap and the high wind drove the chaff on to the terrace, but no one told the servants to be more careful.

Debts of Honor

This midnight work was, for me, so mysterious.

Only once I saw that Lorand turned round as he stood, and began to weep; thereupon grandmother rose, and they fell each upon the other's breast.

I clutched their garments and gazed up at them trembling. Not a single lamp burned upon the terrace.

"Sh!" whispered grandmother, "don't weep so loudly," she was herself choking with sobs. "Come, let us go."

With that she took my hand, and, leaning upon my brother's arm, came down with us into the courtyard, down to the wagon, which stood before the garden gate. Two or more heaps of straw hid *it* from the eye; it was visible only when we reached the bottom of the wagon.

On that wagon lay the coffin of my father.

So this it was that in the dead of night we had stealthily brought into the village, that we had in so skulking a manner escorted, and had so concealed; and of which we had spoken in whispers. This it was that we had wept over in secret—my father's coffin. The four retainers lifted it from the wagon, then carried it on their shoulders toward the garden. We went after it, with bared heads and silent tongues.

A tiny rivulet flowed through our garden; near this rivulet was a little round building, whose gaudy door I had never seen open.

From my earliest days, when I was unable to rise from the ground if once I sat down, the little round building had always been in my mind.

I had always loved it, always feared to be near it; I had so longed to know what might be within it. As a little knickerbockered child I would pick the colored gravel-stones from the mortar, and play with them in the dust; and if perchance one stone struck the iron door, I would run away from the echo the blow produced.

In my older days it was again only around this building that I would mostly play, and would remark that upon its façade were written great letters, on which the ivy, that so actively clambered up the walls, scarcely grew. At that time how I longed to know what those letters could mean!

When the first holiday after I had made the acquaintance of those letters came, and they took me again to our country-seat, one after another I spelled out the ancient letters of the inscription on that mysterious little house, and pieced them together in my mind. But I could not arrive at their meaning; for they were written in some foreign tongue.

Many, many times I wrote those words in the dust even before I understood them:

"NE NOS INDUCAS IN TENTATIONEM."

I strove to reach one year earlier than my school-fellows the so-called "student class," where Latin was taught.

My most elementary acquaintance with the Latin tongue had always for its one aim the discovery of the meaning of that saying. Finally I solved the mystery—

"Lead us not into temptation." It is a sentence of the Lord's Prayer, which I myself had repeated a thousand times; and now I knew its meaning still less than before.

And still more began to come to me a kind of mysterious abhorrence of that building, above whose door was to be found the prayer that God might guard us against temptations.

Perhaps this was the very dwelling of temptations?

We know what children understand by "temptations."

To-day I saw this door open, and knew that this building was our family vault.

This door, which hitherto I had only seen covered with ivy, was now swung open, and through the open porch glittered the light of a lamp. The two great Virginia creepers which were planted before the crypt hid the glass so that it was not visible from the garden. The brightness was only for us.

The four men set the coffin down on the steps; we followed after it.

So this was that house where temptations dwell; and all our prayers were in vain; "lead us not into temptation." Yet to temptation we were forced to come. Down a few steps we descended, under a low, plastered arch, which glittered green from the moisture of the earth. In the wall were built deep niches, four on either side, and six of them were already filled. Before them stood slabs of marble, with inscriptions telling of those who had fallen asleep. The four servants placed the coffin they had brought on their shoulders in the seventh niche; then the aged retainer clasped his hands, and with simple devotion repeated the Lord's Prayer; the other three men softly murmured after him: "Amen. Amen."

Then they left us to ourselves.

Grandmother all this while had without a word, without a movement, stood in the depth of the crypt, holding our hands within her own; but when we were alone, in a frenzy she darted to the coffined niche and flung herself to the ground before it.

Oh! I cannot tell what she said as she raved there. She wept and sobbed, flinging reproaches—at the dead! She scolded, as one reproves a child that has cut itself with a knife. She asked why he did *this*. And again she heaped grave calumny upon him, called him coward, wretch, threatened him with God, with God's wrath, and with eternal damnation;—then asked pardon of him, babbled out words of conciliation, called him back, called him dear, sweet, and good; related to him what a faithful, dear, loving wife waited at home, with his two sweet children,—how could he forget them? Then with gracious, reverent words begged him to turn Christian, to come to God, to learn to believe, to hope, to love; to trust to the boundless mercy; to take his rest in the paths of Heaven. And then she uttered a scream, tore the tresses of her dove-white hair, and cursed God. Methought it was the night of the Last Judgment.

Every fire-breathing monster of the Revelation, the very disgorging of the dead from the rent earth, were as naught to me compared with the terror which that hour heaped upon my head.

'Twas hither we had brought father, who died suddenly, in the prime of life. Hither we had brought him, in stealth, and slinking; here we had concealed him without any Christian ceremony, without psalm or toll of bell; no priest's blessing followed him to his grave, as it follows even the poorest beggar; and now here, in the house of the dead, grandmother had cursed the departed, and anathematized the other world, on whose threshold we stand, and in her mad despair was knocking at the door of the mysterious country as she beat upon the coffin-lid with her fist.

Now, in my mature age, when my head, too, is almost covered with winter's snow, I see that our presence there was essential; drop by drop we were to drain to the dregs this most bitter cup, which I would had never fallen to our lot!

Grandmother fell down before the niche and laid her forehead upon the coffin's edge; her long white hair fell trailing over her.

Long, very long, she lay, and then she rose; her face was no more distorted, her eyes no longer filled with tears. She turned toward us and said we should remain a little longer here.

She herself sat down upon the lowest step of the stone staircase, and placed the lamp in front of her, while we two remained standing before her.

She looked not at us, only peered intensely and continuously with her large black eyes into the light of the lamp, as if she would conjure therefrom something that had long since passed away.

All at once she seized our hands, and drew us toward her to the staircase.

"You are the scions of a most unhappy house, every member of which dies by his own hand."

Debts of Honor

So this was that secret that hung, like a veil of mourning before the face of every adult member of our family! We continuously saw our elders so, as if some mist of melancholy moved between us; and this was that mist.

"This was the doom of God, a curse of man upon us!" continued grandmother, now no longer with terrifying voice. Besides, she spoke as calmly as if she were merely reciting to us the history of some strange family. "Your great-grandfather. Job Áronffy, he who lies in the first niche, bequeathed this terrible inheritance to his heirs; and it was a brother's hand that hurled this curse at his head. Oh, this is an unhappy earth on which we dwell! In other happy lands there are murderous quarrels between man and man; brothers part in wrath from one another; the 'mine and thine,'[3] jealousy, pride, envy, sow tares among them. But this accursed earth of ours ever creates bloodshed; this damned soil, which we are wont to call our 'dear homeland,' whose pure harvest we call love of home, whose tares we call treason, while every one thinks his own harvest the pure one, his brother's the tares, and, for that, brother slays brother! Oh! you cannot understand it yet.

> [3] That is, the disputes as to the superiority of each other's possessions, or as to each other's right to possession.

"Your great-grandfather lived in those days when great men thought that what is falling in decay must be built afresh. Great contention arose therefrom, much knavery, much disillusion; finally the whole had to be wiped out.

"Job's parents educated him at academies in Germany; there his soul became filled with foreign freedom of thought; he became an enthusiastic partisan of common human liberty. When he returned, this selfsame idea was in strife with an equally great one, national feeling. He joined his fortunes with the former idea, as he considered it the just one. In what patriots called relics of antiquity he saw only the vices of the departed. His elder brother stood face to face with him; they met on the common field of strife, and then began between them the unending feud. They had been such good brothers, never had they deserted each other in time of trouble; and on this thorn-covered field they must swear eternal enmity. Your great-grandfather belonged to the victorious, his brother to the conquered army. But the victory was not sweet.

"Job gained a powerful, high position, he basked in the sunshine of power, but he lost that which was—nothing; merely the smiles of his old acquaintances. He was a seigneur, from afar they greeted him, but did not hurry to take his hand; and those who of yore at times of meeting would kiss his face from right and left, now after his change of dignity would stand before him, and bow their greetings askance with cold obeisance. Then there was one man who did not even bow, but sought a meeting only that he might provoke him with his obstinate sullenness, and gaze upon him with his piercing eyes—his own brother. Yet they were both honorable, good men, true Christians, benefactors of the poor, the darlings of their family, and once so fond of each other! Oh, this sorrowful earth here below us!

"Then this new order of things that had been built up for ten years, fell into ruins, and Joseph II. on his death-bed drew a red line through his whole life-work; what had happened till then faded into mere remembrance.

"The earth re-echoed with the shouts of rejoicing—this earth, this bitter earth. Job for his part wended his way to the Turkish bath in Buda, and, that he might meet with his brother no more, opened his arteries and bled to death.

"Yet they were both good Christians; true men in life, faithful to honor, no evil-doers, no godless men; in heart and deed they worshipped God; but still the one brother took his own life, that he might meet no more with the other; and the other said of him: 'He deserved his fate.'

"Oh, this earth that is drenched with the flow of our tears!"

Here grandmother paused, as if she would collect in her mind the memories of a greater and heavier affliction.

Not a sound reached us down there—even the crypt door was closed; the moaning of the wind did not reach so far; no sound, only the beating of the hearts of three living beings.

Grandmother sought with her eyes the date written upon the arch, which the moisture that had sweated out from the lime had rendered illegible.

"In this year they built this house of sorrow. Job was the first inhabitant thereof. Just as now, without priest, without toll of bell, hidden in a wooden chest of other form, they brought him here; and with him began that melancholy line of victims, whose legacy was that one should draw the other after him. The shedding of blood by one's own hand is a terrible legacy. That blood besprinkles children and brothers. That malicious tempter who directed the father's hand to strike the sharp knife home into his own heart stands there in ambush forever behind his successors' backs; he is ever whispering to them; 'Thy father was a suicide, thy brother himself sought out death; over thy head, too, stands the sentence; wherever thou runnest from before it, thou canst not save thyself; thou carriest with thyself thy own murderer in thine own right hand.' He tempts and lures the undecided ones with blades whetted to brilliancy, with guns at full cock, with poison-drinks of awful hue, with deep-flowing streams. Oh, it is indeed horrible!

"And nothing keeps them back! they never think of the love, the everlasting sorrow of those whom they leave behind here to sorrow over their melancholy death. They never think of Him whom they will meet there beyond the grave, and who will ask them: 'Why did you come before I summoned you?'

"In vain was written upon the front of this house of sorrow, 'Lead us not into temptation.' You can see. Seven have already taken up their abode here. All the seven have cast at the feet of Providence that treasure, an account of which will be asked for in Heaven.

"Job left three children: Ákos, Gerö, and Kálmán. Ákos was the eldest, and he married earliest. He was a good man, but thoughtless and passionate. One summer he lost his whole fortune at cards and was ruined. But even poverty did not drive him to despair. He said to his wife and children: 'Till now we were our own masters; now we shall be the servants of others. Labor is not a disgrace. I shall go and act as steward to some landowner.' The other two brothers, when they heard of their elder's misfortune, conferred together, went to him, and said: 'Brother, still two-thirds of our father's wealth is left; come, let us divide it anew.'

"And each of them gave him a third of his property, that they might be on equal terms again.

"That night Ákos shot himself in the head.

"The stroke of misfortune he could bear, but the kindness of his brothers set him so against himself that when he was freed from the cares of life he did not wish to know further the enjoyments thereof.

"Ákos left behind two children, a girl and a boy.

"The girl had lived some sixteen summers—very beautiful, very good. Look! there is her tomb: 'Struck down in her sixteenth year!' She loved; became unhappy; and died.

"You cannot understand it yet!

"So already three lay in the solitary vault.

"Gerö was your grandfather—my good, never-to-be-forgotten husband. No tear wells in my eyes as I think of him; every thought that leads me back to him is sweet to me; and I know that he was a man of high principles; that every deed of his—his last deed, too—was proper and right, it is as it should be. It happened before my very eyes; and I did not seize his hand to stay his action."

How my old grandmother's eyes flashed in this moment! A glowing warmth, hitherto unknown to me, seemed to pervade my whole being; some glimmering ray of enthusiasm—I knew not what! How the dead can inspire one with enthusiasm!

"Your grandfather was the very opposite of his own father; as it is likely to happen in hundreds, nay, in thousands of cases that the sons restore to the East the fame and glory that their fathers gathered in the West.

"But you don't understand that, either!

"Gerö was in union with those who, under the leadership of a priest of high rank, wished at the end of the last century, to prepare the country for another century. No success crowned their efforts; they fell with him—and fell without a head. One afternoon your grandfather was sitting in the family circle—it was toward the end of dinner—when a strange officer entered in the midst of us, and, with a face utterly incapable of an expression of remorse, informed Gerö that he had orders to put him under guard. Gerö displayed a calm face, merely begged the stranger to allow him to drink his black coffee. His request was granted without demur. My husband calmly stirred his coffee, and entered into conversation with the stranger, who did not seem to be of an angry disposition. Indeed, he assured my husband that no harm would come of this incident. My husband peacefully sipped his coffee.

"Then having finished it, he put down his cup, wiped his beautiful long beard, turned to me, drew me to his breast, and kissed me on both cheeks, not touching my mouth. 'Educate our boy well,' he stammered. Then, turning to the stranger: 'Sir, pray do not trouble yourself further on my account. I am a dead man; you will be welcome at my funeral.'

"Two minutes later he breathed his last. And I had clearly seen, for I sat beside him, how with his thumb he opened the seal of the ring he wore on his little finger, how he shook a white powder therefrom into the cup standing before him, how he stirred it slowly till it dissolved, and then sipped it up little by little; but I could not stay his hand, could not call to him, 'Don't do it! Cling to life!'"

Grandmother was staring before her, with the ecstatic smile of madness. Oh! I was so frightened that even now my mind wanders at the remembrance.

This smile of madness is so contagious! Slowly nodding with her gray head, she again fell all in a heap. It was apparent that some time must elapse before this recollection, once risen in her mind, could settle to rest again. After what seemed to us hours she slowly raised herself again and continued her tragic narrative.

"He was already the fourth dweller in this house of temptations.

Debts of Honor

"After his death his brother Kálmán came to join our circle. To the end he remained single; very early in life he was deceived, and from that moment became a hater of mankind.

"His gloom grew year by year more incurable; he avoided every distraction, every gathering; his favorite haunt was this garden—this place here. He planted the beautiful juniper-trees before the door; such trees were in those days great rarities.

"He made no attempt to conceal from us—in fact, he often declared openly to us that his end could be none other than his brothers' had been.

"The pistol, with which Ákos had shot himself, he kept by him as a souvenir, and in sad jest declared it was his inheritance.

"Here he would wander for hours together in reverie, in melancholy, until the falling snow confined him to his room. He detested the winter greatly. When the first snowflake fell, his ill-humor turned to the agony of despair; he loathed the atmosphere of his rooms and everything to be found within the four walls. We so strongly advised him to winter in Italy, that he finally gave in to the proposal. We carefully packed his trunks; ordered his post-chaise. One morning, as everything stood ready for departure, he said that, before going for this long journey, he would once again take leave of his brothers. In his travelling-suit he came down here to the vault, and closed the iron door after him, enjoining that no one should disturb him. So we waited behind; and, as hour after hour passed by and still he did not appear, we went after him. We forced open the closed door, and there found him lying in the middle of the tomb—he had gone to the country where there is no more winter.

"He had shot himself in the heart, with the same pistol as his brother, as he had foretold.

"Only two male members of the family remained: my son and the son of Ákos. Lörincz—that was the name of Ákos' son—was reared too kindly by his poor, good mother; she loved him excessively, and thereby spoiled him. The boy became very fastidious and sensitive. He was eleven years old when his mother noticed that she could not command his obedience. Once the child played some prank, a mere trifle; how can a child of eleven years commit any great offence? His mother thought she must rebuke him. The boy laughed at the rebuke; he could not believe his mother was angry; then, in consequence, his mother boxed his ears. The boy left the room; behind the garden there was a fishpond; in that he drowned himself.

"Well, is it necessary to take one's life for such a thing? For one blow, given by the soft hand of a mother to a little child, to take such a terrible revenge! to cut the thread of life, which as yet he knew not; How many children are struck by a mother, and the next day received into her bosom, with mutual forgiveness and a renewal of reciprocal love? Why, a blow from a mother is merely one proof of a mother's love. But it brought him to take his life."

The cold perspiration stood out in beads all over me.

That bitterness I, too, feel in myself. I also am a child, just as old as that other was; I have never yet been beaten. Once my parents were compelled to rebuke me for wanton petulance; and from head to foot I was pervaded through and through by one raving idea: "If they beat me I should take my own life." So I am also infected with the hereditary disease—the awful spirit is holding out his hand over me; captured, accursed, he is taking me with him. I am betrayed to him! Only instead of thrashing me, they had punished me with fasting fare; otherwise, I also should already be in this house.

Grandmother clasped her hands across her knees and continued her story.

"Your father was older at the time of this event—seventeen years of age. Ever since his birth the world has been rife with discord and revolutions; all the nations of the world pursued a bitter warfare one against another. I scarce expected my only son would live to be old enough to join the army. Thither, thither, where death with a scythe in both hands was cutting down the ranks of the armed warriors; thither, where the children of weeping mothers were being trampled on by horses' hoofs; thither, thither, where they were casting into a common grave the mangled remains of darling first-borns; only not hither, not into this awful house, into these horrible ranks of tempting spectres! Yes, I rejoiced when I knew that he was standing before the foe's cannons; and when the news of one great conflict after another spread like a dark cloud over the country, with sorrowful tranquillity, I lay in wait for the lightning-stroke which, bursting from the cloud, should dart into my heart with the news: 'Thy son is dead! They have slain him, as a hero is slain!' But it was not so. The wars ceased. My son returned.

"No, it is not true; don't believe what I said,—'If only the news of his death had come instead!'

"No; surely I rejoiced, surely I wept in my joy and happiness, when I could clasp him anew in my arms, and I blessed God for not having taken him away. Yet, why did I rejoice? Why did I triumph before the world, saying, 'See, what a fine, handsome son I have! a dauntless warrior, fame and honor he has brought home with him. My pride—my gladness? Now they lie here! What did I gain with him—he, too, followed the rest! He, too! he, whom I loved best of all—he whose every Paradise was here on earth!"

My brother wept; I shivered with cold.

Then suddenly, like a lunatic, grandmother seized our hands, and leaped up from her sitting-place.

"Look yonder! there is still *one* empty niche—room for *one* coffin. Look well at that place; then go forth into the world and think upon what the mouth of this dark hollow said.

"I had thought of making you swear here never to forsake God, never to continue the misfortunes of this family; but why this oath? That some one should take with him to the other world one sin more, in that in the hour of his death he forswore himself? What oath would bind him who says: 'The mercy of God I desire not'?

"But instead, I brought you here and related you the history of your family. Later you shall know still more therefrom, that is yet secret and obscure before you. Now look once more around you, and then—let us go out.

"Now you know what is the meaning of this melancholy house, whose door the ivy enters with the close of a man's life from time to time. You know that the family brings its suicides hither to burial, because elsewhere they have no place. But you know also that in this awful sleeping-room there is space for only *one* person more, and the second will find no other resting-place than the grave-ditch!"

With these words grandmother passionately thrust us both from her. In terror we fell into each other's arms before her frenzied gaze.

Then, with a shrill cry, she rushed toward us and embraced us both with all the might of a lunatic; wept and gasped, till finally she fainted utterly away.

CHAPTER II

THE GIRL SUBSTITUTE[4]

[4] In former days it was the custom for a Magyar and a German family to interchange children, with a view to their learning the two languages perfectly. So Fanny Fromm is interchanged with Desiderius Áronffy.

A pleasant old custom was then in fashion in our town: the interchange of children,—perhaps it is in fashion still. In our many-tongued fatherland one town is German-speaking, the other Magyar-speaking, and, being brothers, after all to understand each other was a necessity. Germans must learn Magyar and Magyars, German. And peace is restored.

So a method of temporarily exchanging children grew up: German parents wrote to Magyar towns, Magyar parents to German towns, to the respective school directors, to ask if there were any pupils who could be interchanged. In this manner one child was given for another, a kind, gentle, womanly thought!

The child left home, father, mother, brother, only to find another home among strangers: another mother, other brothers and sisters, and his absence did not leave a void at home; child replaced child; and if the adopted mother devoted a world of tenderness to the pilgrim, it was with the idea that her own was being thus treated in the far distance; for a mother's love cannot be bought at a price but only gained by love.

It was an institution that only a woman's thought could found: so different from that frigid system invented by men which founded nunneries, convents, and closed colleges for the benefit of susceptible young hearts where all memory of family life was permanently wiped out of their minds.

After that unhappy day, which, like the unmovable star, could never go so far into the distance as to be out of sight, grandmother more than once said to us in the presence of mother, that it would not be good for us to remain in this town; we must be sent somewhere else.

Mother long opposed the idea. She did not wish to part from us. Yet the doctors advised the same course. When the spasms seized her, for days we were not allowed to visit her, as it made her condition far worse.

At last she gave her consent, and it was decided that we two should be sent to Pressburg. My brother, who was already too old to be exchanged, went to the home of a Privy Councillor, who was paid for taking him in, and my place was to be taken by a still younger child than myself, by a little German girl, Fanny, the daughter of Henry Fromm, baker. Grandmother was to take us in a carriage—in those days in Hungary we had only heard rumors of steamboats—and to bring the girl substitute back with her.

For a week the whole household sewed, washed, ironed and packed for us; we were supplied with winter and summer clothing: on the last day provisions were prepared for our journey, as if we had intended to make a voyage to the end of the world, and in the evening we took supper in good time, that we might rise early, as we had to start before daybreak. That was my first departure from my home. Many a time since then have I had to say adieu to what was dearest to me; many sorrows, more than I could express, have afflicted me: but that first parting caused me the greatest pain of all, as is proved by the fact that after so long an interval I remember it so well. In the solitude of my own chamber, I bade farewell separately to all those little trifles that surrounded me: God bless the good old clock that hast so oft awakened me. Beautiful raven, whom I taught to speak and to say "Lorand," on whom wilt thou play thy sportive tricks? Poor old doggy, maybe thou wilt not be living when I return? Forsooth old Susie herself will say to me, "I shall never see you again Master Desi." And till now I always thought I was angry with Susie; but now I remark that it will be hard to leave her.

And my dear mother, the invalid, and grandmother, already so grey-haired!

Thus the bitter strains swept onward along the strings of my soul, from lifeless objects to living, from favorite animals to human acquaintances, and then to those with whom we were bound soul to soul, finally dragging one with them to the presence of the dead and buried. I was sorely troubled by the thought that we were not allowed to enter, even for one moment, that solitary house, round the door of which the ivy was entwining anew. We might have whispered "God be with thee! I have come to see thee!" I must leave the place without being able to say to him a single word of love. And perhaps he would know without words. Perhaps the only joy of that poor soul, who could not lie in a consecrated chamber, who could not find the way to heaven because he had not waited till the guardian angel came for him, was when he saw that his sons love him still.

"Lorand, I cannot sleep, because I have not been able to take my leave of that house beside the stream."

My brother sighed and turned in his bed.

My whole life long I have been a sound sleeper (what child is not?) but never did it seem such a burden to rise as on the morning of our departure. Two days later a strange child would be sleeping in that bed. Once more we met together at breakfast, which we had to eat by candle-light as the day had not yet dawned.

Dear mother often rose from her seat to kiss and embrace Lorand, overwhelmed him with caresses, and made him promise to write much; if anything happened to him, he must write and tell it at once, and must always consider that bad news would afflict two hearts at home. She only spoke to me to bid me drink my coffee warm, as the morning air would be chilly.

Grandmother, too, concerned herself entirely with Lorand: they enquired whether he had all he required for the journey, whether he had taken his certificates with him—and a thousand other matters. I was rather surprised than jealous at all this, for as a rule the youngest son gets all the petting.

When our carriage drove up we took our travelling coats and said adieu in turn to the household. Mother, leaning on Lorand's shoulder, came with us to the gate whispering every kind of tender word to him; thrice she embraced and kissed him. And then came my turn.

She embraced me and kissed me on the cheek, then tremblingly whispered in my ear these words:

"My darling boy,—take care of your brother Lorand!" I take care of Lorand? the child of the young man? the weak of the strong? the later born guide the elder. The whole journey long this idea distracted me, and I could not explain it to myself.

Of the impressions of the journey I retain no very clear recollections: I think I slept very much in the carriage. The journey to Pressburg lasted from early morning till late evening; only as twilight came on did a new thought begin to keep me awake, a thought to which as yet I had paid no attention: "What kind of a child could it be, for whom I was now being exchanged? Who was to usurp my place at table, in my bed-room, and in my mother's heart? Was she small or large? beautiful or ugly? obedient or contrary? had she brothers or sisters, to whom I was to be a brother? was she as much afraid of me as I was of her?"

For I was very much afraid of her.

Naturally, I dreaded the thought of the child who was meeting me at the cross-roads with the avowed intention of taking my place as my mother's child, giving me instead her own parents. Were they reigning princes, still the loss would be mine. I confess that I felt a kind of sweet bitterness in the idea that my substitute might be some dull, malicious creature, whose actions would often cause mother to remember me. But if, on the contrary, she were some quiet, angelic soul, who would soon steal my mother's love from me! In every respect I trembled with fear of that creature who had been born that she might be exchanged for me.

Towards evening grandmother told us that the town which we were going to was visible. I was sitting with my back to the horses, and so

Debts of Honor

I was obliged to turn round in order to see. In the distance I could see the four-columned white skeleton of a building, which was first apparent to the eye.

"What a gigantic charnel-house," I remarked to grandmother.

"It is no charnel-house, my child, but it is the ruin of the citadel of (Pressburg) Pozsony."[5]

[5] Pozsony. A town in Hungary is called by the Germans Pressburg.

A curious ruin it is. This first impression ever remained in my mind: I regarded it as a charnel-house.

It was quite late when we entered the town, which was very large compared to ours. I had never seen such elegant display in shop-windows before and it astonished me as I noticed that there were paved sidewalks reserved for pedestrians. They must be all fine lords who live in this city.

Mr. Fromm, the baker, to whose house I was to be taken, had informed us that we need not go to an hotel as he had room for all of us, and would gladly welcome us, especially as the expense of the journey was borne by us. We found his residence by following the written address. He owned a fine four-storied house in the Fürsten allee,[6] with his open shop in front on the sign of which peaceful lions were painted in gold holding rolls and cakes between their teeth.

[6] Princes avenue.

Mr. Fromm himself was waiting for us outside his shop door, and hastened to open the carriage door himself. He was a round-faced, portly little man, with a short black moustache, black eyebrows, and close-cropped, thick, flour-white hair. The good fellow helped grandmother to alight from the carriage: shook hands with Lorand, and began to speak to them in German: when I alighted, he put his hand on my head with a peculiar smile:

"Iste puer?"

Then he patted me on the cheeks.

Debts of Honor

"Bonus, bonus."

His addressing me in Latin had two advantages; firstly, as I could not speak German, nor he Magyar, this use of a neutral tongue removed all suspicions of our being deaf and dumb; secondly, it at once inspired me with a genuine respect for the honest fellow, who had dabbled in the sciences, and had, beyond his technical knowledge of his own business, some acquaintance with the language of Cicero. Mr. Fromm made room for grandmother and Lorand to pass before him up a narrow stone staircase, while he kept his hand continuously on my head, as if that were the part of me by which he could best hold me.

"Veni puer. Hic puer secundus, filius meus."

So there was a boy in the house, a new terror for me.

"Est studiosus."

What, that boy! That was good news: we could go to school together.

"Meus filius magnus asinus."

That was a fine acknowledgment from a father.

"Nescit pensum nunquam scit."

Then he discontinued to speak of the young student, and pantomimically described something, from which I gathered that "meus filius," on this occasion was condemned to starve, until he had learnt his lessons, and was confined to his room.

This was no pleasant idea to me.

Well, and what about "mea filia?"

I had never seen a house that was like Mr. Fromm's inside. Our home was only one-storied, with wide rooms, and broad corridors, a courtyard and a garden: here we had to enter first by a narrow hall: then to ascend a winding stair, that would not admit two abreast. Then followed a rapid succession of small and large doors, so that when we came out upon the balconied corridor, and I gazed down into the deep, narrow courtyard, I could not at all imagine how I had reached that point, and still less how I could ever find my way out. "Father" Fromm led us directly from the corridor into the reception room, where two candles were burning (two in our honor), and the table laid for "gouter." It seemed they had expected us earlier. Two women were seated at the window, Mrs. Fromm and her mother. Mrs. Fromm was a tall slender person; she had grey curls (I don't know why I should not call them "Schneckles," for that is their name) in front, large blue eyes, a sharp German nose, a prominent chin and a wart below her mouth.

The "Gross-mamma" was the exact counterpart of Mrs. Fromm, only about thirty years older, a little more slender, and sharper in feature: she had also grey "Schneckles"—though I did not know until ten years later that they were not her own:—she too had that wart, though in her case it was on the chin.

In a little low chair was sitting that certain personage with whom they wished to exchange me.

Fanny was my junior by a year:—she resembled neither father nor mother, with the exception that the family wart, in the form of a little brown freckle, was imprinted in the middle of her left cheek. During the whole time that elapsed before our arrival here I had been filled with prejudices against her, prejudices which the sight of her made only more alarming. She had an ever-smiling, pink and white face, mischievous blue eyes, and a curious snub-nose; when she smiled, little dimples formed in her cheeks and her mouth was ever ready to laugh. When she did laugh, her double row of white teeth sparkled; in a word she was as ugly as the devil.

All three were busy knitting as we entered. When the door opened, they all put down their knitting. I kissed the hands of both the elder ladies, who embraced me in return, but my attention was entirely devoted to the little lively witch, who did not wait a moment, but ran to meet grandmother, threw herself upon her neck, and kissed her passionately; then, bowing and curtseying before us, kissed Lorand twice, actually gazing the while into his eyes.

A cold chill seized me. If this little snub-nosed devil dared to go so far as to kiss me, I did not know what would become of me in my terror.

Yet I could not avoid this dilemma in any way. The terrible little witch, having done with the others, rushed upon me, embraced me, and kissed me so passionately that I was quite ashamed; then twining her arm in mine, dragged me to the little arm-chair from which she had just risen, and compelled me to sit down, though we could scarcely find room in it for us both. Then she told many things to me in that unknown tongue, the only result of which was to persuade me that my poor good mother would have a noisy baggage to take the place of her quiet, obedient little son; I felt sure her days would be embittered by that restless tongue. Her mouth did not stop for one moment, yet I must confess that she had a voice like a bell.

That was again a family peculiarity. Mother Fromm was endowed with an inexhaustible store of that treasure called eloquence: and a sharp, strong voice, too, which forbade the interruption of any one else, with a flow like that of the purling stream. The grandmamma had an equally generous gift, only she had no longer any voice: only every second word was audible, like one of those barrel-organs, in which an occasional note, instead of sounding, merely blows.

Our business was to listen quietly.

For my part, that was all the easier, as I could not suspect what was the subject of this flow of barbarian words; all I understood was that, when the ladies spoke to me, they addressed me as "Istok,"[7] a jest which I found quite out of place, not knowing that it was the German for "Why don't you eat?" For you must know the coffee was brought immediately, with very fine little cakes, prepared especially for us under the personal supervision of Father Fromm.

> [7] "Issdoch," the German for "but eat." (Why don't you eat?)
> While Istok is a nickname for Stephan in Magyar.

Even that little snub-nosed demon said "Issdoch," seized a cake, dipped it in my coffee, and forcibly crammed it into my mouth, when I did not wish to understand her words.

Debts of Honor

But I was not at all hungry. All kinds of things were brought onto the table, but I did not want anything. Father Fromm kept calling out continually in student guise "Comedi! Comedi!" a remark which called forth indignant remonstrances from mamma and grossmamma; how could he call his own dear "Kugelhuff"[8] a "comedy!!!"

[8] A cake eaten everywhere in Hungary.

Fanny in sooth required no coaxing. At first sight anyone could see that she was the spoiled child of the family, to whom everything was allowed. She tried everything, took a double portion of everything and only after taking what she required did she ask "darf ich?"[9] — and I understood immediately from the tone of her voice and the nodding of her head, that she meant to ask "if she might."

[9] i. e., darf ich, "may I?"

Then instead of finishing her share she had the audacity to place her leavings on my plate, an action which called forth rebuke enough from Grossmamma. I did not understand what she said, but I strongly suspected that she abused her for wishing to accustom the "new child" to eating a great deal. Generally speaking, I had brought from home the suspicion that, when two people were speaking German before me, they were surely hatching some secret plot against me, the end of which would be, either that I would not get something, or would not be taken somewhere, where I wished to go.

I would not have tasted anything the little snub-nose gave me, if only for the reason that it was she who had given it. How could she dare to touch my plate with those dirty little hands of hers, that were just like cats-paws?

Then she gave everything I would not accept to the little kitten; however, the end of it all was, that she again turned to me, and asked me to play with the kitten.

Incomprehensible audacity! To ask me, who was already a school-student, to play with a tiny kitten.

Debts of Honor

"Shoo!" I said to the malicious creature; a remark which, notwithstanding the fact that it seemed to belong to some strange-tongued nationality, the animal understood, for it immediately leaped down off the table and ran away. This caused the little snub-nose to get angry with me, and she took her sensitive revenge upon me, by going across to my grandmother, whom she tenderly caressed, kissing her hand, and then nestled to her bosom, turning her back on me; once or twice she looked back at me, and if at the moment my eye was on her, sulkily flung back her head; as if that was any great misfortune to me.

Little imp! She actually occupied my place beside my grandmother—and before my eyes too.

Well, and why did I gaze at her, if I was so very angry with her? I will tell you truly; it was only that I might see to what extremes she would carry her audacity. I would far rather have been occupied in the fruitless task of attempting to discover something intelligent in a conversation that was being carried on before me in a strange tongue: an effort that is common to all men who have a grain of human curiosity flowing in their veins, and that, as is well-known, always remains unsuccessful.

Still one combination of mine did succeed. That name "Henrik" often struck my ear. Father Fromm was called Henrik, but he himself uttered the name: that therefore could not be other than his son. My grandmother spoke of him in pitiful tones, whereas Father Fromm assumed a look of inexorable severity, when he gave information on this subject; and as he spoke I gathered frequently the words "prosodia,"—"pensum"—"labor"—"vocabularium"—and many other terms common to dog-Latin: among which words like "secunda"—"tertia"—"carcer" served as a sufficiently trustworthy compass to direct me to the following conclusion: My friend Henrik might not put in an appearance to-day at supper, because he did not know his lessons, and was to remain imprisoned in the house until he could improve his standing by learning to repeat, in the language of a people long since dead, the names of a host of eatables.

Poor Henrik!

I never had any patience with the idea of anyone's starving, and moreover starving by way of punishment. I could understand anyone being done to death at once: but the idea of condemning anyone in cold blood to starve, to wrestle with his own body, to strive with his own heart and stomach, I always regarded as cruelty. I deemed that if I took one of those little cakes, which that audacious girl had piled up before me so forcibly, and put it in my pocket, it would not be wasted.

I waited cautiously until nobody was looking my way, and then slipped the cake into my pocket without accident.

Without accident? I only remarked it, when that little snub-nose laughed to herself. Just at that moment she had squinted towards me. But she immediately closed her mouth with her hand, giggling between her fingers, the while her malicious, deceitful eyes smiled into mine. What would she think? Perhaps that I am too great a coward to eat at table, and too insatiable to be satisfied with what I received. Oh! how ashamed I was before her! I would have been capable of any sacrifice to secure her secrecy, perhaps even of kissing her, if she would not tell anyone.... I was so frightened.

My fright was only increased by the grandmother, who first looked at the cake-dish, and then looked at each plate on the table in turn, subsequently resetting her gaze upon that cake-dish; then she gazed up to the ceiling, as if making some calculation, which she followed up by considerable shaking of her head.

Who could not understand that dumb speech? She had counted the cakes; calculated how many each had devoured; how many had been put on the dish, had added and subtracted, with the result that one cake was missing: what had become of it? An inquisition would follow: the cake would be looked for, and found in my pocket, and then no water could ever wash away my shame.

Every moment I expected that little demoniacal curiosity to point to me with that never-resting hand of hers, and proclaim: "there in the new child's pocket is the cake."

She was already by my side, and I saw that father, mother and Grandmother Fromm turned to me all with inquiring looks, and addressed some terrible "interpellatio" to me, which I did not understand, but could suspect what it was. And Lorand and grandmother did not come to my aid to explain what it all meant.

Instead of which snub-nose swept up to me and, repeating the same question, explained it by pantomimic gestures; laying one hand upon the other, then placing her head upon them, gently closed her eyes.

Oh, she was asking, if I were sleepy? It was remarkable, how this insufferable creature could make me understand everything.

Never did that question come more opportunely. I breathed more freely. Besides, I made up my mind never to call her "snub-nose devil" any more.

Grandmother allowed me to go: little Fanny was to show me to my room: I was to sleep with Henrik: I said good-night to all in turn, and so distracted was I that I kissed even Fanny's hand. And the little bundle of malice did not prevent me, she merely laughed at me for it.

This girl had surely been born merely to annoy me.

She took a candle in her hand and told me to follow her: she would lead the way.

I obeyed her.

We had not quite reached the head of the corridor when the draught blew out the candle.

We were in complete darkness, for there was no lamp burning here of an evening on the staircase, only a red glimmer, reflected probably from the bakery-chimney, lit up the darkness, and even that disappeared as we left the corridor.

Fanny laughed when the candle went out, and tried for a time to blow the spark into a flame: not succeeding, she put down the candle-stick, and leaning upon my arm assured me that she could show me the way in this manner too.

Then, without waiting for a remark from me, she took me with her into the pitchy darkness. At first she spoke, to encourage me, and then began to sing, perhaps to make me understand better; and felt with her hands for the doors, and with her feet for the steps of the staircase. Meanwhile I continually reflected: "this terrible malicious trifler is plotting to lead me into some flour-bin, shut the door upon me, and leave me there till the morning: or to let me step in the darkness into some flue, where I shall fall up to my neck into the rising dough;—for of that everything is full."

Poor, kind, good Fanny! I was so angry with you, I hated you so when I first saw you!... And now, as we grow old....

I should never have believed that anyone could lead me in such subterranean darkness through that winding labyrinth, where even in broad daylight I often entirely lost my whereabouts. I only wondered that this extraordinarily audacious girl could refrain from pulling my hair as she led me through that darkness, her arm in mine, though she had such a painful opportunity of doing so. Yes, I quite expected her to do so.

Finally we reached a door, before which there was no need of a lamp to assure a man of the room he was seeking. Through the door burst that most sorrowful of all human sounds, the sound of a child audibly wrestling with some unintelligible verse, twenty, fifty, a thousand times repeated anew, and anew, without becoming intelligible, while the verse had not yet taken its place in the child's head. Through the boards sounded afar a spiral Latin phrase.

"His atacem, panacem, phylacem, coracem que facemque." Then again:

"His acatem, panacem, phylacem, coracem que facemque."

And again the same.

Fanny placed her ear against the door and seized my hand as a hint to be quiet. Then she laughed aloud. How can anyone find an amusing subject in a poor hard-brained "studiosus," who cannot grasp that rule, inevitable in every career in life, that the second syllable of dropax, antrax, climax "et caethra graeca" in the first case is long, in the second short—a rule extremely useful to a man later in life when he gets into some big scrape?

But Fanny found it extremely ridiculous. Then she opened the door and nodded to me to follow her.

It was a small room under the staircase. Within were two beds, placed face to face; on one I recognized my own pillows which I had brought with me, so that must be my sleeping place. Beside the window was a writing-table on which was burning a single candle, its wick so badly trimmed as to prove that he who should have trimmed it had been so deeply engaged in work that he had not remarked whether darkness or light surrounded him.

Weeping, his head buried in his hands, my friend Henrik was sitting at that table; as the door opened he raised his head from the book over which he was poring. He greatly resembled his mother and grandmother: he had just such a pronounced nose; but he had bristly hair, like his father, only black and not so closely cropped. He, too, had the family wart, actually in the middle of his nose.

As he looked up from his book, in a moment his countenance changed rapidly from fear to delight, from delight to suspicion. The poor boy thought he had gained a respite, and that the messenger had come with the white serviette to invite him to supper: he smiled at Fanny entreating compassion, and then, when he saw me, became embarrassed.

Fanny approached him with an enquiring air, placed one hand on his thigh, with the other pointed to the open book, probably intending to ask him whether he knew his lessons.

The great lanky boy rose obediently before his little confessor, who scarce reached to his shoulder, and proceeded to put himself to rights. He handed the book to Fanny, casting a farewell glance at the disgusting, insufferable words; and with a great gulp by which he hoped to remove all obstacles from the way of the lines he had to utter, cleared his throat and began:—

"His abacem, phylacem ..."

Fanny shook her head. It was not good.

Henrik was frightened. He began again:

"His abacem, coracem...."

Again it was wrong. The poor boy began over five or six times, but could not place those pagan words in the correct order, and as the mischievous girl shook her head each time he made a mistake, he finally became so confused that he could not even begin; then he reddened with anger, and, gnashing his teeth, tore the graceless book out of Fanny's hand, threw it down upon the table and commenced an assault upon the heathen words, and with glaring eyes read the million-times repeated incantation: "His abacem, panacem, phylacem, coracem facemque," striking the back of his head with clinched fist at every word.

Fanny burst into uncontrollable laughter at this scene.

I, however, was very sorry for my companion. My learning had been easy enough, and I regarded him with the air of a lord who looks from his coach window at the bare-footed passers-by.

Fanny was unmerciful to him.

Henrik looked up at her, and though I did not understand her words, I understood from his eyes that he was asking for something to eat.

The strong-headed sister actually refused his request.

I wished to prove my goodness of heart—my vanity also inclined me to inform this mischievous creature that I had not put away the bun for my own sake—So I stepped up to Henrik and, placing my hand on his shoulder with condescending friendliness, pressed into his hand the cake I had reserved for him.

Henrik cast a glance at me like some wild beast which has an aversion to petting, then flung the bun under the table with such violence that it broke into pieces.

"Dummer kerl!"[10]

    [10] "Stupid fellow!"

I remember well, that was the first title of respect I received from him.

Planting his knuckles on the top of my head, he performed a tattoo with the same all over my head.

That is called, in slang, "holz-birn."[11] By this process of "knuckling" the larger boys showed their contempt for the smaller, and it belongs to that kind of teasing which no self-respecting boy ever would allow to pass unchallenged. And before this girl, too!

    [11] Literally "Wild-pear" (*wood-pear*) a method of "knuckling" down the younger boys.

Henrik was taller than I, by a head, but I did not mind. I grasped him by the waist, and grappled with him. He wished to drag me in the direction of my bed, in order to throw me on to it, but with a quick movement I cast him on his own bed, and holding his two hands tight on his chest, cried to him:

"Pick up the bun immediately!"

Henrik kicked and snarled for a moment, then began to laugh, and to my astonishment begged me, in student tongue, to release him: "We should be good friends." I released him, we shook hands, and the fellow became quite lively.

What astonished me most was that, at the time I was throwing her brother, Fanny did not come to his aid nor tear out my eyes, she merely laughed, and screamed her approval. She seemed to be thoroughly enjoying herself.

After this we all three looked for the fragments of Henrik's broken bun, which the good fellow with an expression of contentment dispatched on its natural way; then Fanny produced a couple of secreted apples which she had "sneaked" for him. I found it remarkable beyond words that this impertinent child's thoughts ran in the same direction as my own.

From that hour Henrik and I were always fast friends; we are so to this day. When we got into bed I was curious as to the dreams I should have in the strange house. There is a widely-spread belief that what one dreams the first night in a new house will in reality come to pass.

I dreamed of the little snub-nose.

She was an angel with wings, beautiful dappled wings, such as I had read of not long since in the legend of Vörösmarty.[12] All around me she fluttered: but I could not move, my feet were so heavy, albeit there was something from which I ought to escape, until she seized my hand and then I could run so lightly that I did not touch the earth even with the tips of my feet.

> [12] A great Hungarian poet who lived and died in the early part of this century. He wrote legends and made a remarkable translation of some of Shakespeare's works.

How I worried over that dream! A snub-nosed angel— What mocking dreams a man has, to be sure.

The next day we were early astir; to me it seemed all the earlier, as the window of our little room looked out on to the narrow courtyard, where the day dawned so slowly, but Márton, the principal assistant, was told off to brawl at the schoolboy's door, when breakfast was being prepared:

"Surgendum disciple!"

I could not think what kind of an assault it was, that awoke me from my dream, when first I heard the clamorous clarion call. But Henrik jumped to his feet at once, and roused me from my bed, explaining, half in student language, half by gesture, that we should go down now to the bakery to see how the buns and cakes were baked. There was no need to dress; we might go in our night clothes, as the bakers wear quite similar costumes. I was curious, and easily persuaded to do anything; we put on our slippers and went down together to the bakery.

It was an agreeable place; from afar it betrayed itself by that sweet confectionery smell, which makes a man imagine that if he breathes it in long enough he will satisfy his hunger therewith. Everything in the whole place was as white as snow; everything so clean; great bins full of flour; huge vessels full of swelling dough, from which six white-dressed, white-aproned assistants were forming every conceivable kind of cake and bun; piled upon the shelves of the gigantic white oven the first supply was gradually baking, filling the whole room with a most agreeable odor.

Master Márton, when he caught sight of me, began to welcome me in a kind of broken Hungarian "Jo reggelt jo reggelt!"[13]

[13] Good morning.

He had a curious knack of putting the whole of his scalp into motion whenever he moved his eyebrows up or down; a comical peculiarity of which he availed himself whenever he wished to make anyone laugh, and saw that his words did not have the desired effect.

Henrik set to work and competed with the baker's assistants; he was clever at making dainty little titbits of cakes quite as clever as anyone there; and pleasure beamed on his face when the old assistant praised his efforts.

"You see," Márton said to me, "what a ready assistant he would make! In two years he might be free. But the old man is determined he shall learn and study; he wants to make a councillor of him." With these words Márton, by a movement of his eyebrows, sent the whole of the skin on his head to form a bunch on the crown, for all the world as if it had been a wig on springs.

"Councillor, indeed! a councillor who gnaws pens when he is hungry! Thanks; not if they gave me the tower of St. Michael. A councillor, who, with paper in hand and pen behind ear, goes to visit the bakers in turn, and weighs their loaves in the balance to see if they are correct weight."

It seemed that Márton did not take into consideration any other duties that a councillor might have besides the examining of bakers' loaves—and that one could hardly gain his approval.

"Yet, if you take a little pains for their sake, you will find them as gentle as lambs. Give them a 'heitige striozts,'[14] or All Saints Day, and you will secure your object. Such is Mr. Dintenklek." At this point Márton could not refrain from breaking out into an unmelodious "Gassenhauer"[15] the refrain of which was, "Alas! Mr. Dintenklek."

[14] A kind of dainty bit suitable to this "holy" occasion.

[15] A popular air sung in the streets.

Two or three assistants joined in the refrain, of which I did not understand a word; but as Márton uttered the final words, "Alas Mr. Dintenklek," his gestures were such as to lead me to suspect that this Mr. Dintenklek must be some very ridiculous figure in the eye of baker's assistants.

"Why, of course, Henrik must learn law. The old man says he, too, might have become a councillor if he had concluded his studies at school. What a blessing he did not. As it is, he almost murders us with his learning. He is always showing off how much Latin he knows. Yes, the old man Latinizes."

As he said this Márton could scarcely control the skin of his head, so often did he have to twitch his eyebrows in order to express the above opinion, which he held about his master's pedantry.

Then with a sudden suspicion he turned to me:

"You don't wish to be a councillor, I suppose?"

I earnestly assured him that, on the contrary, I was preparing for a vacancy in the county.

"Oho! lieutenant-governor? That is different, quite another thing; travelling in a coach. No putting on of mud boots when it is muddy. That I allow." And, in order to show how deep a respect he bore towards my presumptive office position, he drew his eyebrows up so high that his cap fell back upon his neck.

"Enough of dough-kneading for the present, Master Henrik. Go back to your room and write out your 'pensum,' for you will again be forbidden breakfast, if it is not ready."

Henrik did not listen to him, but worked away for all the world as if he was not being addressed.

Meanwhile Márton was cutting a large piece of dough into bits of exactly equal size, out of which the "Vienna" rolls were to be formed. This delicate piece of work needs an accurate eye to avoid cheating either one's master or the public.

"You see, he is at home here; he does not want his books. And there is nothing more beautiful, more refined than our art; nothing more remunerative; we deal with the blessing of God, for we prepare the daily bread. The Lord's Prayer includes the baker, 'Give us this day our daily bread.' Is there any mention anywhere of butchers, of tailors or of cobblers? Well, does anyone pray for meat, for coats, or for books? Let me hear about him. But they do pray for their daily bread, don't they? And does the prayer-book say anything concerning councillors? What? Who knows anything on that score?"

Some young assistant interrupted: "Why, of course, 'but deliver us from the evil one.'"

This caused everybody to laugh; it caused Henrik to spoil his buns, which had to be kneaded afresh. He was annoyed by the idea that he had learned all he had merely in order to be ridiculed here in the bakery.

"Ha, yes," remarked Master Márton, smiling. "It is a great misfortune that a man is never asked how he wishes to die, but a still greater misfortune if he is not asked how he wishes to live. My father destined me to be a butcher. I learned the whole trade. Then I suddenly grew tired of all that ox-slaughtering, and cow-skinning. I was always fascinated by these beautiful brown-backed rolls in the shop-window; whenever I passed before the confectionery window, the pleasant warm bread-odors just invited me in:—until at last I deserted my trade, and joined Father Fromm. At that time my moustache and beard were already sprouting, but I have never regretted my determination. Whenever I look at my clean, white shirt, I am delighted at the idea that I have not to sprinkle it with blood, and wear the blood-stained garment the rest of the day. Everyone should follow his own bent, should he not, Henrik?"

"True," muttered the youth in a tone of anger. "And yet the butcher's trade is as far above the councillor's as the weather-cock on St. Michael's tower is above our own vane. I do not like blood on my hands, yet at least I could wash it off; but if a drop of ink gets on my finger from my pen, for three days no pumice stone would induce it to depart. Yes, it is a glorious thing to be a baker's assistant."

Márton now busied himself in shovelling several dozen loaves of white bread into the heated oven. Meantime the whole "ménage" commenced with one voice to sing a peculiar air, which I had already heard several times resounding through the bakers' windows.

It runs as follows:

> "Oh, the kneading trough is fine,
> Very beautiful and fine.
>
> Straight and crooked, round in form
> Thin and long, three-legged too,
> Here's a stork, and here's a 'ticker,'
> While here's a pair of snuffers too,
> Stork and ticker, snuffers too,
> Bottles, tipsy Michael with them.
> Bottles, tipsy Michael with them,
> Stork and ticker, snuffers too,
> Thin and long, three-legged too,
> Straight and crooked, round in form.
>
> Oh! the kneading trough is fine,
> Very beautiful and fine."

Debts of Honor

They sang this air with such a passionate earnestness that, to this day I must believe, was caused, not by the beauty of the verses, or the corresponding melody, but rather by some superstitious feeling that their chanting would prevent the plague infecting the bread while it was baking, or perhaps the air served as an hour-glass telling them by its termination that now was the time to take the bread out of the oven. As they who are wont to use the Lord's Prayer for the boiling of eggs—God save the mark.

Henrik joined in. I saw he had no longer any idea of finishing his school tasks, and when the "Oh, the kneading trough" began anew, I left him in the bakery, and went upstairs to our room. On the table lay Henrik's unfortunate exercise-book open, full of corrections made in a different ink; of the new exercise only the first line had been begun. Immediately I collected the words wanted from a dictionary, and wrote the translation down on a piece of paper.

Not till an hour later did he return from the scene of his operations, and even then did not know to what he should turn his hand first. Great was his delight, then, to see the task already finished; he merely had to copy it.

He gazed at me with a curious peevishness and said: "Guter kerl."[16]

[16] Good fellow.

From his countenance I could not gather what he had said but the word kerl made me prepare myself for a repetition of the struggle of yesterday, for which I did not feel the least inclination.

Scarcely was the copying ready when the steps of Father Fromm resounded on the staircase. Henrik hastily thrust my writing into his pockets and was poring over the open book, when the old man halted before the door, so that when he opened it, such a noise resounded in the room as if Henrik were trying to drive an army of locusts out of the country: "his abacem."

"Ergo, ergo; quomodo?" said the old man, placing the palm of his hand upon my head. I saw that this was his manner of showing affection.

Debts of Honor

I ventured to utter my first German word, answering his query with a "Guter morgen;"[17] at which the old fellow shook his head and laughed. I could not imagine why. Perhaps I had expressed myself badly, or had astonished him with my rapid progress?

[17] Correctly, "Guten Morgen" (wunsch ich): "I wish (you) (a) good morning."

He did not enlighten me on the subject; instead he turned with a severe confessorial face to Henrik: "No ergo! Quid ergo? Quid seis? Habes pensum? Nebulo!"

Henrik tried whether he could move the skin of his head like Master Márton did, when he spoke of Mr. Fromm's Latin. For the sake of greater security he first of all displayed the written exercise to his father, thinking it better to leave his weaker side until later.

Father Fromm gazed at the deep learning with a critical eye, then graciously expressed his approval.

"Bonus, Bonus."

But the lesson?

That bitter piece!

Even yesterday, when he had only to recite them to the little snub-nose, Henrik did not know the verses, and to-day, the book was in the old man's hand! If he had merely taken the book in his hands! But with his disengaged hand he held a ruler with the evident intention of immediately pulling the boy up, if he made a mistake.

Poor Henrik, of course, did not know a single word. He gazed ever askance at Father Fromm's ruler, and when he reached the first obstacle, as the old fellow raised the ruler, probably merely with the intention of striking Henrik's mental capacity into action by startling him, Henrik was no more to be seen; he was under the bed, where he had managed to hide his long body with remarkable agility; nor would he come forth until Father Fromm promised he would not hurt him, and would take him to breakfast.

And Father Fromm kept the conditions of the armistice, only verbally denouncing the boy as he wriggled out of his fortress; I did not understand what he said, I only gathered by his grimaces and gestures that he was annoyed over the matter—by my presence.

The morning was spent in visiting professors. The director was a strongly-built, bony-faced, moustached man, with a high, bald forehead, broad-chested, and when he spoke, he did not spare his voice, but always talked as if he were preaching. He was very well satisfied with our school certificates, and made no secret of it. He assured grandmother he would take care of us and deal severely with us. He would not allow us to go astray in this town. He would often visit us at our homes; that was his custom; and any student convicted of disorderliness would be punished.

"Are the boys musicians?" he asked grandmother in harsh tones.

"Oh, yes; the one plays the piano, the other the violin."

The director struck the middle of the table with his fist: "I am sorry—but I cannot allow violin playing under any circumstances."

Lorand ventured to ask, "Why not?"

"Why not, indeed? Because that is the fountain-head of all mischief. The book, not the violin, is for the student. What do you wish to be? a gypsy, or a scholar? The violin betrays students into every kind of mischief. How do I know? Why, I see examples of it every day. The student takes the violin under his coat, and goes with it to the inn, where he plays for other students who dance there till morning with loose girls. So I break into fragments every violin I find. I don't ask whether it was dear; I dash it to the ground. I have already smashed violins of high value."

Grandmother saw it would be wiser not to allow Lorand to answer, so she hastened to anticipate him:

"Why, it is not the elder boy, sir, who plays the violin, but this younger one; besides, neither has been so trained as to wish to go to any undesirable place of amusement."

"That does not matter. The little one has still less need of scraping. Besides, I know the student; at home he makes saintly faces, as if he would not disturb water, but when once let loose, be it in an inn, be it in a coffee-house, there he will sit beside his beer, and join in a competition, to see who is the greatest tippler, shout and sing 'Gaudeamus igitur.' That is why I don't allow students to carry violins under their top-coats to inns, under any circumstances. I break the violin in pieces, and have the top-coat cut into a covert-coat. A student with a top-coat! That's only for an army officer. Then, I cannot suffer anyone to wear sharp-pointed boots which are especially made for dancing; flat-toed boots are for honest men; no one must come to my school in pointed boots, for I put his foot on the bench and cut away the points."

Grandmother hurried her visit to prevent Lorand having an opportunity of giving answer to the worthy man, who carried his zeal in the defence of morality to such a pitch as to break up violins, have top-coats cut down, and cut off the points of pointed boots.

It was a good habit of mine (long, long ago, in my childhood days), to regard as sacred anything a man, who had the right to my obedience, might say. When we came away from the director's presence, I whispered to Lorand in a distressed tone:

"Your boots seem to me a little too pointed."

"Henceforward I shall have them made still more pointed," replied Lorand,—an answer with which I was not at all satisfied.

In my eyes every serious man was surrounded by a "nimbus" of infallibility; no one had ever enlightened me on the fact that serious-minded men had themselves once been young, and had learned the student jargon of Heidelberg; that this director himself, after a noisy youth, had arrived at the idea that every young man has malicious propensities, and that what seems good in him is only make-believe, and so he must be treated with the severity of military discipline.

Then we proceeded to pay a visit to my class-master, who was the exact opposite of the director: a slight, many-cornered little man, with long hair brushed back, smooth shaved face, and such a thin, sweet voice that one might have taken every word of his as a supplication. And he was so familiar in his dealings with us. He received us in a dressing gown, but when he saw a lady was with us, he hastily changed that for a black coat, and asked pardon—why, I do not know.

Then he attempted to drive a host of little children out of his room, but without success. They clung to his hands and arms and he could not shake them off; he called out to some lady to come and help him. A sleepy face appeared at the other door, and suddenly withdrew on seeing us. Finally, at grandmother's request, he allowed the children to remain.

Mr. Schmuck was an excellent "paterfamilias," and took great care of children. His study was crammed with toys; he received us with great tenderness, and I remember well that he patted me on the head.

Grandmother immediately became more confident of this good man than she had been of his colleague, whom we had previously visited. For he was so fond of his own children. To him she related the secret that made her heart sad; explained why we were in mourning; told him that father was unfortunately dead, and that we were the sole hopes of our sickly mother; that up till now our behaviors had been excellent, and finally asked him to take care of me, the younger.

The good fellow clasped his hands and assured grandmother that he would make a great man of me, especially if I would come to him privately; that he might devote particular attention to the development of my talents. This private tuition would not come to more than seven florins a month. And that is not much for the whetting of one's mind; as much might be paid even for the grinding of scissors.

Grandmother, her spirits depressed by the previous reception, timidly ventured to introduce the remark that I had a certain inclination for the violin, but she did not know whether it was allowed?

The good man did not allow her to speak further. "Of course, of course. Music ennobles the soul, music calms the inclinations of the mind. Even in the days of Pythagoras lectures were closed by music. He who indulges in music is always in the society of good spirits. And here it will be very cheap; it will not cost more than six florins[18] a month, as my children have a music-master of their own."

[18] 1 florin equals 2s English money or 40 cents.

Dear grandmother, seeing his readiness to acquiesce, thought it good to make some more requests (this is always the way with a discontented people, too, when it meets with ready acquiescence in the powers that be). She remarked that perhaps I might be allowed to learn dancing.

"Why, nothing could be more natural," was the answer of the gracious man. "Dancing goes hand-in-hand with music; even in Greek days it was the choral revellers that were accompanied by the harp. In the classics there is frequent mention of the dance. With the Romans it belonged to culture, and according to tradition even holy David danced. In the world of to-day it is just indispensable, especially to a young man. An innocent enjoyment! One form of bodily exercise. It is indispensable that the young man of to-day shall step, walk, stand properly, and be able to bow and dance, and not betray at once, on his appearance, that he has come from some school of pedantry. And in this respect I obey the tendency of the age. My own children all learn to dance, and as the dancing-master comes here in any case my young friend may as well join my children; it will not cost more than five florins."

Grandmother was extraordinarily contented with the bargain; she found everything quite cheap.

"By coöperation everything becomes cheap. A true mental 'ménage.' Many learn together, and each pays a trifle. If you wish my young friend to learn drawing, it will not cost more than four florins; four hours weekly, together with the others. Perhaps you will not find it superfluous, that our young friend should make acquaintance with the more important European languages; he can learn, under the supervision of mature teachers, English and French, at a cost of not more than three florins, three hours a week. And if my young friend has a few hours to spare, he cannot do better than spend them in the gymnasium; gymnastic exercise is healthy, it encourages the development of the muscles along with that of the brain, and it does not cost anything, only ten florins entrance fee."

Grandmother was quite overcome by this thoughtfulness. She left everything in order and paid in advance.

I do not wish anyone to come to the conclusion, from the facts stated above, that in course of time I shall come to boast what a Paganini I became in time, what a Mezzofanti as a linguist, what a Buonarotti in art, what a Vestris in the dance, or what a Michael Toddy in fencing:—I hasten to remark that I do not even yet understand anything of all these things. I have only to relate how they taught them to me.

When I went to my private lessons—"together with the others"—the professor was not at home; we indulged in an hour's wrestling.

When I went to my dancing lessons—"together with the others"—the dancing master was missing: again an hour's wrestling.

During the French lessons we again wrestled, and during the drawing and violin hours we spent our time exactly as we did during the other hours; so that when the gymnastic lessons came round we had no more heart for wrestling.

I did just learn to swim,—in secret, seeing that it was prohibited, and truly without paying:—unless I may count as a forfeit penalty that mass of water I swallowed once, when I was nearly drowned in the Danube. None even dared to acquaint the people at home with the fact; Lorand saved me, but he never boasted of his feat.

As we left the house of this very kind man, who quite overcame grandmother and us, with his gracious and amiable demeanors, Lorand said:

"From this hour I begin to greatly esteem the first professor: he is a noble, straight-forward fellow."

I did not understand his meaning—that is, I did not wish to understand. Perhaps he wished to slight "my" professor.

According to my ethical principles it was purely natural that each student should admire and love that professor who was the director of his own class, and if one class is secretly at war with another, the only reason can be that the professor of one class is the opponent of the other. My kingdom is the foe of thy kingdom, so my soldiers are the enemies of thy soldiers.

I began to look at Lorand in the light of some such hostile soldier.

Fortunately the events that followed drove all these ideas out of my head.

CHAPTER III

MY RIGHT HONORABLE UNCLE

We were invited to dine with the Privy Councillor Bálnokházy, at whose house my brother was to take up his residence.

He was some very distant relation of ours; however, he received a payment for Lorand's board, seven hundred florins, a nice sum of money in those days.

My pride was the greatest that my brother was living in a privy councillor's house, and, if my school-fellows asked me where I lived, I never omitted to mention the fact that "my brother was living with Bálnokházy, P. C.," while I myself had taken up my abode merely with a baker.

Baker Fromm was indeed very sorry that we were not dining "at home." At least they might have left me alone there. That he did not turn to stone as he uttered these words was not my fault; at least I fixed upon him such basilisk eyes as I was capable of. What an idea! To refuse a dinner with my P. C. uncle for his sake! Grandmother, too, discovered that I also must be presented there.

We ordered a carriage for 1:30; of course we could not with decency go to the P. C.'s on foot. Grandmother fastened my embroidered shirt under my waistcoat, and I was vain enough to allow the little pugnose to arrange my tie. She really could make pretty bows, I thought. As I gazed at myself in the looking-glass, I found that I should be a handsome boy when I had put on my silver-buttoned attila.[19] And if only my hair was curled! Still I was completely convinced that in the whole town there did not exist any more such silver-buttoned attilas as mine.

[19] The coat worn by the hussars, forming part, as it does, of all real Magyar *levée* dresses.

Only it annoyed me to watch the little pugnose careering playfully round me. How she danced round me, without any attempt to conceal the fact that I took her fancy; and how that hurt my pride!

At the bottom of the stairs the comical Henrik was waiting for me, with a large brush in his hand. He assured me that my attila had become floury—surely from Fanny's apron, for that was always floury—and that he must brush it off. I only begged him not to touch my collar with the hair brush; for that a silk brush was required, as it was velvet.

I believe I set some store by the fact that the collar of my attila was velvet.

From the arched doorway old Márton, too, called after me, as we took our seats, "Good appetite, Master Sheriff!" and five or six times moved his cap up and down on the top of his head.

How I should have loved to break his nose! Why is he compromising me here before my brother? He might know that when I am in full dress I deserve far greater respect from when he sees me before him in my night clothes.—But so it is with those whose business lies in flour.

But let us speak no more of bakers; let us soar into higher regions.

Our carriage stopped somewhere in the neighborhood of the House of Parliament, where there was a two-storied house, in which the P. C. lived.

The butler—pardon! the chamberlain—was waiting for us downstairs at the gate (it is possible that it was not for us he was waiting). He conducted us up the staircase; from the staircase to the porch; from the porch to the anteroom; from the anteroom to the drawing-room, where our host was waiting to receive us.

I used to think that at home we were elegant people—that we lodged and lived in style; but how poor I felt we were as we went through the rooms of the Bálnokházys. The splendor only incited my admiration and wonder, which was abruptly terminated by the arrival of the host and hostess and their daughter, Melanie, by three different doors. The P. C. was a tall, portly man, broad-shouldered, with black eyebrows, ruddy cheeks, a coal-black moustache curled upward; he formed the very ideal I had pictured to myself of a P. C. His hair also was of a beautiful black, fashionably dressed.

He greeted us in a voice rich and stentorian; kissed grandmother; offered his hand to my brother, who shook it; while he allowed me to kiss his hand.

What an enormous turquoise ring there was on his finger!

Then my right honorable aunt came into our presence. I can say that since that day I have never seen a more beautiful woman. She was then twenty-three years of age; I know quite surely. Her beautiful face, its features preserved with the enamel of youth, seemed almost that of a young girl; her long blonde tresses waved around it; her lips, of graceful symmetry, always ready for a smile; her large, dark blue, and melancholy eyes shadowed by her long eyelashes; her whole form seemed not to walk—rather fluttered and glided; and the hand which she gave me to kiss was transparent as alabaster.

My cousin Melanie was truly a little angel. Her first appearance, to me, was a phenomenon. Methinks no imagination could picture anything more lovely, more ethereal than her whole form. She was not yet more than eight years of age, but her stature gave her the appearance of some ten years. She was slender, and surely must have had some hidden wings, else it were impossible she could have fluttered as she did upon those symmetrical feet. Her face was fine and *distingué*, her eyes artful and brilliant; her lips were endowed with such gifts already—not merely of speaking four or five languages—such silent gifts as brought me beside myself. That child-mouth could smile enchantingly with encouraging calmness, could proudly despise, could pout with displeasure, could offer tacit requests, could muse in silent melancholy, could indulge in enthusiastic rapture—could love and hate.

How often have I dreamed of that lovely mouth! how often seen it in my waking hours! how many horrible Greek words have I learned while musing thereon!

I could not describe that dinner at the Bálnokházys to the end. Melanie sat beside me, and my whole attention was directed toward her.

How refined was her behavior! how much elegance there was in every movement of hers! I could not succeed in learning enough from her. When, after eating, she wiped her lips with the napkin, it was as if spirits were exchanging kisses with the mist. Oh, how interminably silly and clumsy I was beside her! My hand trembled when I had to take some dish. Terrible was the thought that I might perchance drop the spoon from my hand and stain her white muslin dress with the sauce. She, for her part, seemed not to notice me; or, on the contrary, rather, was quite sure of the fact that beside her was sitting now a living creature, whom she had conquered, rendered dumb and transformed. If I offered her something, she could refuse so gracefully; and if I filled her glass, she was so polite when she thanked me.

No one busied himself very particularly with me. A young boy at my age is just the most useless article; too big to be played with, and not big enough to be treated seriously. And the worst of it is that he feels it himself. Every boy of twelve years has the same ambition—"If only I were older already!"

Now, however, I say, "If I could only be twelve years old still!" Yet at that time it was a great burden to me. And how many years have passed since then!

Only toward the end of dinner, when the younger generation also were allowed to sip some sweet wine from their tiny glasses, did I find the attention of the company drawn toward me; and it was a curious case.

The butler filled my glass also. The clear golden-colored liquor scintillated so temptingly before me in the cut glass, my little neighbor would so enchantingly deepen the ruddiness of her lips with the liquor from her glass, that an extraordinarily rash idea sprang up within me.

Debts of Honor

I determined to raise my glass, clink glasses with Melanie, and say to her, "Your health, dear cousin Melanie." The blood rushed into my temples as I conceived the idea.

I was already about to take my glass, when I cast one look at Melanie's face, and in that moment she gazed upon me with such disheartening pride that in terror I withdrew my hand from my glass. It was probably this hesitating movement of mine that attracted the P. C.'s attention, for he deigned to turn to me with the following condescending remark (intended perhaps for an offer):

"Well, nephew, won't you try this wine?" With undismayed determination I answered:

"No."

"Perhaps you don't wish to drink wine?"

Cato did not utter the phrase "Victrix causa diis placuit, sed victa Catoni," with more resolution than that with which I answered:

"Never!"

"Oho! you will never drink wine? We shall see how you keep your word in the course of time!"

And that is why I kept my word. Till to-day I have never touched wine. Probably that first fit of obstinacy caused my determination; in a word, slighted in the first glass, I never touched again any kind of pressed, distilled, or burnt beverage. So perhaps my house lost in me an after-dinner celebrity.

"Don't be ashamed, nephew," encouragingly continued my uncle; "this wine is allowed to the young also, if they dip choice Pressburg biscuits in it; it is a very celebrated biscuit, prepared by M. Fromm."

My blood rose to my cheeks. M. Fromm! My host! Immediately the conversation will turn upon him, and they will mention that I am living with him; furthermore, they will relate that he has a little pug-nosed daughter, that they are going to exchange me with her. I should sink beneath the earth for very shame before my cousin Melanie! And surely, one has only to fear something and it will indeed come to pass. Grandmother was thoughtless enough to discover immediately what I wished to conceal, with these words:

"Desiderius is going to live with that very man."

"Ha ha!" laughed uncle, in high humor (his laughter penetrated my very marrow). "With the celebrated 'Zwieback'[20] baker! Why, he can teach my nephew to bake Pressburg biscuits."

[20] Biscuit.

How I was scalded and reduced to nothing, how I blushed before Melanie! The idea of my learning to bake biscuits from M. Fromm! I should never be able to wash myself clean of that suspicion.

In my despair I found myself looking at Lorand. He also was looking at me. His gaze has remained lividly imprinted in my memory. I understood what he said with his eyes. He called me coward, miserable, and sensitive, for allowing the jests of great men to bring blushes to my cheeks. He was a democrat always!

When he saw that I was blushing, he turned obstinately toward Bálnokházy, to reply for me.

But I was not the only one who read his thoughts in his eyes; another also read therein, and before he could have spoken, my beautiful aunt took the words out of his mouth, and with lofty dignity replied to her husband:

"Methinks the baker is just as good a man as the privy councillor."

I shivered at the bold statement. I imagined that for these words the whole company would be arrested and thrown into prison.

Bálnokházy, with smiling tenderness, bent down to his wife's hand and, kissing it, said:

"As a man, truly, just as good a man; but as a baker, a better baker than I."

Now it was Lorand's turn to crimson. He riveted his eyes upon my aunt's face.

My right honorable uncle hastened immediately to close the rencontre with a vanquishing kiss upon my aunt's snow-white hand, a fact which convinced me that their mutual love was endless. In general, I behaved with remarkable respect toward that great relation of ours, who lived in such beautiful apartments, and whose titles would not be contained in three lines.

I was completely persuaded that Bálnokházy, my uncle, had few superiors in celebrity in the world, for personal beauty (except, perhaps, my brother Lorand) none; his wife was the most beautiful and happiest woman under the sun; and my cousin Melanie such an angel that, if she did not raise me up to heaven, I should surely never reach those climes.

And if some one had said to me then, "Let us begin at the beginning; that rich hair on Bálnokházy's head is but a wig," I should have demanded pardon for interrupting: I can find nothing of the least importance to say against the wearing of wigs. They are worn by those who have need of them; by those whose heads would be cold without them, who catch rheumatism easily with uncovered head. Finally, it is nought else but a head-covering for one of æsthetic tastes; a cap made of hair.

This is all true, all earnest truth; and yet I was greatly embittered against that some one who discovered to me for the first time that my uncle Bálnokházy wore a wig, and painted his moustache (with some colored unguent, of course, nothing else). And I am still the enemy of that some one who repeated that before me. He might have left me in happy ignorance.

Even if some one had said that this showy wealth, which indicated a noble affluence, was also such a mere wig as the other, covering the baldness of his riches; if some one had said that these hand-kissing companions, in whose every word was melody when they spoke the one to the other, that they did not love, but hated and despised one another; if some one had said that this lovely, ideal angel of mine even—but no farther, not so much at once!

At the end of dinner our noble relations were so gracious as to permit my cousin Melanie to play the piano before us. She was only eight years old as yet, still she could play as beautifully as other girls of nine years.

I had very rarely heard a piano; at home mother played sometimes, though she did not much care for it. Lorand merely murdered the scales, which was not at all entertaining for me.

My cousin Melanie executed opera selections, and a French quadrille which excited my extremest admiration. My beautiful aunt laid stress upon the fact that she had only studied two years. A very intricate plan began to develop within me.

Melanie played the piano, I the violin. Nothing could be more natural than that I should come here with my violin to play an obligato to Melanie's piano; and if afterward we played violin and piano together perseveringly for eight or nine years, it would be impossible that we should not in the end reach the goal of life on that road.

In consequence I strove to display my usefulness by turning over the leaves of the music for her; and my pride was greatly hurt by the fact that my noble relations did not ask grandmother how I understood how to read music. Finally the end came to this, as to every good thing; my cousin Melanie was not quite "up" in the remaining pieces, though I would have listened even to half-learned pieces, but my grandmother was getting ready to return to the Fromms'. The Bálnokházys asked her to spend the night with them, but she replied that she had been there before, and that I was there too; and she would remain with the younger. I detested myself so for the idea that I was a drag upon my good grandmother; why, I ought to have kissed the dust upon her feet for those words:

"I shall remain with the younger." My brother I envied, who for his part was "at home" with the P. C.

When I kissed my relations' hands at parting, Bálnokházy thrust a silver dollar[21] into my hand, adding with magnificent munificence:

    [21] Thaler.

"For a little poppy-cake, you know."

Why, it is true, that in Pressburg very fine poppy-biscuits are made; and it is also true, that many poppy-goodies might be bought, a few at a time, for a dollar; likewise I cannot deny that so much money had never been in my hand, as my very own, to spend as I liked. I would not have exchanged it for two other dollars, if it had not been given me before Melanie. I felt that it degraded me in her eyes. I could not discover what to do with that dollar. I scarce dared to look at Melanie when he departed; still I remarked that she did not look at me either when I left.

At the door Lorand seized my hand.

"Desi," said he severely, "that thing that the P. C. thrust into your hand you must give to the butler, when he opens the carriage door."

I liked the idea. By that they would know who I was; and my eyes would no longer be downcast before cousin Melanie.

But, when I thrust the dollar into the butler's hand, I was so embarrassed by his matter-of-fact grandeur that any one who had seen us might have thought the butler had presented me with something. I hoped uncle would not exclude me from his house for that.

Long did that quadrille sound in my ears; long did that phenomenon-pianist haunt me; how long I cannot tell!

She was the standard of my ambition, the prize of a long race, which must be won. In my imagination the whole world thronged before her. I saw the roads by which one might reach her.

I too wished to be a man like them. I would learn diligently; I would be the first "eminence" in the school, my teacher would take pride in me, and would say at the public examination: "This will be a great man some day." I would pass my barrister's exams, with distinction; would serve my time under a sheriff; would court the acquaintance of great men of distinction; would win their favor by my gentle, humble conduct; I would be ready to serve; any work intrusted to me I would punctually perform; would not mix in evil company; would make my talent shine; would write odes of encomium, panegyrics, on occasions of note; till finally, I should myself, like my uncle, become "secretarius," "assessor," "septemvir," and "consiliarius."

Ha, ha, ha!

When we returned to Master Fromm's, the delicate attention of little Miss Pugnose was indeed burdensome. She would prattle all kinds of nonsense. She asked of what the fine dinner consisted; whether it was true that the daughter of the "consiliarius" had a doll that danced, played the guitar, and nodded its head. Ridiculous! As if people of such an age as Melanie and I interested themselves in dolls! I told Henrik to interpret this to her; I observed that it put her in a bad temper, and rejoiced that I had got rid of her.

I remarked that I must go and study, and the lesson was long. So I went to my room and began to study. Two hours later I observed that nothing of what I had learnt remained in my head; every place was full of that councillor's daughter.

In the evening we again assembled in Master Fromm's dining-room. Fanny again sat next to me, was again in good humor, treating me as familiarly as if we had been the oldest acquaintances; I was already frightened of her. It would be dreadful for the Bálnokházys to suspect that one had a baker's daughter as an acquaintance, always ready to jump upon one's neck when she saw one.

Well, fortunately she would be taken away next day, and then would be far away, as long as I remained in the house; we should be like two opposite poles, that avoid each other.

Before bedtime grandmother came into the room once more. She gave me my effects, counted over my linen. She gave me pocket-money, promising to send me some every month with Lorand's.

"Then I beg you," she whispered in my ear, "take care of Lorand!"

Again that word!

Again that hint that I, the child, must take care of my brother, the young man! But the second time the meaning, which the first time I had not understood, burst at once clearly upon me; at first I thought,

"Perhaps some mistaken wisdom or serious conduct on my part has deserved this distinction of looking after my brother." Now I discovered that the best guardian was eternal love; and mother and grandmother knew well that I loved Lorand better than he loved himself.

And indeed, what cause had they to fear for him? And from what could I defend him?

Was he not living in the best place in the world? And did I not live far from him?

Grandmother exacted from me a promise to write a diary of all that happened about us, and to send the same to her at the end of each month. I was to write all about Lorand too; for he himself was a very bad letter-writer.

I promised.

Then we kissed and took leave. They had to start early in the morning.

But the next day, when the carriage stood at the door, I was waiting ready dressed for them.

The whole Fromm family came down to the carriage to say adieu to the travellers.

That girl who was going to occupy my place was sad herself. Methought she was much more winning, when sadness made her eyes downcast.

One could see from her eyes that she had been weeping, that she was even now forcibly restraining herself from weeping. She spoke a few short words to me, and then disappeared behind grandmother in the carriage.

The whip cracked, the horses started, and my substitute departed for my dear home, while I remained in her place.

As I pondered for the first time over my great isolation, in a place where everybody was a stranger to me, and did not even understand my speech, at once all thought of the great man, the violin-virtuoso, the first eminence, the P. C., the heroic lover, disappeared from within me; I leaned my head against the wall, and would have wept could I have done so.

Debts of Honor

CHAPTER IV

THE ATHEIST AND THE HYPOCRITE

Let us leave for a while the journal of the student child, and examine the circumstances of the family circle, whose history we are relating.

There was living at Lankadomb an old heretic Samuel Topándy by name, who was related equally to the Bálnokházy and Áronffy families; notwithstanding this, the latter would never visit him on account of his conspicuously bad habits. His surroundings were of the most unfortunate description, and in distant parts it was told of him that he was an atheist of the most pronounced type.

But do not let any one think that the more modern freedom of thought had perhaps made Topándy cling to things long past, or that out of mental rationalism he had attempted, as a philosopher, to place his mind far beyond the visible tenets of religion. He was an atheist merely for his own amusement, that, by his denial of God, he might annoy those people—priests and the powers that be—with whom he came in contact.

For to annoy, and successfully annoy, has always been held as an amusement among frail humanity. And what can more successfully annoy than the ridiculing of that which a man worships?

The County Court had just put in a judicial "deed of execution," and had sent a magistrate, and a lawyer, supported by a posse of twelve armed gendarmes, for the purpose of putting an end, once for all, to those scandals, by which Topándy had for years been arousing the indignation of the souls of the faithful, causing them to send complaint after complaint in to the court.

Topándy offered cigars to the official "bailiffs." The magistrate, Michael Daruszegi, a young man of thirty, appeared to be still younger from his fair face. They had sent the under, not the chief magistrate, because he was a new hand, and would be more zealous. There is more firmness in a young man, and firmness was necessary when face to face with the disbeliever in God.

"We did not come here to smoke, sir," was the dry reply of the young officer. "We are on official business."

"The devil take official business. Don't 'sir' me, my dear fellow, but come, let us drink a 'chartreuse,' and then tell your business, in company with the lawyer, to my steward. If money is required, break open the granaries, take as much wheat as will settle your claims, then dine with me; there will be some more good fellows, who are coming for a little music. And to-morrow morning we can make out the report and enter it in the protocol."

As he said this he kept continuous hold on the "bailiff's" wrist, and led him inward into the inner room: and as he was far stronger by nature than the latter, it practically amounted to the leader of the attacking force being taken prisoner.

"I protest! I forbid every kind of confidence! This is serious business!"

In vain did the magistrate protest against his enforced march.

Soon the second part of the "legale testimonium;" Mr. Francis Butzkay, the lawyer, came to his aid with his stumpy, short-limbed figure: he had gazed for a time in passive inactivity at the fruitless struggle of his principal with the "in causam vocatus."

"I hope the gentleman will not give cause for the use of force; for we shall fetter him hand and foot in such a manner that no better safeguard will be necessary." So saying, our friend the lawyer smiled complaisantly, all over his round face, looking, with his long moustache, for all the world like the moon, when a long cloud is crossing its surface.

"Fetters indeed!" Topándy guffawed, "I should just like to see you! I beg you, pray put those fetters on me, merely for the sake of novelty, that I may be able to say: I also have had chains on me: at any rate on one of my legs, or one of my arms. It would be a damned fine amusement."

"Sir," exclaimed the magistrate, freeing his hand. "You must learn to respect in us the 'powers that be.' We are your judges, sent by the

County Court, entrusted with the task of putting an end to those scandals caused by you, which have filled every Christian soul with righteous indignation."

Topándy raised his eyes in astonishment at the envoys of the "powers that be."

"Oho, so it is not a case of a 'deed of execution?'"

"By no means. It is a far more important matter that is at stake. The Court considers the atheistical irreligious 'attentats' have gone too far and therefore has sent us—"

"—To preach me a sermon? No, sir magistrate, now you must really bring those irons, and put me in chains, and bind me, for unbound I will not listen to your sermon. Hold me down if you wish to preach words of devotion to me, for otherwise I shall bite, like a wild animal."

The magistrate retreated, in spite of his youthful daring; but the lawyer only smiled gently and did not even take his hands from behind his back.

"Really, sir, you must not get mad, or we shall have to take you to the Rókus hospital,[22] and put the strait-jacket on you."

[22] A hospital in Pest.

"The devil blight you!" roared Topándy, making for the two judges, and then retiring before the undisturbed smiling countenance of the lawyer. "Well, and what complaint has the Court to make of me? Have I stolen anything from anybody? Have I committed incendiarism? Have I committed a murder, that they come down so hard upon me?"

The magistrate was a ready speaker: immediately he answered with:

"Certainly, you have committed a theft: you have stolen the welfare of others' souls. Certainly you are an incendiary: you have set fire to the peace of faithful souls. Certainly you are a murderer: you have murdered the souls entrusted to you!"

Topándy, seeing there was no escape, turned entreatingly to the gendarmes who accompanied the magistrate.

"Boys, cherubims without wings, two of you come here and seize me, that I may not run away."

They obeyed him and laid hands on him.

"Well, my dear magistrate, fire away."

The worthy magistrate was annoyed, that this sorry business could not in any way assume a serious aspect.

"In the first place I come to see the execution of that judgment which the honorable Court has passed upon you."

"I bow my head,"—growled Topándy in a tone of derisive subservience.

"You have in your household youths and young girls growing up in various branches of service, who, born here, have never yet been baptized, thanks to your sinful neglect."

"Excuse me, the general drying up of wells...."

"Don't interrupt me," bawled the magistrate. "You should have produced your defence then and there, when and where you were accused; but as you did not appear at the appointed time, and obstinately procrastinated, you must listen to the sentence. All those boys and girls brought up within your premises must be taken into the country town and baptized according to the ordinances of religion."

"Could not the matter be finished here at once by the spring?"

The magistrate was beside himself with anger. But the good lawyer only smiled and said:

"Pray, sir, show a little common sense. The County Court compels none, against his will, to be a Christian: still one must belong to some religion. So if your lordship will not take the trouble to go with his household to the 'pater,' well, we shall take him to the rabbi: that will do just as well."

Topándy laughingly shook a menacing fist at the lawyer.

"You're a great gibbet! You always manage me. Well, let us rather go to the 'pater' than to the rabbi; but at least let my servants keep their old names."

"That is also inadmissible," answered the magistrate severely. "You have given your servants names, of a kind not usually borne by men. One is called Pirók,[23] another Czinke:[24] the name of one little girl—God save the mark—is Beelzebub! Who would register such names as these? They will all receive respectable names to be found in the Christian calendar; and any one, who dares to call them by the names they have hitherto borne shall pay as great a fine as if he had purposely calumniated a fellow-man. How many are there whom you have kept back in this manner from the water of Christianity?"

[23] Chaffinch.

[24] Titmouse, names of birds given as pet names to these servants.

"Four butlers, three maid-servants and two parrots."

"Perjurer! Your every word is spittle in the face of the true believers."

"Oh, gag me. I beg you to save me from perjury."

"Kindly call the people in question."

Topándy turned round and called to his butler who stood behind him:

"Produce Pirók, Estergályos,[25] Seprünyél,[26] then Kakukfü,[27] and Macskaláb;[28] comfort them with the news that they are going to enter Heaven, and will receive a fur-coat, a pair of boots, and a good gourd, from which the wine will never fail: all the gift of the honorable County Court."

[25] Turner.

[26] Broom.

[27] Thyme.

[28] Catsfoot.

"For my part," said the young representative of the law, standing on tip-toe, "I must ask you seriously to answer, with the moderation due to our presence, have you hidden any one?"

"Whether I have stolen away someone on hell's account? No, my dear fellow, I don't court Satan's acquaintance either: let him catch men for himself, if he can."

"I have a mandatum for your examination on oath."

"Keep your mandatum in your pocket, and measure out thirty florins' worth of oats from my granary: that's the fine. For I don't intend to be examined on oath."

"Indeed?"

"Of course. If you bid me, I will swear: I'm a rare hand at it; I can swear for half an hour at a stretch without repeating myself."

Again the smiling lawyer intervened:

"Give us your word of honor, then, that besides those produced, there is no servant in your household who has not yet been baptized."

"Well, I give you my word of honor that there is not 'in my household' even a living creature who is a pagan."

Topándy's word of honor only just escaped being broken for that gypsy-girl, whom he had bought in her sixth year from encamping gypsies for two dollars and a sucking pig, now, ten years later, did not belong any more to the household, but presided at table when gentlefolk came to dinner. But she still bore that heathen name, which she had received in the reedy thicket. She was still called Czipra.

And the godless fellow had snatched her away from the water of Christianity.

"Has the honorable Court any other complaint to make against me?"

"Yes, indeed. Not merely do you force your household to be pagan, but you are accused of disturbing in their religious services others who make no secret of their devout feelings."

"For example?"

"Just opposite you is the courtyard of Mr. Nepomuk John Sárvölgyi,[29] who is a very righteous man."

[29] Mud-valley.

"As far as I know, quite the opposite: he is always praying, a fact which proves that his sins must be very numerous."

"It is not your business to judge him. In our common world it is a merit, if someone dares to display to the public eye the fact that he still respects religion, and it is the duty of the law to protect him."

"Well, and how have I scandalized the good fellow?"

"Not long ago Mr. Sárvölgyi had a large Saint Nepomuk painted on the façade of his house, in oils on a sheet of bronze, and before the chief figure he was himself painted, in a kneeling position."

"I know: I saw it."

"From the lips of St. Nepomuk was flowing down in 'lapidarig' letters to the kneeling figure the following Latin saying: 'Mi fili, ego te nunquam deseram.'"

"I read the words."

"An iron grating was placed before the picture, and covered the whole niche, that infamous hands might not be able to touch it."

"A very wise idea."

"One morning following a very stormy night, to the astonishment of all, the Latin inscription had disappeared from the picture, and in its place there stood: 'Soon thou wilt pass from before me, thou old hypocrite!'"

"I can't help it, if the person in question changed his views."

"Why, certainly you can help it. The painter who prepared that picture, upon being cross-questioned, confessed and publicly affirmed that, in consideration of a certain sum of money paid by you, he had painted the latter inscription in oils, and over it, in water-colours, the former: so that the first shower washed off the upper surface from the picture, making the honest, zealous fellow an object of ridicule and contempt in his own house. Do you believe, sir, that such practical jokes are not punished by the hand of justice?"

"I am not in the habit of believing much."

"Among other things, however, you are bound to believe that justice will condemn you, first to pay a fine for blackmail; secondly, to pay for the repairs your tricks have made necessary."

"I don't see an atom of plaintiff's counsel here."

"Because plaintiff left the amount due him to the pleasure of the Court, to be devoted to charitable purposes."

"Good: then please break into the granaries."

"That we shall not do," interrupted the lawyer: "later on we shall take it out of the 'regalia.'"

Topándy laughed.

"My dear, good magistrate. Do you believe all that is in the Bible?"

"I am a true Christian."

"Then I appeal to your faith. In one place it stands that some invisible hand wrote, in the room of some pagan king—Belshazzar, if the story be true,—the following words,'Mene, Tekel, Upharsin.' If that hand could write then, why could it not now have written that second saying? And if it was the rain that washed away the righteous fellow's words, you must accuse the rain, for the fault lies there."

"These are indeed very weighty counter-charges: and you might have declared them all before the Court, to which you were summoned: you might have appealed even to the septemvirate, but as you did not appear then, you must bear the consequences of your obstinacy."

"Good; I shall pay the price," said Topándy laughing: — "But it was a good joke on my part after all, wasn't it?"

The magistrate showed an angry countenance.

"There will be other good jokes, too. Kindly wait until the end."

"Is the list of crimes still longer?"

"A severe enquiry into the sources would never find an end. The gravest charge against you is the profanation of holy places."

"I profane some holy place? Why, for twenty years I have not been in the precincts even of a church steeple."

"You desecrated a place used long ago for holy ceremonies by riotous revels."

"Oh, you mean that, do you? Let us make distinctions, if you please. Great is the difference between place and place. Do you mean the convent of the Red Brothers? That is no church. The late Emperor Joseph drove them out, and their property was put up to auction by the State, together with all the buildings situate thereon. Thus it was that I came into possession of the convent garden: I was there at the auction; I bid and it was knocked down to me. There were buildings on it, but whether any kind of church had been there I do not know, for they took away all the movables, and I found only bare walls. No kind of 'servitus' (engagement), as to what I would use the building for, had been included in the agreement of purchase. In this matter I know of others who were no more scrupulous. I know of a convent at Maria-Eich,[30] where in place of the ancient altar stands the peasant-chimney, and here the Swabian, into whose hands this honorable antiquity passed, keeps his maize; why, in a town beside the Danube may be seen what was once a convent, the 'aerarium' of which has been turned into a hospital."

[30] A place in Austria where sacred relics exist.

"Examples cannot help you. If the Swabian peasant keeps 'the blessing of God' in that place, from which they had once prayed for it, that is not profanity: the 'aerarium' too is pursuing an office of righteousness, in nursing bodily sufferings in the place where once mental sufferings gained comfort; but you have had disgusting pictures painted all over the walls that have come into your possession."

"I beg your pardon, the subjects are all chosen from classical literature: illustrations to the poems of Beranger and Lafontaine — 'Mon Curé,' 'Les Clefs Du Paradis,' 'Les Capulier,' 'Les Cordeliers Du Catalogue,' etc. Every subject a pious one."

"I know: I am acquainted with the originals of them. You may cover the walls of your own rooms with them, if you please: but I have brought four stone-workers with me, who, according to the judgment of the Court, are to erase all those pictures."

"Genuine iconoclasm!" guffawed Topándy, who found great amusement in arousing a whole county against him by his caprices. "Iconoclasts! Picture-destroyers!"

"There is something else we are going to destroy!" continued the magistrate. "In that place there was a crypt. What has become of it?"

"It is a crypt still."

"What is in it?"

"What is usually in a crypt: dead men of hallowed memory, who are lying in wooden coffins and waiting for the great awakening."

The magistrate made a face of doubt. He did not know whether to believe or not.

"And when you and your revelling companions hold your Bacchanalia there?"

"I object to the word 'Bacchanalia.'"

"True, it is still more. I should have used a stronger expression for that riot, when in scandalous undress, carrying in front a steak on a spit, the whole company sings low songs such as 'Megálljon Kend'[31] and 'Hetes, nyloczas,'[32] and in this guise makes scandalous processions from castle to cloister."

> [31] "Stop (you)," "Kend" being the pleasant abbreviation for "Kegyed," one method of addressing (literally "your grace"), corresponding to our "you."

> [32] "Seven and eight," referring to the number on the playing cards: the Austrian National Hymn is sung by great patriots to these words: the "king" and "ace" being the highest two cards, come together; and this is in Magyar király (king), diszno (ace); is also "swein."

"The authorities must indeed be greatly embittered against me, if they see anything scandalous in the fact that a body of good-humored men undress to the skin, when they are warm. As far as the so-called low songs are concerned, they have such innocent words, they might be printed in a book, while the melodies are very pious."

"The scandal is just that, that you parody pious songs, setting them to trivial words. Tell me what is the good of singing the eight cards of the pack[33] as a hymn. And if you are in a good humor, why do you go with it to the crypt?"

> [33] In Magyar cards the pack begins with the 7.

"You know we go there for a little mumony feast."

"Yes, for a little 'Mumon,'" interrupted the lawyer.

"That's just what I meant," said the atheist, laughing.

"What?" roared the magistrate, who now began to understand the enigma of the dead lying in their wooden coffins: "perhaps that is a cellar?"

"Of course: I never had a better cellar than that."

"And the dead, and the coffins?"

"Twenty-five round coffins, full of wine. Come, my dear sir, taste them all. I assure you you won't regret it."

The magistrate was now really in a fury: fury made a lion of him, so that he was quite capable of tearing his wrists by sheer force out of the imprisoning hands.

"An end to all familiarity! You stand before the authority of the law, with whom you cannot trifle. Give me the keys of the cloister, that I may clean the profaned place."

"Please break open the door."

"Would you not be sorry to ruin a patent lock?" suggested the lawyer.

"Well, promise me that you will taste at least 'one' brand: then I will open the door, for I don't intend to open any door under the title of 'cloister,' but any number under the title of 'cellar;' and in that case I shall pay in ready money."

The worthy lawyer tugged at the magistrate's sleeve; prudence yielded, and there are bounds to severity, too.

"Very well, the lawyer will taste the wine, but I am no drinker."

Topándy whispered some words in his butler's ears, whereupon that worthy suddenly disappeared.

"So you see, my dear fellow, we are agreed at last: now I should like to see the account of how much I owe to the county for my slight upon the Brotherhood."

"Here is the calculation: two hundred florins with costs, which amount to three florins, thirty kreuzer."

Debts of Honor

(This happened thirty years ago.)

"Further?"

"Further, the repair of the damage caused by you, the expenses of the present expedition, the daily pay and sustenance of the stonemasons aforesaid: making in all a sum total of two hundred and forty-three florins, forty kreuzers."

"A large sum, but I shall produce it from somewhere."

With the words Topándy drew out from his chest a drawer, and carrying it bodily as it was, put it down on the great walnut table, before the authorities of the law.

"Here it is!"

The interesting members of the law first drew back in alarm, and then commenced to roar with laughter. That drawer was filled with—I cannot express it in one word—but generally speaking—with paper.

A great variety of aged bank notes, some before the depreciation of value, others of a late date, still in currency: long bank-notes, black bank-notes, red spotted bank-notes; then, old cards: Hungarian, Swiss, French; old theatre-tickets, market pictures, the well-known product of street-humor; the tailor riding on a goat, the devil taking off bad women, a portrait of the long-moustached mayor of Nuremberg: a pile of envelopes, all heaped together in a huddle.

That was Topándy's savings bank.

He would always spend silver and gold money, but money paid to him in bank-notes, which he had to accept, he would put by year by year among this collection of cards, funny pictures, and theatrical programmes; this heap of value was never disturbed except when, as at present, some enforced visit had to be put up with, some so-called "execution."

"Please, help yourselves."

"What?" cried the magistrate. "Must we pick out the value from the non-value in this rubbish?"

"Now I am not so well-informed an expert as to distinguish what is recalled from what is still in circulation. Still my good friend is right, it is my duty to count out, yours to receive."

Then he plunged his hand into the treasure-heap, and counted over the bits of paper.

"This is good, this is not. This is still new, this is surely torn. Here's a five florin, here a ten florin note. This is the Knave of Hearts."

A little discussion occurred when he counted a label that had been removed from an old champagne bottle, as a ten florin note.

The gentlemen took exception to that: it must be thrown away.

"What, is this not money? It must be money. It is a French bank-note. There is written on it ten florins. Cliquot will pay if you take it to him."

Then he began to explain several comical pictures, and bargained with the authorities—how much would they give for them? he had paid a big price for them.

Finally the worthy lawyer had again to intervene: otherwise this liquidation might have lasted till the following evening; then, after a strict search in a critical manner, he withdrew two hundred and forty-three florins from the pile.

"A little water if you please, I should like to wash my hands," said the lawyer after his work, feeling like one who has separated the raw wheat from the tares.

"Like Pilate after passing judgment," jested Topándy. "You shall have all you want at once. Already there is an end to the legal manipulation: we are no longer 'legale testimonium' and 'incattus,' but guest and host."

"God forbid," repudiated the magistrate retiring towards the door. "We did not come in that guise. We do not wish to trouble you any longer."

"Trouble indeed!" said the accused, guffawing. "What, do you think this matter has been any trouble to me?—on the contrary, the most exquisite amusement! This annoyance of the county against me I would not sell for a thousand florins. It was glorious. 'Execution!' Legally erased pictures! An investigation into my private behavior! I shall live for a year on this joke. And you will see, my friends, I shall do so again soon. I shall find out some plan for getting them to take me in irons to the Court: a battalion of soldiers shall come for me, and they shall make me the son of the warden! Ha! ha! May I be damned if I don't succeed in my project! If they would but put me in prison for a year, and make me saw wood in the courtyard of the County Court, and clean the boots of the Lieutenant Governor. That is a capital idea! I shall not die until I reach that."

In the meantime a butler arrived with the water, while a second opened another door and invited the guests with much ceremony to partake in the pleasure of the table.

"Her ladyship invites the honorable gentlemen's company at déjeuner."

The magistrate looked in perplexity at the lawyer, who turned to the basin and hid his laughing face in his hands.

"You are married?" the magistrate enquired of Topándy.

"Oh dear no," he answered, "she is not my wife, but my sister."

"But we are invited to dinner in the neighborhood."

"By Mr. Sárvölgyi? That does not matter. If a man wishes to dine at Sárvölgyi's, he will be wise to have déjeuner first. Besides I have your word to drink a glass as a 'conditio sine qua non;' besides a chivalrous man cannot refuse the invitation of a lady."

The last pretext was conclusive; it was impossible to refuse a lady's invitation, even if a man has armed force at his command. He is obliged to yield to the superior power.

The magistrate allowed the third attempt to succeed, and was dragged by the arm into the dining-room.

Topándy audibly bade the butlers look after the wants of the gendarmes and stone-masons, and give them enough to eat and drink: and, when our friend, the magistrate, prepared to object, interrupted him with: "Kindly remember the 'execution' is over, and consider that those good fellows are tearing off plaster from the cloister walls, and the paint-dust will go to their lungs: and it shall not be my fault if any harm touches the upholders of public security. This way, if you please: here comes my sister."

Through the opposite door came the above mentioned "ladyship."

She could not have been taken for more than fifteen years old: she was wearing a pure white dress, trimmed with lace, according to the fashion of the time, and bound round her slender waist with a broad rose-colored riband; her complexion was brunette, and pale, in contrast to her ruddy round lips, which allowed to flash between their velvet surfaces the most lovely pearly set of teeth imaginable: her two thick eyebrows almost met on her brow, and below her long eyelashes two restless black eyes beamed forth: like coal, that is partly aglow.

Sir Magistrate was surprised that Topándy had such a young sister.

"My guests," said Topándy, presenting the servants of the law to her ladyship.

"Oh! I know," remarked the young lady in a gay light-hearted tone. "You have come to put in an 'execution' against his lordship. You did quite right: you ought to treat him so. You don't know the hundredth part of his godless dealings. For did you know, you would long since have beheaded him three times over."

The magistrate found this sincere expression of sisterly opinion most remarkable; still, notwithstanding that he took his seat beside her ladyship.

The table was piled with cold viands and old wines.

Her ladyship entertained the magistrate with conversation and tasty tit-bits, meanwhile the lawyer was quietly drinking his glasses with the host,—nor was it necessary to ask him to help himself.

"Believe me," remarked her ladyship: "if this man ever reaches hell, they will give him a special room, so great are his merits. I have already grown tired of trying to reform him."

"Has your ladyship been staying long in this house?" enquired the magistrate.

"Oh, ten years already."

("How old could the lady have been then?" the magistrate thought to himself: but he could not answer.)

"Just imagine what he does. A few days ago he put up an old saint among the vines as a scarecrow, with a broken hat on his head."

The magistrate turned with a movement of scorn towards the accused. It would not be good for him if that, too, came to the ears of the Court.

"Do not speak, for you do not understand what you're saying," replied Topándy by way of explanation. "It was an ugly statue of Pilate, a relic of the ancient Calvary."[34]

> [34] Many such Calvaries exist in Hungary: they may be seen by the roadside, and are used as places of pilgrimage by pious peasants and others: there is always a picture of Christ crucified or a figure of the same.

"Well, and wasn't that holy?" enquired the flashing-eyed damsel.

The magistrate began to rise from his chair. (Her ladyship must have had a curious education if she did not even know who Pilate was.)

Topándy broke out in unrestrained laughter. Then, as if he desired by an earnest word to repair the insult his language had given, he said to the lady with a pious face:

"Well, if you are right, was it not a gracious act on my part to give a permanent occupation to such an honest fellow, who had been degraded from office; and as he was bare-headed I gave him a hat to protect him against changes of the weather. However, don't treat our friend to a series of incriminations, but rather to that deer-steak; you see he does not venture to taste it."

Her ladyship did as she was told.

The magistrate was obliged to eat: in the first place because it was a beautiful woman that offered the viands to him, secondly because everything she offered was so good. He had to drink, too, because she kept filling his glass and calling on him to "clink" with her, herself setting the example. She drained that sparkling liquor from her glass just as if it had been pure water. And those wines were truly remarkably strong. The magistrate could not refuse the appeal of her ladyship's beautiful eyes.

"Forbidden fruit is sweet." The magistrate experienced the truth of the saying keenly, in so far as one may place among forbidden fruit the *déjeuner* of which a man partakes in the house of a godless fellow, destroying his appetite for the ensuing dinner to which he is invited by a pious man.

The courses seemed endless: cold viands were followed by hot, and the beautiful young damsel could offer so kindly, that the magistrate was powerless to resist.

"Just a little of this 'majoraine' sausage. I myself made it yesterday evening."

The magistrate was astonished. Her ladyship busied herself with such things? When the sausage had disappeared, he made a remark about it.

"Yet no one would imagine that these delicate hands could busy themselves with other things than sewing, piano-playing, and the turning over of gold-bordered leaves. Have you read the almanacs of the parliament?"

At this question Topándy burst into loud laughter, while the lawyer covered his mouth with his napkin, the laughter stuck in his throat: the magistrate could not imagine what there could be to ridicule in this question.

Her ladyship answered quite unconsciously:

"Oh! there are some fine airs in it: I know them. If you will listen, I will sing them."

The magistrate thought there must be some misunderstanding: still, if her ladyship cared to sing, he would be only too delighted to listen.

"Which do you want 'Vienna Town' or 'Rose-bud?'"

"Both," said the host, "and into the bargain the latest parliamentary air, 'Come Down from the Cross, and Fly to the Poplar-tree.' But let us go out of the dining-room to hear the songs; the forks and plates are rattling too much here: we'll go to my sister's room. There she will sing to the accompaniment of a Magyar piano. Have you ever seen a Magyar piano, my friend?"

"I don't remember having done so."

"Well, it is beautiful: you must hear it. My sister plays it wonderfully."

The magistrate offered his arm to her ladyship, and the company entered the next room, which was the lady's apartment.

It was an elegant, finely-decorated room, with mahogany and ebony furniture, richly carved and gilded, with huge glass-panelled chests, and heavy silk curtains yet there was a striking difference between this room and those of other ladies; all these expensive draperies, as far as their form and ordering was concerned, did not at all correspond with the usual appanage of a boudoir.

In one corner stood a loom of mahogany, richly inlaid with ivory: it was still covered with some half-finished work, in which flowers, butterflies, and birds had been worked with remarkable refinement.

"You see," said the lady, "this is my work-table. I am responsible also for that table-cloth on which we breakfasted to-day."

Indeed she had received an unusual education.

Beside the loom was a spinning wheel.

"And this is my library," said the lady, pointing to the cupboards against the wall.

Through the glass panels was to be seen a host of every kind of culinary bottles. On the bottom shelf the great folios; every kind of vinegar that grows in hot-houses; the second row was full of preserved cucumbers; and then on the top shelf different sorts of confitures in brilliant perfection; last of all, a row of fruit extracts was visible, in colors as numerous as the bottles that contained them.

"A magnificent library!" said the lawyer. But the magistrate could not yet clearly make out what kind of lady it might be, who called such things a library.

The heavy velvet curtains, which made a kind of tent of the alcove, also had their secret: the young lady; raised the curtain and said naively,

"This is my sleeping place."

An embroidered quilt laid out on a plank, nothing more.

Indeed, a curious, most remarkable education.

Beside the bed stood a large copper cage.

"This is my pet bird," said the fair lady, pointing at the creature within.

It was a large black cock, which rose angrily as the strangers approached, and crowed in an agonized manner, shaking its red comb furiously.

"You see, this is my old comrade, who takes care of me! and is at the same time my clock, waking me at daybreak." And the lady's look became quite tender, as she placed her hand on the wrathful creature. At her gentle touch the bird clucked his satisfaction.

"When I go outside, he accompanies me, loose, like a dog."

The black monster, as long as he saw strangers, only noted in quiet tones the fact that he had remarked their presence, but as soon as Topándy stepped forward, he suddenly broke out into a clarion cry, as if he wished to arouse every hen-roost in the property to the fact that there was a fox in the garden. Every feather on his neck stood bolt upright, like a Spanish shirt-collar.

"He will soon be quiet," the young lady assured the guests:—"for he will listen to music."

So we are about to see the Magyar piano? It was but a "czimbalom."[35] It is true that it was a marvellous work of art, inlaid with ebony and mother-of-pearl; the nails on which the strings were stretched were of silver, the groundwork a mosaic of coloured woods; the two drumsticks lying upon the strings had handles of red coral; the stand on which the "czimbalom" rested was a marvellously perfected specimen of the carpenter's art, giving a strong tone to the instrument; and before it was a little, round, armless chair covered with red velvet, its feet golden tiger-claws. Yet it was certainly strange that a young lady should play the "czimbalom," that country instrument which they are wont to carry under the covering of a ragged coat, and to place upon inn-tables, or up-turned barrels.—Here it appeared among mahogany furniture, to serve as accompaniment to a young lady's voice, while she herself with her delicate fingers beat the melody out of the plaintive instrument for all the world as if she were seated beside a piano. Incongruous enough, for we have always thought of the "czimbalom-artist" as a gawky bushy-bearded fellow with the indispensable short-stemmed clay-pipe—all burned out and being sucked only for its bitter taste.

> [35] The peculiar and characteristic Magyar instrument which is indispensable to every gypsy orchestra, taking the place of

harp and piano. It is in the form of a zither of large size, played with padded sticks, and forms the foundation of these wandering bands.

And the whole "czimbalom" playing is such a jest, so grotesque; the player's arms jerk and wave continuously; his whole shoulder and head are in perpetual motion; whereas, with the piano, the five fingers do all; the artist's relation to the piano is that of my lord to his children, whom he addresses from a far-off height; the czimbalom-player is *"per tu"* with his instrument.

But the young lady had the grace of one born to the instrument. As she took the sticks in her hands and struck a chord upon the outstretched strings, her face assumed a new expression; so far, we must confess, there had been much "naiveté" in it, now she felt at home; this was her world.

She sang two songs to the guests, both taken from what are called in our country "Parliamentary airs;" they used to break forth in "juratus" coffee-houses, during the sitting of Parliament, when there was more spirit in the youths of the country than now.

The one had a fine impassioned refrain: "From Vienna town, from west to east, the wind hath a cold blast." The end of it was that the Danube water is bitter, for at Pressburg many bitter tears have flowed into it, "Which the great ones of our land have shed, because Ragályi was not sent to be ambassador." Now patriots are more sparing with their tears; but in those days much bitterness was expressed with the air of "Vienna town."

The other air was "Rose-bud, laurel," which had also a pretty refrain; it is full of such expressions as "altars of freedom," "angels of freedom," "wreaths of freedom," and other such mythological things. How the strings responded to the young woman's touch, what expression was in her refrain! It was as if she felt the meaning of those beautiful "flosculi" best of all, and must suffer more than all for them.

Then she introduced a third parliamentary song, the contents of which were satirical; but the satire was purely local and personal, and would not be intelligible to people of modern days.

Topándy was inexpressibly pleased by it: he asked for it again. Someone had ridiculed the priests in it, but in such a manner that no one, unless he had had it explained could understand it.

The magistrate was quite enraptured by the simple instrument; he would never have believed that anyone could play it with such masterly skill.

"Tell me," he asked her ladyship, not being able any longer to conceal his astonishment, "where you learned to play this instrument."

At these words her ladyship broke into such a fit of laughter, that, if she had not suddenly steadied herself with her feet against the czimbalom stand, she would have fallen over. As it was, her hair being, according to the fashion of the day, coiled up "à la Giraffe" round a high comb, and the comb falling from her head, her two tresses of raven hair fell waving over her shoulders to the floor.

At this the young lady discontinued laughing, and not succeeding at all in her efforts to place her dishevelled hair around the comb again, suddenly twisted it together on her head and fastened it with a spindle she snatched from the spinning wheel.

Then to recover her previous high spirits, she again took up the czimbalom sticks, and began to play some quiet melody on the instrument.

It was no song, no variations on well-known airs; it was some marvellous reverie; a frameless picture, a landscape without horizon. A plaint, in a voice rather playful over something serious that is long past, and that can never come back again, avowed to no one by word of mouth, only handed down from generation to generation on the resounding strings—the song of the beggar who denies that he has ever been king:—the song of the wanderer, who denies that he ever had a home and yet remembers it, and the pain of the recollection is heard in the song. No one knows or understands, perhaps not even the player, who merely divines it and meditates thereon. It is the desert wind, of which no one knows whence it comes and whither it goes; the driving cloud, of which no one knows whence it arose, and whither it disappears. A homeless, unsubstantial, immaterial bitterness ... a flowerless, echoless, roadless desert ... full of mirages.

The magistrate would have listened till evening, no matter what became of the neighbor's dinner, if Topándy had not interrupted him with the sceptical remark that this lengthened steel wire has far more soul than a certain two-footed creature, who affirms that he was the image of God.

And thus he again drew the attention of the worthy gentleman to the fact that he was in the home of a denier of God.

Then they heard the mid-day curfew, which made the black cock, with fluttering wings, begin his monotonous clarion, for all the world like the bugle call of some watch-tower, whose *taran-tara!* gives the sign to its inhabitants.

At this the lady's face suddenly lost its sad expression of melancholy; she put down the czimbalom-sticks, leaped up from her chair, and with natural sincerity asked,

"It was a beautiful song, was it not?"

"Indeed it was. What is it?"

"Hush! that you may not ask."

The lawyer had to call the magistrate's attention to the fact that it was already time to depart, as there was still another "entertainment" in store for them.

At this they all laughed.

"I am very sorry that it was my fortune to make your acquaintance, on such an occasion as the present," said the young officer of the law, as he bade farewell, and shook hands with his host.

"But I rejoice at the honor, and I hope I may have the pleasure of seeing you again—on the occasion of the next 'execution'."

Then the magistrate turned to her ladyship, to thank her for her kind hospitality.

To do so he sought the young lady's hand with intention to kiss it; but before he could fulfill his intention, her ladyship suddenly threw her arms around his neck and imprinted as healthy a kiss on his face as anyone could possibly wish for.

The magistrate was rather frightened than rejoiced at this unexpected present. Her ladyship had indeed peculiar habits. He scarcely knew how he arrived in the road; true, the wine had affected his head a little, for he was not used to it.

From Topándy's castle to Sárvölgyi's residence one had to cross a long field of clover.

The lawyer led his colleague as far as the gate of this field by the arm, sauntering along by his side. But, as soon as they were within the garden, Mr. Buczkay said to the magistrate:

"Please go in front, I will follow behind; I must remain behind a little to laugh myself out."

Thereupon he sat down on the ground, clasped his hands over his stomach, and commenced to guffaw; he threw himself flat upon the grass, kicking the earth with his feet, and shouting with merriment the while.

The young officer of the law was beside himself with vexation, as he reflected: "This man is horribly tipsy; how can I enter the house of such a righteous man with a drunken fellow?"

Then when Mr. Buczkay had given satisfaction to the demands of his nature, according to which his merriment, repressed almost to the bursting point, was obliged to break loose in a due proportion of laughter, he rose again from the earth, dusted his clothes, and with the most serious countenance under the sun said, "Well, we can proceed now."

Sárvölgyi's house was unlike Magyar country residences, in that the latter had their doors night and day on the latch, with at most a couple of bulldogs on guard in the courtyard—and these were there only with the intention of imprinting the marks of their muddy paws on the coats of guests by way of tenderness. Sárvölgyi's residence was completely encircled with a stone wall, like some town building: the gate and small door always closed, and the stone wall crowned with a continuous row of iron nails:—and,—what is unheard of in country residences—there was a bell at the door which he who desired to enter had to ring.

The gentlemen rang for a good quarter of an hour at that door, and the lawyer was convinced that no one would come to open it; finally footsteps were heard in the hall, and a hoarse, shrill woman's voice began to make enquiries of those without.

"Who is there?"

"We are."

"Who are 'we'?"

"The guests."

"What guests?"

"The magistrate and the lawyer."

Thereupon the bolts were slipped back with difficulty, and the questioner appeared. She was, as far as age was concerned, a little "beyond the vintage." She wore a dirty white kitchen apron, and below that a second blue kitchen apron, and below that again a third dappled apron. It was this woman's custom to put on as many dirty aprons as possible.

"Good day, Mistress Boris," was the lawyer's greeting. "Why, you hardly wished to let us in."

"I crave your pardon. I heard the bell ring, but could not come at once. I had to wait until the fish was ready. Besides, so many bad men are hereabouts, wandering beggars, 'Arme Reisenden,'[36] that one must always keep the door closed, and ask 'who is there?'"

[36] Poor travellers.

"It is well, my dear Boris. Now go and look after that fish, that it may not burn; we shall soon find the master somewhere. Has he finished his devotions?"

"Yes; but he has surely commenced anew. The bells are ringing the death-toll, and at such times he is accustomed to say one extra prayer for the departed soul. Don't disturb him, I beg, or he will grumble the whole day."

Mistress Boris conducted the gentlemen into a large room, which, to judge from the table ready laid, served as dining room, though the intruder might have taken it for an oratory, so full was it of pictures of those hallowed ones, whom we like to drag down to ourselves, it being too fatiguing to rise up to them.

And in that idea there is much that is sublime. A picture of Christ in the mourning widow's chamber; a "mater dolorosa," in the distracted mother's home; a "kerchief" of the Holy Virgin, spotlessly white, like the glorious spirit, above the bed of olden times, are surely elevating, and honorable presences, the recollections which lead us to them are holy and imperishable, as is the devotion which bows the knee before them. But a repugnant sight is the home of the Pharisee, who surrounds himself with holy images that men may behold them.

Sárvölgyi allowed his guests to wait a long time, though they were, as it happened, not at all impatient.

Great ringing of bells announced his coming; this being a sign he was accustomed to give to the kitchen, that the dinner could be served. Soon he appeared.

He was a tall, dry man, of slight stature, and so small was his head that one could scarce believe it could serve for the same purposes as another man's. His smoothly shaven face did not betray his age; the skin of his cheeks was oil yellow, his mouth small, his shoulders rounded, his nose large, mal-formed and unpleasantly crooked.

He shook hands very cordially with his guests; he had long had the honor of the lawyer's acquaintance, but it was his supreme pleasure to see the magistrate to-day for the first time. But he was extremely courteous, not a feature of his countenance betraying any emotion.

The magistrate seemed determined not to say a word. So the brunt of the conversation fell on the lawyer.

"We have happily concluded the 'execution'."

That was naturally the most convenient topic for the commencement of the conversation.

"I am sorry enough that it had to be so," sighed Sárvölgyi. "Apart from the fact that Topándy is unceasingly persecuting me, I respect and like him very much. I only wish he would turn over a new leaf. He would be an excellent fellow. I know I made a great mistake when I accused him out of mere self-love. I am sorry I did so. I ought to have followed the command of scripture, 'If he smite thee on thy right cheek, offer him thy left cheek also.'"

"Under such circumstances there would be very few criminal processes for the courts to consider."

"I confess I rejoiced this morning when the commission of execution arrived. I felt an inward happiness, due to the fact that this foe of mine had fallen, that he was trampled under my feet. I thought: he is now gnashing his teeth and snapping at the heels of justice that stamp upon his head. And I was glad if it. Yet my gladness was sinful, for no one may rejoice at the destruction of the fallen, and the righteous cannot be glad at the danger of a fellow creature. It was a sin for which I must atone."

The simplest atonement, thought the lawyer, would be for him to return the amount of the fine.

"For this I have inflicted a punishment upon myself," said Sárvölgyi, piously bowing his head. "Oh, I have always punished myself for any misdemeanor, I now condemn myself to one day's fasting. My punishment will be, to sit here beside the table and watch the whole dinner, without touching anything myself."

Debts of Honor

It will be very fine! thought the lawyer. He is determined to fast, while we have taken our fill yonder. So we shall all look at the whole dinner, without tasting anything,—and Mistress Boris will sweep us out of the house.

"My friend the magistrate's head is doubtless aching after his great official fatigue!" Sárvölgyi said, hitting the nail right on the head.

"It is indeed true," remarked the lawyer assuringly. The young official was in need rather of rest than of feasting. There are good, blessed mortals, whom two glasses of wine immediately send to sleep, and to whom it is the most exquisite torture to be obliged to remain awake.

"My suggestion is," said the lawyer, "that it would be good for the magistrate to repose in an armchair and rest himself, until the cleaning of the cloister is finished, and we can again take our seats in the carriage."

"Sleep is the gift of Heaven," said the man of piety: "it would be a sin to steal it from a fellow-man. Kindly make yourself comfortable at once in this room."

It was an extremely difficult process to make oneself comfortable on that apology for an arm-chair; it seemed to have been prepared as a resting place for ascetics and body-torturers: still the magistrate sat down in it, craved pardon,—and fell asleep. And then he dreamed that he saw before him again that laid-out table, where one guest sat two yards from the other while all round holy pictures were hanging on the walls, with their faces turned away, as if they did not wish to gaze upon the scene. In the middle of the room there was hanging from the ceiling a heavy chandelier with twelve branches, and on it was swaying the host himself.

What a cursed foolery is a dream! The host was actually sitting there vis-à-vis with the lawyer, at the other end of the long table; for Mistress Boris had so laid the places. And as the magistrate's place remained empty, host and guest sat so far apart that the one was incapable of helping the other.

At last the door opened, with such a delicate creaking that the lawyer thought somebody was ringing to be admitted:—It was Mistress Boris bringing in the soup.

The lawyer was determined to make some sacrifice, in order to maintain the dignity of the "legale testimonium," by dining a second time. He thought himself capable of this heroic deed.

He was deceived.

There is a peculiarity of the Magyar which has not yet been the subject of song: his stomach will not stand certain things.

This a stranger cannot understand: it is a "specificum."

When Vörösmarty sang that "in the great world outside there is no place for thee,"[37] he found it unnecessary to add the reason for that, which every man knows without his telling them:—"in every land abroad they cook with butter."

> [37] From the celebrated Szózat (appeal) calling on the Hungarian to be true to his fatherland.

A Magyar stomach detests what is buttery. He becomes melancholy and sickly from it; he runs away from the very mention of it, and if some sly housekeeper deceitfully gives him buttery things to eat, all his life long he considers that as an attempt upon his life, and will never again sit down to such a poison-mixer's table.

You may place him where you like abroad, still he will long to return from the cursed butter-smelling world, and if he cannot he grows thin and fades away: and like the giraffe in the European climate, he cannot reproduce his kind in a foreign land. Roughly speaking, all his neighbors cook with butter, oil and dripping: and "be harsh or kind, the hand of fate, here thou must live, here die."[38]

> [38] Also from the "Szózat."

The lawyer was a true Magyar of the first water. And when he perceived that the crab soup was made with butter, he put down his spoon beside his plate and said he could not eat crabs. Since he had learned that the crab was nought else but a beetle living in water, and since a company had been formed in Germany for making beetles into preserves for dessert, he had been unable to look with undismayed eye upon these retrograde monsters.

"Ach, take it away, Boris," sighed the host. He himself was not eating, for was he not atoning for his sins?

Mistress Boris removed the dish with an expression of violent anger.

Just imagine a housekeeper, whose every ambition is the kitchen, when her first dish is despatched away from the table without being touched.

The second dish—eggs stuffed with sardines—suffered the same fate.

The lawyer declared on his word of honor that they had buried his grandfather for tasting a dish of sardines, and that every female in the family immediately went into spasms from the smell of the same. He would rather eat a whale than a sardine.

"Take this away, too, Mistress Boris. No one will touch it." Mistress Boris began to mutter under her breath that it was absurd and affected to turn up one's nose at these respectable eatables, which were quite as good as those they had eaten in their grandfather's house. Her last words were rather drowned by the creaking of the door as she went out.

Then followed some kind of salad, with bread crumbs. The lawyer had in his university days received such a dangerous fever from eating such stuff, that it would indeed be a fatal enterprise to tackle it now.

This was too much for the housekeeper. She attacked Mr. Sárvölgyi:

"Didn't I tell you not to cook a fasting dinner? Didn't I say so? You think everyone is as devout as you are in keeping Friday? Now you have it. Now I am disgraced."

"It is part of the punishment I have inflicted on myself," answered Sárvölgyi, with humble acquiescence.

"The devil take your punishment; it is me that will come in for ridicule if they hear about it yonder. You become more of a fool every day."

"Say what is on your tongue, my good Boris; heaven will order you to do penance as well as me."

Mistress Boris slammed the door after her, and cried outside in bitter disappointment.

The lawyer swore to himself that he would eat whatever followed, even if it were poison.

It was worse: it was fish.

We have medical certificates to enable us to assert that whenever the lawyer ate fish he promptly had to go to bed. He was forced to say that if they chased him from the house with boiling water he could not venture to put his teeth into it.

Mistress Boris said nothing now. She actually kept silent. As we all know, the last stage but one of a woman's anger is when she is silent, and cannot utter a word. There is one stage more, which was imminent. The lawyer thought the dinner was over, and with true sincerity begged Mistress Boris to prepare a little coffee for him and the magistrate.

Boris left the room without a word, placing the coffee machine before Sárvölgyi himself; he did not allow anyone else to make it, and occupied himself with the preparations till Mistress Boris came back.

The magistrate was just dreaming that that fellow swinging from the ceiling turned to him, and said "will you have a cup of coffee?" It did him good starting from his doze, to see his host, not on the chandelier, but sitting in a chair before him, saying: "Will you have a cup of coffee?"

The magistrate hastened to taste it, with a view to driving the sleepiness from his eyes, and the lawyer poured some out for himself.

Debts of Honor

Just at that moment Mistress Boris entered with a dish of omelette.

Mistress Boris with a face betraying the last stage of anger, approached the lawyer:—she smiled tenderly.

It is not the pleasantest sight in the world when a lady with a plate of omelette in her hand, smiles tenderly upon a man who is well aware of the fact that only a hair's breadth separates him from the catastrophe of having the whole dish dashed on his head.

"Kindly help yourself."

The lawyer felt a cold shiver run down his back.

"You will surely like this!—omelette."

"I see, my dear woman, that it is omelette," whispered the lawyer; "but no one of my family could enjoy omelette after black coffee."

The catastrophe had not yet arrived. The lawyer had his eyes already shut, waiting for the inevitable; but the storm, to his astonishment, passed over his head.

There was something else to attract the thunderbolt. The magistrate had again taken his seat at the table, and was putting sugar in his coffee; he could not have any such excuse.

"Kindly help yourself ..."

The magistrate's hair stood on end at her awful look. He saw that this relentless dragon of the apocalypse would devour him, if he did not stuff himself to death with the omelette. Yet it was utterly impossible. He could not have eaten a morsel even if confronting the stake or the gallows.

"Pardon, a thousand pardons, my dear woman," he panted, drawing his chair farther away from the threatening horror: "I feel so unwell that I cannot take dinner."

Then the storm broke.

Mistress Boris put the dish down on the table, placed her two hands on her thighs, and exploded:

"No, of course not," she panted, her voice thick with rage. "Of course you can't dine here, because you were simply crammed over yonder by—the gypsy girl."

The hot coffee stuck in the throats of the two guests at these words! In the lawyer's from uncontrollable laughter, in the magistrate's from still more uncontrollable consternation.

This woman had indeed wreaked a monstrous vengeance.

The good magistrate felt like a boy thrashed at school, who fears that his folks at home may learn the whole truth.

Luckily the sergeant of gendarmes entered with the news that the unholy pictures had been already erased from the walls, and the carriages were waiting. He too "got it" outside, for, as he made inquiries after his masters, Mistress Boris told him severely to go to the depths of hell: "he too smelt of wine; of course, that gypsy girl had given him also to drink!"

That gypsy girl!

The magistrate, in spite of his crestfallen dejection, felt an actual sense of pleasure at being rid of this cursed house and district.

Only when they were well on their dusty way along the highroad did he address his companion:

"Well, my dear old man, that fine lady was only a gypsy girl after all."

"Surely, my dear fellow."

"Then why did you not tell me?"

"Because you did not ask me."

"That is why you lay on your stomach and laughed, is it?"

"Naturally."

The magistrate heaved a deep sigh.

"At least, I implore you, don't tell my wife that the gypsy girl kissed me!"

CHAPTER V

THE WILD CREATURE'S HAUNT

In those days the Tisza regulations did not exist—that plain around Lankadomb where now turnips are hoed with four-bladed machines was at that time still covered by an impenetrable marsh, that came right up to Topándy's garden, from which it was separated by a broad ditch. This ditch wound in a meandering, narrow course to the great waste of rushes, and in dry summer gave the appearance of a rivulet conveying the water of the marsh down to the Tisza. When the heavy rains came, naturally the stream flowed back along the same route.

The whole marsh covered some ten or twelve square miles. Here after a heavy frost, they used to cut reeds, and on the occasion of great hunting matches[39] they would drive up masses of foxes and wolves; and all the huntsmen of the neighborhood might lie in wait in its expanse for fowl from morn till eve, and if they pleased, might roam at will in a canoe and destroy the swarms of winged inhabitants of the fen: no one would interrupt them.

> [39] A hunting match in which the vassals of the landlord form a ring of great extent and advancing and narrowing the circle by degrees, drive the animals together towards a place where they can be conveniently shot. (Walter Scott.)

Some ancestor of Topándy had given the peasantry permission to cut peat in the bog, but the present proprietor had discontinued this industry, because it completely defiled the place: the ditches caused by the old diggings became swampy morasses, so that neither man nor beast could pass among them without danger.

Anyone with good eyes could still descry from the castle tower that enormous hay-rick which they had filled up ten or twelve years before in the middle of the marsh; it was just in the height of summer and they had mown the hillocks in the marsh; then followed a mild winter, and neither man nor sleigh could reach it. The hay was lost, it was not worth the trouble of getting; so they had left it there, and it was already brown, its top moss-covered and overgrown with weeds.

Topándy would often say to his hunting comrades, who, looking through a telescope, remarked the hay-rick in the marsh:

"Someone must be living in that rick; often of an evening have I seen smoke coming from it. It might be an excellent place for a dwelling. Rain cannot penetrate it, in winter it keeps out the cold, in summer the heat. I would live in it myself."

They often tried to reach it while out hunting; but every attempt was a failure; the ground about the rick was so clogged with turfy peat that to approach it by boat was impossible, and one who trusted himself on foot came so near being engulfed that his companions could scarcely haul him out of the bog with a rope. Finally they acquiesced in the idea that here within distinct view of the castle, some wild creature, born of man, had made his dwelling among the wolves and other wild beasts; a creature whom it would be a pity to disturb, as he never interfered with anybody.

The most enterprising hunter, therefore, even in broad daylight avoided the neighborhood of the suspicious hay-rick; who then would be so audacious as to dare to seek it out by night when the circled moon foretelling rain, was flooding the marsh-land with a silvery, misty radiance, adding a new terror to the face of the landscape; when the exhalations of the marsh were sluggishly spreading a vaporous heaviness over the lowland; while the eerie habitants of the bog (whose time of sleep is by day, their active life at night) the millions of frogs and other creatures were reëchoing their cries, announcing the whereabouts of the slimy pools, where foul gases are lord and master; when the he-wolf was howling to his comrades; and when, all at once, some mysterious-faced cloud drew out before the moon, and whispered to her something that made all nature tremble, so that for one moment all was silent, a death-like silence, more terrible than all the night voices speaking at once;—at such a time whose steps were those that sounded in the depths of the morass?

A horseman was making his way by the moonlight, in solitude.

His steed struggled along up to the hocks in the swamp which showed no paths at all; the tracks were immediately sucked up by the mud:—nothing lay before to show the way, save the broken reed. No sign remained that anyone had ever passed there before.

The sagacious mare carefully noted the marks from time to time, instinctively scenting the route, that tracks trodden by wild beasts should not lead her astray; cleverly she picked out with her sharp eyes the places where the ground was still firm; at times she would leap from one clod of peat to another. The space between these spots might be overgrown by green grass, with yellow flowers dotted here and there, but the sagacious animal knew, felt, perhaps had even experienced, that the depth there was deceptive; it was one of those peat-diggings, filled in by mud and overgrown by the green of water-moss; he who stepped thereon would be swallowed up in an instant. Then she trotted on picking her way among the dangerous places.

And the rider?

He was asleep.

Asleep on horseback, while his steed was going with him through an accursed spot: where to right and left were graves, where below was hell and around him the gloom of night. The horseman was sleeping, his head nodding backwards and forwards, swaying to and fro. Sometimes he started, as those who travel in carriages are wont to do when the jolting is more pronounced than ordinary, and then settled down again. Though asleep he kept his seat as if he had grown to the saddle. His hands seemed wide awake for all he held the reins in one and a double-barrelled gun in the other.

By the light of the moon his dark face seemed even darker; his long, crisp, curly hair, his hat pressed down over his eyes, his black beard and moustache, his strongly aquiline nose, all proclaimed his gypsy origin. He wore a threadbare blue doublet, braided with cords, which were buttoned here and there at random, and over this was fastened some tattered lambskin covering.

Debts of Honor

The rider was really fast asleep: surely he must have travelled at such a pace that he had no time, or thought for sleep, and now, strangely enough, he felt at home.

Here, where no one could pursue him, he bowed his head upon his horse's neck.

And the horse seemed to know that his master was sleeping, for he did not shake himself once, even to rid himself of the crowds of biting, sucking insects that preyed upon his skin, knowing that such a motion would wake his master.

As the mare broke through a clump of marsh-willows, in the darkness of the willow forest, little dancing fire-flies came before her in scores, leaping from grass to grass, from tree to tree, dissolving one into the other, then leaping apart and dancing alone; their flames assumed a pale, lustreless brilliance in the darkness, like some fire of mystery or the burning gases of some moldering corpses.

The mare merely snorted at the sight of these flickering midnight flames; surely she had often met them, in journeys across the marsh, and already knew their caprices: how they lurked about the living animals, how they ran after her if she passed before them, how they fluttered around, how they danced beside her continuously, how they leaped across above her head, how they strove to lead her astray from the right path.

There they were darting around the heads of horse and horseman as if they were burning night-moths; one lighted upon the horseman's hat, and swayed with it, as he nodded his head.

The steed snorted and breathed hard upon those living lights. But the snorting awakened the rider. He gazed askance at his brilliant demon-companions, one of which was on the brim of his hat; he dug the spurs into the mare's flanks, to make her leap more speedily from among the jeering spirits of the night.

When they came to a turn in the track, the crowd of graveyard mystery-lights parted in twain: most of them joined the rushing air-current, while some careful guardians remained constantly about the rider, now before, now behind him.

Darting from the willows, a cold breeze swept over the plain: before it every mystery-light fled back into the darkness, and still kept up its ghostly dance. Who knows what kind of amusement that was to them?

The horseman was sleeping again. The terrible hay-rick was now so near that one might have gone straight to it, but the steed knew better; instead, she went around the spot in a half-circle, until she reached a little lake that cut off the hay-rick. Here she halted on the water's edge and began to toss her head, with a view to quietly awakening the rider from his sleep.

The latter looked up, dismounted, took saddle and bridle off his horse, and patted her on the back. Therewith the steed leaped into the water, which reached to her neck, and swam to the other side.

Why did she not cross over dry ground? Why did she go only through the water? The horseman meanwhile squatted down among the broom, rested his gun upon his knee, made sure that it was cocked and that the powder had not fallen from the pan, and noiselessly crouched down, gazing after the retreating steed, as she reached the opposite bank. Suddenly she drew in her tail, bristled her mane, pricked up her ears. Her eyes flashed fire, her nostrils expanded. Slowly and cautiously she stepped forward, so as to make no noise, bowed her head to the earth, like some scenting hound, and stopped to listen.

On the southern side of the hay-rick,—the side away from the village,—there was a narrow entrance cut into the pile of hay: a plaited door of willow-twigs covered it, and the twigs were plaited together in their turn with sedges to make the color harmonize with that of the rick. This was done so perfectly that no one looking at it, even from a short distance, would have suspected anything. As the steed reached the vicinity of the door, she cautiously gazed upon it: below the willow-door there was an opening, through which something had broken in.

The mare knew already what it was. She scented it. A she-wolf had taken up her abode there in the absence of the usual occupants, she had young ones with her, and was just now giving suck; otherwise she would have noticed the horse's approach; the whining of the whelps could be heard from the outside. The mare seized the door with her teeth, and suddenly wrenched it from its place.

From the hollow of the hay-rick a lean, hungry wolf crept out. At first in wonder she raised her eyes, which shone in the green light, astonished at this disturbance of her repose; and she seemed to take counsel within herself, whether this was the continuation of her sweet dreams. The providential joint had come very opportunely to the mother of seven whelps. Two or three of these were still clinging to her hanging udders, and left her only that she might prepare herself for the fight. The old animal merely yawned loudly,—in a man it would be called a laugh,—a yawn that declared her delight in robbery, and with her slatternly tail beat her lean, hollow sides. The mare, seeing that her foe was in no hurry for the combat, came nearer, bowed her head to the earth, and in this manner stepped slowly forward, sniffing at the enemy; when the wolf seemed in the act of springing on her neck she suddenly turned, and dealt a savage kick at the wolf's chin that broke one of its great front teeth. Then the furious wild creature, snarling and hissing, darted upon the steed, which at the second attack kicked so viciously with both hind legs that the wolf turned a complete somersault in the air; but this only served to make it more furious: gnashing its teeth, its mouth foaming and bloody, it sprang a third time upon the mare, only to receive from the sharp hoof a long wound in its breast; but that was not all: before it could rise from the ground, the mare dealt another blow that crushed one of its fore paws.

The wolf then gave up the battle. Terrified, with broken teeth and feet, it hobbled off from the scene of the encounter, and soon appeared on the roof of the rick. The coward had sought a place of refuge from the victorious foe, whither that foe could not follow it.

The steed galloped round the rick: she wished to deceive her enemy, who merely sat on the roof licking its broken leg, its bruised side, and bloody jaws.

All at once the proud mare halted, with a haughtier look than man is capable of, as who might say: "You are not coming?"

Debts of Honor

Suddenly she seized one of the whelps in her teeth. They had slunk out of the hollow, whining after their mother. She shook it cruelly in the air, then dashed it to the ground violently so that in a moment its cries ceased.

The mother-wolf hissed with agonized fury on the roof of the rick.

The mare seized another one of the whelps and shook it in the air.

As she grasped the third by the neck, the mother, mad with rage, leaped down upon her from the pile and, with the energy of despair, made so fierce an assault that her claws reached the steed's neck; but her crushed leg could take no hold, and she fell in a heap at the mare's feet; the triumphant foe then trampled to death first the old mother, then all the whelps. At last, proudly whinnying, she galloped in frisky triumph around the rick, and then quickly swam back to the place where she had left her master.

"Well, Farao, is there anything the matter?" said the horseman, embracing his horse's head.

The horse replied to the question with a familiar neigh, and rubbed her nose against her master's hip.

The horseman thereupon tied saddle and bridle together into one bundle, and leaped upon his steed's back, who then, without harness of any kind, readily swam with him to the place she had already visited, and halted before the opening in the rick. The master dismounted. The steed, thus freed, rolled on the grass, neighing and whinnying, then leaped up, shook herself, and with great delight grazed in the rich swampy pasture.

The gypsy was not surprised to see the bloody signs of the late struggle. He had many a time discovered dead wolves in the track of his grazing horse.

"This will serve splendidly for a skin-cloak, as the old one is torn."

Then something occurred to him.

"This was a female: so the male must be here somewhere—I know where." The rick was surrounded by wolf-ditches in double rows, so made that the inner ditch corresponded to the space left between the two outer ones: the whole crafty work of defence was covered over with thin brush and reeds, which had been overgrown by process of time by moss, so that even a man might have been deceived by their appearance. Here was the reason why the steed had not approached the rick in a straight line. This was a fortified place, and the only entrance to the stronghold was that lake which lay before it: that was the gate. The she-wolf, too, had undoubtedly come across the water, but the male had not been so prudent and had entrapped himself in one of the ditches.

The gypsy at once noticed that one ditch had been broken in, and, as he gazed down into the depths, two blazing blood-red eyes told him that what he was looking for was there.

"Well, you are in a fine position, old fellow: in the morning I shall come for you: and I'll ask for your skin, if you'll give it to me. If you give, you give; if you don't give, I take. That is the order of things in the world. I have none, you have: I want it, you don't. One of us must die for the other's sake: that one must be you."

Then it occurred to him to remove the skin of the she-wolf at once, for, if he left it to cool, the work would be more difficult. He stretched the fur on poles and left it to dry in the moonlight; the carcass he dragged to the end of the rick and buried it there; then he made a fire of rushes, took his seven days' old bread and rancid bacon from his greasy wallet and ate. As the darting flames threw a flickering light upon his face, he looked no more peaceful than that wild creature, whose hollow he had usurped.

It was just a sagacious, courageous, wily, resolute—*animal* face.

"Either you eat me, or I eat you." That was its meaning. "You have, I have not; I want, you don't:—if you give, you give; if you don't, I take."

At every bite with his brilliant white teeth into the bread and bacon, you could see it in his face; his gnashing teeth, and ravenous eyes declared it.

That bacon, and bread, had surely cost something, if not money.

Money? How could the gypsy purchase for money? Why, when he took that bright dollar from his knapsack, people would ask him where he got it. Should he show one of those red-eyed bank-notes, they would at once arrest, imprison him: whom had he murdered to obtain them?

Yet he has dollars and bank-notes in plenty. He gathers them from his leathern purse with his hands, and scatters them around him on the grass.

Bright silver and gold coins glitter around him in the firelight. He gazes at the curious notes of the imperial banks, and fears within himself that he cannot make out the worth of any of them. Then he sweeps them all together in one heap, along with snail shells and rush-seeds. After a while the man enters the hollow interior of the rick, and draws from the hay a large, sooty copper vessel, partly moldy with the mold of money. He pours the new pile in with two full hands. Then he raises the cauldron to see how much heavier it has become.

Is he satisfied with his work?

He buries his treasure once more in the depths of the rick; he himself knows not how much there might be. Then he attacks anew the hard, stale bread, the rancid bacon, and devours it to the last morsel. Perhaps some ready-prepared banquet awaited him on the morrow. Or perhaps he is accustomed to feasting only every third day. At last he stretches himself out on the grass, and calls to Farao.

"Come here, graze about my head, let me hear you crunch the grass."

And quickly he fell asleep beside her, as it were one whose brain was of the quietest and his conscience the most peaceful.

CHAPTER VI

"FRUITS PREMATURELY RIPE"

At first I was invited to my P. C. uncle's every Sunday to dinner: later I went without invitation. As soon as I was let out of school, I hastened thither. I persuaded myself that I went to visit my brother. I found an excuse, too, in the idea that I must make progress in art, and that it was in any case an excellent use of time, and a very good "entrée" to art, if I played waltzes and quadrilles of an afternoon from five to eight on the violin to Melanie's accompaniment on the piano, while the rest of the company danced to our music.

For the Bálnokházys had company every day. Such a change of faces that I could scarcely remember who and what they all were. Gay young men and ladies they were, who loved to enjoy themselves: every day there was a dance there.

Sometimes others would change places with Melanie at the piano: a piece of good fortune for me, for she was able to then have a dance — with me.

I have never seen any one dance more beautifully than she; she fluttered above the floor, and could make the waltz more agreeable than any one else before or after her. That was my favorite dance. I was exclusively by her side at such times, and we could not gaze except into each other's eyes. I did not like the quadrille so well: in that one is always taking the hands of different persons, and changing partners; and what interest had I in those other lady-dancers?

And I thought Melanie, too, rejoiced at the same thing that pleased me.

And, if by chance—a very rare event—the P. C. had no company, we still had our dance. There were always two gentlemen and two lady dancers in the house party; the beautiful wife of the P. C. and Fraülein Matild, the governess: Lorand and Pepi[40] Gyáli.

[40] A nickname for Joseph.

Pepi was the son of a court agent at Vienna, and his father was a very good friend of Bálnokházy; his mother had once been ballet-dancer at the Vienna opera—a fact I only learned later.

Pepi was a handsome young fellow "en miniature;" he was a member of the same class as Lorand, a law student in the first year, yet he was no taller than I. Every feature of his face was fine and tender, his mouth, small, like that of a girl, yet never in all my life have I met one capable of such backbiting as was he with his pretty mouth.

How I envied that little mortal his gift for conversation, his profound knowledge, his easy gestures, his freedom of manners, that familiarity with which he could treat women! His beauty was plastic!

I felt within myself that such ought a man to be in life, if he would be happy.

The only thing I did not like in him was that he was always paying compliments to Melanie: he might have desisted from that. He surely must have remarked on what terms I was with her.

His custom was, in the quadrille, when the solo-dancing gentlemen returned to their lady partners, to anticipate me and dance the turn with Melanie. He considered it a very good joke, and I scowled at him several times. But once, when he wished to do the same, I seized his arm, and pushed him away; I was only a grammar-school boy, and he was a first-year law student; still I did push him away.

With this heroic deed of mine not only myself but my cousin Melanie also was contented. That evening we danced right up till nine o'clock. I always with Melanie, and Lorand with her mother.

When the company dispersed, we went down to Lorand's room on the ground floor, Pepi accompanying us.

I thought he was going to pick a quarrel with me, and vowed inwardly I would thrash him.

But instead he merely laughed at me.

"Only imagine," he said, throwing himself on Lorand's bed, "this boy is jealous of me."

My brother laughed too.

It was truly ridiculous: one boy jealous of another.

Yes, I was surely jealous, but chivalrous too. I think I had read in some novel that it was the custom to reply in some such manner to like ridicule:

"Sir, I forbid you to take that lady's name in vain."

They laughed all the more.

"Why, he is a delightful fellow, this Desi," said Pepi. "See, Lorand, he will cause you a deal of trouble. If he learns to smoke, he will be quite an Othello."

This insinuation hit me on a sensitive spot. I had never yet tasted that ambrosia, which was to make me a full-grown man; for as every one knows, it is the pipe-stem which is the dividing line between boyhood and manhood; he who could take that in his mouth was a man. I had already often been teased about that.

I must vindicate myself.

On my brother's table stood the tobacco-box full of Turkish tobacco, so by way of reply I went and filled a church warden, lit and began to smoke it.

"Now, my child, that will be too strong," sneered Pepi, "take it away from him, Lorand. Look how pale he is getting: remove it from him at once."

But I continued smoking: the smoke burned and bit the skin of my tongue; still I held the stem between my teeth, until the tobacco was burned out.

That was my first and last pipe.

"At any rate, drink a glass of water," Lorand said.

"No thank you."

"Well, go home, for it will soon be dark."

"I am not afraid in the streets."

Yet I felt like one who is a little tipsy.

"Have you any appetite?" inquired Pepi scornfully.

"Just enough to eat a gingerbread-hussar like you."

Lorand laughed uncontrollably at this remark of mine.

"Gingerbread-hussar! you have got it from him, Pepi."

I was quite flushed with pride at being able to make Lorand laugh.

But Pepi, on the contrary, became quite serious.

"Ho, ho, old fellow," (when he spoke seriously to me he always addressed me "old fellow," and on other occasions as "my child"). "Never be afraid of me; now Lorand might have reason to be: we both want what is ready; we do not court your little girl, but her mother. If the old wigged councillor is not jealous of us, don't you be so."

I expected Lorand to smite that fair mouth for this despicable calumny.

Instead of which he merely said, half muttering:

"Don't; before the child..."

Pepi did not allow himself to be called to order.

"It is true, my dear Desi: and I can tell you that you will have a far more grateful part to play around Melanie, if she marries someone else."

Then indeed I went home. This cynicism was something quite new to my mind. Not only my stomach, but my whole soul turned sick. How could I measure the bitterness of the idea that Lorand was paying court to a married woman? Such a thing was not to be seen in the circle in which we had been brought up. Such a case had been mentioned in our town, perhaps, as the scandal of the century, but only in whispers that the innocent might not hear: neither the man nor the woman could have shown their faces in our street. Surely no one would have spoken another word to them.

And Lorand had been so confused when Pepi uttered this foul thing to his face before me. He did not deny it, nor was he angry.

I arrived at home in an agony of shame. The street-door was already closed: so I had to pass in by the shop door. I wished to open it softly that the bell should not betray my coming, but Father Fromm was waiting for me. He was extremely angry: he stopped my way.

"Discipulus negligens! Do you know 'quote hora?' Decem. Every day to wander out of doors till after nine, hoc non pergit.—Scio, scio, what you wish to say. You were at the P. C.'s. That is 'unum et idem' for me. The other 'asinus' has been learning his lessons ever since midday, so much has he to do, while you have not even so much as glanced at them; do you wish to be a greater 'asinus' than he? Now I say 'semel propter semper,' 'finis' to the carnival! Don't go any more a-dancing; for if you stay out once more, 'ego tibi umsicabo.' Now 'pergus, dixi.'"

Old Márton during this well-deserved drubbing kept moving the scalp of his head back and forth in assent, and then came after me with a candle, to light me along the corridor to the door of my room, singing behind me these jesting verses:

> "Hab i ti nid gsagt
> Komm um halbe Acht?
> Und du Kummst mir jetzt um halbe naini
> Jetzt ist de Vater z'haus, kannst nimmer aini."[41]

[41] "Did I not tell thee, 'come at half-past seven?' and thou comest now at half-past eight? Now the father is at home, thou canst no more come in."

And after me he called out "Prosit, Sir Lieutenant-Governor." I had no desire to be angry with him. I felt too sad to quarrel with any one.

Debts of Honor

Henrik was indeed slaving away at the table, and the candle, burnt to the end, proved that he had been at it a long time.

"Welcome, Desi," he said good humoredly. "You come late; a terrible amount of 'labor' awaits you to-morrow. I have finished mine: you will be behind with yours, so I have written the exercises in your place. Look and see if it is good."

I was humbled.

That heavy-headed boy, on whom I had been wont to look down from such a height, whose work I had prepared in play, work which he would have broken his head over, had now in my place finished the work I had neglected. What had become of me?

"I waited for you with a little pleasant surprise," said Henrik, taking from his drawer something which he held in his hand before me. "Now guess what it is."

"I don't care what it is."

I was in a bad humor, I longed to lay my head on the bed.

"Of course you care. Fanny has written a letter from her new home. She has written to you in Magyar, about your dear mother."

These words roused me from my lethargy.

"Show me: give it me to read."

"You see, you are delighted after all."

I tore the letter from him.

First Fanny wrote to her parents in German, on the last page in Magyar to me. She had already made such progress.

She wrote that they often spoke of me at home; I was a bad boy not to write mother a letter: she was very ill and it was her sole delight to be able to speak of me. As often as her parents or brother wrote to Fanny, she would add a few lines after opening the letter, in my name, then take it to my mother and read it to her, as if I had written. How delighted she was! She did not know my German writing, so she readily believed it was I who had written. But I must be a good boy and write myself, for some day mother and grandmother would discover the deceit and would be angry.

My heart was almost bursting.

I pored over the letter I had read, and sobbed bitterly as I had never before done in my life.

My dear only mother! thou saint, thou martyr! who sufferest, weepest, and anguishest so much for my sake, while I mix in a society where they mock women, and mothers! Canst thou forgive me?

When I had cried myself out, my face was covered with tears. Henrik raised me from my seat upon the floor.

"Give me this letter," I panted; and I kissed him for giving it to me.

Many great historical documents have been torn up since then, but that letter is still in my possession.

"Now I cannot go to bed. I will stay up until morning and finish the work I have neglected. I thank you for what you have written in my stead, but I cannot accept it. I shall do it myself. I shall do everything in which I am behindhand."

"Good, Desi, my boy, but you see our candle has burned down; and grandmother is already asleep, so I cannot ask her for one. Still, if you do wish to sit up, go down to the bakehouse, they are working all night, as to-morrow is Saturday: take your ink, paper, and books with you. There you can write and learn your lessons."

I did so. I descended to the court, washed my head beside the fountain, then took my books and writing material and descended to the bakehouse, begging Márton to allow me to work there by lamp-light. Márton irritated me the whole night with his satire, the assistants jostled me, and drove me from my place; they sang the "Kneading-trough" air, and many other street-songs: and amid all these abominations I studied till morning; what is more, I finished all my work.

That night, I know, was one of the turning-points in my life.

Two days later came Sunday: I met Pepi in the street.

"Well, old fellow: are you not coming to-day to see little Melanie? There will be a great dance-rehearsal."

"I cannot: I have too much to do."

Pepi laughed loudly. "Very well, old fellow."

His laughter did not affect me in the least.

"But when you have learned all there is to learn will you come again?"

"No. For then I shall write a letter to my mother."

Some good spirit must have whispered to this fellow not to laugh at these words, for he could not have anticipated the box on the ears I would have given him, because he could not for an instant forget that I was a grammar-school boy, and he a first-year law student.

CHAPTER VII

THE SECRET WRITINGS

One evening Lorand came to me and laid before me a bundle of papers covered with fine writing.

"Copy this quite clearly by to-morrow morning. Don't show the original to any one, and, when you have finished, lock it up in your trunk with the copy, until I come for it."

I set to work in a moment and never rose from my task until I had completed it.

Next morning Lorand came for it, read it through, and said: "Very good," handing me two pieces of twenty.

"What do you mean?"

"Take it," he said, "It is not my gift, but the gift of someone else: in fact, it is not a gift, but a fixed contract-price. Honorable work deserves honorable payment. For every installment[42] you copy, you get two pieces of twenty. It is not only you that are doing it: many of your school-fellows are occupied in the same work."

[42] *i. e.*, A printed sheet of sixteen pages.

Then I was pleased with the two pieces of twenty.

My uneasiness at receiving money from anybody except my parents, who alone were entitled to make me presents, was only equalled by my pleasure at the possession of my first earnings, the knowledge that I was at last capable of earning something, that at last the tree of life was bearing fruit, which I might reach and pluck for myself.

I accepted the work and its reward. Every second day, punctually at seven o'clock in the evening, Lorand would come to me, give me the matter to be copied, 'matter written, as I recognized, in his own hand writing,' and next day in the morning would come for the manuscript.

I wrote by night, when Henrik was already asleep: but, had he been awake, he could not have known what I was writing, for it was in Magyar.

And what was in these secret writings?

The journal of the House of Parliament. It was the year 1836. Speeches held in Parliament could not be read in print; the provisional censor ruled the day, and a few scarecrow national papers fed their reading public on stories of the Zummalacarregu type.

So the public helped itself.

In those days shorthand was unknown in our country; four or five quick-fingered young men occupied a bench in the gallery of the House, and "skeletonized" the speeches they heard. At the end of a sitting they pieced their fragments together: in one would be found what was missing in the other: thus they made the speeches complete. They wrote the result out themselves four times, and then each one provided for the copying forty times, of his own copy. The journals of Parliament, thus written, were preserved by the patriots, who were members at that time,—and are probably still in preservation.

The man of to-day, who sighs after the happy days of old, will not understand how dangerous an enterprise, was the attempt made by certain young men "in the glorious age of noble freedom," to make the public familiar, through their handwriting, with the speeches delivered in Parliament.

These writings had a regenerating influence upon me.

An entirely new world opened out before me: new ideas, new impulses arose within my mind and heart. The name of that world which opened out before me was "home." It was marvellous to listen for the first time to the full meaning of "home." Till then I had had no idea of "home:" now every day I passed my nights with it:—the lines, which I wrote down night after night, were imprinted upon those white pages, that are left vacant in the mind of a child. Nor was I the only one impressed.

There is still deeply engraved on my memory that kindling influence, by which the spirit of the youth of that age was transformed through the writing of those pages.

One month later I had no more dreams of becoming Privy-Councillor:—then I knew not how I could ever approach my cousin Melanie.

All at once the school authorities discovered where the parliamentary speeches were reproduced. It was done by the school children, that hundred-handed typesetting machine.

The danger had already spread far; finding no ordinary outlet, it had found its way through twelve-year-old children: hands of children supplied the deficiency of the press.

Great was the apprehension.

The writing of some (among them mine) was recognized. We were accused before the school tribunal.

I was in that frame of mind that I could not fear. The elder boys they tried to frighten with greater things, and yet they did not give way: I would at least do no worse. I was able to grasp it all with my child's mind, the fact that we, who had merely copied for money, could not be severely punished. Probably we never understood what might be in those writings lying before us. We merely piled up letter after letter. But the gravest danger threatened those who had brought those original writings before us.

Twenty-two of the students of the college were called up for trial.

On that day armed soldiers guarded the streets that led to the council-chamber, because the rumor ran that the young members of parliament wished to free the culprits.

On the day in question there were no lessons—merely the accused and their judges were present in the school building.

It is curious that I did not fear, even when under the surveillance of the pedellus,[43] I had to wait in the ante-room of the school tribunal.

And I knew well what was threatening. They would exclude either me or Lorand from the school.

> [43] Warden of the school.

That idea was terrible for me.

I had heard thrilling stories of expelled students. How, at such times, they rang that cracked bell, which was used only to proclaim, to the whole town, that an expelled student was being escorted by his fellows out of the town, with songs of penitence. How the poor student became thenceforth a wanderer his whole lifetime through, whom no school would receive, who dared not return to his father's house. Now I merely shrugged my shoulders when I thought of it.

At other times the least rebuke would break my spirit, and drive me to despair; now—I was resolved not even to ask for pardon. As I waited in the ante-room, I met the professors, one after another, as they passed through into the council-chamber. Fittingly I greeted them. Some of them did not so much as look at me. As Mr. Schmuck passed by he saw me, came forward, and very tenderly addressed me:—

"Well, my child, and you have come here too. Don't be afraid: only look at me always. I shall do all I can for you, as I promised to your dear, good grandmother. Oh how your devoted grandmother would weep if she knew in what a position you now stand. Well, well, don't cry: don't be afraid. I intend to treat you as if you were my own child: only look at me always."

I was glad when he went away. I was angry that he wished to soften me. I must be strong to-day.

The director also noticed me, and called out in harsh tones:

"Well, famous fiddler: now you can show us what kind of a gypsy[44] you are."

> [44] The czigány (gypsy) is celebrated for his sneaking cowardice, and his fiddle playing, he being a naturally gifted

musician, as any one who has heard czigány music in Budapest can testify.

That pleased me better.

I would be no gypsy!

The examination began: my school-fellows, the greater part of whom were unknown to me, as they were students of a higher class, were called in one by one into the tribunal chamber, and one by one they were dismissed; then the pedellus led them into another room, that they might not tell those without what they had been asked, and what they had answered.

I had time enough to scrutinize their faces as they came out.

Each one was unusually flushed, and brought with him the impression of what had passed within.

One looked obstinate, another dejected. Some smiled bitterly: others could not raise their eyes to look at their fellows. Each one was suffering from some nervous perturbation which made his face a glaring contrast to the gaping, frozen features without.

I was greatly relieved at not seeing Lorand among the accused. They did not know one of the chief leaders of the secret-writing conspiracy.

But when they left me to the last, I was convinced they were on the right track; the copyers one after another had confessed from whom they had received the matter for copying. I was the last link in the chain, and behind me stood Lorand.

But the chain would snap in two, and after me they would not find Lorand.

For that one thing I was prepared.

At last, after long waiting, my turn came. I was as stupefied, as benumbed, as if I had already passed through the ordeal.

No thought of mother or grandmother entered my head; merely the one idea that I must protect Lorand with body and soul: and then I felt as if that thought had turned me to stone: let them beat themselves against that stone.

"Desiderius Áronffy," said the director, "tell us whose writing is this?"

"Mine," I answered calmly.

"It is well that you have confessed at once: there is no necessity to compare your writing, to equivocate, as was the case with the others.—What did you write it for?"

"For money."

One professor-judge laughed outright, a second angrily struck his fist upon the table, a third played with his pen. Mr. Schmuck sat in his chair with a sweet smile, and putting his hands together twirled his thumbs.

"I think you did not understand the question, my son," said the director in a harsh dry voice. "It is not that I wished to know for how much you wrote that trash: but with what object."

"I understood well, and answered accordingly. They gave me writings to copy, they paid me for them: I accepted the payment because it was honorable earnings."

"You did not know they were secret writings?"

"I could not know it was forbidden to write what it was permitted to say for the hearing of the whole public, in the presence of the representative of the King and the Prince Palatine."

At this answer of mine one of the younger professors uttered a sound that greatly resembled a choked laugh. The director looked sternly at him, rebuked with his eyes the sympathetic demonstration, and then bawled angrily at me:—

"Don't play the fool!"

The only result of this was that I gazed still more closely at him, and was already resolved not to move aside, even if he drove a coach and four at me. I had trembled before him when he had rebuked me for my violin-playing; but now, when real danger threatened me, I did not wince at his gaze.

"Answer me, who gave into your hands that writing, which you copied?"

I clenched my teeth. I would not answer. He might cut me in two without finding within me what he sought.

"Well, won't you answer my question?"

Indeed, what would have been easier than to relate how some gentleman, whom I did not know, came to me; he had a beard that reached to his knees, wore spectacles, and a green overcoat: they must then try to find the man, if they could:—but then—I could not any longer have gazed into the questioning eyes.

No! I would not lie: nor would I play the traitor.

"Will you answer?" the director cried at me for the third time.

"I cannot answer."

"Ho ho, that is a fine statement. Perhaps you don't know the man?"

"I know, but will not betray him."

I thought that, at this answer of mine, the director would surely take up his inkstand and hurl it at my head.

But he did not: he took a pinch of snuff from his snuff-box, and looked askance at his neighbor, Schmuck, as much as to say, "It is what I expected from him."

Thereupon Mr. Schmuck ceased to twirl his thumbs and turning to me with a tender face he addressed me with soothing tones:—

"My dear Desider, don't be alarmed without cause: don't imagine that some severe punishment awaits you or him from whom you received the writing. It was an error, surely, but not a crime, and will only become a crime in case you obstinately hold back some of the truth. Believe me, I shall take care that no harm befall you; but in that case it is necessary you should answer our questions openly."

These words of assurance began to move me from my purpose. They were said so sweetly, I began to believe in them.

But the director suddenly interrupted: —

"On the contrary! I am forced to contradict the honored professor, and to deny what he has brought forward for the defence of these criminal young men. Grievous and of great moment is the offence they have committed, and the chief causers thereof shall be punished with the utmost rigor of the law."

These words were uttered in a voice of anger and of implacable severity; but all at once it dawned upon me, that this severe man was he who wished to save us, while that assuring, tender paterfamilias was just the one who desired to ruin us.

Mr. Schmuck continued to twirl his thumbs.

The director then turned again to me.

"Why will you not name the man who entrusted you with that matter for copying?"

I gave the only answer possible. "When I copied these writings I could not know I was engaged on forbidden work. Now it has been told me that it was a grievous offence, though I cannot tell why. Still I must believe it. I have no intention of naming the man who entrusted that work to me, because the punishment of me who did not know its object, will be far lighter than that of him, who knew."

"But only think, my dear child, what a risk you take upon your own shoulders," said Mr. Schmuck in gracious tones; "think, by your obduracy you make yourself the guilty accomplice in a crime, of which you were before innocent."

"Sir," I answered, turning towards him: "did you not teach me the heroic story of Mucius Scævola? did you not yourself teach me to recite 'Romanus sum civis?'

"Do with me what you please: I shall not prove a traitor: if the Romans had courage, so have I to say 'longus post me ordo idem petentium decus.'"

"Get you hence," brawled the director; and the pedellus led me away.

Two hours afterwards they told me I might go home; I was saved. Just that implacable director had proved himself the best in his efforts to rescue us. One or two "primani," who had amused the tribunal with some very broad lies, were condemned to a few days' lock-up. That was all.

I thought that was the end of the joke. When they let me go I hurried to Lorand. I was proudly conscious of my successful attempt to rescue my elder brother.

CHAPTER VIII

THE END OF THE BEGINNING

Her ladyship, the beautiful wife of Bálnokházy, was playing with her parrot, when her husband entered her chamber.

The lady was very fond of this creature—I mean of the parrot.

"Well, my dear," said Bálnokházy, "has Kokó learned already to utter Lorand's name?"

"Not yet."

"Well, he will soon learn. By the bye, do you know that Parliament is dissolved. Mr. Bálnokházy may now take his seat in peace beside his wife."

"As far as I am concerned, it may dissolve."

"Well, perhaps you will be interested so far; the good dancers will now go home. The young men of Parliament will disperse to their several homes."

"I don't wish to detain them."

"Of course not. Why, Lorand will remain here. But even Lorand will with difficulty be able to remain here. He must fly."

"What do you say?"

"What I ought not to say out. Nor would I tell anyone other than you, my dear, as we agreed. Do you understand?"

"Partly. You are referring to the matter of secret journalism?"

"Yes, my dear, and to other matters which I have heard from you."

"Yes, from me. I told you frankly, what Lorand related to me in confidence, believing that I shared his enthusiastic ideas. I told you that you might use your knowledge for your own elevation. They were gifts of honor, as far as you are concerned, but I bound you not to bring any disgrace upon him from whom I learned the facts, and to inform me if any danger should threaten him."

Bálnokházy bent nearer to his wife and whispered in her ear:

"To-night arrests will take place."

"Whom will they arrest?"

"Several leaders of the Parliamentary youths, particularly those responsible for the dissemination of the written newspaper."

"How can that affect Lorand? He has burned every writing; no piece of paper can be found in his room. The newspaper fragments, if they have come into strange hands, cannot be compared with his handwriting. If hitherto he wrote with letters leaning forwards, he will now lean them backwards: no one will be able to find any similarity in the handwritings. His brother, who copied them, has confessed nothing against him."

"True enough; but I am inclined to think that he has not destroyed everything he has written in this town. Once he wrote some lines in the album of a friend. A poem or some such stupidity; and that album has somehow come into the hands of justice."

"And who gave it over?" enquired the lady passionately.

"As it happens, the owner of the album himself."

"Gyáli?"

"The same, my dear. He too thought that one must use a good friend's shoulders to elevate himself."

Madam Bálnokházy bit her pretty lips until blood came.

"Can you not help Lorand further?" she inquired, turning suddenly to her husband.

"Why, that is just what I am racking my brain to do."

"Will you save him?"

"That I cannot do, but I shall allow him to escape."

"To escape?"

"Surely there is no other choice, than either to let himself be arrested, or to escape secretly."

"But in this matter we have made no agreement. It was not this you promised me."

"My darling, don't place any confidence in great men's promises. The whole world over, diplomacy consists of deceit: you deceive me, I deceive you: you betrayed Lorand's confidence, and Lorand deserved it: why did he confide in you so? You cannot deny that I am the most polite husband in the world. A young man pays his addresses to my wife: I see it, and know it; I am not angry; I do not make him leap out of the window, I do not point my pistol at him: I merely slap him on the shoulder with perfect nonchalance, and say, 'my dear boy, you will be arrested to-night in your bed.'"

Bálnokházy could laugh most jovially at such sallies of humor. The whole of his beautiful white teeth could be seen as he roared with laughter—(even the gold wire that held them in place.)

My lady Hermine rose from beside him, and seemed to be greatly irritated.

"You are only playing the innocent before me, but I know quite surely that you put Gyáli up to handing over the album to the treasury."

"You only wish to make yourself believe that, my dear, so that when Lorand disappears from the house, you may not be compelled to be angry with Gyáli, but with me; for of course somebody must remain in the house."

"Your insults cannot hurt me."

"I did not wish to hurt you. My every effort was and always will be to make your life, my dear, ever more agreeable. Have I ever showed jealousy? Have I not behaved towards you like a father to a daughter about to be married?"

"Don't remind me of that, sir. That is your most ungracious trait. It is true that you yourself have introduced into our house young men of every class of society. It is true that you have never guarded me against them:—but then in a short time, when you began to remark that I felt some affection towards some of them, you discovered always choice methods to make me despise and abhor them. Had you shut me up and guarded me with the severity of a convent, you would have shown me more consideration. But you are playing a dangerous game, sir: maybe the time will come when I shall not cast out him whom I have hated!"

"Well, that will be your own business, my dear. But the first business is to tell our relation Lorand that by ten o'clock this evening he must not be found here: for at that hour they will come to arrest him."

Hermine walked up and down her room in anger.

"And it is all your work: it is useless for you to defend yourself," said she, tossing away her husband's hat from the arm-chair, and then throwing herself in a spiritless manner into it.

"Why, I have no intention of defending myself," said Bálnokházy, good-humoredly picking up his rolling hat. "Of course I had a little share in it: why, you know it well enough, my dear. A man's first business is to create a career. I have to rise: you approve of that yourself; it is a man's duty to make use of every circumstance that comes to hand. Had I not done so, I should be a mere magistrate, somewhere in Szabolcs, who at the end of every three years kisses the hands of all the 'powers that be,' that they may not turn him out of office.[45] The present chancellor, Adam Reviczky, was one class ahead of me in the school. He too was the head of his class, as I was of mine. Every year I took his place: at every desk, where I sat in the first place, I found his name carved, and always carved it out, putting mine in its place. He reached the height of the 'parabola,' and is now about to descend. Who knows what may happen next? At such times we must not mind if we make celebrated men of a few lads, whom at other times we did not remark."

[45] Every three years new magistrates and officials were elected to the various posts in the counties.

"But consider, Lorand is a relation of ours."

"That only concerns me, not you."

"It is, notwithstanding, terrible to ruin the career of a young man."

"What will happen to him? He will fly away to the country to some friend of his, where no one will search for him. At most he will be prohibited from being 'called to the bar.' But it will not prevent him from being elected lawyer to the county court at the first renovation.[46] Besides, Lorand is a handsome fellow: and the harm the persecution of men has done him will soon be repaired by the aid of women."

[46] As explained above.

"Leave me to myself. I shall think about the matter."

"I shall be deeply obliged to you. But, remember, please, ten o'clock this evening must not find here—the dear relation."

Hermine hastened to her jewel-case with ostentation. Bálnokházy, as he turned in the doorway, could see with what feverish anxiety she unlocked it and fumbled among her jewels.

With a smile on his face the husband went away. It is a fine instance of the irony of fate, when a woman is obliged to pawn her jewels in order to help someone escape whom she has loved, and whom she would love still to see about her,—to send him a hundred miles from her side.

Hermine did indeed collect her jewels, and threw them into a travelling-bag.

Then she sat down at her writing-table, and very hurriedly wrote something on some lilac-coloured letter paper on which the initials of her name had been stamped; this she folded up, sealed it and sent it by her butler to Lorand's room.

Lorand had not yet stirred from the house that day; he did not know that part of the Parliamentary youth, gaining an inkling of the movement against them, had hurried to depart.

Debts of Honor

When he had read the letter of the P. C.'s wife, he begged the butler to go to Mr. Gyáli and ask him in his name to pay him a visit at once: he must speak a few words to him without fail.

When the butler had gone, Lorand began to walk swiftly up and down his room. He was in search of something which he could not find, an idea.

He sat again, driving his fist into his hand: then sprang up anew and hastened to the window, as if in impatient expectation of the new-comer.

Suddenly a thought came to him: he began to put on gloves, fine, white kid gloves. Then he tried to clench his fist in them without tearing them.

Perhaps he does not wish to touch, with uncovered hands, him for whom he is waiting!

At last the street door opened, and steps made direct for his door.

Only let him come! but he, whom he expected did not come alone: the first to open his door was not Pepi Gyáli, but his brother, Desiderius. By chance they had met.

Lorand received his brother in a very spiritless manner. It was not he whom he wished to see now. Yet he rushed to embrace Lorand with a face beaming triumph.

"Well, and what has happened, that you are beaming so?"

"The school tribunal has acquitted me: yet I drew everything on myself and did not throw any suspicion on you."

"I hope you would be insulted if I praised you for it. Every ordinary man of honor would have done the same. It is just as little a merit not to be a traitor as it is a great ignominy to be one. Am I not right? Pepi,—my friend?"

Pepi Gyáli decided that Lorand could not have heard of his treachery and would not know it until he was placed in some safe place. He answered naturally enough that no greater disgrace existed on earth than that of treachery.

"But why did you summon me in such haste," he enquired, offering his hand confidently to Lorand; the latter allowed him to grasp his hand—on which was a glove.

"I merely wished to ask you if you would take my vis-à-vis in the ball to-night following my farewell banquet?"

"With the greatest pleasure. You need not even have asked me. Where you are, I must be also."

"Go upstairs, Desi, to the governess and ask her whether she intends to come to the ball to-night, or if the lady of the house is going alone."

Desiderius listlessly sauntered out of the room.

He thought that to-day was scarcely a suitable day to conclude with a ball; still he did go upstairs to the governess.

The young lady answered that she was not going for Melanie had a difficult "Cavatina" to learn that evening, but her ladyship was getting ready, and the stout aunt was going with her.

As Desiderius shut the door after him, Lorand stood with crossed arms before the dandy, and said:

"Do you know what kind of dance it is, in which I have invited you to be my vis-à-vis?"

"What kind?" asked Pepi with a playful expression.

"A kind of dance at which one of us must die." Therewith he handed him the lilac-coloured letter which Hermine had written to him: "Read that."

Gyáli read these lines:

"Gyáli handed over the album-leaf you wrote on. All is betrayed."

The dandy smiled, and placed his hands behind him.

"Well, and what do you want with me?" he enquired with cool assurance.

"What do you think I want?"

"Do you want to abuse me? We are alone, no one will hear us. If you wish to be rough with me, I shall shout and collect a crowd in the street: that will also be bad for you."

"I intend to do neither. You see I have put gloves on, that I may not befoul myself by touching you. Yet you can imagine that it is not customary to make a present of such a debt."

"Do you wish to fight a duel with me?"

"Yes, and at once: I shall not allow you out of my sight until you have given me satisfaction."

"Don't expect that. Because you are a Hercules, and I a titmouse, don't think I am overawed by your knitted eyebrows. If you so desire, I am ready."

"I like that."

"But you know that as the challenged, I have the right to choose weapons and method."

"Do so."

"And you will find it quite natural that I have no intention of being pummelled into a loaf of bread and devoured by you. I recommend the American duel. Let us put our names into a hat and he whose name is drawn is compelled to shoot himself."

Lorand was staggered. He recalled that night in the crypt.

"One of us must die; you said so yourself," remarked Gyáli. "Good, I am not afraid of it. Let us draw lots, and then he whom fate chooses, must die."

Lorand gazed moodily before him, as if he were regarding things happening miles away.

"I understand your hesitation: there are others whom you would spare. Well, let us fix a definite time for dying. How long can those, of whom you are thinking, live? Let us say ten years. He, whose name is drawn must shoot himself—to-day ten years."

"Oh," cried Lorand in a tone of vexation, "this is merely a cowardly subterfuge by which you wish to escape."

"Brave lion, you will fall just as soon, if you die, as the mouse. Your whole valor consists in being able to pin, with a round pin, a tiny little fly to the bottom of a box, but if you find an opponent, like yourself, you draw back before him."

"I shall not draw back," said Lorand irritated; and there appeared before his soul all those figures, which, pointing their fingers threateningly, rose before him from the depths of the earth. Headless phantoms returned to the seven cold beds; and the eighth was bespoken.

"Be it so," sighed Lorand: "let us write our names." Therewith he began to look for paper. But not a morsel was there in his room: all had been burned, clean paper too, that the water mark might not betray him. At last he came across Hermine's note. There was no other alternative. Tearing it in two,—one part he threw to Gyáli, on the other he inscribed his own name.

Then they folded the pieces of paper and put them into a hat.

"Who shall draw?"

"You are the challenger."

"But you proposed the method."

"Wait a moment. Let us entrust the drawing of lots to a third party."

"To whom?"

"There is your brother, Desi."

"Desi?"—Lorand felt a twitching pain at his heart:—"that one's own brother should draw one's death warrant!"

"As yet his hand is innocent. Nor shall he know for what he is drawing. I will tell him some tale. And so both of us may be tranquil during the drawing of lots."

Just at that moment Desiderius opened the door.

He related that the governess was not going, but the stout aunt was to accompany "auntie" to the ball. And the "fraülein" had sent Lorand a written dance-programme, which Desiderius had torn up on the way.

He tore it up because he was angry that other people were in so frivolous a mood at a time when he felt so exalted. For that reason he had no intention of handing over the programme.

Hearing of the stout aunt, Pepi laughed and then began to feign horror.

"Great heavens, Lorand: the seven fat kine of the Old Testament will be there in one: and one of us must dance with this monster. One of us will have to move from its place that mountain, which even Mahomet could not induce to stir, and waltz with it. Please undertake it for my sake."

Lorand was annoyed by the ill-timed jest which he did not understand.

"Well, to be sure I cannot make the sacrifice: it must be either you or I. I don't mind, let's draw lots for it, and see who must dance this evening with the tower of St. Stephen's."

"Very well,"—Lorand now understood what the other wanted.

"Desi will draw lots for us."

"Of course. Just step outside a moment, Desi, that you may not see on which paper which of our names was written." Desiderius stepped outside.

"He must not see that the tickets are already prepared," murmured Lorand:— —

"You may come in now."

"In this hat are both our names," said Gyáli, holding the hat before Desiderius: "draw one of them out: open it, read it, and then put both names into the fire. The one whose name you draw will do the honors to the Cochin-China Emperor's white elephant."

The two foes turned round toward the window. Lorand gazed out, while Gyáli played with his watch-chain.

The child unsuspectingly stepped up to the hat that served as the "urna sortis," and drew out one of the pieces of paper.

He opened it and read the name,

"Lorand Áronffy."

"Put them in the fire," said Gyáli.

Desiderius threw two pieces of lilac paper into the fire.

They were cold May days; outside the face of nature had been distorted, and it was freezing; in Lorand's fire-place a fire was blazing. The two pieces of paper were at once burnt up.

Only they were not those on which the two young men had written their names. Desiderius, without being noticed, had changed them for the dance programme, which he had cast into the fire. He kept the two fatal signatures to himself.

He had a very good reason for doing so, and a still better reason for saying nothing about it.

Lorand said:

"Thank you, Desi."

He thanked him for drawing that lot.

Pepi Gyáli took up his hat and said to Lorand in playful jesting:

"The white elephant is yours. Good night." And he went away unharmed.

Debts of Honor

"And now, my dear Desi, you must go home," said Lorand, gently grasping his brother's hand.

"Why I have only just come."

"I have much to do, and it must be done to-day."

"Do it: I will sit down in a corner, and not say a word; I came to see you. I will be silent and watch you."

Lorand took his brother in his arms and kissed him.

"I have to pay a visit somewhere where you could not come with me."

Desiderius listlessly felt for his cap.

"Yet I did so want to be with you this evening."

"To-morrow will do as well."

Lorand was afraid that the officers of justice might come any moment for him. For his part he did not mind: but he did not wish his brother to be present.

Desiderius sorrowfully returned home.

Lorand remained by himself.

By himself? Oh no. There around him were the others—seven in number: those headless dead.

Well, fate is inevitable.

Family misfortune is inherited. One is destroyed by the family disease, another by the hereditary curse.

And again the cause is the "sorrowful soil beneath them."

From that there is no escape.

A terrible inheritance is the self-shed blood, which besprinkles the heads of sons and grandsons!

And his inheritance was — the pistol, with which his father had killed himself.

It were vain for the whole Heaven to be here on earth. He must leave it, must go, where the others had gone.

The eighth niche was still empty, but was already bespoken.

For later comers there was room only in the ditch of the graveyard.

And there were still ten years left to think thereon! But ten years is a long time. Meanwhile that field might open where an honourable death, grasping a scythe in its two hands, cuts a way through the ranks of armed warriors: — where the children of weeping mothers are trampled to death by the hoofs of horses: — where they throw the first-born's mangled remains into the common burying-pit: perhaps there the son will find what the father sought in vain: — those who fled from before the resting-chamber of that melancholy house, on the façade of which was to be read the inscription, covered by the creepers since days long gone by.

"Ne nos inducas in tentationem."

CHAPTER IX

AGED AT SEVENTEEN

How beautiful it is to be young! How fair is the spring! Yours is life, joy, hope; the meadows lavish flowers upon you; the earth's fair halo of love surrounds you with glory: a nation, a fatherland, mankind entrusts to you its future; old men are proud of you; women love you: every brightening day of heaven is yours.

Oh, how I love the spring! how I love youth! In spring I see the fairest work of God, the earth, take new life; in youth I see the fairest work of man, his nation, reviving.

"In those days" I did not yet belong to the "youth:" I was a child.

Never do I remember a brighter promise of spring, than in that year; never were the eyes of the old men gladdened by the sight of a more spirited "youth" than was that of those days.

Spring began very early: even at the end of February the fields were green, parks hastened to bedeck themselves in their leafy wings, the blossoms hastened to bloom and fall; the opening days of May saw fruit on the apple-trees; and prematurely ripe cherries were "hawked" in the streets, beside bouquets of late blooming violets.

Of the "youths" of that year the historian has written: "These youths were in general very serious, very lavish in patriotic feeling, fiery and spirited in the defence of freedom and national dignity. The new tendency which manifested itself so vividly in our country was reflected by their impetuous and susceptible natures with all its noble yearnings, its virtues and excesses exaggerated. The frivolous pastimes, the senseless or dissolute amusements that were so fashionable in those days were abandoned for serious reading, gathering of information and investigation of current events. They had already opinions of their own, which not rarely they could utter with striking audacity."—I could only envy these lines of gold; not one word of them had any reference to me: for I was still but a child. During a night that followed a lovely May day, the weather suddenly changed: winter, who was during the days of his dominion, watching how the warm breezes played with the flower-bells of the trees, all at once returned: with the full vigor of vengeance he came, and in three days destroyed everything, in which man happened to delight. To the last leaf everything was frozen off the trees.

On this most inclement of the three wintry May evenings Lorand was standing alone at his window, and gazing abstractedly at the street through the ice-flower pattern of the window-panes.

Just such ice-flowers lay frozen before his soul. The lottery of fate has appointed his time: ten years his life would last; then he must die.

From seventeen to twenty-seven is just the fairest part of life. Many had made their whole earthly career during that period.

And what awaits him?

His ardent yearning for freedom, his audacious plans, his misplaced confidence; friends' treason, and the consequent freezing rigor, where were they leading to?...

Every leaf had fallen from the trees. Only ten years to live: the decree was unalterable.

From the opponent, whom he despised, it is not possible even to accept as a present, that to which chance has once given him the right.

And these ten years, with what will they begin? Perhaps with a long imprisonment? The time which is so short—(ten years are light!) will seem so long *there*! (ten years are heavy!) Would it not be better not to wait for the first day? To say: if it is time, take it away: let me not take the days on lease from thee! The hateful, freezing days.

Why, when nature dies in this wise, man himself would love to die after her.

If only there were not that weeping face at home, that white-haired head, mother and grandmother.

In vain Fate is inevitable. The eighth bed was already made;—but *that* no one must know for ten years. Should someone learn, he might perpetrate the outrage of occupying earlier the eighth niche in the family vault; and then his successor would have nothing left but the church-yard grave.

What a thought, a youthful spring with these frozen leaves!

He did not think for the next few moments. Is it worth while to try to avoid the fate, which is certain? Let it come. The keystone of the arch had been removed, the downfall of the whole must follow. His room was already in darkness, but he did not light a lamp. The dancing flames of the fire-place gazed out sometimes above the embers, in curiosity, as if they would know whether any living being were there: and still he did not stir.

In this dim twilight Lorand was thinking upon those who had passed away before him.

That bony-faced figure, whose death face he was painting,—his ordinary physiognomy was terrible enough: those empty eye-sockets, into which he fears to gaze:—suppose between these two hollows a third was darkling, the place of the bullet that pierced his forehead!

Lorand now knew what torture must have been theirs, who had left him this sorrowful bequest, before they could make up their minds to raise their own hands against their own lives! with what power of God they must have struggled, with what power of devils have made a compact! Oh, if they would only come for him now!

Who?

Those who picked the fruit that dared so early to ripen?

Yes, rather those, than these quiet, bloodless faces, in their bloody robes. Rather those who come with clank of arms, tearing open the door with drawn sword, than those who with inaudible step steal in, gently open the door, whisperingly speak and tremblingly pronounce your name.

Debts of Honor

"Lorand."

"Ha! Who is that?"

Not one of the dead, though her robe is white: one far worse than they:—a beautiful woman.

It was Hermine who opened the door and entered Lorand's room so silently, with inaudible steps. Her ball-robe was on her: she had dressed for the dance in her room above, and thus dressed had descended.

"Are you ready now, Lorand?"

"Oh, good evening: pardon me. I will light a candle in a moment."

"Never mind about that," whispered the woman. "It is quite light enough as it is. To-day no candle may burn in this room."

"You are going to a ball," said Lorand, masking the sorrow of his soul by a display of good spirits: "and you wish me to accompany you?"

"Fancy the thought of dancing coming into my head just now!" replied Hermine, coming so close to Lorand that she could whisper in his ear. "Did you get my letter?"

"Yes, thank you. Don't be alarmed, there is no danger."

"Indeed there is. I know it well. The danger is in the hands of Bálnokházy: therefore certain."

"What great harm can happen to me?"

Hermine placed her hand on Lorand's shoulder and tremblingly hissed:

"They will arrest you to-night."

"They may do so."

"Oh no, they may not, kind Heaven! That they shall not do. You must escape, immediately, this hour."

"Is it sure they will arrest me?"

"Believe me, yes."

"Then just for that reason I shall not stir from my place."

"What are you saying? Why? Why not?"

"Because I should be ashamed, if they who wanted me should draw me out from under my bed in my mother's house, like a child who has played some mischief."

"Who is speaking now of your mother's house? You must fly far: away to foreign lands."

"Why?" asked Lorand coldly.

"Why? My God, what questions you put. I don't know how to answer! Can you not see that I am in despair, that every limb of my body trembles for my fear on your account? Believe me, I cannot possibly allow them to take you away from before my eyes, to imprison you for years, so that I shall never see you again."

To appeal the more to Lorand's feelings, and to show him how her hands trembled she tore off her beautiful ball gloves, and grasped his hands in her own and then sobbed before him.

As she touched him Lorand began to feel, instead of his previous tomblike chillness, a kind of agitating heat as if the cold bony hand of death had given over his hand to some other unknown demon.

"What shall I do in a foreign country? I have no one, nothing, no way there. Everyone I love is here, in this land. There I should go mad."

"You will not be alone there, because the one who loves you best on earth, who worships you above all, who loves you better than her health, her soul, better than heaven itself, goes with you and will never leave you."

The young man could make no mistake as to whom she meant: Hermine encircled his young neck with her beautiful arms and overwhelmed his face with kisses.

Lorand was no longer his own. In one hour he lost his home, his fortune, and his heart.

CHAPTER X

I AND THE DEMON

It was already late in the evening when Bálnokházy's butler brought me a letter, and then hurriedly departed, before I could read it.

It was Lorand's writing. The message was short:

"My dear brother:—I have been betrayed and must escape: comfort our dear parents. Good-bye."

I leaped up from my bed:—I had already gone to bed that I might get up early on the morrow:—and hastened to dress.

My first idea was to go to Bálnokházy. He was my uncle and relation, and was extremely fond of us: besides, he was very influential; he could accomplish anything he wished, I would tell him everything frankly, and beg him to do for my brother what he was capable of doing: to prevent his prosecution and arrest, or, if he was convicted, to secure his pardon. Why, to such a great man nothing could be impossible.

I begged old Márton to open the door for me.

"What! discipulus negligens! To slip out of the house at night is not proper. He who wanders about at night can be no Lieutenant Governor—at most a night-watchman."

"No joking now; they are prosecuting my brother! I must go and help him."

"Why didn't you tell me at once? Prosecute indeed? You should have told me that. Who? Perhaps the butcher clerks? If so, let us all six go with clubs to his aid."

"No, they are not butcher clerks. What are you thinking of?"

"Why, in past years the law-students were continually having brawls with butcher clerks."

"They want to arrest him," I whispered to him, "to put him in prison, because he was one of the 'Parliamentary youth' lot."

"Aha," said Márton, "that's where we are is it? That is beyond my assistance. And, what can you do?"

"I must go to my uncle Bálnokházy at once and ask him to interfere."

"That's surely a wise thing to do. Under those circumstances I shall go with you. Not because I think you would be afraid to go by yourself at night, but that I may be able to tell the old man by-and-bye that you were not in mischief."

The old fellow put on a coat in a moment, and a pair of boots, then accompanied me to the Bálnokházys.

He did not wish to come in, but told me that, on my way back, I should look for him at the corner beer-house, where he would wait for me.

I hurried up stairs.

I was greatly disappointed to find my brother's door closed: at other times that had always been my first place of retreat.

I heard the piano in the "salon": so I went in there.

Melanie was playing with the governess.

They did not seem surprised that I came at so late an hour; I only noticed that they behaved a little more stiffly towards me than on other occasions.

Melanie was deeply engrossed in studying the notes. I enquired whether I could speak with my uncle.

"He has not yet come home from the club," said the governess.

"And her ladyship."

"She has gone to the ball."

That annoyed me a little.

"And when do they come home?"

"The Privy Councillor at eleven o'clock, he usually plays whist till that hour; her ladyship probably not until after midnight. Do you wish to wait?"

"Yes, until my uncle returns."

"Then you can take supper with us."

"Thank you, I have already had supper."

"Do they have supper so early at the baker's?"

"Yes."

I then sat down beside the piano, and thought for a whole hour what a stupid instrument the piano was; a man's head may be full of ideas, and it will drive them all out.

Yet I had so much to ponder over. What should I say to my uncle when he came. With what should I begin? How could I tell him what I knew? What should I ask from him?

But how was it possible that neither was at home at such a critical time? Surely they must have been informed of such a misfortune. I did not dare to introduce Lorand's name before the governess. Who knows what others are? Besides, I had no sympathy for her. For me a governess seemed always a most frivolous creature.

In the room there was a large clock that caused me most annoyance. How long it took for those hands to reach ten o'clock! Then, when it did strike, its tone was of that aristocratic nasal quality that it must have acquired from the voices of the people around it.

Sometimes the governess laughed, when Melanie made some curious mistake; Melanie, too, laughed and peeped from behind her music to see if I was smiling.

I had not even noticed it.

Then my pretty cousin poutingly tossed back her curly hair, as if she were annoyed that I too was beginning to play a part of indifference towards her.

At last the street-door bell rang. From the footsteps I knew my uncle had come. They were so dignified.

Soon the butler entered and said I could speak with his lordship, if I so desired.

Trembling all over, I took my hat, and wished the ladies good-night.

"Are you not coming back, to hear the end of the Cavatina;" inquired Melanie.

"I cannot," I answered, and left them there.

My uncle's study was on the farther side of the hall; the butler lighted my way with a lamp, then he put it down on a chest, that I might find my way back.

"Well, my child, what do you want?" inquired my uncle, in that gay, playful tone, which we are wont to use in speaking to children to express that we are quite indifferent as to their affairs.

I answered languidly, as if some gravestone were weighing upon my breast,

"Dear uncle, Lorand has left us."

"You know already?" he asked, putting on his many colored embroidered dressing-gown.

"You know too?" I exclaimed, taken aback.

"What, that Lorand has run away?" remarked my uncle, coolly buttoning together the silken folds of his dressing gown; "why I know more than that:—I know also that my wife has run away with him, and all my wife's jewels, not to mention the couple of thousand florins that were at home—all have run away with your brother Lorand."

How I reached the street after those words; whether they opened the door for me; whether they led me out or kicked me out, I assure you I do not know. I only came to myself, when Márton seized my arm in the street and shouted at me:

"Well sir Lieutenant-Governor, you walk right into me without even seeing me. I got tired of waiting in the beer-house and began to think that they had run you in too. Well, what is the matter? How you stagger."

"Oh! Márton," I stammered, "I feel very faint."

"What has happened?"

"I cannot tell anyone that."

"Not to anyone? No! not to Mr. Brodfresser,[47] nor to Mr. Commissioner:—but to Márton, to old Márton? Has old Márton ever let out anything? Old Márton knows much that would be worth his while to tell tales about: have you ever heard of old Márton being a gossip? Has old Márton ever told tales against you or anyone else? And if I could help you in any way?"

[47] The name given to Desiderius' professor ("bread devourer").

There was a world of frank good-heartedness in these reproaches; besides I had to catch after the first straw to find a way of escape.

"Well, and what did my old colleague say?—You know the reason I call him 'colleague,' is that my hair always acts as if it were a wig, while his wig always acts as it if were hair."

"He said," I answered tremblingly, hanging on to his arm, "he knew more than I. Lorand has not merely run away, but has stolen my uncle's wife."

At these words Márton commenced to roar with laughter. He pressed his hands upon his stomach and just roared, then turned round, as if he wished to give the further end of the street a taste of his laughter; then he remarked that it was a splendid joke, at which remark I was sufficiently scandalized.

"And then he said—that Lorand had stolen his money."

At this Márton straightened himself and raised his head very seriously.

"That is bad. That is 'a mill,' as Father Fromm would say. Well, and what do you think of it, sir?"

"I think, it cannot be true; and I want to find my brother, no matter what has become of him.

"And when you have found him?"

"Then, if that woman is holding him by one hand, I shall seize the other and we shall see which of us will be the stronger."

Márton gave me a sound slap on the back, saying "Teufelskerl.[48] What are you thinking of?—would other children mind, if a beautiful woman ran away with their brother? But this one wishes to stand between them. Excellent. Well, shall we look for Master Lorand? How will you begin?"

[48] Devil's fellow: *i. e.*, devil of a fellow.

"I don't know."

"Let me see; what have you learned at school? What can you do, if you are suddenly thrown back on your own resources? Which way will you start? Right or left: will you cry in the street, 'Who has seen my brother?'"

Indeed I did not know how to begin.

"Well,—you shall see that you can at times make use of that old fellow Márton. Trust yourself to me. Listen to me now, as if I were Mr. Brodfresser. If two of them ran away together, surely they must have taken a carriage. The carriage was a fiacre. Madame has always the same coachman, number 7. I know him well. So first of all we must find Móczli: that is coachman No. 7. He lives in the Zuckermandel. It's a cursed long way, but that's all the better, for by the time we get to his house we shall be all the surer to find him at home."

"If he was the one who took them."

"Don't play the fool now, sir studiosus. I know what cab-horses are. They could not take anyone as far as the border; at most as far as some wayside inn, where speedy country horses can be found: there the runaways are waiting while the fiacre is returning."

In astonishment I asked what made him surmise all this: when it seemed to me that with speedy country horses they might already be far beyond the frontier.

"Sir Lieutenant-Governor," was Márton's hasty reproof; "How could you have such ideas? You expect to become Lieutenant-Governor some day, yet you don't know that he who wishes to pass the frontiers must be supplied with a passport. No one can go without a pass from Pressburg to Vienna; Madame has quite surely despatched Móczli back to bring to her the gentleman with whose 'pass' they are to escape farther."

"What gentleman?"

"An actor from the theatre here, who will arrange that the young gentleman shall pass the frontier with his passport."

"How can you figure it all out?"

Márton paused for a moment, made an ugly mouth, closed his left eye, and hissed through his teeth, as if he would express by all this pantomime that there are things which cannot be held under children's noses.

"Well, never mind; you do wish to be a county officer or something of the kind. So you must know about such things sooner or later, when you will have to examine people on such questions. I will tell you—I know because Móczli once told me just such a story about madame."

"Once before?"

"Certainly," said Márton chuckling wickedly. "Ha ha! Madame is a cute little woman. But then no one knows of it—only Móczli and I; and Madame's husband. Her husband has already pardoned her for it: Móczli was well paid; and what business is it of Márton's? All three of us hold our tongues, like a broiled fish. But it is not the first time it has happened."

I do not know why, but this discovery somehow relieved my bitterness. I began to surmise that Lorand was not the most deeply implicated in the crime.

"Well, let us go first of all to Móczli," said Márton; "But I have a promise to exact from you. Don't say a word yourself; leave the talking to me. For he is a cursed fellow, this Móczli; if he finds that we wish to get information out of him, he will lie like a book: but I will suddenly drive in upon him, so that he will not know whether to turn to the right or to the left. I will spring something on him as if I knew all about it, that will scare him out of his wits and then I'll press him close, so that it'll take his breath away, and before he knows it I'll have that secret squeezed out of him to the very last drop. You must observe how it is done, so that you can make use of similar methods in the future when in the position of Lieutenant-Governor you will have to cross-question some suspicious rascal in order to wring the truth out of him!"

By this time we had started at a brisk pace along the banks of the Danube. I wasn't dressed for such a dismal night, and old Márton was doing his best to shield me with the wing of his coat against the chilling gusts that rushed against us from the river. At the same time he made every effort to make me believe that what we were engaged in was one of the finest jokes he had ever taken a hand in, and that our recollections of it will afford us no end of amusement in the future. At the foot of the castle-hill, along the banks of the Danube was a group of tottering houses; tottering because in spring, when the ice broke up, the Danube roared and dashed among them. Here lived the fiacre drivers. Here were the cab-horses in tumble-down stables.

It was a ball-night: in the windows of the tumble-down houses candles were burning, for the cabmen were waiting till midnight, when they would again harness their horses and return to fetch their patrons from the ball-room.

Márton looked in at one window so lighted; he had to climb up on something to do so, for the ground floor was built high, in order that the water might not enter at the windows.

"He is at home," he remarked, as he stepped down, "but he is evidently preparing to go out again, for he has his top-coat on."

The gate was open; the carriage was in the courtyard, the horses in the shafts, covered with rugs.

Their harness had not even been taken off: they must have just arrived and had to start again at once.

Márton motioned to me to follow him at his heels while he made his way into the house.

The door we ran up against could not be opened unless one knew the tricks that made it yield. Márton seemed to be well acquainted with the peculiarities of the entrance to Móczli's den: first he pressed down on the door knob and raised the whole door bracing against it with his shoulder, then turning the knob and giving the door a severe kick it flew open and in the next moment we found ourselves in a dingy, narrow hole of a room smelling horribly of axle-grease, tallow and tobacco-smoke.

On a table, which was leaning against the wall with the side where a leg was broken, stood a burning tallow-dip stuck into the mouth of an empty beer-jug, and by its dim light Móczli was seated eating— no, devouring his supper. With incredible rapidity he was piling in and ramming down, as it were, enormous slices of blood-sausage in turn with huger chunks of salted bread.

His many-collared coat was thrown over his huge frame, and his broad-brimmed hat that was pressed over his eyes was still covered with hoar-frost that had no chance of thawing in that cold, damp room, the wall of which glistened like the sides of some dripping cave.

Móczli was a well-fed fellow, with strongly protruding eyes, which seemed almost to jump out of their sockets as he stared at us for bursting in upon him without knocking.

"Well, where does it 'burn?'" were his first words to Márton.

"Gently, old fellow; don't make a noise. There is other trouble! You are betrayed and they will pinch the young gentleman at the frontier."

Móczli was really scared for a moment. A tremendous three-cornered chunk of bread that he had just thrust in his mouth stuck there staring frightenedly at us like Móczli himself and looking for all the world as if a second nose was going to grow on his face; however he soon came to himself, continued the munching process, gulped it all down, and then drank a huge draught out of a monstrous glass, his protruding eyes being all the while fixed on me.

"I surely thought there was a fire somewhere, and I must go for a fire-pump again with my horses.—I must always go for the pump, if a fire breaks out anywhere. Even if there is a fire in the mill quarter, it is only me they drive out: why does not the town keep horses of her own?"

"Do you hear, Móczli," Márton interrupted, "don't talk to me now of the town pumps don't sprinkle your throat either, for it's not there that it is burning, but your back will be burning immediately, if you don't listen to me. Her ladyship's husband learned all. They will forestall the young gentleman at the frontier, and bring him back."

Móczli endeavored to display a calm countenance, though his eyes belied him.

"What 'young gentleman' do you mean, and what 'ladyship?'"

Márton bent over him and whispered,

"Móczli, you don't want to make a fool of yourself before me, surely. Was it not you that took away Bálnokházy's wife in the company of a young gentleman? Your number is on your back: do you think no one can see it?"

"If I did take them off, where did I drive them to? Why to the ball."

"A fine ball, indeed. You know they want to arrest the 'juratus.' He will find one for you soon where they play better music. Here is his younger brother, just come from seeing his lordship, who told him his wife had eloped with the young gentleman whom they would search for in every direction."

Móczli was at this moment deeply engaged in picking his teeth. First with his tongue, then with his fingers, until he found a wisp of straw with which to clean them, and at which, like drowning people, he clutched to save himself.

"Well, do you think I care: anyone may send for anyone else for all I mind. I have seen no one, have taken no one away. And if I did take someone, what business of mine is it to know what the one is doing with the other? And even if I did know that someone has eloped with someone else's wife, what business is it of mine? I am no 'syndic' that I should bother my head to ask questions about it: I carry woman or man, who pays, according to the tariff of fares. Otherwise I know absolutely nothing."

"Well, good-bye, and God bless you, Móczli," said Márton hastily. "If you don't know about it, someone else must know about it. However, we didn't come here to gaze into your dreamy eyes, but to free this young gentleman's brother: we shall search among the other fiacres, until we find the right one, for it is a critical business: and if we find that fiacre in which the young fellow came to harm and cannot manage to secure his escape, I would not like to be in his shoes."

"In whose shoes?" inquired Móczli, terrified.

"In the young gentleman's not at all, but still less in the fiacre-driver's. Well, good-night, Móczli."

At these words Móczli leaped up from his chair and sprang after Márton.

"Wait a moment: don't be a fool. Come with me. Take your seats in my fiacre. But the devil take me if I have seen, heard or said anything."

Therewith he removed the rugs from his horses, placed me inside the carriage, covering me with a rug, took Márton beside him on the box, and drove desperately along the bank of the Danube.

Long did I see the lamps of the bridge glittering in the water; then suddenly the road turned abruptly, and, to judge by the almost intolerable shaking of the carriage and the profound darkness, we had entered one of those alleys, the paving of which is counted among the curses of civilization, the street-lamps being entrusted to the care of future generations.

The carriage suddenly proceeded more heavily: perhaps we were ascending a hill: the whip was being plied more vigorously every moment on the horses' backs: then suddenly the carriage stopped.

Móczli commenced to whistle as if to amuse himself, at which I heard the creaking of a gate, and we drove into some courtyard.

When the carriage stopped, the coachman leaped off the box, and addressed me through the window.

"We are here: at the end of the courtyard is a small room; a candle is burning in the window. The young gentleman is there."

"Is the woman with him too?" I inquired softly.

"No. She is at the 'White Wolf,' waiting with the speedy peasant cart, until I bring the gentleman with whom she must speak first."

"He cannot come yet, for the performance is not yet over."

Móczli opened his eyes still further.

"You know that too?"

I hastened across the long dark courtyard and found the door of the little room referred to. A head was to be seen at the lighted window. Lorand was standing there melting the ice on the panes with his breath, that he might see when the person he was expecting arrived.

Oh how he must have loved her. What a desperate struggle awaited me!

Debts of Honor

When he saw me from the window, he disappeared from it, and hurried to meet me.

At the door we met and in astonishment he asked:

"How did you get here?"

I said nothing, but embraced him, and determined that even if he cut me in pieces, I would never part from him.

"Why did you come after me? How did you find your way hither?"

I saw he was annoyed. He was displeased that I had come.

"Those, who saw you take your seat in a carriage, directed me."

He visibly shuddered.

"Who saw me?"

"Don't be afraid. Someone who will not betray you."

"But what do you want? Why did you come after me?"

"You know, dear Lorand, when we left home mother whispered in my ear, 'take care of Lorand,' when grandmother left us here, she whispered in my ear, 'take care of your brother.' They will ask me to give account of how I loved you. And what shall I tell them, if they ask me 'where were you when Lorand stood in direst danger?'"

Lorand was touched; he pressed me close to his heart, saying: —

"But, how can you help me?"

"I don't know. I only know that I shall follow you, wherever you go."

This very naive answer roused Lorand to anger.

"You will go to hell with me! Do I want irons on my feet to hinder my steps when I scarce know myself whither I shall fly? I know not how to rescue myself, and must I rescue you too?"

Lorand was in a violent rage and strove to shake me off from him. Yet I would not leave go of him.

"What if I intend to rescue you?"

"You?" he said, looking at me, and thrusting his hands in his pockets. "What part of me will you defend?"

"Your honor, Lorand."

Lorand drew back at these words.

"My honor?"

"And mine:—You know that father left us one in common, one we cannot divide—his unsullied name. It is entirely mine, just as it is entirely yours."

Lorand shrugged his shoulders indifferently.

"Let it be yours entirely: I give over my claim."

This indifference towards the most sacred ideas quite embittered me. I was beside myself, I must break out.

"Yes, because you wish to take the name of a wandering actor, and to elope with a woman who has a husband."

"Who told you?" Lorand exclaimed, standing before me with clenched fists.

I was far from being afraid of anyone: I answered coolly.

"That woman's husband."

Lorand was silent and began to walk feverishly up and down the narrow, short, little room. Suddenly he stopped, and half aside addressed me, always in the same passionate tones.

"Desi, you are still a child."

"I know."

"There are things which cannot yet be explained to you."

"On such subjects you may hold your peace."

"You have spoken with that woman's husband?"

"He said, you had eloped with his wife."

"And that is why you came after me?"

"Yes."

"Now what do you want?"

"I want you to leave that woman."

"Have you lost your senses?"

"Mine? Not yet."

"You wish perhaps to hint that I have lost mine: it is possible, very possible."

Therewith he sat down beside the table, and leaning his chin on his hands, began to gaze abstractedly into the candle-flames like some real lunatic.

I stepped up to him, and laid my head on his shoulder.

"Dear Lorand, you are angry with me."

"No. Only tell me what else you know."

"If you wish I will leave you here and return."

"Do as you wish."

"And what shall I tell dear mother, if she asks questions about you?"

Lorand dispiritedly turned his head away from me.

"You wrote to me to cheer and comfort mother and grandmother:— tell me then, what shall I write to them, if they enquire after you?"

Lorand answered defiantly,

"Write that Lorand is dead."

At his answer the blood boiled within me. I seized my brother's hands and cried to him:

"Lorand, till now the fathers were suicides in our family: do you wish that the mothers should continue the list?"

It was a pitiless remark of mine, I knew. Lorand commenced to shiver, I felt it. He stood up before me and became so pale.

I wished I had addressed him more gently.

"My dear brother Lorand, could you bear to become responsible for a mother, who left her child, and for another who died for her child?"

Lorand clasped his hands and bowed his head.

"If you only knew what you are saying to me now?" he said with such bitter reproach that I can never forget it.

"But I have not yet told you all I know."

"What do you know? As yet you are happy—your life mere play—passion does not yet trouble you. But I am already lost, through what, you have no idea, and may you never have!"

How he must love that woman!

It would have cost me few words to make him hate and despise her, but I did not wish to break his heart. I had other means with which to steel his heart, that he might wake up, as from a delirious dream, to another life.

I too had had visions about my piano-playing beauty: but I had forgotten that ideal for ever and ever, for being able to play, after she knew her mother had run away.—But that was mere childish love, a child's thought—-there is something, however, in the heart which is awakened earlier, and dies later than passion, that is a feeling of honor, and I had as much of that as Lorand: let us see whose was the stronger.

"Lorand, I don't know what enchantment it was, with which this woman could lure you after her. But I know that I too have a magic word, which will tear you from her."

"Your magic word?—Do you wish to speak of mother? Do you wish to stand in my way with her name?—Do so.—The only effect you will produce, by worrying me very much, will be that I shall blow my brains out here before you: but from that woman you can never tear me."

"I have no intention to speak of poor mother. It is a different subject I have in mind."

"Something, or someone else."

"It is Bálnokházy, for whose sake you are going to leave this woman."

Lorand shrugged his shoulders.

"Do you think I am afraid of Bálnokházy's prosecution?"

"He has no intention of prosecuting you. He has been very considerate to his wife in similar cases. Well, don't knit your eyebrows so; I am not saying a word about his wife. I have no business with women. Bálnokházy will not prosecute you, he will merely tell the world what has happened to him."

Lorand, with a bitter smile of scorn, asked me:

"What will he relate to the world?"

"That his wife broke open his safe, stole his jewels, and his ready money, and eloped with a young man."

Lorand turned abruptly to me like one whom a snake has bitten,

"What did he say?"

"That his faithless wife in company with a young man, whom he had treated like his own child, has stolen his money, and then run away, like a thief—with her companion in theft!"

Lorand clutched at the table for support.

"Don't, don't say any more."

"I shall. I have seen the safes, empty, in which the family treasures were wont to be piled. I heard from the cabman, who handed in her travelling bag after her that 'it must have been full of gold, it was so heavy.'"

Lorand's face was burning now like the clouds of a storm-swept sky at sunset.

"Did you have the bag in your hands?" I asked him.

"Not a word more!" Lorand cried, pressing my arm so that it pained me. "That woman shall never see me again."

Then he sank upon the table and sobbed.

How glad I felt that I had been able to move him.

Soon he raised his tear-stained face, stood up, came to me, embraced and kissed me.

"You have conquered! — Now tell me what else you want with me?"

I was incapable of uttering a word, so oppressed was my heart in my delight, my anguish. It was no child's play, this. Fate is not wont to entrust such a struggle to a child's hands.

"Brother, dear!" more I could not say: I felt as he must have when he brought me up from the bottom of the Danube.

"You will not allow anyone," he whispered, "to utter such a calumny against me."

"You may be sure of that."

"You will not let them degrade me before mother?"

"I shall defend you. You see that after all I am capable of defending you. — But time is precious: — they are prosecuting you for another crime too, you know, from which to escape is a duty. There is not a moment to lose. Fly!"

"Whither? I cannot take new misfortunes to mother's house."

"I have an idea. We have a relation of whom we have heard much, far off in the interior of the country, where they will never look for you, since we were never on good terms with him, Uncle Topándy."

"That infidel?" exclaimed Lorand; then he added bitterly, "It was a good idea of yours, indeed: I shall have a very good place in the house of an atheist, who lives at enmity with the whole earth, and with Heaven besides."

"There you will be well hidden."

"Well and for ever."

"Don't say that. This danger will pass away."

"Listen to me, Desi," said Lorand severely. "I shall abide by what you say: I shall go away, without once looking behind: I shall bury myself, but on one condition, which you must accept, or I shall go to the nearest police station and report myself."

"What do you wish?"

"That you shall never tell either mother or grandmother, where I have gone to."

"Never?" I inquired, frightenedly.

"No, only after ten years, ten years from to-day."

"Why?"

"Don't ask me: only give me your word of honor to keep my secret. If you do not do so, you will inflict a heavy sorrow on me, and on all our family."

"But if circumstances change?"

Debts of Honor

"I said, not for ten years. And, if the whole world should dance with delight, still keep peace and don't call for me, or put my mother on my tracks. I have a special reason for my desire, and that reason I cannot tell you."

"But if they ask me, if they weep before me?"

"Tell them nothing ails me, I am in a good place. I shall take another name, [49]Bálint Tátray. Topándy also shall know me under that name. I shall find my way to his place as bailiff, or servant, whichever he will accept me as, and then I shall write to you once every month. You will tell my loved ones at home what you know of me. And they will love you twice as well for it: they will love you in place of me."

[49] A name peculiarly Magyar.

I hesitated. It was a difficult promise.

"If you love me, you must undertake it for my sake."

I clung to him and said I would undertake to keep the secret. For ten years I would not say before mother or grandmother where their dearest son had gone.

Would they reach the end of those ten years?

"You undertake that—on your word of honor?" said Lorand, gazing deeply into my eyes; "on that honor by which you just now so proudly appealed to me? Look, the whole Áronffy name is borne by you alone. Do you undertake it for the honor of that whole name, not to mention this secret before mother or grandmother?"

"I do—on my word of honor."

He grasped my hand. He trusted so much to that word!

"Well, now be quick. The carriage is waiting."

"Carriage? With that I cannot travel far. Besides it is unnecessary. I have two good legs, they will carry me, if necessary, to the end of the world, without demanding payment afterwards."

I took a little purse, on the outside of which mother had worked a design, from my pocket, and wished to slip it into Lorand's side-pocket without attracting attention.

He discovered it.

"What is this?"

"A little money. I thought you might want it for the journey."

"How did you come by it?" enquired my brother in astonishment.

"Why, you know, you yourself paid me two twenties a sheet, when I copied those writings."

"And you have kept it?"—Lorand opened the purse, and saw within it about twenty florins. He began to laugh.

How glad I was to see him laugh now, I cannot tell you, his laughter infected me too, then I do not know why, but we laughed together, very good-spiritedly. Now as I write these words the tears stand in my eyes—and I did laugh so heartily.

"Why, you have made a millionaire of me."

Then cheerfully he put my purse into his pocket. And I did not know what to do in my delight at Lorand's accepting my money.

"Now comrade mine, I could go to the end of the world. I don't have to play 'armen reisender'[50] on the way."

[50] Poor traveller.

When we stepped out again through the low door into the narrow dark courtyard, Márton and Móczli were standing in astonishment before us. Anyone could see they could not comprehend what they had seen by peeping through the window.

"I am here," said Móczli, touching the brim of his hat, "where shall I drive, sir?"

Debts of Honor

"Just drive where you were told to," said Lorand, "take him for whom you were sent, to her who sent you for him.—I am going in another direction."

At these words Márton grasped my arm so savagely I almost cried out with pain. It was his peculiar method of showing his approval.

"Very good, sir," said Móczli, without asking any further questions, and clambering up onto the box.

"Stop a moment," Lorand exclaimed, taking out his purse. "Let no one say that you were paid for any services you did me with other people's money."

"Wha-at?" roughly grumbled Móczli. "Pay me? Am I a 'Hanák fuvaros'[51] that someone should pay me for helping a 'juratus' to escape? That has never happened yet."

[51] A Slavonian coachman who hires out his coach and carriages.

With that he whipped up his horses, and drove out of the courtyard.

"That's the trump for you," said Márton, "that's Móczli. I know Móczli, he's a sharp fellow, without him we should never have found our way here. Well, sir, and whither now?"

This remark was made to Lorand. My brother was acquainted with the jesting old fellow, and had often heard his humorous anecdotes, when he came to see me.

"At all events away from Pressburg, old man."

"But which way? I think the best would be over the bridge, through the park."

"But very many people pass there. Someone might recognize me."

"Then straight along the Danube, down-stream; by morning you will reach the ferry at Mühlau, where they will ferry you over for two kreuzers. Have you some change? You must always have that. Men on foot must always pay in copper, or they will be suspected. It's a pity I didn't know sooner, I could have lent you a passport. You might have travelled as a baker's assistant."

"I shall travel as a 'legátus.'[52]"

[52] A travelling preacher. A kind of missionary sent out by the "Legatio."

"That will do finely."

Meantime we reached the end of the street. Lorand wished to bid us farewell.

"Oho!" said Márton, "we shall accompany you to the outskirts of the town; we cannot leave you alone until you are in a secure place, on the high-road. Do you know what? You two go on in advance and I shall remain close behind, pretending to be a little drunk. Patrols are in the street. If I sing loudly they will waste their attention on me, and will not bother you. If necessary, I shall pitch into them, and while they are running me in, you can go on. To you, Master Lorand, I give my stick for the journey. It's a good, honest stick. I have tramped all over Germany with it. Well, God bless you."

The old fellow squeezed Lorand's hand.

"I have a mind to say something. But I shall say nothing. It is well just as it is,—I shall say nothing. God bless you, sir."

Therewith the old man dropped back, and began to brawl some yodling air in the street, and to thump the doors with his fists, in accompaniment, like some drunken reveller.

"Hai-dia-do."

Taking each other's hand we hastened on. The streets were already very dark here.

At the end of the town are barracks, before which we had to pass: the cry of the sentinel sounded in the distance. "Who goes there? Guard out!" and soon behind our backs we heard the squadron of horsemen clattering on the pavement.

Márton did just as he had said. He pitched into the guard. Soon we heard a dream-disturbing uproar, as he fell into a noisy discussion with the armed authorities.

"I am a citizen! A peaceful, harmless citizen! Fugias Mathias (this to us)! Ten glasses of beer are not the world! I am a citizen, Fugias Mathias is my name! I will pay for every thing. If I have broken any bottles I will pay for them. Who says I am shouting? I am singing. 'Hai-dia-do;' let any one who doesn't like it try to sing more beautifully himself!"

We were already outside of the town, and still we heard the terrible noise which he made in his self-sacrifice for our sakes.

As we came out into the open, we were both able to breathe more freely; the starry sky is a good shelter.

The cold, too, compelled us to hasten. We had walked a good half-hour among the vineyards, when suddenly something occurred to Lorand.

"How long do you wish to accompany me?"

"Until day breaks. In this darkness I should not dare to return to the town alone."

Now he became anxious for me too. What could he do with me? Should he let me go home alone at midnight through these clusters of houses in that suburb of ill-repute. Or should he take me miles on his way with him? From there I should have to return alone in any case.

At that moment a carriage approached rapidly, and as it passed before us, somebody leaped down upon us from the back seat, and laughing came where we were beside the hedge.

In him we recognized old Márton.

"I have found you after all," said the old fellow, smiling. "What a fine time I have had. They really thought I was drunk. I quarrelled with them. That was the 'gaude!' They tugged and pulled, and beat my back with the flat of their sabres: it was something glorious!"

Debts of Honor

"Well, how did you escape?" I asked, not finding that entertainment to the accompaniment of sabre-blows so glorious.

"When I saw a carriage approaching, I leaped out from their midst and climbed up behind:—nor did they give me a long chase. I soon got away from them."

The good old man was quite content with the fine amusement which he had procured for himself.

"But now we must really say adieu, Master Lorand. Don't go the same way as the carriage went: cut across the road here in the hills to the lower road; you can breakfast at the first inn you come to: you will reach it by dawn. Then go in the direction of the sunrise."

We embraced each other. We had to part. And who knew for how long?

Márton was nervous. "Let us go! Let Lorand too hurry on *his* way."

Why, ten years is a very long way. By that time we should be growing old.

"Love mother in my place. Then remember your word of honor." Lorand whispered these words. Then he kissed me and in a few moments had disappeared from my sight down the lower road among the hills.

Who knew when I should see him again?

Márton's laugh awoke me from my reverie.

"You know—" he inquired with a voice that showed his inclination to laugh—"You know ha! ha—you know why I told Master Lorand not to go in the same direction as the carriage?"

"No."

"Did you not recognize the coachman? It was Móczli."

"Móczli?"

"Do you know who was inside the carriage?—Guess!—Well, it was Madame."

"Bálnokházy's wife?"

"The same—with that certain actor."

"With whose passport Lorand was to have eloped?"

"Well if one is on his way to elope—it is all the same:—one must have a companion, if not the one, then the other.'"

It was all a fable to me. But such a mysterious fable that it sent a cold chill all over me.

"But where could they go?"

"Where?—Well, as far as the frontier, perhaps. Anyhow, as far as the contents of that bag, which Móczli handed into the carriage after her ladyship, will last.—Hai-dia-do."

Now it was really exuberance of spirits that made old Márton sing in Tyrolese manner, that refrain, "hai-hai-dia-hia-do."

He actually danced on the dusty road—a galop.

Was it possible? That madonna face, than which I have never seen a more beautiful, more enchanting—either before or since that day!

CHAPTER XI

"PAROLE D'HONNEUR"

Two days after Lorand's disappearance a travelling coach stopped before Mr. Fromm's house. From the window I recognized coach-horses and coachman: it was ours.

Some one of our party had arrived.

I hastened down into the street, where Father Fromm was already trying very excitedly to turn the leather curtain that was fastened round the coach....

No, not "some one!" the whole family was here! All who had remained at home. Mother, grandmother, and the Fromms' Fanny.

Actually mother had come: poor mother!

We had to lift her from the carriage: she was utterly broken down. She seemed ten years older than when I had last seen her.

When she had descended, she leaned upon Fanny on the one side, on the other upon me.

"Only let us go in, into the house!" grandmother urged us on, convinced that poor mother would collapse in the street.

All who had arrived were very quiet: they scarcely answered me, when I greeted them. We led mother up into the room, where we had had our first reception.

Mother Fromm and grandmother Fromm were not knitting stockings on this occasion; it seemed they were prepared for this appearance. They too received my parents very quietly and solemnly: as if everyone were convinced that the first word addressed by anyone to this broken-down, propped up figure would immediately reduce it to ashes, as the story goes about some figures they have found in old tombs. And yet she had come on this long, long journey. She had not waited for the weather to grow warmer.

Debts of Honor

She had started in the teeth of a raw, freezing spring wind, when she heard that Lorand was gone.

Oh, is there any plummet to sound the depths of a mother's love?

Poor mother did try so hard to appear strong. It was so evident, that she was struggling to combat with her nervous attacks, just in the very moment which awoke every memory before her mind.

"Quietly, my daughter—quietly," said grandmother. "You know what you promised: you promised to be strong. You know there is need of strength. Don't give yourself over. Sit down."

Mother sat down near the table where they led her, then let her head fall on her two arms, and, as she had promised not to weep—she did not weep.

It was piteous to see her sorrowful figure as, in this strange house, she was leaning over the table with her face buried in her hands in mute despair; determined, however, not to cry, for so she had promised.

Everyone kept at a distance from her: great sorrow commands great respect. Only one person ventured to remain close to her, one of whom I had not even taken notice as yet,—Fanny.

When she had taken off her travelling cloak I found she was dressed entirely in blue. Once that had been my mother's favorite color; father too had been exceedingly fond of it. She stood at mother's side and whispered something into her ear, at which mother raised her head and, like one who returns from the other world, sighed deeply, seemed to come to herself, and said with a peaceful smile, turning to the host and hostess:

"Pardon me, I was exceedingly abstracted." Merely to hear her speak agonized me greatly. Then she turned to Fanny, embraced her, kissed her forehead twice, and said to the Fromms,

"You will agree, will you not, to Fanny's staying a little longer with me? She is already like a child of my own."

I was no longer jealous of Fanny. I saw how happy she made mother, if she could embrace her.

Fanny again whispered something in mother's ear, at which mother rose, and seemed quite herself again: she approached Mrs. Fromm resolutely, with no faltering steps, and grasping both her hands, said, "I thank you," and once again repeated whisperingly, "I thank you."

All this I regarded speechlessly from a corner. I feared my mother's gaze inexpressibly.

Then grandmother interrupted,

"We have no time to lose, my daughter. If you are capable of coming at once, come."

Mother nodded assent with her head, and gazed continually upon Fanny.

"Meanwhile Fanny remains here," added grandmother. "But Desiderius comes with us."

At these words mother looked at me, as if it had only just occurred to her that I too was here, still it was Fanny's fair curls only that she continued stroking.

Father Fromm hurriedly sent Henrik for a cab. Not a soul asked us where we were going. Everyone wondered, where, and why? What purpose? But, only I knew what would be the end of to-day's journey.

I did not distress myself about it. I waited merely until my turn should come. I knew nothing could happen without me.

The cab was there, and the Fromms led mother down the steps. They set her down first of all, and, when we were all seated; Father Fromm called to the cabman:

"To the house of Bálnokházy!"

He knew well that we must go there now. During the whole journey there we did not exchange a single word: what could those two have said to me?

When we stopped before Bálnokházy's residence, it seemed to me, my mother was endowed with a quite youthful strength; she went before us, her face burning, her step elastic, her head carried on high.

I don't know whether it was our good fortune, or whether my parents' arrival had been announced previously, but the P. C. was at home, when we came to look for him.

I was curious to see with what countenance he would receive us.

I knew already much about him, that I ought never to have known.

As we stepped into his room, he came to meet us, with more courtesy than pleasure apparent on his countenance. Some kind of displeasure strove to display itself thereon, but it was just as if he had studied the expression for hours in the mirror; it seemed to be an artificial, affected, calculated displeasure.

Mother straightway hastened to him, and taking both his hands, impetuously introduced the conversation with these words:

"Where is my son Lorand?"

My right honorable uncle shrugged his shoulders, and with gracious mien answered this mother's passionate outburst:

"My dear lady cousin, it is I who ought to urge that question; for it is my duty to prosecute your son. And if I answer that I do not know where he is, I think thereby I shall display the most kinsmanlike feeling."

"Why prosecute my son?" said mother, tremblingly. "Is it possible to eternally ruin anyone for a mere schoolboy escapade?"

"Not one but many 'schoolboy escapades' justify me in my action: it is not merely in my official capacity that I am bound to prosecute him."

As he said this, Bálnokházy fixed his eyes sharply upon me: I did not wince before him. I knew I had the right and the power to withstand his gaze. Soon my turn would come.

"What?" asked mother. "What reason could you have to prosecute him?"

Bálnokházy shrugged his shoulders more than ever, bitterly smiling.

"I scarcely know, in truth, how to tell you this story, if you don't know already. I thought you were acquainted with all the facts. He who told you the news of the young man's disappearance, wrote to you also the reasons for it."

"Yes," said mother, "I know all. The misfortune is great: but there is no ignominy."

"Indeed?" interrupted Bálnokházy, drawing his shoulders derisively together: "I did not know that such conduct was not considered ignominious in the provinces. Indeed I did not. A young man, a law student, a mere stripling, shows his gratitude for the fatherly thoughtfulness of a man of position,—who had received him into his house as a kinsman, treating him as one of the family,—by seducing and eloping with his wife, and helping her to break open his money-chest, and steal his jewelry, disappearing with the shameless woman beyond the confines of the country. Oh, really, I did not know that they did not consider that a crime deserving of prosecution!"

Poor mother was shattered at this double accusation, as if she had been twice struck by thunder-bolts, and deadly pale clutched at grandmother's hand. The latter had herself in this moment grown as white as her grizzled hair. She took up the conversation in mother's place, for mother was no longer capable of speaking.

"What do you say? Lorand a seducer of women?"

"To my sorrow, he is. He has eloped with my wife."

"And thief?"

"A harsh word, but I can give him no other name."

"For God's sake, gently, sir!"

"Well, you can see that hitherto I have behaved very quietly. I have not even made a noise about my loss: yet, besides the destruction of my honor, I have other losses.

"This faithless deed has robbed me and my daughter of 5,000 florins.[53] If the matter only touched me, I would disdain to notice it: but that sum was the savings of my little daughter."

[53] Above £415—$2,000.

"Sir, that sum shall be repaid you," said grandmother, "but I beg you not to say another word on the subject before this lady. You can see you are killing her with it."

As she was speaking, Bálnokházy gazed intently at me, and in his gaze were many questions, all of which I could very well have answered.

"I am surprised," he said at last, "that these revelations are entirely new to you. I thought that the same person who had acquainted you with Lorand's disappearance, had unfolded to you therewith all those critical circumstances, which caused his disappearance, seeing that I related all myself to that person."

Now mother and grandmother too turned their gaze upon me.

Grandmother addressed me: "You did not write a word about all this to us."

"No."

"Nor did you mention a word about it here when we arrived."

"Yet I told it all myself to my nephew."

"Why don't you answer?" queried my grandmother impetuously.

Mother could not speak: she merely wrung her hands.

"Because I had certain information that this accusation was groundless."

"Oho! you young imp!" exclaimed Bálnokházy in proud, haughty tones.

"From beginning to end groundless," I repeated calmly; although every muscle of mine was trembling from excitement. But you should have seen, how mother and grandmother rushed into my arms: how they grasped one my right, the other my left hand, as drowning men clutch at the rescuer's hands, and how that proud angry man stood before me with flashing eyes. All sobriety had left the three, together they cried to me in voices of impetuousity, of anger, of madness, of hope, of joy: "speak! tell us what you know."

"I will tell you.—When his lordship acquainted me with these two terrible charges against Lorand, I at once started off to find my brother. Two honorable poor men came in my way to help me find him: two poor workmen, who left their work to help me to save a lost life. The same will be my witness that what I relate is all true and happened just as I tell you: one is Márton Braun, the baker's man, the other Matthias Fleck."

"My wife's coachman," interrupted the P. C.

"Yes. He conducted me to where Lorand was temporarily concealed. He related to me that her ladyship was elsewhere. He had taken her ladyship across the frontier—without Lorand. My brother started at the same time on foot, without money, towards the interior of Hungary: Márton and I accompanied him into the hills, and my pocket money, which he accepted from me, was the only money he had with him, and Márton's walking stick was the only travelling companion that accompanied him further."

I noticed that mother kneeled beside me and kissed me.

That kiss I received for Lorand's sake.

"It is not true!" yelled Bálnokházy; "he disappeared with my wife. I have certain information that this woman passed the frontier with a young smooth-faced man and arrived with him in Vienna. That was Lorand."

"It was not Lorand, but another."

"Who could it have been?"

"Is it possible that you should not know? Well, I can tell you. That smoothed-faced man who accompanied her ladyship to Vienna was the German actor Bleissberg;—and not for the first time."

Ha, ha! I had stabbed him to the heart: right to the middle of the liver, where pride dwells. I had thrust such a dart into him, as he would never be able to draw out. I did not care if he slew me now.

And he looked as if he felt very much like doing it—but who would have dared touch me and face the wrath of those two women—no—lionesses, standing next to me on either side! They seemed ready to tear anyone to pieces who ventured as much as lay a finger on me.

"Let us go," said mother, pressing my hand. "We have nothing more to do here."—Mother passed out first: they took me in the middle and grandmother, turning back addressed a categorical "adieu" to Bálnokházy, whom we left to himself.

My cousin Melanie was playing that cavatina even now, though now I did not care to stop and listen to it. That piano was a good idea after all; quarrels and disputes in the house were prevented thereby from being heard in the street.

When we were again seated in the cab, mother pressed me passionately to her, and smothered me with kisses.

Oh, how I feared her kisses! She kissed me because she would soon ask questions about Lorand. And I could not answer them.

"You were obedient: you took care of your poor brother: you helped him: my dear child." Thus she kept whispering continually to me.

I dared not be affected.

"Tell me now, where is Lorand?"

I had known she would ask that. In anguish I drew away from her and kept looking around me.

"Where is Lorand?"

Grandmother remarked my anguish.

"Leave him alone," she hinted to mother. "We are not yet in a sufficiently safe place: the driver might hear. Wait until we get home."

So I had time until we arrived home. What would happen there? How could I avoid answering their questions.

Scarcely had we returned to Master Fromm's house, scarce had Fanny brought us into a room which had been prepared for my parents, when my poor mother again fell upon my neck, and with melancholy gladness asked me:

"You know where Lorand is?"

How easy it would have been for me to answer "I know not!" But what should I have gained thereby? Had I done so, I could never have told her what Lorand wrote from a distance, how he greeted and kissed them a thousand times!

"I know, mother dear."

"Tell me quickly, where he is."

"He is in a safe place, mother dear," said I encouragingly, and hastened to tell all I might relate.

"Lorand is in his native land in a safe place, where he has nothing to fear: with a relation of ours, who will love and protect him."

"But when will you tell us where he is?"

"One day, soon, mother dear."

"But when? When? Why not at once? When?"

"Soon,—in ten years."—I could scarce utter the words.

Both were horrified at my utterance.

"Desi, do you wish to play some joke upon us?"

Debts of Honor

"If it were only a joke? It is true: a very heavy truth! I promised Lorand to tell neither mother nor grandmother, for ten years, where he is living."

Grandmother seemed to understand it all: she hinted with a look to Fanny to leave us alone: she thought that I did not wish to reveal it before Fanny.

"Don't go Fanny," I said to her. "Even in your absence I cannot say more than I have already said."

"Are you in your senses then?" grandmother sternly addressed me thinking harsh words might do much with me. "Do you wish to play mysteries with us: surely you don't think we shall betray him?"

"Desi," said mother, in that quiet, sweet voice of hers. "Be good."

So, they were deceived in me. I was no longer that good child, who could be frightened by strong words, and tamed by a sweet tongue,—I had become a hard, cruel unfeeling boy:—they could not force me to confession.

"That I cannot tell you."

"Why not? Not even to us?" they asked both together.

"Why not? That I do not know myself. But not even to you can I tell it. Lorand made me give him my word of honor, not to betray his whereabouts—not to his mother and grandmother. He said he had a great reason to ask this, and said any neglect of my promise would produce great misfortune. I gave him my word, and that word I must keep."

Poor mother fell on her knees before me, embraced me, showered kisses upon me, and begged me so to tell her where Lorand was. She called me her dear "only" son: then burst into tears: and I,—could be so cruel as to answer to her every word, "No—no—no."

I cannot describe this scene. I am incapable of reflecting thereupon. At last mother fainted, grandmother cursed me, and I left the room, and leaned against the door post.

During this indescribable scene the whole household hastened to nurse my mother, who was suffering terrible pain; then they came to me one by one, and tried in turn their powers of persuasion upon me. First of all came Mother Fromm, to beg me very kindly to say that one word that would cure my mother at once; then came Grandmother Fromm with awful threats: then Father Fromm, who endeavored to persuade me with sage reasoning, declaring that my honor would really be greatest if I should now break my word!

It was all quite useless. Surely no one knew how to beg, as my mother begged kneeling before me! No one could curse as my terrible grandmother had done, and no one knew the wickedness of my character as well as I did myself.

Let them only give me peace! I could not tell them.

Last of all Fanny came to me: leaned upon my shoulder, and began to stroke my hair.

"Dear Desi."

I jerked my shoulder to be rid of her.

"'Dear Desi,' indeed!—Call me 'wicked, bad, cursed Desi!'—that is what I am."

"But why?"

"Because no other name is possible. I promised because I was *obliged* to promise: and now I am keeping my word, because I promised."

"Your poor mother says she will die, if you do not tell her where Lorand is."

"And Lorand told me he will die if I do tell her. He told me that, when I discovered his whereabouts to mother or grandmother, he will either report himself at the nearest military station, or will shoot himself, according as he feels inclined. And in our family such promises are not wont to dissolve in thin air."

"What might have been his reason for exacting such a promise from you?"

"I do not know. But I know he would not have done it without cause. I beg you to leave me."

"Wait a moment," said Fanny, standing before me. "You said Lorand made you swear not to tell your mother or grandmother where he had gone to. He did not forbid you to tell another?"

"Naturally not," I answered with irritated pride. "He knew all along that there has not yet been born into the world that other who could force the truth out of me with red-hot pincers."

"But that other has been born," interrupted Fanny with wild earnestness. "Just twelve years, eight months and five days ago."

I looked at her.

"I should tell you? is that what you think?"

I admired her audacity.

"Certainly, me. For your parole forbids you to speak only to your mother and grandmother. You can tell me: and I shall tell them. You will not have told anybody anything, and they still will know it."

"Well, and are you 'nobody?'"

Fanny gazed into my eyes, became serious, and with trembling lips said:

"If you wish it—I am nobody. As if I had never been born."

From that moment Fanny began to be "someone," in my eyes.

Her little sophism pleased me. Perhaps on these terms we might come to an agreement.

"You have asked something very difficult of me, Fanny; but it is not impossible. Only you must wait a little: give me time to think it over. Until I have done so, be our go-between. Go in and tell grandmother what you have recommended to me, and that I said in answer, 'it is well.'"

I was cunning. I was dissembling. I thought in that moment, that, if Fanny should burst in childish glee into the neighboring room, and in triumphant voice proclaim the concession she had wrung out of me, I might tell her on her return the name of some place that did not exist, and so throw the responsibility off my own shoulders.

But she did not do that.

She went back quietly, and waited long, until her friends had retired by the opposite door: then she came and whispered:—

"I have been long: but I did not wish to speak before my mother. Now your parents are alone: go and speak."

"Something more first. Go back, Fanny, and say that I can tell them the truth, only on the condition that mother and grandmother promise not to seek him out, until I show them a letter from Lorand, in which he invites them to come to him: nor to send others in search of him: and, if they wish to send a letter to him, they must first give it to me, that I may send it off to him, and they never show, even by a look, to anyone that they know aught of Lorand's whereabouts."

Fanny nodded assent, and returned into the neighboring room.

A few minutes later she came out again, and held open the door before me.

"Come in."

I went in. She shut the door after me, and then, taking my hand, led me to mother's bedside.

Poor dear mother was now quiet, and pale as death. She seemed to beckon me to her with her eyes. I went to her side, and kissed her hand.

Fanny bent over me, and held her face near my lips, that I might whisper in her ear what I knew.

I told her all in a few words. She then bent over mother's pillow and whispered in her ear what she had heard from me.

Mother sighed and seemed to be calmed. Then grandmother bent over dear mother, that she might learn from her all that had been said.

As she heard it, her grey-headed figure straightened, and clasping her two hands above her head, she panted in wild prophetic ecstasy:

"O Lord God! who entrustest Thy will to children: may it come to pass, as Thou hast ordained!"

Then she came to me and embraced me.

"Did you counsel Lorand to go there?"

"I did."

"Did you know what you were doing? It was the will of God. Every day you must pray now for your brother."

"And you must keep silent for him. For when he is discovered, my brother will die and I cannot live without him."

The storm became calm: they again made peace with me. Mother, some minutes later, fell asleep, and slumbered sweetly. Grandmother motioned to Fanny and to me to leave her to herself.

We let down the window-blinds and left the room.

As we stepped out, I said to Fanny:

"Remember, my honor has been put into your hands."

The girl gazed into my eyes with ardent enthusiasm and said:

"I shall guard it as I guard mine own."

That was no child's answer, but the answer of a maiden.

CHAPTER XII

A GLANCE INTO A PISTOL-BARREL

The weather changed very rapidly, for all the world as if two evil demons were fighting for the earth: one with fire, the other with ice. It was the middle of May; it had become so sultry that the earth, which last week had been frozen to dry bones, now began to crack.

The wanderer who disappeared from our sight we shall find on that plain of Lower Hungary, where there are as many high roads as cart-ruts.

It is evening, but the sun had just set, and left a cloudless ruddy sky behind it. On the horizon two or three towers are to be seen so far distant that the traveller who is hurrying before us cannot hope to reach any one of them by nightfall.

The dust had not so overlaid him, nor had the sun so tanned his face that we cannot recognize in these handsome noble features the pride of the youth of Pressburg, Lorand.

The long journey he has accomplished has evidently not impaired the strength of his muscles, for the horseman who is coming behind him, has to ride hard to overtake him.

The latter leaned back in his shortened stirrups, after the manner of hussars, and wore a silver-buttoned jacket, a greasy hat, and ragged red trousers. Thrown half over his shoulders was a garment of wolf-skins; around his waist was a wide belt from which two pistol-barrels gleamed, while in the leg of one of his boots a silver-chased knife was thrust. The horse's harness was glittering with silver, just as the ragged, stained garments of its master.

The rider approached at a trot, but the traveller had not yet thought it worth while to look back and see who was coming after him. Presently he came up to the solitary figure, trudging along, doggedly.

"Good evening, student."

Lorand looked up at him.

"Good evening, gypsy."

At these words the horseman drew aside his skin-mantle that the student might see the pistol-barrels, and consider that even if he were a gypsy, he was something more than a mere musician. But Lorand did not betray the slightest emotion: he did not even take down from his shoulder the stick, on which he was carrying his boots. He was walking bare-footed. It was cheaper.

"Oh, you are proud of your red boots!" sneered the rider, looking down at Lorand's bare-feet.

"It's easy for you to say so," was Lorand's sharp reply; "sitting on that hack."

But "hack" means a kind of four-footed animal which this rider found no pleasure in hearing mentioned.[54]

> [54] The Magyar word has a double meaning; besides a horse it means a peculiar whipping-bench with which gypsies used to be particularly well acquainted.

"My own training," he said proudly, as if in self-defence against this cutting remark.

"I know. I knew that even in my scapegrace days."

"Well, and where are you hobbling to now, student?"

"I am going to Csege, gypsy, to preach."

"What do you get from the 'legatio' for that, student?"

"Twenty silver florins, gypsy."

"Do you know what, student? I have an idea—don't go just yet to Csege, but turn aside here to the shepherd's where you see that fold. Wait there for me till to-morrow, when I shall come back, and preach your sermon to me: I have never yet heard anything of the kind, and I'll give you forty florins for it."

"Oh no, gypsy; do you turn aside to yonder fold. Don't go just now to the farm, but wait a week for me; when I shall come back; then you can fiddle my favorite tune, and I'll give you ten florins for it."

"I am no musician," replied the horseman, extending his chest.

"What's that rural fife doing at your side?" The gypsy roared at the idea of calling his musket a "rural fife!" Many had paid dearly so as not to hear its notes!

"You student, you are a deuce of a fellow. Take a draught from my 'noggin.'"

"No, thanks, gypsy; it isn't spiritual enough to go with my sermon."[55]

> [55] Lorand really quoted a sentence from a popular ditty, but it is impossible in such cases to do proper justice to the original.
>
> The whole passage between Lorand and the gypsy is full of allusions intelligible only to Hungarians, *in Hungarian*, a proper rendering of which, in my opinion, baffles all attempts. Of course the force of the original is lost, but it is unavoidable.

The gypsy laughed still more loudly.

"Well, good night, student."

He drove his spurs into his horse and galloped on along the high-road.

Then the evening drew in quietly. Lorand reached a grassy mound, shaded by juniper bushes. This spot he chose for his night-camp in preference to the wine-reeking, stenching rooms of the way-side inns. Putting on his boots, he drew from his wallet some bread and bacon, and commenced eating. He found it good: he was hungry and young.

Scarcely had he finished his repast when, along the same road on which the horseman had come, rapidly approached a five-in-hand.

The three leaders were supplied with bells and their approach could be heard from afar off.

Lorand called out to the coachman,

"Stop a moment, fellow-countryman."

The coachman pulled up his horses.

"Quickly," he said to Lorand, with a hoarse voice, "get up at once, sir 'legatus,' beside me. The horses will not stand."

"That was not what I wanted to say," remarked Lorand. "I did not want to ask you to take me up, but to tell you to be on your guard, for a highwayman has just gone on in front, and it would be ill to meet with him."

"Have you much money?"

"No."

"Nor have I. Then why should we fear the robber?"

"Perhaps those who are sitting inside the carriage?"

"Her ladyship is sitting within and is now asleep. If I awake her and frighten her, and then we don't find the highwayman she will break the whip over my back. Get up here. It will be good to travel as far as Lankadomb in a carriage, 'sblood.'"

"Do you live at Lankadomb?" asked Lorand in a tone of surprise.

"Yes. I am Topándy's servant. He is a very fine fellow, and is very fond of people who preach."

"I know him by reputation."

"Well, if you know him by reputation, you will do well to make his personal acquaintance, too. Get up, now."

Lorand put the meeting down as a lucky chance. Topándy's weakness was to capture men of a priestly turn of mind, keep them at his house and annoy them. That was just what he wanted, a pretext for meeting him.

He clambered up beside the coachman and under the brilliance of the starry heaven, the five steeds, with merry tinkling of bells, rattled the carriage along the turfy road.

The coachman told him they had come from Debreczen: they wished to reach Lankadomb in the morning, but on the way they would pass an inn, where the horses would receive feed, while her ladyship would have some cold lunch: and then they would proceed on their journey. Her ladyship always loved to travel by night, for then it was not so hot: besides she was not afraid of anything.

It was about midnight when the carriage drew up at the inn mentioned.

Lorand leaped down from the box, and hastened first into the inn, not wishing to meet the lady who was within the carriage. His heart beat loudly, when he caught a glimpse of that silver-harnessed horse in the inn-yard, saddled and bridled. The steed was not fastened up, but quite loose, and it gave a peculiar neigh as the coach arrived, at which there stepped out from a dark door the same man whom Lorand had met on the plain.

He was utterly astonished to see Lorand.

"You are here already, student?"

"You can see it with your own eyes, gypsy."

"How did you come so quickly?"

"Why, I ride on a dragon: I am a necromancer."

By this time the occupants of the carriage had entered: her ladyship and a plump, red-faced maid-servant. The former was wrapped in a thick fur cloak, her head bound with a silken kerchief; the latter wore a short red mantle, fastened round her neck with a kerchief of many colors, while her hair was tied with ribbons. Her two hands were full of cold viands.

"So that was it, eh?" said the rider, as he perceived them. "They brought you in their carriage." Then, he allowed the new-comers to enter the parlor peacefully, while he himself took his horse, and, leading it to the pump, pumped some water into the trough.

Lorand began to think he was not the rascal he thought him, and he now proceeded into the parlor.

Her ladyship threw back her fur cloak, took off the silken kerchief and put two candles before her. She trimmed them both, like one who "loves the beautiful."

You might have called her face very beautiful: she had lively, sparkling eyes, strong brown complexion, rosy lips, and arched eyebrows: it was right that such light as there was in the room should burn before her.

In the darkness, on the long bench at the other end of the table, sat Lorand, who had ordered a bottle of wine, rather to avoid sitting there for nothing, than to drink the sour vintage of the Lowland.

Beside the bar, on a straw mattress, was sleeping a Slavonian pedler of holy images, and a wandering jack-of-all-trades; at the bar the bushy-headed host grinned with doubtful pleasure over such guests, who brought their own eatables and drinkables with them, and only came to show their importance.

Lorand had time enough calmly to take in this "ladyship," in whose carriage he had come so far, and under whose roof he would probably live later.

She must be a lively, good-natured creature. She shared every morsel with her servant, and sent what remained to the coachman. Perhaps if she had known she had another nameless travelling companion, she would have invited him to the repast. As she ate she poured some rye-whiskey into her tin plate; to this she added figs, raisins and sugar, and then lighted it. This beverage is called in our country "krampampuli." It must be very healthy on a night journey for a healthy stomach.

When the repast was over, the door leading to the courtyard opened: and there entered the rogue who had been left outside, his hat pressed over his eyes, and in his hand one of his pistols that he had taken from his girdle.

"Under the table! under the bed! all whose lives are dear to them!" he cried, standing in the doorway. At these terrible words the Slavonian and the other who were sleeping on the floor clambered up into the chimney-place, the host disappeared into the cellar, banging the door after him, while the servant hid herself under the bench; then the robber stepped up to the table and extinguished both candles with his hat, so that there remained no light on the table save that of the burning spirit.

The latter gave a weird light. When sugar burns in spirits, a sepulchral light appears on everything: living faces look like faces of the dead; all color disappears from them, the ruddiness of the countenance, the brilliance of the lips, the glitter of the eyes, —all turn green. It is as if phantoms rose from the grave and were gazing at one another.

Lorand watched the scene in horror.

This gay, smiling woman's face became at once like that of one raised from the tomb; and that other who stood face to face with her, weapon in hand, was like Death himself, with black beard and black eyelids.

Yet for one moment it seemed to Lorand as if both were laughing— the face of the dead and the face of Death, but it was only for a moment; and perhaps, too, that was merely an illusion.

Then the robber addressed her in a strong, authoritative voice:

"Your money, quickly!"

The woman took her purse, and without a word threw it down on the table before him.

The robber snatched it up and by the light of the spirit began to examine its contents.

Debts of Honor

"What is this?" he asked wrathfully.

"Money," replied the lady briefly, beginning to make a tooth-pick from a chicken bone with her silver-handled antique knife.

"Money! But how much?" bawled the thief.

"Four hundred florins."

"Four hundred florins," he shrieked, casting the purse down on the table. "Did I come here for four hundred florins? Have I been lounging about here a week for four hundred florins? Where is the rest?"

"The rest?" said the lady. "Oh, that is being made at Vienna."

"No joking, now. I know there were two thousand florins in this purse."

"If all that has ever been in that purse were here now, it would be enough for both of us."

"The devil take you!" cried the thief, beating the table with his fist so that the spirit flame flickered in the plate. "I don't understand jokes. In this purse just now there were two thousand florins, the price of the wool you sold day before yesterday at Debreczen. What has become of the rest?"

"Come here, I'll give you an account of it," said the lady, counting on her fingers with the point of the knife. "Two hundred I gave to the furrier—four hundred to the saddler—three hundred to the grocer—three hundred to the tailor:—two hundred I spent in the market: count how much remains."

"None of your arithmetic for me. I only want money, much money! Where is much money?"

"As I said already, at Körmöcz, in the mint."

"Enough of your foolery!" threatened the highwayman. "For if I begin to search, you won't thank me for it."

"Well, search the carriage over; all you find in it is yours."

Debts of Honor

"I shan't search the coach, but you, too, to your skin."

"What?" cried the woman, in a passion; and at that moment her face, with her knitted eyebrows, became like that of a mythical Fury. "Try it,"—with these words dashing the knife down into the table, which it pierced to the depth of an inch.

The thief began to speak in a less presumptuous tone.

"What else will you give me?"

"What else, indeed?" said the lady, throwing herself defiantly back in her chair. "The devil and his son."

"You have a bracelet on your arm."

"There you are!" said the woman, unclasping the emerald trinket from her arm, and dashing it on the table.

The thief began to look at it critically.

"What is it worth?"

"I received it as a present: you can get a drink of wine for it in the nearest inn you reach."

"And there is a beautiful ring sparkling on your finger."

"Let it sparkle."

"I don't believe it cannot come off."

"It will not come off, for I shall not give it." At this moment the thief suddenly grasped the woman's hand in which she held the knife, seizing it by the wrist, and while she was writhing in desperate struggle against the iron grip, with his other hand thrust the end of his pistol in her mouth.

This awful scene had till now made upon Lorand the impression of the quarrel of a tipsy husband with his obstinate wife, who answers all his provocations with jesting: the lady seemed incapable of being frightened, the thief of frightening. Some unnatural indifference seemed to give the lie to that scene, which youthful imagination would picture so differently. The meeting of a thief with an unprotected lady, at night, in an inn on the plain! It was impossible that they should speak so to one another.

But as the robber seized the lady's hand, and leaning across the table, drew her by sheer force towards him, continually threatening the screaming woman with a pistol, the young man's blood suddenly boiled up within him. He leaped forward from the darkness, unnoticed by the thief, crept toward him and seized the rascal's right hand, in which he held the pistol, while with his other hand he tore the second pistol from the man's belt.

The highwayman, like some infuriated beast, turned upon his assailant, and strove to free his arm from the other's grip.

He felt he had to do with one whose wrist was as firm as his own.

"Student!" he snarled, with lips tightly drawn like a wolf, and gnashing his gleaming white teeth.

"Don't stir," said Lorand, pointing the pistol at his forehead.

The thief saw plainly that the pistol was not cocked: nor could Lorand have cocked it in this short time. Lorand, as a matter of fact, in his excitement had not thought of it.

So the highwayman suddenly ducked his head and like a wall-breaking, battering ram, dealt such a blow with his head to Lorand, that the latter fell back on to the bench, and while he was forced to let go of the rascal with his left, he was obliged with his armed right hand to defend himself against the coming attack.

Then the robber pointed the barrel of the second pistol at his forehead.

"Now it is my turn to say, 'don't stir,' student."

In that short moment, as Lorand gazed into the barrel of the pistol that was levelled at his forehead, there flashed through his mind this thought:

"Now is the moment for checkmating the curse of fate and avoiding the threatened suicide. He who loses his life in the defence of persecuted and defenceless travellers dies as a man of honor. Let us see this death."

He rose suddenly before the levelled weapon.

"Don't move or you are a dead man," the thief cried again to him.

But Lorand, face to face with the pistol levelled within a foot of his head calmly put his finger to the trigger of the weapon he himself held and drew it back.

At this the thief suddenly sprang back and rushed to the door, so alarmed that at first he attempted to open it the wrong way.

Lorand took careful aim at him.

But as he stretched out his arm, the lady sprang up from the table, crept to him and seized his arm, shrieking:

"Don't kill him, oh, don't!"

Lorand gazed at her in astonishment.

The beautiful woman's face was convulsed in a torture of terror: the staring look in her beautiful eyes benumbed the young man's sinews. As she threw herself upon his bosom and held down his arms, the embrace quite crippled him.

The highwayman, seeing he could escape, after much fumbling undid the bolt of the door. When he was at last able to open it, his gypsy humor returned to take the place of his fear. He thrust his dishevelled head in at the half-opened door, and remarked in that broken voice which is peculiarly that of the terrified man:

"A plague upon you, you devil's cur of a student: student, inky-fingered student. Had my pistol been loaded, as the other was, which was in your hand, I would have just given you a pass to hell. Just fall into my hands again! I know that...."

Then he suddenly withdrew his head, affording a very humorous illustration to his threat: and like one pursued he ran out into the court. A few moments later a clatter of hoofs was heard—the robber was making his escape. When he reached the road he began to swear godlessly, reproaching and cursing every student, legatus, and hound of a priest, who, instead of praising God at home, prowled about the high-roads, and spoiled a hard working man's business. Even after he was far down the road his loud cursing could still be heard. For weeks that swearing would fill the air in the bog of Lankadomb, where he had made himself at home in the wild creature's unapproachable lair.

To Lorand this was all quite bewildering.

The arrogant, almost jesting, conversation, by the light of that mysterious flame, between a murderous robber and his victim:—the inexplicable riddle that a night-prowling highwayman should have entered a house with an empty pistol, while in his belt was another, loaded:—and then that woman, that incomprehensible figure, who had laughed at a robber to his face, who had threatened him with a knife as he pressed her to his bosom, and who, could she have freed herself, would surely have dealt him such a blow as she had dealt the table:—that she, when her rescuer was going to shoot her assailant, should have torn aside his hand in terror and defended the miscreant with her own body!

What could be the solution of such a riddle?

Meanwhile the lady had again lighted the candles: again a gentle light was thrown on all things. Lorand gazed at her. In place of her previous green-blue face, which had gazed on him with the wild look of madness, a smiling, good-humored countenance was presented. She asked in a humorous tone:

"Well, so you are a student, what kind of student? Where did you come from?"

"I came with you, sitting beside the coachman."

"Do you wish to come to Lankadomb?"

"Yes."

"Perhaps to Sárvölgyi's? He loves prayers."

"Oh no. But to Mr. Topándy."

"I cannot advise that: he is very rude to such as you. You are accustomed to preach. Don't go there."

"Still I am going there: and if you don't care to let me sit on the box, I shall go on foot, as I have done until to-day."

"Do you know what? What you would get there would not be much. The money, which that man left here, you have by you as it is. Keep it for yourself: I give it to you. Then go back to the college."

"Madame, I am not accustomed to live on presents," said Lorand, proudly refusing the proffered purse.

The woman was astonished. This is a curious legatus, thought she, who does not live by presents.

Her ladyship began to perceive that in this young man's dust-stained features there was something of that which makes distinctions between man. She began to be surprised at this proud and noble gaze.

Perhaps she was reflecting as to what kind of phenomenon it could be, who with unarmed hand had dared to attack an armed robber, in order to free from his clutch a strange woman in whom he had no interest, and then refused to accept the present he had so well deserved.

Lorand saw that he had allowed a breach to open in his heart through which anyone could easily see the secret of his character. He hastened to cover his error.

"I cannot accept a present, your ladyship, because I wish more. I am not a preaching legatus, but an expelled school-boy. I am in search of a position where I can earn my living by the work of my hands. When I protected your ladyship it occurred to me, 'This lady may have need for some farm steward or bailiff. She may recommend me to her husband.' I shall be a faithful servant, and I have given a proof of my faithfulness, for I have no written testimonials."

"You wish to be Topándy's steward? Do you know what a godless man he is?"

"That is why I am in search of him. I started direct for him. They expelled me from school for my godlessness. We cannot accuse each other of anything."

"You have committed some crime, then, and that is why you avoid the eyes of the world? Confess what you have done. Murdered? Confess. I shall not be afraid of you for it, nor shall I tell any one. I promise that you shall be welcomed, whatever the crime may be. I have said so. Have you committed murder?"

"No."

"Beaten your father or mother?"

"No, madame:—My crime is that I have instigated the youth against their superiors."

"What superiors? Against the magistrate?"

"Even superior to the magistrate."

"Perhaps against the priest. Well, Topándy will be delighted. He is a great fool in this matter."

The woman uttered these words laughingly; then suddenly a dark shadow crossed her face. With wandering glance she stepped up to the young man, and, putting her hand gently on his arm, asked him in a whisper:

"Do you know how to pray?"

Lorand looked at her, aghast.

"To pray from a book—could you teach some one to pray from a book? Would it require a long time?"

Lorand looked with ever-increasing wonder at the questioner.

Debts of Honor

"Very well—I did not say anything! Come with us. The coachman is already cracking his whip. Will you sit inside with us, or do you prefer to sit outside beside the coachman in the open? It is better so; I should prefer it myself. Well, let us go."

The servant, who had crawled out from under the bench, had already collected the silver and crockery; her ladyship paid mine host, and they soon took their seats again in the carriage:—and both thought deeply the whole way. The young man, of that woman, who playfully defied a thief, and struggled for a ring; then of that robber, who came with an empty pistol, and again of that woman, who when he spoke of the powers that be, understood nothing but a magistrate, and had inquired whether he knew how to pray from a book;—and who meanwhile wore golden bracelets, ate from silver, was dressed in silk and carried the fire of youth in her eyes. While the woman thought of that young man who could fight like a hero; was ready to work like a day laborer, to throw money away like a noble, to fascinate women like an angel, and to blaspheme the powers that be like a devil!

CHAPTER XIII

WHICH WILL CONVERT THE OTHER?

In the morning the coach rolled into the courtyard of the castle of Lankadomb.[56]

[56] *i. e.,* Orchard-hill.

Topándy was waiting on the terrace, and ran to meet the young lady, helped her out of the coach and kissed her hand very courteously. At Lorand, who descended from his seat beside the coachman, he gazed with questioning wonder.

The lady answered in his place:

"I have brought an expelled student, who desires to be steward on your estate. You must accept him."

Then, trusting to the hurrying servants to bring her travelling rugs and belongings after her, she ascended into the castle, without further waste of words, leaving Lorand alone with Topándy.

Topándy turned to the young fellow with his usual satirical humor.

"Well, fellow, you've got a fine recommendation! An expelled student; that's saying a good deal. You want to be steward, or bailiff, or præfectus here, do you? It's all the same; choose which title you please. Have you a smattering of the trade?"

"I was brought up to a farm life: it is surely no hieroglyphic to me."

"Bravo! So I shall tell you what my steward has to do. Can you plough with a team of four? Can you stack hay, standing on the top of the sheaves? Can you keep order among a dozen reapers? Can you...?"

Lorand was not taken aback by his questions. He merely replied to each one, "yes."

"That's splendid," said Topándy. "Many renowned and well-versed gentlemen of business have come to me, to recommend themselves as farm bailiffs, in buckled shoes; but when I asked them if they could heap dung on dung carts, they all ran away. I am pleased my questions about that did not knock you over. Do you know what the 'conventio'[57] will be?"

[57] The payment. The honorarium.

"Yes."

"But how much do *you* expect?"

"Until I can make myself useful, nothing; afterwards, as much as is required from one day to the next."

"Well said; but have you no claims to bailiff's lodgings, office, or something else? That shall be left entirely to your own discretion. On my estate, the steward may lodge where he likes—either in the ox-stall, in the cow-shed, or in the buffalo stable. I don't mind; I leave it entirely to your choice."

Topándy looked at him with wicked eyes, as he waited for the answer.

Lorand, however, with the most serious countenance, merely answered that his presence would be required most in the ox-stall, so he would take up his quarters there.

"So on that point we are agreed," said Topándy, with a loud laugh. "We shall soon see on what terms of friendship we shall stand. I accept the terms; when you are tired of them, don't trouble to say so. There is the gate."

"I shall not turn in that direction."

"Good! I admire your determination. Now come with me; you will receive at once your provisions for five days—take them with you. The shepherd will teach you how to cook and prepare your meals."

Lorand did not make a single grimace at these peculiar conditions attached to the office of steward; he acquiesced in everything, as if he found everything most correct.

"Well, come with me, Sir bailiff!"

So he led him into the castle, without even so much as inquiring his name. He thought that in any case he would disappear in a day or two.

Her ladyship was just in the ante-room, where breakfast was usually served.

While Topándy was explaining to Lorand the various quarters from which he might choose a bedroom, her ladyship had got the coffee ready, for déjeuner, and had laid the fine tablecloth on the round table, on which had been placed three cups, and just so many knives, forks and napkins.

As Topándy stepped into the room, letting Lorand in after him, her ladyship was engaged in pouring out the coffee from the silver pot into the cups, while the rich buffalo milk boiled away merrily on the glittering white tripod before her. Topándy placed himself in the nearest seat, leaving Lorand to stand and wait until her ladyship had time to weigh out his rations for him.

"That is not your place!" exclaimed the fair lady.

Topándy sprang up suddenly.

"Pardon. Whose place is this?"

"That gentleman's!" she answered, and nodded at Lorand, both her hands being occupied.

"Please take a seat, sir," said Topándy, making room for Lorand.

"You will always sit there," said the lady, putting down the coffee-pot and pointing to the place which had been laid on her left. "At breakfast, at dinner, at supper."

This had a different sound from what the gentleman of the house had said. Rather different from garlic and black bread.

"This will be your room here on the right," continued the lady. "The butler's name is George; he will be your servant. And John is the coachman, who will stand at your orders."

Lorand's wonder only increased. He wished to make some remark, but he did not know himself what he wanted to say. Topándy, however, burst into a Homeric laugh, in which he quite lost himself.

"Why, brother, didn't you tell me you had already arranged matters with the lady? You would have saved me so much trouble. If matters stand so, sleep on my sofa, and drink from my glass!"

Lorand wished to play the proud beggar. He raised his head defiantly.

"I shall sleep in the hay, and shall drink from——"

"I advise you to do as I tell you," said the lady, making both men wince with the flash of her gaze.

"Surely, brother," continued Topándy, "I can give you no better counsel than that. Well, let us sit down, and drink 'Brotherhood' with a glass of cognac."

Lorand thought it wise to give way before the commanding gaze of the lady, and to accept the proffered place, while the latter laughed outright in sudden good-humor. She was so lovable, so natural, so pleasant, when she laughed like that, Topándy could not forbear from kissing her hands.

The lady laughingly, and with jesting prudery, extended the other hand toward Lorand.

"Well, the other too! Don't be bashful!"

Lorand kissed the other hand.

Upon this, she clapped her hands over her head, and burst into laughter.

"See, see! I have brought you a letter from town," said the lady, drawing out her purse. "It's a good thing the thief left me this, or your letter would have been lost as well."

"Thief?" asked Topándy earnestly. "What thief?"

"Why, at the 'Skull-smasher' inn, where we stopped to water our horses, a thief attacked us, and then wanted to empty our pockets. I threw him my money and my bracelet, but he wanted to tear this ring from my finger, too. That I would not give up. Then he caught hold of my hand, and to prevent my screaming, thrust the butt-end of his pistol into my mouth—the fool!"

The lady related all this with such an air of indifference that Topándy could not make out whether she was joking or not.

"What fable is this?"

"Fable indeed!" was the exclamation that greeted him on two sides, on the one from her ladyship, on the other from the neat little maid, the latter crying out how much she had been frightened; that she was still all of a tremble; the former turned back her sleeve and held out her arm to Topándy.

"See how my arm got scratched by the grasp of the robber! and look here, how bruised my mouth is from the pistol," said she, parting her rosy lips, behind which two rows of pearly teeth glistened. "It's a good thing he didn't knock out my teeth."

"Well, that would have been a pity. But how did you get away from him," asked Topándy, in an anxious tone.

"Well, I don't know whether you would ever have seen me again, if this young man had not dashed to our assistance; for he sprang forward and snatched the pistol from the hand of the robber,—who immediately took to his heels and ran away."

Topándy again shook his head, and said it was hard to believe.

"No doubt he still has the pistol in his pocket."

"Give it to me."

Debts of Honor

"But don't fool with it; it might go off and hurt somebody."

Lorand handed the pistol in question to Topándy. The barrel was of bronze, highly chased in silver.

"Curious!" exclaimed Topándy, examining the ornamentation. "This pistol bears the Sárvölgyi arms."

Without another word he put the weapon in his pocket, and shook hands with Lorand across the table.

"My boy, you are a fine fellow. I honor you for so bravely defending my people. Now I have the more reason in agreeing to your living henceforward under the same roof with me; unless you fear it may, through fault of mine, fall in upon you. What was the robber like?" he said, turning again to the women.

"We could not see him, because he put out the candle and ran away."

Lorand was struck by the fact that the woman did not seem inclined to recall the robber's features, which she must, however have been able to see by the help of the spirit-lamp; he noticed, too, that she did not utter a word about the robber's being a gypsy.

"I don't know what he was like," she repeated, with a meaning look at Lorand. "Neither of us could see, for it was dark. For the same reason our deliverer could not shoot at him, because it was difficult to aim in the dark. If he had missed him, the robber might have murdered us all."

"A fine adventure," muttered Topándy. "I shall not allow you to travel alone at night another time. I shall go armed myself. I shall not put up with the existence of that den in the marsh any longer or it will always be occupied by such as mean to harm us. As soon as the Tisza overflows, I shall set fire to the reeds about the place, when the stack will catch fire, too."

During this conversation the woman had produced the letter.

"There it is," she cried, handing it to Topándy.

"A lady's handwriting!" exclaimed Topándy, glancing at the direction.

"What, you can tell by the letters whether it is the writing of a man or a woman?" queried the beautiful lady, throwing a curious glance at the writing.

Lorand looked at it, too, and it seemed to him as if he had seen the writing before, but he could not remember where.

It was a strange hand; the characters did not resemble the writing of any of his lady acquaintants, and yet he must have seen it somewhere.

You may cast about and reflect long, Lorand, before you discover whose writing it is. You never thought of her who wrote this letter. You never even noticed her existence! It is the writing of Fanny, of the jolly little exchange-girl. It was Desi who once showed you that handwriting for a moment, when your mother sent her love in Fanny's letter. Now the unknown hand had written to Topándy to the effect that a young man would appear before him, bespattered and ragged. He was not to ask whence he came, or whither he went; but he was to look well at the noble face, and he would know from it that the youth was not obliged to avoid persecution of the world for some base crime.

Topándy gazed long at the youthful face before him. Could this be the one she meant?

The story of the Parliamentary society of the young men was well known to him.

He asked no questions.

After the first day Lorand felt himself quite at home in Topándy's home.

Topándy treated him as a duke would treat his only son, whom he was training to be his heir; Lorand's conduct toward Topándy was that of a poor man's son, learning to make himself useful in his father's home. Each found many extraordinary traits in the other, and each would have loved to probe to the depths of the other's peculiarities.

Lorand remarked in his uncle a deep, unfathomable feeling underlying his seeming godlessness. Topándy, on his side, suspected that some dark shadow had prematurely crossed the serenity of the young man's mind. Each tried to pierce the depths of the other's soul—but in vain.

Her ladyship had on the first day confided her life secret to Lorand. When he endeavored to pay her the compliment of kissing her hand after supper, she withdrew her hand and refused to accept this mark of respect.

"My dear boy, don't kiss my hand, or 'my ladyship' me any more. I am but a poor gypsy girl. My parents, were simple camp-folk; my name is Czipra. I am a domestic servant here, whom the master has dressed up, out of caprice, in silks and laces, and he makes the servants call me 'madame,' on which account they subsequently mock me,—of course, only behind my back, for if they did it to my face I should strike them; but don't you laugh at me behind my back. I am an orphan gypsy girl, and my master picked me up out of the gutter. He is very kind to me, and I would die for him, if fate so willed. That's how matters stand, do you understand?"

The gypsy girl glanced with dimmed eyes at Topándy, who smilingly listened to her frank confession, as though he approved of it. Then, as if she had gained her master's consent, she turned again to Lorand:

"So call me simply 'Czipra.'"

"All right, Czipra, my sister," said Lorand, holding out his hand.

"Well now, that is nice of you to add that;" upon which she pressed Lorand's hand, and left the men to themselves.

Topándy turned the conversation, and spoke no more to Lorand of Czipra. He first of all wished to find out what impression the discovery would make upon the young man.

The following days enlightened him.

Lorand, from that day, far from showing more familiarity, manifested greater deference towards the reputed lady of the house. Since she had confessed her true position to him, moreover he treated her as one who knew well that the smallest slight would doubly hurt one who was not in a position to complain. He was kind and attentive to the woman, who, beneath the appearance of happiness, was wretched, though innocent. To the uninitiated, she was the lady of the house; to the better informed, she was the favorite of her master, and that was nought but a maiden in the disguise of wife, and Lorand was able to read the riddle aright.

If Topándy watched him, he in his turn observed Topándy; he saw that Topándy did not watch, nor was jealous of the girl. He consented to her traveling alone, confided the greater part of his fortune to her, overwhelmed her with presents, but beyond this did not trouble about her. Still he showed a certain affection which did not arise from mere habit. He would not brook the least harm to her from anybody, making the whole household fear her as much as the master, and if by chance they hesitated as to their duty to one or the other, it was always Czipra who had a prior claim on their services.

Topándy at once perceived that Lorand did not run after a fair face, nor after the face of any woman, who was not difficult to conquer, because she was not guarded, and who might be easily got rid of, being but a gypsy girl. His heart was either fully occupied by one object only, or it was an infinite void which nothing could fill. Topándy led a boisterous life, when he fell in with his chums, but when alone he was quite another man. To fathom nature's mysteries was a passion with him. In a corner of the basement of the castle there was a chemical laboratory, where he passed his time with making physical experiments; he labored with instruments, he probed the secrets of the stars, and of the earth; at such times he only cared to have Lorand at his side; in him he found a being capable of sharing his scientific researches, though he did not share in his doubts.

"All is matter!" such had for centuries been the motto of the naturalist, and therefore the naturalist had ever found a kindred spirit in the agnostic.

Often did Czipra come upon the two men at their quiet pursuits and watch them for hours together; and though she did not understand what in this higher science went beyond her comprehension, yet she could take pleasure in observing Cartesius' diving imps; she dared to sit upon the insulators, and her joy was boundless when Lorand at such a time, approaching her with his finger, called forth electric sparks from her dress or hands. She found enjoyment, too, in peering through the great telescopes at the heavenly wonders. Lorand was always ready to answer her questions; but the poor girl was far from understanding all. Yet how rapturous the thought of knowing all! Once when Lorand was explaining to her the properties of the sun-spectrum, the girl sighed and, suddenly bending down to Lorand, whispered blushingly:

"Teach me to read."

Lorand looked at her in amazement. Topándy, looking over his shoulder, asked her:

"Tell me, what would be the use of teaching you to read?"

The girl clasped her hands to her bosom:

"I should like to learn to pray."

"What? To pray? And what would you pray for? Is there anything that you cannot do without?"

"There is."

"What can it be?"

"That is what I should like to know by praying."

"And you do not know yourself what it is?"

"I cannot express what it is."

"And do you know anybody who could give it you?"

The girl pointed to the sky.

Topándy shrugged his shoulders at her.

"Bah! you goose, reading is not for girls. Women are best off when they know nothing."

Then he laughed in her face.

Czipra ran weeping out of the laboratory.

Lorand pitied the poor creature, who, dressed in silks and finery, did not know her letters, and who was incapable of raising her voice to God. He was in a mood, through long solitude, for pitying others; under a strange name, known to nobody, separated from the world, he was able to forget the lofty dreams to which a smooth career had pointed, and which fate, at his first steps, had mocked. He had given up the idea that the world should acknowledge this title: "a great patriot, who is the holder of a high office." He who does not desire this should keep to the ploughshare. Ambition should only have well-regulated roads, and success should only begin with a lower office in the state. But he whose hobby it is to murmur, will find a fine career in field labor; and he who wishes to bury himself, will find himself supplied, in life, with a beautiful, romantic, flowery wheat-covered cemetery by the fields, from the centre of which the happy dead creatures of life cheerfully mock at those who weary themselves and create a disturbance—with the idea that they are doing something, whereas their end is the same as that of the rest of mankind.

Lorand was even beginning to grow indifferent to the awful obligation that lay before him at the end of the appointed time. It was still afar off. Before then a man might die peacefully and quietly; perhaps that other who guarded the secret might pass away ere then. And perhaps the years at the plough would harden the skin of a man's soul, as it did of his face and hands, so that he would come to ridicule a wager, which in his youthful over-enthusiasm he would have fulfilled; a wager the refusal to accept which would merely win the commendation of everybody. And if any one could say the reverse, how could he find him to say it to his face? As regards his family at home, he was fairly at his ease. He often received letters from Dezső (Desiderius), under another address; they were all well at home, and treated the fate of the expelled son with good grace. He also learned that Madame Bálnokházy had not returned to her husband, but had gone abroad with that actor with whom she had previously been acquainted. This also he had wiped out from his memory. His whole mind was a perfect blank in which there was room for other people's misfortunes.

It was impossible not to remark how Czipra became attached to him in her simplicity. She had a feeling which she had never felt before, a feeling of shame, if some impudent jest was made at her expense by one of Topándy's guests, in the presence of Lorand.

Once, when Topándy and Lorand were amusing themselves at greater length with optical experiments in the lonely scientific apartment, Lorand took the liberty of introducing the subject.

"Is it true that that girl has grown up without any knowledge whatever?"

"Surely; she knows neither God nor alphabet."

"Why don't you allow the poor child to learn to know them?"

"What, her alphabet? Because in my eyes it is quite superfluous. A mad idea once occurred to me of picking some naked gypsy child out of the streets, with the intention of making a happy being therefrom. What is happiness in the world? Ease and ignorance. Had I a child of my own, I should do the same with it. The secret of life is to have a good appetite, sound sleep, and a good heart. If I reflect what bitternesses have been my lot my whole life, I find the cause of each one was what I have learned. Many a night did I lie awake in agonized distraction, while my servants were snoring in peace. I desired to see before me a person as happy as it was my ideal to be; a person free from those distressing tortures, which the civilized world has discovered for the persecution of man by man. Well, I have begun by telling you why I did not teach Czipra her alphabet."

"And God?"

Topándy took his eyes off the telescope, with which he had just been gazing at the starry sky.

"I don't know Him myself."

Lorand turned from him with a distressed air. Topándy remarked it.

"My dear boy, my dear twenty-year-old child, probably you know more than I do; if you know Him, I beg you to teach me."

Lorand shrugged his shoulders, then began to discuss scientific subjects.

"Does Dollond's telescope show stars in the Milky Way?"

"Yes, a million twinkling stars o'erspread the Milky Way, each several star a sun."

"Does it dissipate the mist in the head of the Northern Hound?"

"The mist remains as it was before—a round cloudy mass with a ring of mist around it."

"Perhaps Gregory's telescope, just arrived from Vienna, magnifies better?"

"Bring it here. Since its arrival there has been no clear weather, to enable us to make experiments with it."

Topándy gazed at the heavens through the new telescope with great interest.

"Ah," he remarked in a tone of surprise. "This is a splendid instrument; the star-mist thins, some tiny stars appear out of the ring."

"And the mass itself?"

"That remains mist. Not even this telescope can disperse its atoms."

"Well, shall we not experiment with Chevalier's microscope now?"

"That is a good idea; get it ready."

"What shall we put under it? A rhinchites?"

"That will do."

Lorand lit the spirit-lamp, which threw light on the subject under the magnifying glass; then he first looked into it himself, to find the correct focus. Enraptured, he cried out:

"Look here! That fabled armor of Homer's *Iliad* is not to be compared with this little insect's wing-shields. They are nothing but emerald and enamelled gold."

"Indeed it is so."

"And now listen to me: between the two wings of this little insect there is a tiny parasite or worm, which in its turn has two eyes, a life, and life-blood flowing in its veins, and in this worm's stomach other worms are living, impenetrable to the eye of this microscope."

"I understand," said the atheist, glancing into Lorand's eyes. "You are explaining to me that the immensity of the world of creation reaching to awful eternity is only equalled by the immensity of the descent to the shapeless nonentity; and that is your God!"

The sublime calm of Lorand's face indicated that that was his idea.

"My dear boy," said Topándy, placing his two hands on Lorand's shoulder, "with that idea I have long been acquainted. I, too, fall down before immensity, and recognize that we represent but one class in the upward direction towards the stars, and one degree in the descent to the moth and rust that corrupt; and perhaps that worm, that I killed in order to take rapt pleasure in its wings, thought itself the middle of eternity round which the world is whirling like Plato's featherless two-footed animals; and when at the door of death it uttered its last cry, it probably thought that this cry for vengeance would be noted by some one, as when at Warsaw four thousand martyrs sang with their last breath, 'All is not yet lost.'"

"That is not my faith, sir. The history of the ephemeral insect is the history of a day,—that of a man means a whole life; the history of nations means centuries, that of the world eternity; and in eternity justice comes to each one in irremediable and unalterable succession."

"I grant that, my boy; and I allow, too, that the comets are certainly claimants to the world whose suits have been deferred to this long justice, who one day will all recover their inheritances, from which some tyrant sun has driven them out; but you must also acknowledge, my child, that for us, the thoughtful worms, or stars, if you like, which can express their thoughts in spirited curses, providence has no care. For everything, everything there is a providence: be it so, I believe it. But for the living kind there is none, unless we take into account the rare occasions when a plague visits mankind, because it is too closely spread over the earth and requires thinning."

"Sir, many misfortunes have I suffered on earth, very many, and such as fate distributes indiscriminately; but it has never destroyed — my faith."

"No misfortune has ever attacked me. It is not suffering that has made me sceptical. My life has always been to my taste. Should some one divide up his property in reward for prayer, I should not benefit one crumb from it.—It is hypocrites who have forcibly driven me this way. Perhaps, were I not surrounded by such, I should keep silence about my unbelief, I should not scandalize others with it, I should not seek to persecute the world's hypocrites with what they call blasphemy. Believe me, my boy, of a million men, all but one regard Providence as a rich creditor, from whom they may always borrow—but when it is a question of paying the interest, then only that one remembers it."

"And that one is enough to hallow the ideal!"

"That one?—but you will not be that one!"

Lorand, astonished, asked:

"Why not?"

"Because, if you remain long in my vicinity, you must without fail turn into such a universal disbeliever as I am."

Lorand smiled to himself.

"My child," said Topándy, "you will not catch the infection from me, who am always sneering and causing scandals, but from that other who prays to the sound of bells."

"You mean Sárvölgyi?"

"Whom else could I mean? You will meet this man every day. And in the end you will say just as I do—'If one must go to heaven in this wise, I had rather remain here?'"

"Well, and what is this Sárvölgyi?"

"A hypocrite, who lies to all the saints in turn, and would deceive the eyes of the archangels if they did not look after themselves."

"You have a very low opinion of the man."

"A low opinion? That is the only good thing in my heart, that I despise the fellow."

"Simply because he is pious? In the world of to-day, however, it is a kind of courage to dare to show one's piety outwardly before a world of scepticism and indifference. I should like to defend him against you."

"Would you? Very well. Let us start at once. Draw up a chair and listen to me. I shall be the devil's advocate. I shall tell you a story concerning this fellow; I was merely a simple witness to the whole. The man never did me any harm. I tell you once again that I have no complaint to make either against mankind or against any beings that may exist above or below. Sit beside me, my boy."

Lorand first of all stirred up the fire in the fire-place, and put out the spirit lamp of the microscope, so that the room was lighted only by the red glare of the log-fire and the moon, which was now rising above the horizon and shed her pale radiance through the window.

"In my younger days I had a very dear friend, a relation, with whom I had always gone to school and such fast comrades were we that even in the class-room we sat always side by side. My comrade was unapproachably first in the class, and I came next; sometime between us like a dividing wall came this fellow Sárvölgyi, who was even then a great flatterer and sneak, and in this way sometimes drove me out of my place—and young schoolboys think a great deal of their own particular places. Of course I was even then so godless that they could not make sufficient complaints against me. Later, during the French war, as the schools suffered much, we were both sent together to Heidelberg. The devil brought Sárvölgyi after us. His parents were parvenues. What our parents did they were always bound to imitate. They might have sent their boy to Jena, Berlin, or Nineveh; but he must come just where we were."

"You have never mentioned your friend's name," said Lorand, who had listened in anguish to the commencement of the story.

"Indeed?—Why there's really no need for the name. He was a friend of mine. As far as the story is concerned it doesn't matter what they called him. Still that you may not think I am relating a fable, I may as well tell you his name. It was Lörincz Áronffy."

A cold numbness seized Lorand when he heard his father's name. Then his heart began suddenly to beat at a furious pace. He felt he was standing before the crypt door, whose secret he had so often striven to fathom.

"I never knew a fairer figure, a nobler nature, a warmer heart than he had," continued Topándy. "I admired and loved him, not merely as my relation, but as the ideal of the young men of the day. The common knowledge of all kinds of little secrets, such as only young people understand among themselves, united us more closely in that bond of friendship which is usually deferred until later days. At that time there broke out all over Europe those liberal political views, which had such a fascinating influence generally on young men. Here too there was an awakening of what is called national feeling; great philosophers even turned against one another with quite modern opposition in public as well as in private life. All this made more intimate the relations which had till then been mere childish habit.

"We were two years at the academy; those two years were passed amidst enough noise and pleasure. Had we money, we spent it together; had we none, we starved together. For one another we went empty-handed, for one another, we fought, and were put in prison. Then we met Sárvölgyi very seldom; the academy is a great forest and men are not forced together as on the benches of a grammar-school.

"Just at the very climax of the French war, the idea struck us to edit a written newspaper among ourselves."

(Lorand began to listen with still greater interest.)

"We travestied with humorous score in our paper all that the 'Augsburger' delivered with great pathos: those who read laughed at it.

"However, there came an end to our amusement, when one fine day we received the 'consilium abeundi.'

"I was certainly not very much annoyed. So much transcendental science, so much knowledge of the world had been driven into me already, that I longed to go home to the company of the village sexton, who, still believed that anecdotes and fables were the highest science.

"Only two days were allowed us at Heidelberg to collect our belongings and say adieu to our so-called 'treasures.' During these two days I only saw Áronffy twice: once on the morning of the first day, when he came to me in a state of great excitement, and said, 'I have the scoundrel by the ear who betrayed us!—If I don't return, follow in my tracks and avenge me.' I asked him why he did not choose me for his second, but he replied: 'Because you also are interested and must follow me.' And then on the evening of the second day he came home again, quite dispirited and out of sorts! I spoke to him; he would scarcely answer; and when I finally insisted: 'perhaps you killed someone?' he answered determinedly, 'Yes.'"

"And who was that man?" inquired Lorand, taken aback.

"Don't interrupt me. You shall know soon," Topándy muttered.

"From that day Áronffy was completely changed. The good-humored, spirited young fellow became suddenly a quiet, serious, sedate man, who would never join us in any amusement. He avoided the world, and I remarked that in the world he did his best to avoid me.

"I thought I knew why that was. I thought I knew the secret of his earnestness. He had murdered a man whom he had challenged to a duel. That weighed upon his mind. He could not be cold-blooded enough to drive even such a bagatelle from his head. Other people count it a 'bravour,' or at most suffer from the persecutions of others—not of themselves. He would soon forget it, I thought, as he grew older.

"Yet my dear friend remained year by year a serious-minded man, and when later on I met him, his society was for me so unenjoyable that I never found any pleasure in frequenting it.

"Still, as soon as he returned home, he got married. Even before our trip to Heidelberg he had become engaged to a very pleasant, pretty, and quiet young girl. They were in love with each other. Still Áronffy remained always gloomy. In the first year of his marriage a son was born to him. Later another. They say both the sons were handsome, clever boys. Yet that never brightened him. Immediately after the honeymoon he went to the war, and behaved there like one who thinks the sooner he is cut off the better. Later, all the news I received of him confirmed my idea that Áronffy was suffering from an incurable mental disease.—Does a man, the candle of whose life we have snuffed out deserve that?"

"What was the name of the man he murdered?" demanded Lorand with renewed disquietude.

"As I have told you, you shall know soon: the story will not run away from me! only listen further.

"One day—it might have been twelve years since the day we shook off the dust of the Heidelberg school from our boots—I received a parcel from Heidelberg, from the Local Council, which informed me that a certain Dr. Stoppelfeld had left me this packet in his will.

Debts of Honor

"Stoppelfeld? I racked my brains to discover who it might be that from beyond the border had left me something in his testament. Finally it occurred to me that a long light-haired medical student, who was famous in his days among the drinking clubs, had attended the same lectures as we had. If I was not deceived, we had drunk together and fought a duel.

"I undid the packet, and found within it a letter addressed to me.

"I have that letter still, but I know every word by heart so often have I read it. Its contents were as follows:

"'My Dear Comrade:

"'You may remember that, on the day before your departure from Heidelberg, one of our young colleagues, Lörincz Áronffy, looked among his acquaintances for seconds in some affair of honor. As it happened I was the first he addressed. I naturally accepted the invitation, and asked his reason and business. As you too know them—he told me so—I shall not write them here. He informed me, too, why he did not choose you as his second, and at the same time bound me to promise, if he should fall in the duel, to tell you that you might follow the matter up. I accepted, and went with him to the challenged. I explained that in such a case a duel was customary, and in fact necessary; if he wished to avoid it, he would be forced to leave the academy. The challenged did not refuse the challenge, but said that as he was of weak constitution, shortsighted and without practice with any kind of weapons, he chose the American duel of drawing lots!'"

... Topándy glanced by chance at Lorand's face, and thought that the change of color he saw on his countenance was the reflection of the flickering flame in the fire-place.

"The letter continued:

"'At our academy at that time there was a great rage for that stupid kind of duel, where two men draw lots and the one whose name comes out, must blow his brains out after a fixed time. Asses! At that time I had already enough common sense, when summoned to act as second in such cases, to try to persuade the principals to fix a longer period, calculating quite rightly that within ten or twelve years the bitterest enemies would become reconciled, and might even become good friends: the successful principal might be magnanimous, and give his opponent his life, or the unsuccessful adversary might forget in his well-being, such a ridiculous obligation.

"'In this case I arranged a period of sixteen years between the parties. I knew my men: sixteen years were necessary for the education of the traitorous schoolfox[58] into a man of honor, or for his proud, upright young adversary to reach the necessary pitch of *sang froid* that would make a settlement of their difference feasible.

[58] *i. e.*, Schoolfox, a term of contempt.

"'Áronffy objected at first: "At once or never!" but he had finally to accept the decision of the seconds: and we drew lots.

"'Áronffy's name came out.'"

... Lorand was staring at the narrator with fixed eyes, and had no feeling for the world outside, as he listened in rapt awe to this story of the past.

"'The name that was drawn out we gave to the successful party, who had the right to send this card, after sixteen years were passed, to his adversary, in order if the latter deferred the fulfilment of his obligation, to remind him thereof.

"'Then we parted company, you went home and I thought we should forget the matter as many others have done.

"'But I was deceived. To this, the hour of my death, it has always remained in my memory, has always agonized and persecuted me. I inquired of my acquaintances in Hungary about the two adversaries, and all I learned only increased my anguish. Áronffy was a proud and earnest man. It is surely stupidity for a man to kill himself, when he is happy and faring well: yet a proud man would far rather the worms gnawed his body than his soul, and could not endure the idea of giving up to a man, whom yesterday he had the right to despise, of his own accord, that right of contempt. He can die, but he cannot be disgraced. He is a fool for his pains: but it is consistent.'"

Lorand was shuddering all over.

"'I am in my death-struggles,' continued Stoppelfeld's letter: 'I know the day, the hour in which I shall end all; but that thought does not calm me so much, seeing that I cannot go myself and seek that man, who holds Áronffy in his hands, to tell him: "Sir, twelve years have passed. Your opponent has suffered twelve years already because of a terrible obligation: for him every pleasure of life has been embittered, before him the future eternity has been overclouded; be contented with that sacrifice, and do not ask for the greatest too. Give back one man to his family, to his country, and to God—" But I cannot go. I must sit here motionless and count the beats of my pulse, and reckon how many remain till the last.

"'And that is why I came to you: you know both, and were a good friend to one: go, speak, and act. Perhaps I am a ridiculous fool: I am afraid of my own shadow; but it agonizes and horrifies me; it will not let me die. Take this inheritance from me. Let me rest peacefully in my ashes. So may God bless you! The man who has Áronffy's word, as far as I know, is a very gracious man, it will be easy for you to persuade him—his name is Sárvölgyi.'"

... At these words Topándy rose from his seat and went to the window, opening both sides of it: so heavy was the air within the room. The cold light of the moon shone on Lorand's brow.

Topándy, standing then at the window, continued the thrilling story he had commenced. He could not sit still to relate it. Nor did he speak as if his words were for Lorand alone, but as if he wished the dumb trees to hear it too, and the wondering moon, and the shivering stars and the shooting meteors that they might gainsay if possible the earthy worm who was speaking.

"I at once hurried across to the fellow. I was now going with tender, conciliatory countenance to a man whose threshold I had never crossed, whom I had never greeted when we met. I first offered him my hand that there might be peace between us. I began to appraise his graciousness, his virtues. I begged him to pardon the annoyances I had previously caused him; whatever atonement he might demand from me I would be glad to fulfill.

"The fellow received me with gracious obeisance, and grasped my hand. He said, upon his soul, he could not recall any annoyance he had ever suffered from me. On the contrary he calculated how much good I had done him in my life, beginning from his school-boy years:—I merely replied that I certainly could not remember it.

"I hastened to come straight to the point. I told him that I had been brought to his home by an affair the settlement of which I owed to a good old friend, and asked him to read the letter that I had received that day.

"Sárvölgyi read the letter to the end. I watched his face all the time he was reading it. He did not cease for a moment that stereotyped smile of tenderness which gives me the shivers whenever I see it in my recollections.

"When he was through with the letter, he quietly folded it and gave it back.

"'Have you not discovered,' he said to me with pious face, 'that the man who wrote that letter is—mad?'

"'Mad?' I asked, aghast.

"'Without doubt,' answered Sárvölgyi; 'he himself writes that he has a disease of the nerves, sees visions, and is afraid of his shadow. The whole story is—a fable. I never had any conflict with our friend

Áronffy, which would have given occasion for an American or even a Chinese duel. From beginning to end it is—a poem.'

"I knew it was no poem: Áronffy had had a duel, but I had never known with whom. I had never asked him about it any more after he had, to my question, 'perhaps you have murdered someone?' answered, 'Yes.' Plainly he had meant himself. I tried to penetrate more deeply into that man's heart.

"'Sir, neighbor, friend,—be a man! be the Christian you wish to be thought: consider that this fellow-man of ours has a dearly-loved family. If you have that card which the seconds gave you twelve years ago, don't agonize or terrify him any more; write to him that "the account is settled," and give over to him that horrible deed of contract. I shall honor you till my death for it. I know that in any case you will do it one day before it is too late. You will not take advantage of that horrible power which blind fate has delivered into your hand, by sending him his card empty to remind him that the time is up. You would pardon him then too. But do so now. This man's life during its period of summer, has been clouded by this torturing obligation, which has hung continuously above his happiness; let the autumn sunbeams shine upon his head. Give, give him a hand of reconciliation now, at once!'

"Sárvölgyi insisted that he had never had any kind of 'cartell': how could I imagine that he would have the heart to maintain his revenge for years? His past and present life repudiated any such charge. He had never had any quarrel with Áronffy, and, had there been one, he would long ago have been reconciled to him.

"I did not yet let the fellow out of my hands. I told him to think what he was doing. Áronffy had once told me that, should he perish in this affair, I was to continue the matter. I too knew a kind of duel, which surpassed even the American, because it destroyed a man by pin-pricks. So take care you don't receive for your eternal adversary the neighboring heathen in exchange for the pious, quiet and distant Áronffy.

"Sárvölgyi swore he knew nothing of the affair. He called God and all the saints to witness that he had not the very remotest share in Áronffy's danger.

"'Well, and why is Áronffy so low-spirited?'

"'—As if you should not know that,' said the Pharisee, making a face of surprise: 'not know anything about it?

"'Well I will whisper it to you in confidence. Áronffy has not been happy in his family life. You know, of course, that when he came home he married, and immediately joined the rebel army. With a corps of volunteers he fought till the end of the war, and returned again to his family. But he has still that worm in his soul.'"

It was well that the fire had already died out:—well that a dark cloud rolled up before the moon:—well that the narrator could not see the face of his listener, when he said that:

"And I was fool enough to believe him. I credited the calumny with which the good fame of the angelically pure wife of an honorable man had been defiled. Yes, I allowed myself to be deceived in this underhand way! I allowed myself to rest calm in the belief that there is many a sad man on the earth, whose wife is beautiful.

"Still, once I met by chance Áronffy's mother, and produced before her the letter which had been accredited a fable. Her ladyship was very grateful, but begged me not to say a word about it to Áronffy.

"I believe that from that day she paid great attention to her son's behavior.

"Four years I had managed to keep myself at a respectful distance from Sárvölgyi's person.

"But there came a day in the year, marked with red in my calendar, the anniversary of our departure from Heidelberg.

"Three days after that sixteenth anniversary I received a letter, which informed me that Áronffy had on that red-letter day killed himself in his family circle."

The narrator here held silence, and, hanging down his hands, gazed out into the brilliant night; profound silence reigned in the room, only the large "grandfather's clock" ticked the past and future.

"I don't know what I should have done, had I met the hypocrite then: but just at that time he was away on a journey: he left behind a letter for me, in which he wrote that he, too, was sorry our unfortunate friend—our friend indeed!—had met with such a sad end: certainly family circumstances had brought him to it. He pitied his weakness of mind, and promised to pray for his soul!

"How pious.

"He killed a man in cold blood, after having tortured him for sixteen years! Sent him the sentence of death in a letter! Forced the gracious, quiet, honorable man and father to cut short his life with his own hand!

"With a cold, smiling countenance he took advantage of the fiendish power which fate and the too sensitive feeling of honor of a lofty soul had given into his hand; and then shrugged his shoulders, clasped his hands, turned his eyes to heaven, and said 'there is no room for the suicide with God.'

"Who is he, who gives a true man into the hands of the deceiver, that he may choke with his right hand his breath, with his left his soul.

"Well, philosopher, come; defend this pious man against me! Tell me what you have learned."

But the philosopher did not say what he had learned. Half dead and wholly insensible he lay back in his chair while the moon shone upon his upturned face with its full brilliance.

CHAPTER XIV

TWO GIRLS

Eight years had passed.

The young man who buried himself on the plains had become a man, his face had lengthened, his beard grown round it; few of his old acquaintances would have recognized him. Even he himself had long ago become accustomed to his assumed name.

In Topándy's house the old order of things continued: Czipra did the honors, presiding at the head of the table: Lorand managed the farm, living in the house, sitting at the table, speaking to the comrades who came and went "per tu";[59] with them he drank and amused himself.

[59] A sign of intimacy—addressing a person as "thou."

Drank and amused himself!

What else should a young man do, who has no aim in life?

With Czipra, tête-à-tête, he spoke also "per tu;" before others he miladyed her.

Once at supper Topándy said to Czipra and Lorand:

"Children, in a few days another child will come to the house. The devil has carried off a very dear relation of mine with whom I was on such excellent terms that we never spoke to one another. I should not, logically, believe there is a devil in the world, should I? But for the short period during which he had carried that fellow away, I am willing to acquiesce in his existence. To-day I have received a lamentable letter from his daughter, written in a beautiful tone of sorrow; the poor child writes that immediately after her father's death the house was swooped down upon by those Sadducees who trample all piety under foot, the so-called creditors. They have seized everything and put it under seals; even her own piano; they have even put up at auction the pictures she drew with her own hand;

and have actually sold the 'Gedenkbuch,'[60] in which so many clever and famous men had written so much absurdity: the tobacconist bought it for ten florins for the sake of its title-page. The poor girl has hitherto been educated by the nuns, to whom three quarters' payment is due, and her position is such that she has no roof except her parasol beneath which she may take shelter. She has a mother in name, but her company she cannot frequent, for certain reasons; she has tried her other relations and acquaintances in turn, but they have all well-founded reasons for not undertaking to burden their families in this manner; she cannot go into service, not having been educated to it. Well, it occurred to her that she had, somewhere in the far regions of Asia, a half-mad relation—that is your humble servant: it would be a good plan to find him out at once, and take up her abode with him as a princess. I entirely indorse my niece's argument: and have already sent her the money necessary for the journey, have paid the fees due, and have enabled her to appear among us in the style befitting her rank."

[60] An album in which one writes something "as a souvenir."

Topándy laughed loudly at his own production.

It was only himself that laughed: the others did not share in it.

"Well, there will be one more young lady in the house: a refined, graceful, sentimental woman-in-white, before whom people must take great care what they say, and who will probably correct the behavior of all of us."

Czipra pushed her chair back angrily from the table.

"Oh, don't be afraid. She will not correct you. You may be sure of that. You have absolute authority in the house, as you know already: what you command or order is accomplished, and against your will not even a cat comes to our table. You remain what you were: mistress of life and death in the house. When you wish it, there is washing in the house, and everybody is obliged to render an account even of his last shirt; what you do not like in the place, you may throw out of the window, and you can buy what you wish. The new young lady will not take away from you a single one of those keys which hang on that silver chain dangling from your red girdle; and if only she does not entice away our young friend, she will be unable to set up any opposition against you. And even in that event I shall defend you."

Czipra shrugged her shoulders defiantly.

"Let her do as she pleases."

"And we two shall do as we please, shall we not?"

"You," said Czipra, looking sharply at Topándy with her black eyes. "You will soon be doing what that young lady likes. I foresee it all. As soon as she puts her foot in, everybody will do as she does. When she smiles, everybody will smile at her in return. If she speaks German, the whole house will use that language; if she walks on her tip-toes, the whole house will walk so; if her head aches, everybody in the house will speak in whispers; not as when poor Czipra had a burning fever and nine men came to her bed to sing a funeral song, and offered her brandy."

Topándy laughed still more loudly at these invectives: the poor gypsy girl fixed her two burning eyes on Lorand's face and kept them there till they turned into two orbs swimming in water. Then she sprang up, threw down her chair and fled from the room.

Topándy calmly picked up the overthrown chair and put it in its place, then he went after Czipra and a minute later brought her back on his arm into the dining-room, with an exceedingly humorous expression, and a courtesy worthy of a Spanish grandee, which the poor foolish gypsy girl did not understand in the least.

So readily did she lose her temper, and so readily did she recover it again. She sat down again in her place, and jested and laughed, — always and continuously at the expense of the finely-educated new-comer.

Lorand was curious to know the name of the new member of the family.

"The daughter of one Bálnokházy, P. C." said Topándy, "Melanie, if I remember well."

Lorand was perplexed. A face from the past! How strange that he should meet her there?

Still it was so long since they had seen each other, that she would probably not recognize him.

Melanie was to arrive to-morrow evening. Early in the morning Czipra visited Lorand in his own room.

She found the young man before his looking-glass.

"Oho!" she said laughing, "you are holding counsel with your glass to see whether you are handsome enough? Handsome indeed you are: how often must I say so? Believe me for once."

But Lorand was not taking counsel with his glass on that point: he was trying to see if he had changed enough.

"Come now," said Czipra with a certain indifference. "I will make you pretty myself: you must be even more handsome, so that young lady's eyes may not be riveted upon me. Sit down, I will arrange your hair."

Lorand had glorious chestnut-brown curls, smooth as silk. Madame Bálnokházy had once fallen madly in love with those locks and Czipra was wont to arrange them every morning with her own hands: it was one of her privileges, and she understood it so well.

Lorand was philosopher enough to allow others to do him a service, and permitted Czipra's fine fingers the privilege of playing among his locks.

"Don't be afraid: you will be handsome to-day!" said Czipra, in naive reproach to the young fellow.

Lorand jestingly put his arm round her waist.

"It will be all of no avail, my dear Czipra, because we have to thrash corn to-day, and my hair will all be full of dust. Rather, if you wish to do me a favor, cut off my hair."

Czipra was ready for that, too. She was Lorand's "friseur" and Topándy's "coiffeur." She found it quite natural.

"Well, and how do you wish your hair? Short? Shall I leave the curls in front?"

"Give me the scissors: I will soon show you," said Lorand, and, taking them from Czipra's hand, he gathered together the locks upon his forehead with one hand and with the other cropped them quite short, throwing what he had cut to the ground.—"So with the rest."

Czipra drew back in horror at this ruthless deed, feeling as pained as if those scissors had been thrust into her own body. Those beautiful silken curls on the ground! And now the rest must of course be cut just as short.

Lorand sat down before her in a chair, from which he could look into the glass, and motioned to her to commence. Czipra could scarcely force herself to do so. So to destroy the beauty of that fair head, over which she had so often stealthily posed in a reverie! To crop close that thick growth of hair, which, when her fingers had played among its electric curls, had made her always feel as if her own soul were wrapt together with it. And she was to close-crop it like the head of some convict!

Yet there was a kind of satisfaction in the thought that another would not so readily take notice of him. She would make him so ugly that he would not quickly win the heart of the new-comer. Away with that Samsonian strength, down to the last solitary hair! This thought lent a merciless power to her scissors.

And when Lorand's head was closely shaven, he was indeed curious to see. It looked so very funny that he laughed at himself when he turned to the glass.

The girl too laughed with him. She could not prevent herself from laughing to his face; then she turned away from him, leaned out of the window, and burst into another fit of laughter.

Really it would have been difficult to distinguish whether she was laughing or crying.

"Thank you, Czipra, my dear," said Lorand, putting his arm round the girl's waist. "Don't wait with dinner for me to-day, for I shall be outside on the threshing-floor."

Thereupon he left the room.

Czipra, left to herself, before anyone could have entered, kneeled down on the floor, and swept up from the floor with her hands the curls she had cut off. Every one: not a single hair must remain for another. Then she hid the whole lovely cluster in her bosom. Perhaps she would never take them out again....

With that instinct, which nature has given to women only, Czipra felt that the new-comer would be her antagonist, her rival in everything, that the outcome would be a struggle for life and death between them.

The whole day long she worried herself with ideas about the new adversary's appearance. Perhaps she was some doll used to proud and noble attitudinising: let her come! It would be fine to take her pride down. An easy task, to crush an oppressed mind. She would steal away from the house, or fall into sickness by dint of much annoyance, and grow old before her time.

Or perhaps she was some spoiled, sensitive, fragile chit, who came here to weep over her past, who would find some hidden reproach in every word, and would feel her position more and more unendurable day by day. Such a creature, too, would droop her head in shame—so that every morning her pillow would be bedewed with tears. For she need not reckon on pity! Or perhaps she would be just the opposite: a light-hearted, gay, sprightly bird, who would find herself at home in every position. If only to-day were cheerful, she would not weep for yesterday, or be anxious for the morrow. Care would be taken to clip the wings of her good humor: a far greater triumph would it be to make a weeping face of a smiling one.

Or perhaps a languid, idle, good-for-nothing domestic delicacy, who liked only to make toilettes, to sit for hours together before the mirror, and in the evening read novels by lamp-light. What a jest it would be to mock her, to make her stare at country work, to spoil her precious hands in the skin-roughening house-keeping work, and to laugh at her clumsiness.

Be she what she might, she might be quite sure of finding an adversary who would accept no cry for mercy.

Oh, it was wise to beware of Czipra! Czipra had two hearts, one good, the other bad: with the one she loved, with the other she hated, and the stronger she loved with the one, the stronger she hated with the other. She could be a very good, quiet, blessed creature, whose faults must be discovered and seen through a magnifying-glass: but if that other heart were once awakened, the old one would never be found again.

Every drop of Czipra's blood wished that every drop of "that other's" blood should change to tears.

This is how they awaited Melanie at Lankadomb.

Evening had not yet drawn in, when the carriage, which had been sent for Melanie to Tiszafüred station, arrived.

The traveler did not wait till some one came to receive her; she stepped out of the carriage unaided and found the verandah alone. Topándy met her in the doorway. They embraced, and he led her into the lobby.

Czipra was waiting for her there.

The gypsy girl was wearing a pure white dress, white apron, and no jewels at all. She had done her best to be simple, that she might surprise that town girl. Of course, she might have been robed in silk and lace, for she had enough and to spare.

Yet she ought to have known that the new-comer could not be stylishly dressed, for she was in mourning.

Melanie had on the most simple black dress, without any decoration, only round her neck and wrists were crochet lace trimmings.

She was just as simple as Czipra. Her beautiful pale face, with its still childish features, her calm quiet look,—all beamed sympathy around her.

"My daughter, Czipra," said Topándy, introducing them.

Melanie, with that graciousness which is the mark of all ladies, offered her hand to the girl, and greeted her gently.

"Good evening, Czipra."

Czipra bitterly inquired:

"A foolish name, is it not?"

"On the contrary, the name of a goddess, Czipra."

"What goddess? Pagan?"—the idea did not please Czipra: she knit her eyebrows and nodded in disapproval.

"A holy woman of the Bible was called by this name, Zipporah,[61] the wife of Moses."

> [61] This play upon names is really only feasible in Magyar, where Zipporah-Czippora.

"Of the Bible?" The gypsy girl caught at the word, and looked with flashing eyes at Topándy, as who would say "Do you hear that?"—Only then did she take Melanie's hand, but after that she did not release her hold of it any more.

"We must know much more of that holy woman of the Bible! Come with me. I will show you your room."

Czipra remarked that they had kissed each other. Topándy shrugged his shoulders, laughed, and let them go alone.

The newly arrived girl did not display the least embarrassment in her dealing with Czipra: on the contrary, she behaved as if they had been friends from childhood.

She at once addressed Czipra in the greatest confidence, when the latter had taken her to the room set apart for her use.

"You will have much trouble with me, my dear Czipra, at first, for I am very clumsy. I know now that I have learned nothing, with which I can do good to myself or others. I am so helpless. But you will be all the cleverer, I know: I shall soon learn from you. Oh, you will often find fault with me, when I make mistakes; but when one girl reproaches another it does not matter. You will teach me housekeeping, will you not?"

"You would like to learn?"

"Of course. One cannot remain for ever a burden to one's relations; only in case I learn can I be of use, if some poor man takes me as his wife; if not I must take service with some stranger, and must know these things anyhow."

There was much bitterness in these words; but the orphan of the ruined gentleman said them with such calm, such peace of mind, that every string of Czipra's heart was relaxed as when a damp mist affects the strings of a harp.

Meanwhile they had brought Melanie's travelling-trunk: there was only one, and no bonnet-boxes—almost incredible!

"Very well,—so begin at once to put your own things in order. Here are the wardrobes for your robes and linen. Keep them all neat. The young lady, whose stockings the chamber-maid has to look for, some in one room, some in another, will never make a good housekeeper."

Melanie drew her only trunk beside her and opened it: she took out her upper-dresses.

There were only four, one of calico, one of batiste, then one ordinary, and one for special occasions.

"They have become a little crumpled in packing. Please have them bring me an iron; I must iron them before I hang them up."

"Do you wish to iron them yourself?"

"Naturally. There are not many of them: those I must make respectable—the servant can heat the iron. Oh, they must last a long time."

"Why haven't you brought more with you?"

Melanie's face for a moment flushed a full rose—then she answered this indiscreet inquiry calmly:

"Simply, my dear Czipra, because the rest were seized by our creditors, who claimed them as a debt."

"Couldn't you have anticipated them?"

Melanie clasped her hands on her breast, and said with the astonishment of moral aversion:

"How? By doing so I should have swindled them."

Czipra recollected herself.

"True; you are right."

Czipra helped Melanie to put her things in the cupboards. With a woman's critical eye, she examined everything. She found the linen not fine enough, though the work on it pleased her well. That was Melanie's own handiwork. As regards books, there was only one in the trunk, a prayer-book. Czipra opened it and looked into it. There were steel plates in it. The portrait of a beautiful woman, seven stars round her head, raising her tear-stained eyes to Heaven: and the picture of a kneeling youth, round the fair bowed head of whom the light of Heaven was pouring. Long did she gaze at the pictures. Who could those figures be?

There were no jewels at all among the new-comer's treasures.

Czipra remarked that Melanie's ear-rings were missing.

"You have left your earrings behind too?" she asked, hiding any want of tenderness in the question by delivering it in a whisper.

"Our solicitor told me," said Melanie, with downcast eyes, "that those earrings also were paid for by creditors' money:—and he was right. I gave them to him."

"But the holes in your ears will grow together; I shall give you some of mine."

Therewith she ran to her room, and in a few moments returned with a pair of earrings.

Melanie did not attempt to hide her delight at the gift.

"Why, my own had just such sapphires, only the stones were not so large."

And she kissed Czipra, and allowed her to place the earrings in her ears.

With the earrings came a brooch. Czipra pinned it in Melanie's collar, and her eyes rested on the pretty collar itself: she tried it, looked at it closely and could not discover "how it was made."

"Don't you know that work? it is crochet, quite a new kind of fancy-work, but very easy. Come, I will show you right away."

Thereupon she took out two crochet needles and a reel of cotton from her work-case, and began to explain the work to Czipra: then she gave it to her to try. Her first attempt was very successful. Czipra had learned something from the new-comer, and remarked that she would learn much more from her.

Czipra spent an hour with Melanie and an hour later came to the conclusion that she was only now beginning—to be a girl.

At supper they appeared with their arms round each other's necks.

The first evening was one of unbounded delight to Czipra.

This girl did not represent any one of those hateful pictures she had conjured up in the witches' kettle of her imagination. She was no rival; she was not a great lady, she was a companion, a child of seventeen years, with whom she could prattle away the time, and before whom she must not choose her words so nicely, seeing that she was not so sensitive to insult. And it seemed that Melanie liked the idea of there being a girl in the house, whose presence threw a gleam of pleasure on the solitude.

Czipra might also be content with Melanie's conduct towards Lorand. Her eyes never rested on the young man's face, although they did not avoid his gaze. She treated him indifferently, and the whole day only exchanged words with him when she thanked him for filling her glass with water.

And indeed Lorand had reduced his external advantages to such a severe simplicity by wearing his hair closely cropped, and his every movement was marked by that languid, lazy stooping attitude which is usually the special peculiarity of those who busy themselves with agricultural work, that Melanie's eyes had no reason to be fixed specially upon him.

Oh, the eyes of a young girl of seventeen summers cannot discover manly beauty under such a dust-stained, neglected exterior.

Lorand felt relieved that Melanie did not recognize him. Not a single trace of surprise showed itself on her face, not a single searching glance betrayed the fact that she thought of the original of a well-known countenance when she saw this man who had met her by chance far away from home. Lorand's face, his gait, his voice, all were strange to her. The face had grown older, the gait was that of a farmer, the old beautiful voice had deepened into a perfect baritone.

Nor did they meet often, except at dinner, supper and breakfast. Melanie passed the rest of the day without a break, by Czipra's side.

Czipra was six years her senior, and she made a good protectress; that continuous woman's chattering, of which Topándy had said, that, if one hour passed without its being heard, he should think he had come to the land of the dead:—a man grew to like that after awhile. And side by side with the quick-handed, quick-tongued maiden, whose every limb was full of electric springiness, was that charming clumsiness of the neophyte,—such a contrast! How they laughed together when Melanie came to announce that she had forgotten to put yeast in the cake, both her hands covered with sticky leaven, for all the world as if she were wearing winter gloves; or when, at Cizpra's command, she tried to take a little yellow downy chicken from the cold courtyard to a warm room, keeping up the while a lively duel with the jealous brood-hen, till finally Melanie was obliged to run.

How much two girls can laugh together over a thousand such humorous nothings!

And how they could chatter over a thousand still more humorous nothings, when of an evening, by moonlight, they opened the window looking out on the garden, and lying on the worked window-cushions, talked till midnight, of all the things in which no one else was interested?

Melanie could tell many new things to Czipra which the latter delighted to hear.

There was one thing which they had touched on once or twice jestingly, and which Czipra would have particularly loved to extract from her.

Melanie, now and again forgetting herself, would sigh deeply.

"Did that sigh speak to someone afar off?"

Or when at dinner she left the daintiest titbit on her plate.

"Did some one think just now of some one far away, who is perhaps famishing?"

"Oh, that 'some one' is not famishing"—whispered Melanie in answer.

So there was "somebody" after all.

That made Czipra glad.

That evening during the conversation she introduced the subject.

"Who is that 'some one?'"

"He is a very excellent youth: and is on close terms with many foreign princes. In a short time he won himself great fame. Everyone exalts him. He came often to our house during papa's life-time, and they intended me to be his bride even in my early days."

"Handsome?" inquired Czipra. That was the chief thing to know.

Melanie answered this question merely with her eyes. But Czipra might have been content with the answer. He was at any rate as handsome a man in Melanie's eyes as Lorand was in hers.

"Shall you be his wife?"

At this question Melanie held up her fine left hand before Czipra, raising the fourth finger higher than the rest. On it was a ring.

Czipra drew the ring off her finger and looked closely at it. She saw letters inside it. If she only knew those!

"Is this his name?"

"His initials."

"He is called?"

"Joseph Gyáli."

Czipra put the ring on again. She was very contented with this discovery. The ring of an old love, who was a handsome man, excellent, and celebrated, was there on her finger. Peace was hallowed. Now she believed thoroughly in Melanie, she believed that the indifference Melanie showed towards Lorand was no mere pretence. The field was already occupied by another.

But if she was quite at rest as regards Melanie, she could be less assured as to the peaceful intentions of Lorand's eyes.

How those eyes feasted themselves every day on Melanie's countenance!

Of course, who could be indignant if men's eyes were attracted by the "beautiful?" It has ever been their privilege.

But it is the marvellous gift of woman's eyes to be able to tell the distinction between look and look. Through the prism of jealousy the eye-beam is refracted to its primary colors; and this wonderful optical analysis says: this is the twinkle of curiosity, that the coquettish ogle, this the fire of love, that the dark-blue of abstraction.

Czipra had not studied optics, but this optical analysis she understood very well.

She did not seem to be paying attention; it seemed as if she did not notice, as if her eyes were not at work; yet she saw and knew everything.

Lorand's eyes feasted upon the beautiful maiden's figure.

Every time he saw her, they dwelt upon her: as the bee feasts upon the invisible honey of the flower, and slowly a suspicion dawned upon Czipra. Every glance was a home-returning bee who brings home the honey of love to a humming heart.

Besides, Czipra might have known it from the fact that Lorand, ever since Melanie came to the house, had been more reserved towards her. He had found his presence everywhere more needful, that he might be so much less at home.

Czipra could not bear the agony long.

Once finding Lorand alone, she turned to him in wanton sarcasm.

"It is certain, my friend Bálint," (that was Lorand's alias) "that we are casting glances at that young girl in vain, for she has a fiancé already."

"Indeed?" said Lorand, caressing the girl's round chin, for all the world as if he was touching some delicate flower-bud.

"Why all this tenderness at once? If I were to look so much at a girl, I would long ago have taken care to see if she had a ring on her finger:—it is generally an engagement ring."

"Well, and do I look very much at that girl?" enquired Lorand in a jesting tone.

"As often as I look at you."

That was reproach and confession all in one. Czipra tried to dispose of the possible effect of this gentle speech at once, by laughing immediately.

"My friend Bálint! That young lady's fiancé is a very great man. The favorite of foreign princes, rides in a carriage, and is called 'My Lord.' He is a very handsome man, too: though not so handsome as you. A fine, pretty cavalier."

"I congratulate her!" said Lorand, smiling.

"Of course it is true; Melanie herself told me.—She told me his name, too—Joseph Gyáli."

"Ha, ha, ha!"

Lorand, smilingly and good-humoredly pinching Czipra's cheek, went on his way. He smiled, but with the poisonous arrow sticking in his heart!

Oh, Czipra did herself a bad turn when she mentioned that name before Lorand!

CHAPTER XV

IF HE LOVES, THEN LET HIM LOVE!

Lorand's whole being revolted at what Czipra had told him. That girl was the bride of that fatal adversary! of that man for whose sake he was to die! And that man would laugh when they stealthily transferred him, the victim too sensible of honor, to the crypt, when he would dance with his newly won bride till morning dawned, and delight in the smile of that face, which could not even weep for the lost one.

That thought led to eternal damnation. No, no: not to damnation: further than that, there and back again, back to that unspeakable circle, where feelings of honor remain in the background, and moral insensibility rules the day. That thought was able to drive out of Lorand's heart the conviction, that when an honorable man has given his life or his honor into the hands of an adversary, of the two only the latter can be chosen.

From that hour he pursued quite a different path of life.

Now the work in the fields might go on without his supervision: there was no longer such need of his presence. He had far more time for staying at home.

Nor did he keep himself any farther away from the girls: he went after them and sought them; he was spirited in conversation, choice in his dress, and that he might display his shrewdness, he courted both girls at the same time, the one out of courtesy, the other for love.

Topándy watched them smilingly. He did not mind whatever turn the affair took. He was as fond of Czipra as he was of Melanie, and fonder of the boy than either. Of the three there would be only one pair; he would give his blessing to whichever two should come together. It was a lottery! Heaven forbid that a strange hand should draw lots for one.

But Czipra was already quite clear about everything, It was not for her sake that Lorand stayed at home.

She herself was forced to acknowledge the important part which Melanie played in the house, with her thoughtful, refined, modest behavior; she was so sensible, so clever in everything. In the most delicate situation she could so well maintain a woman's dignity, while side by side she displayed a maiden's innocence. When his comrades were at the table, Topándy strove always by ambiguous jokes, delivered in his cynical, good humor, to bring a blush to the cheeks of the girls, who were obliged to do the honors at table; on such occasions Czipra noisily called him to order, while Melanie cleverly and spiritedly avoided the arrow-point of the jest, without opposing to it any foolish prudery, or cold insensibility;—and how this action made her queen of every heart!

Without doubt she was the monarch of the house: the dearest, most beautiful, and cleverest;—hers was every triumph.

And on such occasions Czipra was desperate.

"Yet all in vain! For, however clever, and beautiful, and enchanting that other, I am still the real one. I feel and know it:—but I cannot prove it! If we could only tear out our hearts and compare them;—but that is impossible."

Czipra was forced to see that everybody sported with her, while they behaved seriously with that other.

And that completely poisoned her soul.

Without any mental refinement, supplied with only so much of the treasure of moral reserve, as nature and instinct had grafted into her heart, with only a dreamy suspicion about the lofty ideas of religion and virtue, this girl was capable of murdering her whom they loved better than herself.

Murder, but not as the fabled queen murdered the fairy Hófehérke,[62] because the gnomes whispered untiringly in her ear "Thou art beautiful, fair queen: but Hófehérke is still more beautiful." Czipra wished to murder her but not so that she might die and then live again.

> [62] Little Snow-white, the step-daughter of the queen, who commanded her huntsman to bring her the eyes and liver of Hófehérke, thinking she would thus become the most beautiful of all, but he brought her those of a wild beast. The queen thought her rival was dead, but her magic mirror told her she was living still beyond hill and sea.

She was a gypsy girl, a heathen, and in love. Inherited tendencies, savage breeding, and passion had brought her to a state where she could have such ideas.

It was a hellish idea, the counsel of a restless devil who had stolen into a defenceless woman's heart.

Once it occurred to her to turn the rooms in the castle upside down; she found fault with the servants, drove them from their ordinary lodgings, dispersed them in other directions, chased the gentlemen from their rooms, under the pretext that the wall-papers were already very much torn: then had the papers torn off and the walls re-plastered. She turned everything so upside down that Topándy ran away to town, until the rooms should be again reduced to order.

The castle had four fronts, and therefore there were two corridors crossing through at right angles: the chief door of the one opened on the courtyard, that of the other led into the garden. The rooms opened right and left from the latter corridor.

During this great disorder Czipra moved Lorand into one of the vis-à-vis rooms. The opposite room she arranged as Melanie's temporary chamber. Of course it would not last long; the next day but one, order would be restored, and everyone could go back to his usual place.

And then it was that wicked thoughts arose in her heart: "if he loves, then let him love!"

At supper only three were sitting at table. Lorand was more abstracted than usual, and scarcely spoke a word to them: if Czipra addressed him, there was such embarrassment in his reply, that it was impossible not to remark it.

But Czipra was in a particularly jesting mood to-day.

"My friend Bálint, you are sleepy. Yet you had better take care of us at night, lest someone steal us."

"Lock your door well, my dear Czipra, if you are afraid."

"How can I lock my door," said Czipra smiling light-heartedly, "when those cursed servants have so ruined the lock of every door at this side of the house that they would fly open at one push."

"Very well, I shall take care of you."

Therewith Lorand wished them good night, took his candle and went out.

Czipra hurried Melanie too to depart.

"Let us go to bed in good time, as we must be early afoot to-morrow."

This evening the customary conversation at the window did not take place.

The two girls shook hands and wished each other good night. Melanie departed to her room. Czipra was sleeping in the room next to hers.

When Melanie had shut the door behind her, Czipra blew out the candle in her own room, and remained in darkness. With her clothes on she threw herself on her bed, and then, resting her head on her elbow, listened.

Suddenly she thought the opposite room door gently opened.

The beating of her heart almost pierced through her bosom.

"If he loves, then let him love."

Then she rose from her bed, and, holding her breath, slipped to the door and looked through the keyhole into Melanie's room.[63]

[63] This was of course through the door that communicated between the rooms of Melanie and Czipra.

The candle was still burning there.

But from her position she could not see Melanie. From the rustling of garments she suspected that Melanie was taking off her dress. Now with quiet steps she approached the table, on which the candle was burning. She had a white dressing-gown on, her hair half let down, in her hand that little black book, in which Czipra had so often admired those "Glory" pictures without daring to ask what they were.

Melanie reached the table, and laying the little prayer-book on the shelf of her mirror, kneeled down, and, clasping her two hands together, rested against the corner of the table and prayed.

In that moment her whole figure was one halo of glory.

She was beautiful as a praying seraph, like one of those white phantoms who rise with their airy figures to Heaven, palm-branches of glory in their hands.

Czipra was annihilated.

She saw now that there was some superhuman phenomenon, before which every passion bowed the knee, every purpose froze to crystals;—the figure of a praying maiden! He who stole a look at that sight lost every sinful emotion from his heart.

Czipra beat her breast in dumb agony. "She can fly, while I can only crawl on the ground."

When the girl had finished her prayer she opened the book to find those two glory-bright pictures, which she kissed several times in happy rapture:—as the sufferer kisses his benefactor's hands, the orphan his father's and mother's portraits, the miserable defenceless man the face of God, who defends in the form of a column of cloud him who bows his head under its shadow.

Debts of Honor

Czipra tore her hair in her despair and beat her brow upon the floor, writhing like a worm.

At the noise she made Melanie darted up and hastened to the door to see what was the matter with Czipra.

As soon as she noticed Melanie's approach, Czipra slunk away from her place and before Melanie could open the door and enter, dashed through the other door into the corridor.

Here another shock awaited her.

In the corner of the corridor she found Lorand sitting beside a table. On the table a lamp was burning; before Lorand lay a book, beside him, resting against his chair, a "tomahawk."[64]

> [64] The Magyar weapon is the so-called "fokos," which is much smaller than a tomahawk, but is set on a long handle like a walking stick, and only to be used with the hand in dealing blows, not for throwing purposes.

"What are you doing here?" inquired Czipra, starting back.

"I am keeping guard over you," answered Lorand. "As you said your doors cannot be locked, I shall stay here till morning lest some one break in upon you."

Czipra slunk back to her room. She met Melanie, who, candle in hand, hastened towards her, and asked what was the matter.

"Nothing, nothing. I heard a noise outside. It frightened me."

No need of simulation, for she trembled in every limb.

"You afraid?" said Melanie, surprised. "See, I am not afraid. It will be good for me to come to you and sleep with you to-night."

"Yes, it will," assented Czipra. "You can sleep on my bed."

"And you?"

"I?" Czipra inquired with a determined glance. "Oh, just here!"

Debts of Honor

And therewith she threw herself on the floor before the bed.

Melanie, alarmed, drew near to her, seized her arm, and tried to raise her. She asked her: "Czipra, what is the matter with you? Tell me what has happened?"—Czipra did not answer, did not move, did not open her eyes.

Melanie seeing she could not reanimate her, rose in despair, and, clasping her hands, panted:

"Great Heavens! what has happened?"—Then Czipra suddenly started up and began to laugh.

"Ha ha! Now I just managed to frighten you."

Therewith rolling uncontrolledly on the floor, she laughed continuously like one who has succeeded in playing a good joke on her companion.

"How startled I was!" panted Melanie, pressing her hands to her heaving breast.

"Sleep in my bed," Czipra said. "I shall sleep here on the floor. You know I am accustomed to sleep on the ground, covered with rugs.

> "'My mother was a gypsy maid
> She taught me to sleep on the ground,
> In winter to walk with feet unbound;
> In a ragged tent my home was made.'"

She sang Melanie this bizarre song twice in her peculiar melancholy strain, and then suddenly threw around her the rug which lay on the bed, put one arm under her head, and remained quite motionless; she would not reply any longer to a single word of Melanie's.

The next day Topándy returned from town; scarce had he taken off his traveling-cloak, when Czipra burst in upon him.

She seized his hand violently, and gazing wildly into his eyes, said:

"Sir, I cannot live longer under such conditions. I shall kill myself. Teach me to pray."

Topándy looked at her in astonishment and shrugged his shoulders sarcastically.

"Whatever possessed you to break in so upon me? Do you think I come from some pilgrimage to Bodajk,[65] all my pockets full of saints' fiddles, of beads, and of gingerbread-saints? Or am I a Levite? Am I a 'monk' that you look to me for prayer?"

> [65] A place visited by pilgrims, like Lourdes, etc., it is in Fehérmegye (white county).

"Teach me to pray. I have long enough besought you to do so, and I can wait no longer."

"Go and don't worry me. I don't know myself where to find what you want."

"It is not true. You know how to read. You have been taught everything. You only deny knowledge of God, because you are ashamed before Him; but I long to see His face! Oh, teach me to pray!"

"I know nothing, my dear, except the soldier's prayer."[66]

> [66] *i. e.*, Blasphemy.

"Very well. I shall learn that."

"I can recite it to you."

"Well, tell it to me."

Czipra acted as she had seen Melanie do: she kneeled down before the table: clasping her hands devotedly and resting against the edge of the table.

Topándy turned his head curiously: she was taking the matter seriously.

Then he stood before her, put his two hands behind him, and began to recite to her the soldier's prayer.

"Adjon Isten három 'B'-ét,

Három 'F'-ét, három 'P'-ét.
Bort, búzát, békességet,
Fát, füvet, feleséget,
Pipát, puskát, patrontást,
Es egy butykos pálinkát!
Ikétum, pikétum, holt! berdo! vivát!"[67]

[67] "God grant three 'B-s,' three 'F-s,' and three 'P-s.' Wine, wheat, peace, wood, grass, wife, pipe, rifle, cartridge-case, and a little cask of brandy.... Hurrah! hurrar!" It is quite impossible to render the verse into English in any manner that would reproduce the original, so I have given the original Magyar with a literal translation.

The poor little creature muttered the first sentences with such pitiable devotion after that godless mouth:—but, when the thing began to take a definitely jesting turn, she suddenly leaped up from her knees in a rage, and before Topándy could defend himself, dealt him such a healthy box on the ears that it made them sing; then she darted out and banged the door after her.

Topándy became like a pillar of salt in his astonishment. He knew that Czipra had a quick hand, but that she would ever dare to raise that tiny hand against her master and benefactor, because of a mere trifling jest, he was quite incapable of understanding.

She must be in some great trouble.

Though he never said a word, nor did Czipra, about the blow he had received, and though when next they met they were the same towards one another as they had ever been, Topándy ventured to make a jest at table about this humorous scene, saying to Lorand:

"Bálint, ask Czipra to repeat that prayer which she has learned from me: but first seize her two hands."

"Oho!" threatened Czipra, her face burning red. "Just play some more of your jokes upon me. Your lives are in my hands: one day I shall put belladonna in the food, and poison us all together."

Topándy smilingly drew her towards him, smoothing her head; Czipra sensitively pressed her master's hand to her lips, and covered it with kisses;—then put him aside and went out into the kitchen,—to break plates, and tear the servants' hair.

CHAPTER XVI

THAT RING

The tenth year came: it was already on the wane. And Lorand began to be indifferent to the prescribed fatal hour.

He was in love.

This one thought drove all others from his mind. Weariness of life, atheism, misanthropy,—all disappeared from his path like will-o'-the-wisps before the rays of the sun.

And Melanie liked the young fellow in return.

She had no strong passions, and was a prudent girl, yet she confessed to herself that this young man pleased her. His features were noble, his manner gentle, his position secure enough to enable him to keep a wife.

Many a time did she walk with Lorand under the shade of the beautiful sycamores, while Czipra sat alone beside her "czimbalom" and thrashed out the old souvenirs of the plain,—alone.

Lorand found it no difficult task to remark that Melanie gladly frequented the spots he chose, and listened cheerfully to the little confessions of a sympathetic heart. Yet he was himself always reserved.—And that ring was always there on her finger. If only that magic band might drop down from there! Two years had already passed since her father's death had thrown her into mourning; she had long since taken off black dresses; nor could she complain against "the bread of orphanhood." For Topándy supplied her with all that a woman holds dear, just as if she had been his own child.

One afternoon Lorand found courage enough to take hold of Melanie's hand. They were standing on a bridge that spanned the brook which was winding through the park, and, leaning upon its railing, were gazing at the flowers floating on the water—or perhaps at each other's reflection in the watery mirror.

Debts of Honor

Lorand grasped Melanie's hand and asked:

"Why are you always so sad? Whither do those everlasting sighs fly?"

Melanie looked into the youth's face with her large, bright eyes, and knew from his every feature that heart had dictated that question to heart.

"You see, I have enough reason for being sad in that no one has ever asked me that question; and that had someone asked me I could never have answered it."

"Perhaps the question is forbidden?"

"I have allowed him, whom I allowed to remark that I have a grief, also to ask me the reason of it. You see, I have a mother, and yet I have none."

The girl here turned half aside.

Lorand understood her well:—but that was just the subject about which he desired to know more; why, his own fate was bound up with it.

"What do you mean, Melanie?"

"If I tell you that, you will discover that I can have no secret any more in this world from you."

Lorand said not a word, but put his two hands together with a look of entreaty.

"About ten years have passed since mother left home one evening, never to return again. Public talk connected her departure with the disappearance of a young man, who lived with us, and who, on account of some political crime, was obliged to fly the same evening."

"His name?" inquired Lorand.

"Lorand Áronffy, a distant relation of ours. He was considered very handsome."

"And since then you have heard no news of your mother?"

"Never a word. I believe she is somewhere in Germany under a false name, as an actress, and is seeking the world, in order to hide herself from the world."

"And what became of the young man? She is no longer with him?"

"As far as I know he went away to the East Indies, and from thence wrote to his brother Desiderius, leaving him his whole fortune — since that time he has never written any news of himself. Probably he is dead."

Lorand breathed freely again. Nothing was known of him. People thought he had gone to India.

"In a few weeks will come again the anniversary of that unfortunate day on which I lost my mother, my mother who is still living: and that day always approaches me veiled: feelings of sorrow, shame, and loneliness involuntarily oppress my spirit. You now know my most awful secret, and you will not condemn me for it?"

Lorand gently drew her delicate little hand towards his lips, and kissed its rosy finger-tips, while all the time he fixed his eyes entreatingly on that ring which was on one of her fingers.

Melanie understood the inquiry which had been so warmly expressed in that eloquent look.

"You ask me, do you not, whether I have not some even more awful secret?"

Lorand tacitly answered in the affirmative.

Melanie drew the ring off her finger and held it up in her hand.

"It is true—but it is for me no longer a living secret. I am already dead to the person to whom this secret once bound me. When he asked my hand, I was still rich, my father was a man of powerful influence. Now I am poor, an orphan and alone. Such rings are usually forgotten."

At that moment the ring fell out of her hand and missing the bridge dropped into the water, disappearing among the leaves of the water-lilies.

"Shall I get it out?" inquired Lorand.

Melanie gazed at him, as if in reverie, and said:

"Leave it there...."

Lorand, beside himself with happiness, pressed to his lips the beautiful hand left in his possession, and showered hot kisses, first on the hand, then on its owner. From the blossoming trees flowers fluttered down upon their heads, and they returned with wreathed brows like bride and bridegroom.

Lorand spoke that day with Topándy, asking him whether a long time would be required to build the steward's house, which had so long been planned.

"Oho!" said Topándy, smiling, "I understand. It may so happen that the steward will marry, and then he must have a separate lodging where he may take his wife. It will be ready in three weeks."

Lorand was quite happy.

He saw his love reciprocated, and his life freed from its dark horror.

Melanie had not merely convinced him that in him she recognized Lorand Áronffy no more, but also calmed him by the assurance that everyone believed the Lorand Áronffy of yore to be long dead and done for: no one cared about him any longer; his brother had taken his property, with the one reservation that he always sent him secretly a due portion of the income. Besides that one person, no one knew anything. And he would be silent for ever, when he knew that upon his further silence depended his brother's life.

Love had stolen the steely strength of Lorand's mind away.

He had become quite reconciled to the idea that to keep an engagement, which bound anyone to violate the laws of God, of man, and of nature, was mere folly.

Who could accuse him to his face if he did not keep it? Who could recognize him again? In this position, with this face, under this name,—was he not born again? Was that not a quite different man whose life he was now leading? Had he not already ended that life which he had played away *then*?

He would be a fool who carried his feeling of honor to such extremes in relations with dishonorable men; and, finally, if there were the man who would say "it is a crime," was there no God to say "it was virtue?"

He found a strong fortress for this self-defence in the walls of their family vault, in the interior of which his grandmother had uttered such an awful curse against the last inhabitant. Why, that implied an obligation upon him too. And this obligation was also strong. Two opposing obligations neutralize each other. It was his duty rather to fulfil that which he owed to a parent, than that which he owed to his murderer.

These are all fine sophisms. Lorand sought in them the means of escape.

And then in those beautiful eyes. Could he, on whom those two stars smiled, die? Could he wish for annihilation, at the very gate of Heaven?

And he found no small joy in the thought that he was to take that Heaven away from the opponent, who would love to bury him down in the cold earth.

Lorand began to yield himself to his fate. He desired to live. He began to suspect that there was some happiness in the world. Calm, secret happiness, only known to those two beings who have given it to each other by mutual exchange.

We often see this phenomenon in life. A handsome cavalier, who was the lion of society, disappears from the perfumed drawing-room world, and years after can scarcely be recognized in the country farmer, with his rough appearance and shabby coat. A happy family life has wrought this change in him. It is not possible that this same happy feeling which could produce that out of the brilliant, buttoned dress-coat, could let down the young man's pride of character, and give him in its stead an easy-going, wide and water-proof work-a-day blouse, could give him towards the world indifference and want of interest? Let his opponent cry from end to end of the country with mocking guffaws that Lorand Áronffy is no cavalier, no gentleman; the smile of his wife will be compensation for his lost pride.

Now the only thing he required was the eternal silence of the one man, who was permitted to know of his whereabouts, his brother.

Should he make everything known to him?—give entirely into his hands the duel he had accepted, his marriage and the power that held sway over his life, that he might keep off the threatening terror which had hitherto kept him far from brother and parents?

It was a matter that must be well considered and reflected upon.

Lorand became very meditative some days later.

Once after dinner Czipra grasped his hand and said playfully:

"You are thinking very deeply about something. You are pale. Come, I will tell you your fortune."

"My fortune?"

"Of course: I shall read the cards for you: you know

> "'A gypsy woman was my mother,
> Taught me to read the cards of fortune,
> In that surpassing many wishes.'"

"Very well, my dear Czipra: then tell me my fortune."

Czipra was delighted to be able to see Lorand once more alone in her strange room. She made him sit down on the velvet camp-stool, took her place on the tiger-skin and drew her cards from her pocket. For two years she had always had them by her. They were her sole counsellors, friends, science, faith, worship—the sooth-saying cards.

A person, especially a woman, must believe something!

At first she shuffled the cards, then, placing them on her hand offered them to Lorand.

"Here they are, cut them: the one, whose future is being told, must cut. Not with the left hand, that is not good. With the right hand, towards you."

Lorand did so, to please her.

Czipra piled the cards in packs before her.

Then, resting her elbows on her knees and laying her beautiful sun-goldened face upon her hand she very carefully examined the well-known picture-cards.

The knave of hearts came just in the middle.

"Some journey is before you," the gypsy girl began to explain, with a serious face. "You will meet the mourning woman. Great delight. The queen of hearts is in the same row:—well met. But the queen of jealousy[68] and the murderer[68] stand between them and separate them. The dog[68] means faithfulness, the cat[68] slyness. The queen of melancholy stands beside the dog.—Take care of yourself, for some woman, who is angered, wishes to kill you."

> [68] These prophecies are made with Magyar cards and the gypsy girl pointing at certain cards, gives an interpretation of her own to them.

Lorand looked with such a pitying glance at Czipra that she could not help reading the young man's thoughts.

She too replied tacitly. She pressed three fingers to her bosom, and silently intimated that she was not "that" girl. The yellow-robed woman, the queen of jealousy in the cards, was some one else. She placed her pointing fingers to the green-robed—that queen of melancholy. And Lorand remarked that Czipra had long been wearing a green robe, like the green-robed lady in the fortune-telling cards.

Czipra suddenly mixed the cards together:

Debts of Honor

"Let us try once more. Cut three times in succession. That is right."

She placed the cards out again in packs.

Lorand noticed that as the cards came side by side, Czipra's face suddenly flushed; her eyes began to blaze with unwonted fire.

"See, the queen of melancholy is just beside you, on the far side the murderer. The queen of jealousy and the queen of hearts are in the opposite corner. On the other side the old lady. Above your head a burning house. Beware of some great misfortune. Some one wishes to cause you great sorrow, but some one will defend you."

Lorand did not wish to embitter the poor girl by laughing in her face at her simplicity.

"Get up now, Czipra, enough of this play."

Czipra gathered the cards up sadly. But she did not accept Lorand's proffered hand, she rose alone.

"Well, what shall I do, when I don't understand anything else?"

"Come, play my favorite air for me on the czimbalom. It is such a long time since I heard it."

Czipra was accustomed to acquiesce: she immediately took her seat beside her instrument, and began to beat out upon it that lowland reverie, of which so many had wonderingly said that a poet's and an artist's soul had blended therein.

At the sound of music Topándy and Melanie came in from the adjoining rooms. Melanie stood behind Czipra; Topándy drew a chair beside her, and smoked furiously.

Czipra struck the responsive strings and meantime remarked that Lorand all the while fixed his eyes in happy rapture upon the place where she sat; though not upon her face, but beyond, above, upon the face of that girl standing behind her. Suddenly the czimbalom-sticks fell from her hand. She covered her face with her two hands and said panting:

Debts of Honor

"Ah—this pipe-smoke is killing me."

For answer Topándy blew a long mouthful playfully into the girl's face.—She must accustom herself to it: and then he hinted to Lorand that they should leave that room and go where unlimited freedom ruled.

But Czipra began to put the strings of the czimbalom out of tune with her tuning-key.

"Why did you do that?" inquired Melanie.

"Because I shall never play on this instrument again."

"Why not?"

"You will see it will be so: the cards always foretell a coffin for me; if you do not believe me, come and see for yourself."

Therewith she spread the cards again out on the table, and in sad triumph pointed to the picture portrayed by the cards.

"See, now the coffin is here under the girl in green."

"Why, that is not you," said Melanie, half jestingly, half encouragingly, "but you are here."

And she pointed with her hand to the queen of hearts.

But Czipra—saw something other than what had been shown her. She suddenly seized Melanie's tender wrist with her iron-strong right hand, and pointed with her ill-foreboding first finger to that still whiter blank circle remaining on the white finger of her white hand.

"Where has *that* ring gone to?"

Melanie's face flushed deeply at these words, while Czipra's turned deathly pale. The black depths of hell were to be seen in the gypsy girl's wide-opened eyes.

CHAPTER XVII

THE YELLOW-ROBED WOMAN IN THE CARDS

Lorand deferred as long as possible the time for coming to an agreement with Desiderius as to what they should both do, when the fatal ten years had passed by.

His mother and grandmother would be sure to press the latter, when the defined period was over, to tell them of Lorand's whereabouts. But if they learned the story and sought him out, there would be an end to his saving alias: the happy man who was living in the person of Bálint Tátray would be obliged to yield place to Lorand Áronffy who would have to choose between death and the sneers of the world.

When he had made Desiderius undertake, ten years before, not to betray his whereabouts to his parents, he had always calculated and intended to fulfil his fatal obligation. Desiderius alone would be acquainted with the end, and would still keep from the two mothers the secret history of his brother. They had during this time become accustomed to knowing that he was far from them, and his brother would, to the day of their death, always put them under the happy delusion that their son would once again knock at the door, and would show them the letters his brother had written; while he would in reality long have gone to the place, from whence men bring no messages back to the light of the sun. Yet the good peaceful mothers would every day lay a place at table for the son they expected, when the glass had long burst of its own accord.

In place of this cold, clean, transparent dream is now that hot chaos. What should he do now that he wished to live, to enjoy life, to see happy days?

Wherever he would go, in the street, in the field, in the house, everywhere he would feel himself walking in that labyrinth; everywhere that endless chain would clank after him, which began again where it had ended.

He did not even notice, when some one passed him, whether he greeted him or not.

To escape, to exchange his word of honor for his life, to shut out the whole world from his secret—what has pride to say to that?—what the memory of the father who in a like case bowed before his self-pride and cast his life and happiness as a sacrifice before the feet of his honor? What would the tears of the two mothers say?—how could tender-handed love fight alone against so strong adversaries?

How could Bálint Tátray shake off from himself that whole world which cleaved like a sea of mud to Lorand Áronffy?

As he proceeded in deep reflection beside the village houses, his hat pressed firmly down over his eyes, he did not even notice that from the other direction a lady was crossing the rough road, making straight for him, until as she came beside him she addressed him with affected gaiety:

"Good day, Lorand."

The young fellow, startled at hearing his name, looked up amazed and gazed into the speaker's face.

She, with the cheery smile of undoubted recognition, grasped his hand.

"Yes, yes! I recognized you again after so long a time had passed, though you know me no more, my dear Lorand."

Oh! Lorand knew her well enough! And that woman—was Madame Bálnokházy....

Her face still possessed the beautiful noble features of yore; only in her manner the noblewoman's graceful dignity had given way to a certain unpleasant freedom which is the peculiarity of such women as are often compelled to save themselves from all kinds of delicate situations by humorous levity.

She was dressed for a journey, quite fashionably, albeit a little creased.

Debts of Honor

"You here?" inquired Lorand, astonished.

"Certainly: quite by accident. I have just left my carriage at the Sárvölgyi's. I have won a big suit in chancery, and have come to the 'old man' to see if I could sell him the property, which he said he was ready to purchase. Then I shall take my daughter home with me."

"Indeed?"

"Of course—poor thing, she has lived long enough in orphan state in the house of a half-madman. But be so kind as to give me your arm to lean on: why I believe you are still afraid of me: it is so difficult, you know, for some one who is not used to it, to walk along these muddy rough country roads.—I am going to sell my property which I have won, because we must go to live in Vienna."

"Indeed?"

"Because Melanie's intended lives there too."

"Indeed?"

"Perhaps you would know him too,—you were once good friends—Pepi Gyáli!"

"Indeed?"

"Oh, he has made a great career! An extraordinarily famous man. Quite a wonder, that young man!"

"Indeed?"

"But you only taunt me with your series of 'indeeds.' Tell me how you came here. How have I found you?"

"I am steward here on Mr. Topándy's estate!"

"Steward! Ha ha! To your kinsman?"

"He does not know I am his kinsman."

"So you are incognito? Ever since *then*? Just like me: I have used six names since that day. That is famous. And now we meet by chance. So much the better; at least you can lead me to Topándy's house: the atheist's dogs will not tear me to pieces if I am under your protection.—But after that you must help again to defend me."

Lorand was displeased by the fact that this woman turned into jest those memories in which the shame of both lay buried.

Topándy was on the verandah of the castle in company with the girls when Lorand led in the strange lady.

Lorand went first to Melanie:

"Here is the one you have so often sighed after," ... then turning to Topándy—"Madame Bálnokházy."

For a moment Melanie was taken aback. She merely stared in astonishment at the new arrival, as if it were difficult to recognize her at once, while her mother, with a passion quite dramatic, rushed towards her, embraced her, clasped her to her bosom, and covered her with kisses. She sobbed and knelt before her; as one may see times without number in the closing scene of the fifth act of any pathetic drama.

"How beautiful you have become! What an angel! My darling, only, beloved Melanie!—for whom I prayed every day, of whom every day I dreamed.—Well, tell me, have you thought sometimes of me?"

Melanie whispered in her mother's ear:

"Later, when we are alone."

The woman understood that well ("later when we are alone, we can talk of cold, prosaic things: but when they see us, let us weep, faint, and embrace.") This scene of meeting was going to begin anew, only Topándy was good enough to kindly request her ladyship to step into the room, where space was confined, and circumstances are more favorable to dramatic episodes. Madame Bálnokházy then became gay and talkative. She thanked Topándy (the old atheistical fool) thousands, millions of times, for giving a place of refuge to her child, for guarding her only treasure. Then she looked around to see whom else she had to thank. She saw Czipra.

"Why," she said to Lorand, "you have not yet introduced me to your wife."

Everybody became embarrassed—with the exception of Topándy, who answered with calm humor:

"She is my ward, and has been so many years."

"Oh! A thousand apologies for my clumsiness. I certainly thought she was already married."

Madame Bálnokházy had time to remark that Czipra's eyes, when they looked upon Lorand, seemed like the eyes of faithfulness: and she had a delicious opportunity of cutting to the heart two, if not three people.

"Well, it seems to me what is not may be, may it not, 'Lorand?'"

"Lorand!" cried three voices in one.

"There we are! Well I have betrayed you now. But what is the ultimate good of secrecy here between good friends and relations? Yes, he is Lorand Áronffy, a dear relation of ours. And you had not yet recognized him, Melanie?"

Melanie turned as white as the wall.

Lorand answered not a word.

Instead of answering he stepped nearer to Topándy, who grasped his hand, and drew him towards him.

Madame Bálnokházy did not allow anyone else to utter a word.

"I shall not be a burden long, my dear uncle. I have taken up my residence here in the neighborhood, with Mr. Sárvölgyi, who is going to buy our property; we have just won an important suit in chancery."

"Indeed?"

Madame Bálnokházy did not explain the genesis of the suit in chancery any further to Topándy, who had himself now fallen into that bad habit of saying, "indeed" to everything, as Lorand did.

"For that purpose I must enjoy myself a few days here."

"Indeed?"

"I hope, dear uncle, you will not deny me the pleasure of being able to have Melanie all this time by my side. I should surely have found it much more proper to take up my quarters directly here in your house, if Sárvölgyi had not been kind enough to previously offer his hospitality."

"Indeed?" (Topándy knew sometimes how to say very mocking "indeeds.")

"So please don't offer any objections to my request that I may take Melanie to myself for these few days. Later on I shall bring her back again, and leave her here until fortune desires you to let us go forever."

At this point Madame Bálnokházy put on an extremely matronly face. She wished him to understand what she meant.

"I find your wish very natural," said Topándy briefly, looking again in the woman's face as one who would say "What else do you know for our amusement?"

"Till then I render you endless thanks for taking the part of my poor deserted orphan. Heaven will reward you for your goodness."

"I didn't do it for payment."

Madame Bálnokházy laughed modestly, as though in doubt whether to understand a joke when the inhabitants of higher spheres were under consideration.

"Dear uncle, you are still as jesting as ever in certain respects."

"As godless—you wished to say, did you not? Indeed I have changed but little in my old age."

"Oh we know you well!" said the lady in a voice of absolute grace: "you only show that outwardly, but everyone knows your heart."

"And runs before it when he can, does he not?"

"Oh, no: quite the contrary," said Madame apologetically, "don't misinterpret our present departures to prove how much we all think of that beneficial public life which you are leading. I shall whisper one word to you, which will convince you of our most sincere respect for you."

That one word she did whisper to Topándy, resting her gloved hand on his shoulder—:

"I wish to ask my dear uncle to give Melanie away, when Heaven brings round the happy day."

At these words Topándy smiled: and, putting Madame Bálnokházy's hand under his arm, said:

"With pleasure. I will do more. If on that certain day of Heaven the sun shines as I desire it, this my godless hand shall make two people happy. But if that day of Heaven be illumined otherwise than I wish, I shall give 'quantum satis' of blessing, love congratulatory verses, long sighs and all that costs nothing. So what I shall answer to this question depends upon that happy day."

Madame Bálnokházy clasped Topándy's hand to her heart and with eyes upturned to Heaven, prayed that Providence might bless so good a relation's choice with good humor, and then drew Melanie too towards him, that she might render thanks to her good uncle for the gracious care he had bestowed upon her.

Lorand gazed at the group dispiritedly, while Czipra, unnoticed, escaped from the room.

"And now perhaps Lorand will be so kind as to accompany us to Sárvölgyi's house."

"As far as the gate."

"Where is your dear friend, Melanie, that beautiful dear creature? Take a short leave of her. But where has she gone to?"

Lorand did not move a muscle to go and look for Czipra.

"Well we shall meet the dear child again soon," said Madame Bálnokházy, noticing that they were waiting in vain. "Give me your arm, Lorand."

She leaned on Lorand's right arm, and motioned to Melanie to take her position on the other side; but the girl did not do so. Instead she clasped her mother's arm, and so they went along the street, the mother waving back affectionately to Topándy, who gazed after them out of the window.

Melanie did not utter a single word the whole way.

"The old fellow, it seems, is on bad terms with Sárvölgyi?"

"Yes."

"Is he still as iconoclastic, as godless, as ever?"

"Yes."

"And you have been able to stand it so long?"

"Yes."

"And yet you were always so pious, so god-fearing; are you still?"

"Yes."

"So Topándy and Sárvölgyi are living on terms of open enmity?"

"Yes."

"Yet you will visit us several times, while we are here?"

"No."

"Heaven be praised that once I hear a 'no' from you! That heap of *yes's* began already to make me nervous. Then you too are among *his* opponents?"

"Yes."

Meantime they had reached the gate of Sárvölgyi's house. Here Lorand stopped and would proceed no further.

Madame Bálnokházy clasped Melanie's hand that she might not go in front.

"Well, my dear Lorand, and are you not going to take leave of us even?"

Lorand gazed at Melanie, who did not even raise her eyes.

"Good-bye, Madame," said Lorand briefly. He raised his hat and was gone.

Madame Bálnokházy cast one glance after him with those beautiful expressive eyes.—Those beautiful expressive eyes just then were full to the brim of relentless hatred.

When Lorand reached home Czipra was waiting for him at the door.

Raising her first finger, she whispered in his ear:

"That was the yellow-robed woman!"

Yet she had nothing yellow on her.

CHAPTER XVIII

THE FINGER-POST OF DEATH

Lorand threw himself exhausted into his arm-chair.

There was an end to every attempt at escape.

He had been recognized by the very woman who ought to detest him more bitterly than anyone in the world.

Nemesis! the liberal hand of everlasting justice!

He had deserted that woman in the middle of the road, on which they were flying together passionately into degradation, and now that he wished to return to life, that woman blocked his way.

There was no hope of pity. Besides, who would accept it—from such a hand? At such a price? Such a present must be refused, were it life itself.

Farewell calm happy life! Farewell, intoxicating love!

There was only one way, a direct one—to the opened tomb.

They would laugh over the fallen, but at least not to his face.

The father had departed that way, albeit he had a loving wife, and growing children:—but he was alone in the world. He owed nobody any duty.

There were two enfeebled, frail shadows on earth, to which he owed a duty of care; but they would soon follow him, they had no very long course to run.

Fate must be accomplished.

The father's blood besprinkled the sons. One spirit drew the other after it by the hand, till at last all would be there at home together.

Only a few days more remained.

These few days he must be gay and cheerful: must deceive every eye and heart, that followed attentively him who approached the end of his journey,—that no one might suspect anything.

There was still one more precaution to be taken.

Desiderius might arrive before the fatal day. In his last letter he had hinted at it. That must be prevented. The meeting must be arranged otherwise.

He hurriedly wrote a letter to his brother to come to meet him at Szolnok on the day before the anniversary, and wait for him at the inn. He gave as his reason the cynicism of Topándy. He did not wish to introduce him as a discord in that tender scene. Then they could meet, and from there could go together to visit their parents.

The plan was quite intelligible and natural. Lorand at once despatched the letter to the post.

So does the cautious traveler drive from his route at the outset, the obstacles which might delay him.

Scarcely had he sent the letter off when Topándy entered his room.

Lorand went to meet him. Topándy embraced and kissed him.

"I thank you that you chose my home as a place of refuge from your prosecutors, my dear Lorand; but there is no need longer to keep in hiding. Later events have long washed out what happened ten years ago, and you may return to the world without being disturbed."

"I have known that long since: why, we read the newspapers; but I prefer to remain here. I am quite satisfied with this world."

"You have a mother and a brother from whom you have no reason to hide."

"I only wish to meet them when I can introduce myself to them as a happy man."

"That depends on yourself."

"A few days will prove it."

"Be as quick as you can with it. Let only one thought possess your mind: Melanie is now in Sárvölgyi's house. The great spiritual delight it will afford me to think of the hypocrite's death-face which that Pharisee will make when that trivial woman discloses to him that the young man, who is living in the neighborhood, is Lörincz Áronffy's son, can only be surpassed by my anxiety for you, caused by his knowledge of the fact. For, believe me, he will leave no stone unturned to prevent you, who will remind him of that night when we spoke of great and little things, from being able to strike root in this world. He will even talk Melanie over."

Lorand, shrugging his shoulders, said with light-hearted indifference:

"Melanie is not the only girl on this earth."

"Well said. I don't care. You are my son: and she whom you bring here is my daughter. Only bring her; the sooner the better."

"It will not take a week."

"Better still. If you want to act, act quickly. In such cases, either quickly or not at all; either courageously or never."

"There will be no lack of courage."

Topándy spoke of marriage, Lorand of a pistol.

"Well in a week's time I shall be able to give my blessing on your choice."

"Certainly."

Topándy did not wish to dive further into Lorand's secret. He suspected the young fellow was choosing between two girls, and did not imagine that he had already chosen a third:—the one with the down-turned torch.[69]

Lorand during the following days was as cheerful as a bridegroom during the week preceding his marriage—so cheerful!—as his father had been the evening before his death.

[69] The torch, which should have been held upright for the marriage festivities, would be held upside down for the festivities of death, just as the life would be reversed.

The last day but one came: May again, but not so chilly as ten years before. The air in the park was flower-perfumed, full of lark trills, and nightingale ditties.

Czipra was chasing butterflies on the lawn.

Ever since Melanie had left the house, Czipra's sprightly mood had returned. She too played in the lovely spring, with the playful birds of song.

Lorand allowed her to draw him into her circle of playmates:

"How does this hyacinth look in my hair?"

"It suits you admirably, Czipra."

The gypsy girl took off Lorand's hat, and crowned it with a wreath of leaves, then put it back again, changing its position again and again until she found out how it suited him best.

Then she pressed his hand under her arm, laid her burning face upon his shoulder, and thus strolled about with him.

Poor girl! She had forgotten, forgiven everything already!

Six days had passed since that ruling rival had left the house: Lorand was not sad, did not pine after her, he was good-humored, witty, and playful; he enjoyed himself. Czipra believed their stars were once more approaching each other.

Lorand, the smiling and gay Lorand, was thinking that he had but one more day to live; and then—adieu to the perfumed fields, adieu to the songster's echo, adieu to the beautiful, love-lorn gypsy girl!

They went arm-in-arm across the bridge, that little bridge that spanned the brook. They stopped in the middle of the bridge and leaning upon the railing looked down into the water;—in the self same place where Melanie's engagement ring fell into the water.

They gazed down into the water-mirror, and the smooth surface reflected their figures; the gypsy girl still wore a green dress, and a rose-colored sash, but Lorand still saw Melanie's face in that mirror.

In this place her hand had been in his: in that place she had said of the lost ring "leave it alone:" in that place he had clasped her in his arms!

And to-morrow even that would cause no pain!

Topándy now joined them.

"Do you know what, Lorand?" said the old Manichean cheerily: "I thought I would accompany you this afternoon to Szolnok. We must celebrate the day you meet your brother: we must drink to it!"

"Will you not take me with you?" inquired Czipra half in jest.

"No!" was the simultaneous reply from both sides.

"Why not?"

"Because it is not fit for you *there*.—There is no room for you *there*!"

Both replied the same.

Topándy meant "You cannot take part in men's carousals; who knows what will become of you?" while Lorand—meant something else.

"Well, and when will Lorand return?" inquired Czipra eagerly.

"He must first return to his parents," answered Topándy.

(—"Thither indeed" thought Lorand, "to father and grandfather"—)

"But he will not remain *there* forever?"

At that both men laughed loudly. What kind of expression was that word "forever" in one's mouth? Is there a measure for time?

"What will you bring me when you return?" inquired the girl childishly.

Lorand was merciless enough to jest: he tore down a leaf which was round, like a small coin; placing that on the palm of her hand, he said:

"Something no greater than the circumference of this leaf."

Two understood that he meant "a ring," but what he meant was a "bullet" in the centre of his forehead.

How pitiless are the jests of a man ready for death.

Their happy dalliance was interrupted by the butler who came to announce that a young gentleman was waiting to speak with Master Lorand.

Lorand's heart beat fast! It must be Desi!

Had he not received the letter? Had he not acceded to his brother's request? He had after all come one day sooner than his deliberate permission had allowed.

Lorand hastened up to the castle.

Topándy called after him:

"If it is a good friend of yours bring him down here into the park: he must dine with us."

"We shall wait here by the bridge," Czipra added: and there she remained on the bridge, she did not herself know why, gazing at those plants on the surface of the water, that were hiding Melanie's ring.

Lorand hastened along the corridors in despondent mood: if his brother had really come, his last hours would be doubly embittered.

That simulation, that comedy of cynical frivolity, would be difficult to play before him.

The new arrival was waiting for him in the reception room.

When Lorand opened the door and stood face to face with him, an entirely new surprise awaited him.

The young cavalier who had thus hastened to find him was not his brother Desi, but—Pepi Gyáli.

Pepi was no taller, no more manly-looking than he had been ten years before; he had still that childish face, those tiny features, the same refined movements. He was still as strict an adherent to fashion: and if time had wrought a change in him, it was only to be seen in a certain, distinguished bearing,—that of those who often have the opportunity of playing the protector toward their former friends.

"Good day, dear Lorand," he said in a gay tone, anticipating Lorand. "Do you still recognize me?"

("Ah," thought Lorand: "you are here as the finger-post of death.")

"I did not want to avoid you: as soon as I knew from the Bálnokházys that you were here, I came to find you."

After all it was *"she"* that had put him on Lorand's track!

"I have business here with Sárvölgyi in Madame Bálnokházy's interest—a legal agreement."

Lorand's only thought, while Gyáli was uttering these words, was—how to behave himself in the presence of this man.

"I hope," said the visitor tenderly extending his hand to Lorand, "that that old wrangle which happened ten years ago has long been forgotten by you—as it has by me."

("He wishes to make me recollect it, if perchance I had forgotten.")

"And we shall again be faithful comrades and true."

One thought ran like lightning in a moment through Lorand's brain. "If I kick this fellow out now as would be my method, everyone would clearly understand the origin of the catastrophe, and take it as satisfaction for an insult. No, they must have no such triumph: this wretch must see that the man who is gazing into the face of his own death is in no way behind him, who burns to persecute him to the end with exquisiteness, in cheerful mood."

So Lorand did not get angry, did not show any sullenness or melancholy, but, as he was wont to do in student days of yore, slapped the dandy's open hand and grasped it in manly fashion.

"So glad to see you, Pepi. Why the devil should I not have recognised you? Only I imagined that you would have aged as much as I have since that time, and now you stand before me the same as ever. I almost asked you what we had to learn for to-morrow?"

"I am glad of that! Nothing has caused me any displeasure in my life except the fact that we parted in anger—we, the gay comrades!—and quarrelled!—why? for a dirty newspaper! The devil take them all!—Taken all together they are not worth a quarrel between two comrades. Well, not a word more about it!"

"Well, my boy, very well, if your intentions are good. In any case we are country fellows who can stand a good deal from one another. To-day we calumniate each other, to-morrow we carouse together."

Ha, ha, ha!

"But you must introduce me to the old man. I hear he is a gay old fool. He does not like priests. Why I can tell him enough tales about priests to keep him going for a week. Come, introduce me. I know his mouth will never cease laughing, once I begin upon him."

"Naturally it is understood that you will remain here with us."

"Of course. Old Sárvölgyi, as it is, had made sour faces enough at the unusual invasion of guests: and he has a cursedly sullen housekeeper. Besides it is disagreeable always to have to say nice things to the two ladies: that's not why a fellow comes to the country. *A propos*, I hear you have a beautiful gypsy girl here."

"You know that too, already?"

"I hope you are not jealous of her?"

"What, the devil! of a gypsy girl?"

("Well just try it with her," thought Lorand, "at any rate you will get 'per procura,' that box on the ears which I cannot give you.")

"Ha, ha! we shall not fight a duel for a gypsy girl, shall we, my boy?"

"Nor for any other girl."

"You have become a wise man like me: I like that. A woman is only a woman. Among others, what do you say to Madame Bálnokházy? I find she is still more beautiful than her daughter. *Ma foi*, on my word of honor! Those ten years on the stage have only done her good. I believe she is still in love with you."

"That's quite natural," said Lorand in jesting scorn.

In the meantime they had reached the park; they found Topándy and Czipra by the bridge. Lorand introduced Pepi Gyáli as his old school-fellow.

That name fairly magnetized Czipra.—Melanie's fiancé!—So the lover had come after his bride. What a kind fellow this Pepi Gyáli was! A really most amiable young man!

Gyáli quite misunderstood the favorable impression his name and appearance made on Czipra: he was ready to attribute it to his irresistible charms.

After briefly making the acquaintance of the old man, he very rapidly took over the part of courtier, which every cavalier according to the rules of the world is bound to do; besides, she was a gypsy girl, and—Lorand was not jealous.

"You have in one moment explained to me something over which I have racked my brains a whole day."

"What can that be?" inquired Czipra curiously.

"How it is that some one can prefer fried fish and fried rolls at Sárvölgyi's to cabbage at Topándy's?"

"Who may that someone be?"

"Why, I could not understand that Miss Melanie was able to persuade herself to change this house for that; now I know: she must have put up with a great persecution here."

Debts of Honor

"Persecution?" said Czipra, astonished:—the gentlemen too stared at the speaker.—"Who would have persecuted her?"

"Who? Why these eyes!" said Gyáli, gazing flatteringly into Czipra's eyes. "The poor girl could not stand the rivalry. It is quite natural that the moon, however sweet and poetic a phenomenon, always flees before the sun."

To Czipra this speech was very surprising. There are many who do not like overburdened sweetness.

"Ah, Melanie is far more beautiful than I," she said, casting her eyes down, and growing very serious.

"Well it is my bounden duty to believe in that, as in all the miracles of the apostles: but I cannot help it, if you have made a heretic of me."

Czipra turned her head aside and gazed down into the water with eyes of insulted pride: while Lorand, who was standing behind Gyáli, thought within himself:

("If I take you by the neck and drown you in that water, you would deserve it, and it will do good to my soul: but I should know I had murdered you: and no one should ever be able to boast of *that*? My name shall never be connected with yours in death.")

For Lorand might well have known that Gyáli's appearance on that day had no other object than that of reminding Lorand of his awful obligation.

"My dear boy," said Lorand patting Gyáli's shoulder playfully, "I must show what a general I should have made. I have an important journey this afternoon to Szolnok."

"Well, go; don't bother yourself on my account. Do exactly as you please."

"That's not how matters lie, Pepi: you must not stay here in the meantime."

"The devil! Perhaps you will turn me out?"

"Oh dear no! To-night we shall have a glorious carnival at Szolnok, in honor of my regeneration. All the gay fellows of the neighborhood are invited to it. You must come with us too."

"Ha! Your regeneration carnival!" cried Gyáli, in a voice of ecstasy, the while gazing at Czipra apologetically. "Albeit other magnets draw me hither with overpowering force—I must go there without fail. I must deliver a 'toast' at your 'regeneration' festival, Lorand."

"My brother Desi will also be there."

"Oho! little Desi? That little rebel. Well all the better. We shall have much in common with him; of old he was an amusing boy, with his serious face. Well I shall go with you. I sacrifice myself. I capitulate. Well we shall go to Szolnok to-night."

Why, anyone might have seen plainly—had he not come that day just to revel in the agony of Lorand?

"Yes, Pepi," Lorand assured him, "we shall be gay as we were once ten years ago. Much hidden joy awaits us: we shall break in suddenly upon it. Well, you are coming with us."

"Without fail: only be so good as to send some one next door for my traveling-cloak. I shall go with you to your 'regeneration' fête!"

And once again he grasped Lorand's hand tenderly, as one who was incapable of expressing in words all the good wishes with which his heart was brimming over.

"You see I should have been a good general after all," said Lorand smiling. "How beautifully I captured the besieging army."

"Oh, not at all; the blockade is still being kept up."

"But starvation will be a difficult matter where the garrison is well nourished."

The poor gypsy girl did not understand a word of all this jesting, which was uttered for her edification: and if she had understood it, was she not a gypsy girl, just to be sported with in this manner?

Were not Topándy and his comrades wont to jest with her after this manner.

But Czipra did not laugh over these jests as much as she had done at other times.

It exercised a distasteful influence upon her heart, when this young dandy spoke so lightly of Melanie, and even slighted her before the eyes of another girl. Did all men speak so of their loved ones? And do men speak so of every girl?

Topándy turned the conversation. He knew his man at the first glance: he had many weak sides. He began to "my lord" him, and made inquiries about those foreign princes, whose plenipotentiary minister M. Gyáli was pleased to be.

That had its effect.

Gyáli became at once a different person: he strove to maintain an imposing bearing with a view to raising his dignity, for all the world as if he had swallowed a poker; he straightened his eyebrows, put his hands behind him under the tails of his lilac-colored dress-coat and formed his mouth into the true diplomatic shape.

It was a supreme opportunity for being able to display his grandiose achievements. Let that other see how high he had flown, while others had remained fastened to the earth.

"I have just concluded a splendid business for his Excellency, the Prince of Hohenelm-Weitbreitstein."

"A ruling prince, of course?" inquired Topándy, in naïve wonder.

"Why, you know that."

"Of course, of course. His possessions lie just where the corners of the great principalities of Lippedetmold, Schwarzburg-Sondershausen and Reuss-major meet."

Oh, Gyáli must have been very full of self-confidence when he answered to the old magistrate's peculiar geographical definition, "yes."

"Your lordship has already doubtless found an excellent situation in the Principality?"

"I have an order and a title, the gift of His Excellency."

"Of course it may lead to more."

"Oh yes. In return for my winning His Excellency's domains, which he inherited on his mother's side, he will settle on me 5,000 acres of land."

"In Hohenelm-Weitbreitstein?"

"No: here in the Magyar country."

"I thought in Hohenelm-Weitbreitstein: for that is a beautiful country."

Gyáli began to see that it was after all something more than simplicity that could give utterance to such easily recognized exaggeration; and when the old man began to inform him, in which section of which chapter of the Corpus Juris would be found inscribed His Excellency's Magyar "indigenatus," etc., etc., Gyáli began to feel exceedingly uncomfortable, and began to again change the course of the conversation. He chattered on about His Excellency being a fine, free-thinking man, related a hundred anecdotes about him, how he turned out the Jesuits from his possessions, what jokes he had played on the monks, how he persecuted the pietists, and other such things as might be very inconvenient incumbrances to the Principality of Hohenelm-Weitbreitstein,—in the case of any such principality existing in the world.

The theme lasted the whole of dinner time.

Czipra wanted to do all she could to-day for herself. For the farewell-dinner she sought out all that she had found Lorand liked, and Lorand was ungrateful enough to allow Gyáli the field of compliment to himself: he could not say one good word to her.

Yet who knew when he would sit at that table again?

Debts of Honor

Dinner over, Lorand spent a few minutes in running over the house: to give instructions to every servant as to what was to be done in the fields, the garden and the forest before his return in two weeks' time. He gave everyone a tip to drink to his health; for to-morrow he was to celebrate a great festival.

Topándy, too, was looking over the preparations for the journey. Czipra was the lady of the house: it was her task, as it had always been, to amuse the guest who remained alone. Topándy never troubled himself to amuse anyone, for whose entertainment he was responsible. Czipra was there, he must listen to what she had to say.

In the meantime the butler, who had been sent to Sárvölgyi's to bring Gyáli's traveling cloak, came back.

He brought also a letter from the young lady for Lorand.

"From the young lady?"

Lorand took the letter from him and told him to take the cloak up to the guest's room.

He himself hastened to his own room.

As he passed through the saloon, Gyáli met him, coming from Czipra's room. The dandy's face was peculiarly flurried.

"My dear friend," he said to Lorand, "that gypsy girl of yours is a regular female panther, and you have trained her well, I can tell you.—Where is there a looking-glass?"

"Yes she is," replied Lorand. He scarcely knew why he said it: he heard, but only unconsciously.

Only that letter! Melanie's letter!

He was in such a hurry to reach his room with it. Once there and alone, he shut the door, kissed the fine rose-colored note, and its azure-blue letters, the red seal upon it; and clasped it to his breast, as if he would find out from his heart what was in it.

Well, and what could be in it?

Lorand put the letter down before him and laid his fist heavily upon it.

"Must I know what is in that letter?

"Suppose she writes that she loves me, and awaits happiness from me, that her love can outbalance a whole lost world, that she is ready to follow me across the sea, beyond the mocking sneers of acquaintances, and to disappear with me among the hosts of forgotten figures!

"No. I shall not break open this letter.

"My last step shall not be hesitating.

"And if what seems such a chance meeting is nought but a well planned revenge? If they have all along been agreed and have only come here together that they may force me to confess that I am humiliated, that I beg for happiness, for love, that I am afraid of death because I am in love with the smiling faces of life; and when I have confessed that, they will laugh in my face, and will leave me to the contempt of the whole world, of my own self....

"Let them marry each other!"

Lorand took the beautiful note and locked it up in the drawer of his table, unopened, unread.

His last thought must be that perhaps he had been loved, and that last thought would be lightened by the uncertainty: only "perhaps."

And now to prepare for that journey.

It was Lorand's wont to carry two good pistols on a journey. These he carefully loaded afresh, then hid them in his own traveling trunk.

He left his servant to pack in the trunk as much linen as would be enough for two weeks, for they were going to journey farther.

Topándy had two carriages ready, his traveling coach and a wagon.

When the carriages drove up, Lorand put on his traveling cloak, lit his pipe and went down into the courtyard.

Czipra was arranging all matters in the carriages, the trunks were bound on tightly and the wine-case with its twenty-four bottles of choice wine, packed away in a sure place.

"You are a good girl after all, Czipra," said Lorand, tenderly patting the girl's back.

"After all?"

Was he really so devoted to that pipe that he could not take it from his mouth for one single moment?

Yet she had perhaps deserved a farewell kiss.

"Sit with my uncle in the coach, Pepi," said Lorand to the dandy, "with me you might risk your life. I might turn you over into the ditch somewhere and break your neck. And it would be a pity for such a promising youth."

Lorand sprang up onto the seat and took the reins in his hands.

"Well, adieu, Czipra!"—The coach went first, the wagon following.

Czipra stood at the street-door and gazed from there at the disappearing youth, as long as she could see him, resting her head sadly against the doorpost.

But he did not glance back once.

He was going at a gallop towards his doom.

And when evening overtakes the travelers, and the night's million lights have appeared, and the tiny glowworms are twinkling in the ditches and hedges, the young fellow will have time enough to think on that theme: that eternal law rules alike over the worlds and the atoms—but what is the fate of the intermediate worms? that of the splendid fly? that of ambitious men and nations struggling for their existence? "Fate gives justice into the two hands of the evil one, that while with the right he extinguishes his life, with the left he may stifle the soul."

CHAPTER XIX

FANNY

Some wise man, who was a poet too, once said: "the best fame for a woman is to have no fame at all." I might add: "the best life history is that, which has no history."

Such is the romance of Fanny's life and of mine.

Eight years had passed since they brought a little girl from Fürsten-Allee to take my place: the little girl had grown into a big girl,—and was still occupying my place.

How I envied her those first days, when I had to yield my place to her, that place veiled with holy memories in our family's mourning circle, in mother's sorrowing heart; and how I blessed fate, that I was able to fill that place with her.

My career led me to distant districts, and every year I could spend but a month or two at home; mother would have aged, grandmother have grown mad from the awful solitude had Heaven not sent a guardian angel into their midst.

How much I have to thank Fanny for.

For every smile of mother's face, for every new day of grandmother's life—I had only Fanny to thank.

Every year when I returned for the holidays I found long-enduring happy peace at home.

Where everyone had so much right every day madly to curse fate, mankind, the whole world; where sorrow should have ruled in every thought;—I found nothing but peace, patience, and hope.

It was she who assured them that there was a limit to suffering, she who encouraged them with renewed hopes, she who allured them by a thousand possible variations on the theme of chance gladness, that might come to-morrow or perhaps the day after.

And she did everything for all the world as if she never thought of herself.

What a sacrifice it must be for a fair lively girl to sacrifice the most brilliant years of her youth to the nursing of two sorrow-laden women, to suffering with them, to enduring their heaviness of disposition.

Yet she was only a substitute girl in the house.

When I left Pressburg and the Fromm's house her parents wished to take her home; but Fanny begged them to leave her there one year longer, she was so fond of that poor suffering mother.

And then every year she begged for another year; so she remained in our small home until she was a full-grown maiden.

Yes Pressburg is a gay, noisy town. The Fromm's house was open before the world and the flower ought to open in spring—the young girl has a right to live and enjoy life.

Fanny voluntarily shut herself off from life. There was no merriment in our house.

My parents often assured her they would take her to some entertainments, and would go with her.

"For my sake? You would go to amusements that I might enjoy myself? Would that be an amusement for me? Let us stay at home.— There will be time for that later."

And when she victimized herself, she did it so that no one could see she was a victim.

There are many good patient-hearted girls, whose lips never complain, but hollow eyes, pale faces, and clouded dispositions utter silent complaints and give evidence of buried ambitions.

Fanny's face was always rosy and smiling: her eyes cheerful and fiery, her disposition always gay, frank and contented; her every feature proved that what she did she did from her heart and her heart was well pleased. Her happy ever-gay presence enlightened the while gloomy circle around her, as when some angel walks in the darkness, with a halo of glory around his figure.

From year to year I found matters so at home when I returned for the holidays: and from year to year one definite idea grew and took shape in our minds mutually.

We never spoke of it: but we all knew.

She knew—I knew, her parents knew and so did mine; nor did we think anything else could happen. It was only a question of time. We were so sure about it that we never spoke of it.

After finishing my course of studies, I became a lawyer; and, when I received my first appointment in a treasury office, one day I drew Fanny's hand within mine, and said to her:

"Fanny dear, you remember the story of Jacob in the Bible?"

"Yes."

"Do you not think Jacob was an excellent fellow, in that he could serve seven years to win his wife?"

"I cannot deny that he was."

"Then you must acknowledge that I am still more excellent for I have already served eight years—to win you."

Fanny looked up at me with those eyes of the summer-morning smile, and with childish happiness replied:

"And to prove your excellence still further, you must wait two years more."

"Why?" I asked, downcast.

"Why?" she said with quiet earnestness. "Do you not know there is a vacant place at our table; and until that is filled, there can be no gladness in this house. Could you be happy, if you had to read every day in your mother's eyes the query, 'where is that other?' All your gladness would wound that suffering heart, and every dumb look she gave would be a reproach for our gladness. Oh, Desi, no marriage is possible here, as long as mourning lasts."

And as she said this to prevent me loving her, she only forced me to love her the more.

"How far above me you are!"

"Why those two short years will fly away, as the rest. Our thoughts for each other do not date from yesterday, and, as we grow old, we shall have time enough to grow happy. I shall wait, and in this waiting I have enough gladness."

Oh how I would have loved to kiss her for those words: but that face was so holy before me, I should have considered it a sacrilege to touch it with my lips.

"We remain then as we were."

"Very well."

"Not a word of it for two years yet, when you are released from your word of honor you gave to Lorand, and may discover his whereabouts. Why this long secrecy? That I cannot understand. I have never had any ambition to dive more deeply into your secret than you yourselves have allowed me to: but if you made a promise, keep it; and if by this promise you have thrown your family, yourself, and me into ten years' mourning, let us wear it until it falls from us."

I grasped the dear girl's hand, I acknowledged how terribly right she was; then with her gay, playful humor she hurried back to mother, and no one could have fancied from her face, that she could be serious for a moment.

I risked one more audacious attempt in this matter.

I wrote to Lorand, putting before him that the horizon all round was already so clear, that he might march round the country to the sound of trumpets, announcing that he is so and so, without finding anyone to arrest him, as it was the same whether it was ten years or eight, he might let us off the last two years, and admit us to him.

Lorand wrote back these short lines in answer:

"We do not bargain about that for which we gave our word of honor."

It was a very brief refusal.

I troubled him no more with that request. I waited and endured, while the days passed.... Ah, Lorand, for your sake I sacrificed two years of heaven on earth!

CHAPTER XX

THE FATAL DAY!

It had come at last!

We had already begun to count the days that remained.

One week before the final day, I received a letter from Lorand, in which he begged me not to go to meet him at Lankadomb, but rather to give a rendezvous in Szolnok: he did not wish the scene of rapture to be spoiled by the sarcasms of Topándy.

I was just as well pleased.

For days all had been ready for the journey. I hunted up everything in the way of a souvenir which I had still from those days ten years before when I had parted from Lorand, even down to that last scrap of paper,[70] which now occupied my every thought.

> [70] The paper of Madame Bálnokházy's letter which was used for the fatal lot-drawing.

It would have been labor lost on my part to tell the ladies how bad the roads in the lowlands are at that time of year, that in any case Lorand would come to them a day later. Nor indeed did I try to dissuade them from making the journey. Which of them would have remained home at such a time? Which of them would have given up a single moment of that day, when she might once more embrace Lorand? They both came to me.

We arrived at Szolnok one day before Lorand: I only begged them to remain in their room until I had spoken with Lorand.

They promised and remained the whole day in one room of the inn, while I strolled the whole day about the courtyard on the watch for every arriving carriage.

An unusual number of guests came on that day to the inn: gay companions of Topándy from the neighborhood, to whom Lorand had given a rendezvous there. Some I knew personally, the others by reputation; the latter's acquaintance too was soon made.

It struck me as peculiar that Lorand had written to me that he did not wish the elegiac tone of our first gathering to be disturbed by the voice of the stoics of Lankadomb, yet he had invited the whole Epicurean alliance here—a fact which was likely to give a dithyrambic tone to our meeting.

Well, amusement there must be. I like fellows who amuse themselves.

It was late evening when a five-horsed coach drove into the courtyard—in the first to get out I recognized Gyáli.

What did he want among us?

After him stepped out a brisk old man whose moustache and eyebrows I remembered of old. It was my uncle, Topándy.

Remarkable!

Topándy came straight towards me.

So serious was his face, when, as he reached me, he grasped my hand, that he made me feel quite confused.

"You are Desiderius Áronffy?" he said: and with his two hands seized my shoulders, that he might look into my eyes. "Though you do not say so, I recognize you. It is just as if I saw your departed father before me. The very image!"

Many had already told me that I was very like what my father had been in his young days.

Topándy embraced me feelingly.

"Where is Lorand?" I inquired. "Has he not come?"

"He is coming behind us in a wagon," he answered, and his voice betrayed the greatest emotion. "He will soon be here. He does not like a coach. Remain here and wait for him."

Then he turned to his comrades who were buzzing around him.

"Let us go and wait inside, comrades. Let us leave these young fellows to themselves when they meet. You know that such a scene requires no audience. Well, right about face, quick march!"

Therewith he drove all the fellows from the corridor: indeed did not give Gyáli time to say how glad he was to meet me again.

The gathering became all the more unintelligible to me.

Why, if Topándy himself knew best what there was to be felt in that hour, what necessity had we to avoid him?

Now the wagon could be heard! The two steeds galloped into the courtyard at a smart pace with the light road-cart. He was driving himself.

I scarcely recognized him. His great whiskers, his closely-cropped hair, his dust-covered face made quite a different figure before me from that which I had been wont to draw in my album,—as I had thought to see, as mother or grandmother directed me, saying "that is missing, that feature is other, that is more, that is less, that is different," times without number we had amused ourselves with that.

Lorand was unlike any portrait of him I had drawn. He was a muscular, powerful, rough country cavalier.

As he leaped out of the wagon, we hastened to each other.

The centre of the courtyard was not the place to play an impassioned scene in. Besides neither of us like comedy playing.

"Good evening, old fellow."

"Good evening, brother."

That was all we said to each other: we shook hands, kissed each other, and hurried in from the courtyard, straight to the room filled with roysterers.

They received Lorand with wall-shaking "hurrahs," and Lorand greeted them all in turn.

Some embittered county orator wished to deliver a speech in his honor, but Lorand told him to keep that until wine was on the table: dry toasts were not to his taste.

Then he again returned to my side and took my face in his hands.

"By Jove! old fellow, you have quite grown up! I thought you were still a child going to school. You are half a head taller than I am. Why I shall live to see you married without my knowing or hearing anything about it."

I took Lorand's arm and drew him into a corner.

"Lorand, mother and grandmother are here too."

He wrenched his arm out of my hand.

"Who told you to do that?" he growled irritatedly.

"Quietly, my dear Lorand. I have committed no blunder even in formalities. It will be ten years to-morrow since you told me I might in ten years tell mother where you are. Then you wrote to me to be at Szolnok to-day. I have kept my promise to mother as regards telling her to-morrow and to you by my appearance here. Szolnok is two days distant from our home:—so I had to bring them here in order to do justice to both my promises."

Lorand became unrestrainedly angry.

"A curse upon every pettifogger in the world! You have swindled me out of my most evident right."

"But, dear Lorand, are you annoyed that the poor dear ones can see you one day earlier?"

"That's right, begin like that.—Fool, we wanted to have a jolly evening all to ourselves, and you have spoilt it."

"But you can enjoy yourselves as long as you like."

Debts of Honor

"Indeed? 'As long as we like,' and I must go in a tipsy drunken state to introduce myself to mother?"

"It is not your habit to be drunk."

"What do you know? I'm fairly uproarious once I begin at it. It was a foolish idea of yours, old fellow."

"Well, do you know what? Put the meeting first, after that the carousal."

"I have told you once for all that we shall make no bargains, sir advocate. No transactions here, sir advocate!"

"Don't 'sir advocate' me!"

"Wait a moment. If you could be so cursedly exact in your calculation of days, I shall complete your astronomical and chronological studies. Take out your watch and compare it with mine. It was just 11:45 by the convent clock in Pressburg, when you gave me your word. To-morrow evening at 11:45 you are free from your obligation to me: then you can do with me what you like."

I found his tone very displeasing and turned aside.

"Well don't be dispirited," said Lorand, drawing me towards him and embracing me. "Let us not be angry with each other: we have not been so hitherto. But you see the position I am in. I have gathered together a pack of dissolute scamps and atheists, not knowing you would bring mother with you, and they have been my faithful comrades ten years. I have passed many bad, many good days with them: I cannot say to them 'Go, my mother is here.' Nor can I sit here among them till morning with religious face. In the morning we shall all be 'soaked.' Even if I conquer the wine, my head will be heavy after it. I have need of the few hours I asked you for to collect myself, before I can step into my dear ones' presence with a clear head. Explain to them how matters stand."

"They know already, and will not ask after you until to-morrow."

"Very well. There is peace between us, old fellow."

Debts of Honor

When the company saw we had explained matters to each other, they all crowded round us, and such a noise arose that I don't know even now what it was all about. I merely know that once or twice Pepi Gyáli wished to catch my eye to begin some conversation, and that at such times I asked the nearest man, "How long do you intend to amuse yourselves in this manner?" "How are you?" and similar surprising imbecilities.

Meanwhile the long table in the middle of the room had been laid: the wines had been piled up, the savory victuals were brought in; outside in the corridors a gypsy band was striking up a lively air, and everybody tried to get a seat.

I had to sit at the head of the table, near Lorand. On Lorand's left sat Topándy, on his right, beside me, Pepi Gyáli.

"Well, old fellow, you too will drink with us to-day?" said Lorand to me playfully, putting his arms familiarly round my neck.

"No, you know I never drink wine."

"Never? Not to-day either? Not even to my health?"

I looked at him. Why did he wish to make me drink to-day especially?

"No, Lorand. You know I am bound by a promise not to drink wine, and a man of honor always keeps his promises, however absurd."

I shall never forget the look which Lorand gave me at these words.

"You are right, old fellow:" and he grasped my hand. "A man of honor keeps his promises, however absurd...."

And as he said so, he was so serious, he gazed with such alarming coldness into the eyes of Gyáli, who sat next to him. But Pepi merely smiled. He could smile so tenderly with those handsome girlish round lips of his.

Lorand patted him on the shoulder.

"Do you hear, Pepi? My brother refused to drink wine, because a man of honor keeps his promises. You are right, Desi. Let him who says something keep his word."

Then the banquet began.

It is a peculiar study for an abstainer to look on at a midnight carousal, with a perfectly sober head, and to be the only audience and critic at this "divina comedia" where everyone acts unwittingly.

The first act commenced with the toasts. He to whom God had given rhetorical talent raises his glass, begs for silence,—which at first he receives and later not receiving tries to assure for himself by his stentorian voice;—and with a very serious face, utters very serious phrases:—one is a master of grace, another of pathos: a third quotes from the classics, a fourth humorizes, and himself laughs at his success, while everybody finishes the scene with clinking of glasses, and embraces, to the accompaniment of clarion "hurrahs."

Later come more fiery declamations, general outbursts of patriotic bitterness. Brains become more heated, everyone sits upon his favorite hobby-horse, and makes it leap beneath him; the socialist, the artist, the landlord, the champion of order, everyone begins to speak of his own particular theme—without keeping to the strict rules of conversation that one waits until the other has finished: rather they all talk at once, one interrupting the other, until finally he who has commenced some thrilling refrain hands over the leadership to all: the song becomes general, and each one is convinced from hearing his own vocal powers, that nowhere on earth can more lovely singing be heard.

And meantime the table becomes covered with empty bottles.

Then the paroxysm grows by degrees to a climax. He who previously delivered an oration now babbles, comes to a standstill, and, cuts short his discomfiture by swearing; there sits one who had already three times begun upon some speech, but his bitterness, mourning for the past, so effectually chokes his over-ardent feelings that he bursts into tears, amidst general laughter. Another who has already embraced all his comrades in turn, breaks in among the gypsies and kisses them one after the other, swearing brotherhood to the bass fiddler and the clarinetist. At the farther end of the table sits a choleric fellow, whose habit it is always to end in riotous fights, and he begins his freaks by striking the table with his fist, and swearing he will kill the man who has worried him. Luckily he does not know with whom he is angry. The gay singer is not content with giving full play to his throat, helping it out with his hands and feet: he begins to dash bottles and plates against the wall, and is delighted that so many smashed bottles give evidence of his triumph. With a half crushed hat he dances in the middle of the room quite alone, in the happy conviction that everybody is looking at him, while a blessed comrade had come to the pass of dropping his head back upon the back of his chair, only waking up when they summon him to drink with him—though he does not know whether he is drinking wine or tanner's ooze.

But the fever does not increase indefinitely.

Like other attacks of fever, it has a crisis, beyond which a turn sets in!

After midnight the uproarious clamor subsided. The first heating influence of the wine had already worked itself out. One or two who could not fight with it, gave in and lay down to sleep, while the others remained in their places, continuing the drinking-bout, not for the sake of inebriety, merely out of principle, that they might show they would not allow themselves to be overcome by wine.

This is where the real heroes' part begins, of those whom the first glass did not loosen, nor the tenth tie their tongues.

Now they begin to drink quietly and to tell anecdotes between the rounds.

One man does not interrupt another, but when one has finished his story, another says, "I know one still better than that," and begins: "the matter happened here or there, I myself being present."

The anecdotes at times reached the utmost pitch of obscenity and at such times I was displeased to hear Lorand laugh over such jokes as expressed contempt for womankind.

Debts of Honor

I was only calmed by the thought that "our own" were long in bed—it was after midnight—and so it were impossible for mother or someone else out of curiosity to be listening at the keyhole, waiting for Lorand's voice.

All at once Lorand took over the lead in the conversation.

He introduced the question "Which is the most celebrated drinking nation in the world?"

He himself for his part immediately said he considered the Germans were the most renowned drinkers.

This assertion naturally met with great national opposition.

They would not surrender the Magyar priority in this respect either.

Two peacefully-inclined spirits interfered, trying to produce a united feeling by accepting the Englishman, then the Servian as the first in drinking matters—a proviso which naturally did not satisfy either of the disputing parties. Lorand, alone against the united opinion of the whole company, had the audacity to assert that the Germans were the greatest drinkers in the world. He produced celebrated examples to prove his theory.

"Listen to me! Once Prince Batthyány sent two barrels of old Göncz wine to the Brothers of Hybern. But the duty to be paid on good Magyar wine beyond the Lajta[71] was terrible. The recipients would have had to pay for the wine twenty gold pieces[72]—a nice sum. So the Brothers, to avoid paying and to prevent the wine being lost, drank the contents of the two barrels outside the frontier."

[71] A river near Pressburg, the boundary between Austria and Hungary.

[72] Probably 200 florins.

Ah, they could produce drinkers three times or four times as great, this side of the Lajta!

But Lorand would not give in.

"Well, your namesake, Pépó Henneberg," related Lorand, turning to Gyáli, "introduced the custom of drawing a string through the ears of his guests, who sat down at a long table with him, and compelled them all to drain their beakers to the dregs, whenever he drank, under penalty of losing the ends of their ears."

"With us that is impossible, for we have no holes bored in our ears!" cried one.

"We drink without compulsion!" replied another.

"The Magyar does all a German can do!"

That assertion, loudly shouted, was general.

"Even draining glasses as they did at Wartburg?" cried Lorand.

"What the devil was the custom at Wartburg?"

"The revellers at Wartburg, when they were in high spirits used to load a pistol, and then to fill the barrel to the brim with wine: then they cocked the trigger, and drained this curious glass one after another for friendship's sake."

(I see you, Lorand!)

"Well, which of you is inclined to follow the German cavaliers' example?"

Topándy interrupted.

"I for one am not, and Heaven forbid you should be."

"I am."

—Which remark came from Gyáli, not Lorand.

I looked at him. The fellow had remained sober. He had only tasted the wine, while others had drunk it.

"If you are inclined, let us try," said Lorand.

"With pleasure, only you must do it first."

"I shall do so, but you will not follow me."

"If you do it, I shall too. But I think you will not do it before me."

One idea flashed clearly before me and chilled my whole body. I saw all: I understood all now: the mystery of ten years was no longer a secret to me: I saw the refugee, I saw the pursuer, and I had both in my hand, in such an iron grip, as if God had lent me for the moment the hand of an archangel.

You just talk away.

Lorand's face was a feverish red.

"Well, well, you scamp! Let us bet, if you like."

"What?"

"Twenty bottles of champagne, which we shall drink too."

"I accept the wager."

"Whoever withdraws from the jest loses the bet."

"Here's the money!"

Both took their purses and placed each a hundred florins on the table.

I too produced my purse and took a crumpled paper out of it:—but it was no banknote.

Lorand cried to the waiter.

"Take my pistols out of my trunk."

The waiter placed both before him.

"Are they really loaded?" inquired Gyáli.

"Look into the barrels, where the steel head of the bullets are smiling at you."

Gyáli found it wiser to believe than to look into the pistol barrels.

"Well, the bet stands; whichever of us cannot drink out his portion pays for the champagne."

Lorand seized his glass to pour the red wine that was in it into the pistol-barrel.

The whole company was silent: some agonized restraint ruled their intoxicated nerves: every eye was rested on Lorand as if they wished to check the mad jest before its completion. On Topándy's forehead heavy beads of sweat glistened.

I quietly placed my hand on Lorand's, in which he held the weapon and amid profound silence asked:

"Would it not be good to draw lots to see who shall do it first?"

Both looked at me in confusion when I mentioned drawing lots.

Could their secret have been discovered?

"Only if you draw lots about it," I continued quietly, "don't omit to be quite sure about the writing of each other's name, lest there be a repetition of that farce which took place ten years ago, when you drew lots as to who was to dance with the white elephant."

I saw Gyáli turn as white as paper.

"What farce?" he panted, beginning to rise from his chair.

"You always were a jesting boy, Pepi: at that time you made me draw lots for you, and told me to put both the one I had drawn and the other in the grate: but instead of doing so I threw the dance programme in the fire, and put those papers aside and kept them. You, instead of your own, wrote my brother's name on the paper, and so whichever was drawn, Lorand Áronffy must have come out of the hat. Look, the two lottery tickets are still in my possession, those same two pieces of paper, a sheet of note paper torn in two, both with the same name on them, and on the other side the writing of Madame Bálnokházy."

Gyáli rose from his seat like one who had seen a ghost, and gazed at me with a look of stone.

Yet I had not threatened him. I had merely playfully jested with him. I smilingly spread out the two pieces of lilac-colored papers, which so exactly fitted together.

But Lorand with flashing eyes glared at him, and as the dignified upright figure stood opposite him, threw the contents of the glass he held in his hand into the fellow's face, so that the red wine splashed all over his laced white waistcoat.

Gyáli with his serviette wiped from his face the traces of insult and with dignified coldness said:

"With men in such a condition no dispute is possible. We cannot answer the taunts of drunken men."

Therewith he began to back towards the door.

Everybody, in amazement at this scene, allowed him to go: for all the world as if everyone had suddenly begun to be sober, and at the first surprise no one knew how to think what should now happen.

But I ... I was not drunk. I had no need to become sober.

I leaped up from my place, with one bound came up to the departing man, and seized him before he could reach the door, just as a furious tiger fastens up a miserable dormouse.

"I am not drunk! I have never drunk wine, you know," I cried losing all self-restraint, and pressing him against the wall so that he shivered like a bat.—"I shall be the one to throw that cursed forgery in your face, miserable wretch!"

And I know well that that single blow would have been the last chapter in his life—which would have been a great pity, not as far as he was concerned, but for my own sake—had not Heaven sent a guardian angel to check me in my wickedness.

Suddenly someone behind seized the hand raised to strike. I looked back, and my arm dropped useless at my side.

It was Fanny who had seized my arm.

"Desi," cried my darling in a frightened voice: "This hand is mine: you must not defile it."

I felt she was right. I allowed my uncontrollable anger to be overcome; with my left hand I threw the trembling wretch out of the door—I do not know where he fell—and then I turned round to clasp Fanny to my breast.

Already mother and grandmother were in the room.

The poor women had spent the whole evening of agony in the neighboring room, keeping perfectly still, so as not to betray their presence there, with the intention of listening for Lorand's voice: and they had trembled through that last awful scene, of which they could hear every word. When they heard my cry of rage, they could restrain themselves no longer, but rushed in, and threw themselves among the revellers with a cry of "My son, my son."

Everyone rose at their honored presence: this solemn picture, two kneeling women embracing a son snatched from the jaws of death.

The surprising horror had reduced everyone to soberness: all tipsiness, all winy drowsiness, had passed away.

"Lorand, Lorand," sobbed mother, pressing him frantically to her breast, while grandmother, unable to speak or to weep, clutched his hand.

"Oh Lorand, dear...."

But Lorand grasped the two ladies' hands and led them towards me.

"It is him you must embrace, not me: his is the triumph."

Then he caught sight of that sweet angel bowed upon my shoulder, who was still holding my hand in hers: he recollected those words with which Fanny a moment before had betrayed our secret. "This hand is mine"—and he smiled at me.

"Is that the way matters stand? Then you have your reward in your hands, ... and you can leave these two weeping women to me."

Therewith he threw himself on his face upon the floor before them, and embracing their feet kissed the dust beneath them.

"Oh, my darlings! My loved ones."

CHAPTER XXI

THAT LETTER

What those who had so long waited, spoke and thought during that night cannot be written down. These are sacred matters, not to be exposed to the public gaze.

Lorand confessed all, and was pardoned for all.

And he was as happy in that pardon as a child who had been again received into favor.

Lorand indeed felt as if he were beginning his life now at the point where ten years before it had been interrupted, and as if all that happened during ten years had been merely a dream, of which only the heavy beard of manhood remained.

It was very late in the morning when he and Desiderius woke. Sleep had proved very pleasant for once.

Sleep—and in place of death too.

"Well old fellow," said Lorand to his brother, "I owe you one more adventurous joke, with which I wish to surprise you."

The threat was uttered so good-humoredly that Desiderius had no cause to be frightened, but he said quietly: "Tell me what it is."

Lorand laughed.

"I shall not go home with you now."

"Well, and what shall you do?" inquired Desiderius quite as astonished as Lorand had expected.

"I shall escape from you," he said, shaking his head good-humoredly.

"Ah, that is an audacious enterprise! But tell me, where are you going to escape to?"

"Ha, ha! I shall not merely tell you where I am going, but I shall take you with me to look after me henceforward as you have done hitherto."

"You are very wise to do so.—May I know whither?"

"Back to Lankadomb."

"To Lankadomb? Perhaps you have lost something there?"

"Yes, my senses.—Well don't look at me so curiously as if you wished to ask whether I ever had any. You and this little girl quite understand each other. I see that mother and grandmother too are sufficiently in love with her to give her to you: but my blessing has yet to come, old man—that you have not received yet."

"Hope assures me that perhaps I have softened your hard heart."

"Not all at once. I shall tell you something."

"I am all ears."

"In my will I passed over all my worldly wealth to you: the sealed letter is in your possession. As far as I know you, I believe I shall cause you endless joy by asking back my will from you, and telling you that you will now be poorer by half your wealth, for the other half I require."

"I know that without waiting for you to teach me. But what has your old testament to do with the gospel of my heart?"

"Oh your head must be very dense, old fellow, if you don't understand yet. Then listen to my ultimatum. I refuse to give my consent to your marrying—before me."

Desiderius threw himself on Lorand's neck; he understood now.

"There is somebody you love?"

Lorand assented with a smile.

"Of course there is. But—you know how that blackguard (by Jove, you gave him a powerful shaking!) confused my calculation for an entire life. I could not make her understand about that of which the continuation begins only to-day. Still, all the more reason for hastening. A half hour is necessary to tell another all about it, half an hour in a carriage: they will remain here meanwhile. We shall fly to Topándy at Lankadomb: by evening we shall have finished all, and to-morrow we shall be here again, like two flying madmen, who are striving to see which can carry the other off more rapidly towards the goal—where happiness awaits him. I shall drive the horses to Lankadomb, you can drive them back."

"Poor horses!"

Desiderius did not dare to go himself with these glad tidings to his mother. He entrusted Fanny to prepare her for them—perhaps so much delight would have killed her.

They told her Lorand had official business which called him to Lankadomb for one day; and they started together with Topándy.

Topándy was let into the secret, and considered it his duty to go with Lorand—he might be required to give the bride away.

The world around Lorand had changed—at least so he thought, but the change in reality was within him.

He was indeed born again: he had become quite a different man from the Lorand of yesterday. The noisy good-humor of yesterday badly concealed the resolve that despised death, just as the dreaminess of to-day openly betrayed the happiness that filled his heart.

The whole way Desiderius could scarcely get one word from him, but he might easily read in his face all upon which he was meditating: and if he did utter once or twice encomiums on the beautiful May fields, Desiderius could see that his heart too felt spring within it.

How beautiful it was to live again, to be happy and gay, to have hopes, expect good in the future, to love and be proud in one's love, to go with head erect, to be all in all to someone!

At noon they arrived at Lankadomb.

Czipra ran out to meet them and clapped her hands.

"You were driven away; how did you get back so soon? Well no one expected you to dinner."

Lorand was the first to leap off the cart, and tenderly offered his hand to the girl.

"We have arrived, my dear Czipra. Even if you did not expect us to dinner, you can give us some of your own."

"Oh, no," said the girl in a whisper, blushing at the same time, "I have been accustomed to eat at the servant's table, when you were not at home, and you have brought a guest too. Who is that gentleman?"

"My brother, Desi, a very good fellow. Kiss him, Czipra."

Czipra did not wait to be told twice, and Desiderius returned the kiss.

"Now give him a room: to-day we shall stay here. Send up water to my room, we have got very dusty on the way, although we wished to be handsome to-day."

"Indeed?"—Czipra took Desiderius' hand, and as she led him to his room, asked him the whole history of his life: where he lived: why he had not visited Lorand sooner: was he married already, and would he ever come back there again?

Desiderius had learned from Lorand's letters about Czipra that he might readily answer any question the poor girl might ask, and might at first sight tell her every secret of his heart. Czipra was delighted.

Lorand, however, did not wait for Topándy, who was coming behind, but rushed to his room.

That letter, that letter!—it had been on his mind the whole way.

His first duty was to take it out of the closed drawer and read it over.

He did not deliberate long now whether to break the seal or not: and the envelope tore in his hand, as the seal would not yield.

And then he read the following words:

"Sir:

"That minute, in which I learned your name, raised a barrier for ever between us. The recollections which are a burden upon you, cannot be continued by an alliance between us. You who dragged my mother down into misfortune, and then faithlessly deserted her, cannot insure me happiness, or expect faithfulness from me. I shall weep over Bálint Tátray, as my departed to whom my dream gave being, and whom cold truth has buried; but Lorand Áronffy I do not know. It is my duty to tell you so, and if you are, as I believe, a man of honor, you will consider it your duty, should we ever meet in life, never again to make mention of what was Bálint Tátray.

Good-bye,

"Melanie."

Lorand fell back in his chair broken-hearted.

That was the contents of the letter he had kissed—the letter which, on the threshold of the house of death he had not dared to open, lest the happiness which would beam upon him should shake the firmness of his tread. Ah, they wished to make death easy for him! To write such a letter to him! To utter such words to one she had loved!...

"Why, she is right. I was not the Joseph of the Bible: but does not love begin with pardon? Did I blame her for the possession of that ring she let fall in the water? And from whom could she know that my crime was worse than that which hung round that ring?

"And if I were steeped in that crime with which she charges me, how can an angel, who may know nothing of what happens in hell, put such a thought in these cold-blooded words.

"They wished to kill me.

"They wished to close the door behind me, as Johanna of Naples did to her husband, when he was struggling with his assassins.

"And they wished to wash clean the murderer's hands, throwing upon me the charge of having killed myself because my love was despised.

"They knew everything well, they calculated all with cold mercilessness. They waited for the hour to come, and whetted the knife before I took it in my hands.

"And yet I can never hate her! She has plunged the dagger into my heart, and I remember only the kiss she gave...."

That moment he felt a quiet pressure on his shoulder.

Confused, he looked up. Czipra was standing behind him. The poor gypsy girl could not allow anyone else to wait on Lorand: she had herself brought him the water.

The girl's face betrayed a tender fear: she might long have been observing him, unknown to him.

"What is the matter?" she asked in trembling anxiety.

Lorand could not speak. He merely showed her the letter he had read.

Czipra could not understand the writing. She did not know how one could poison another with dumb letters, could wound his heart to its depths, and murder it. She merely saw that the letter made Lorand ill.

She recognized that rose-colored paper, those fine characters.

"Melanie wrote that."

By way of reply Lorand in bitter inexpressible pain turned his gaze towards the letter.

And the gypsy girl knew what that gaze said, knew what was written in that letter: with a wild beast's passion she tore it from Lorand's hand and passionately shred it into fragments and cast it on the ground, then trampled upon its pieces, as one tramples upon running spiders.

Thereupon she hid her face in her hands and wept in Lorand's stead.

Lorand went towards her and taking her hand, said sadly:

"You see, such are not the gypsy girls whose faces are brown, who are born under tents, and who cut cards, and make that their religion."

Then with Czipra's hand in his he walked long up and down his room without a word. Neither knew what to say to the other. They merely reflected how they could comfort each other's sorrow—and could not find a way.

This melancholy reverie was interrupted by Topándy's arrival.

"Now I beg you, Czipra, if you love me—" said Lorand.

If she loved him?

"To say not a single word to anybody of what you have seen. Nothing has happened to me.—If from this moment you ever see me sad, ask me 'What is the matter?' and I shall confess to you. But *that* pale face shall never be among those for which I mourn."

Czipra was rejoiced at these words.

"Let us show cheerful faces before my uncle and brother. Let us be good-humored. No one shall see the sting within us."

"And who knows, perhaps the bee will die for it—" Czipra departed with a cheery face as she said that. At the door she turned back once more:

"The cards told me all that last night. Till midnight I kept cutting them. But the murderer always threatens you albeit the green-robed girl always defends you.—See, I am so mad—but there is nothing else in which I can believe."

"There will be something else, Czipra," said Lorand. "Now I am going away with my brother to celebrate his marriage, then I shall return again."

Thereupon there was no more need to insist on Czipra's being good-humored the whole day. Her good-humor came voluntarily.

Poor girl, so little was required to make her happy.

Lorand, as soon as Czipra was gone, collected from the floor the torn, trampled paper fragments, carefully put them together on the table, until the note was complete, then read it over once again.

Before the door of his room he heard steps, and gay talk intermingled with laughter. Topándy and Desiderius had come to see him. Lorand blew the fragments off the table: they flew in all directions: he opened the door and joined the group, a third smiling figure.

CHAPTER XXII

THE UNCONSCIOUS PHANTOM

What were they laughing at so much?

"Do you know what counsel Czipra gave us?" said Topándy. "As she did not expect us to dinner, she advised us to go to Sárvölgyi's, where there will be a great banquet to-day. They are expecting somebody."

"Who will probably not arrive in time for dinner," added Desiderius.

Czipra joined the conversation from the extreme end of the corridor.

"The old housekeeper from Sárvölgyi's was here to visit me. She asked for the loan of a pie-dish and ice: for Mr. Gyáli is expected to arrive to-day from Szolnok."

"Bravo!" was Topándy's remark.

"And as I see you have left the young gentleman behind, just go yourselves to taste Mistress Boris's pies, or she will overwhelm me again with curses."

"We shall go, Czipra," said Lorand: "Yes, yes, don't laugh at the idea. Get your hat, Desi: you are well enough dressed for a country call: let us go across to Sárvölgyi's."

"To Sárvölgyi's?" said Czipra, clasping her hands, and coming closer to Lorand. "You will go to Sárvölgyi's?"

"Not just for Sárvölgyi's sake," said Lorand very seriously,—"who is in other respects a very righteous pious fellow; but for the sake of his guests, who are old friends of Desi's.—Why, I have not yet told you, Desi. Madame Bálnokházy and her daughter are staying here with Sárvölgyi on a matter of some legal business. You cannot overlook them, if you are in the same village with them."

"I might go away without seeing them," replied Desiderius indifferently; "but I don't mind paying them a visit, lest they should think I had purposely avoided them. Have you spoken with them already?"

"Oh yes. We are on very good terms with one another."

Lorand sacrificed the caution he had once exercised in never writing a word to Desiderius about Melanie. It seemed Desi did not run after her either; what had his childish ideal come to? Another ideal had taken its place.

"Besides, seeing that Gyáli is the ladies' solicitor, and seeing that you, my dear friend, have *'manupropria'* despatched Gyáli out of Szolnok—he immediately took the post-chaise and is already in Pest, or perhaps farther—it is your official duty to give an explanation to those who are waiting for their solicitor and to tell them where you have put their man—if you have courage enough to do so."

Desiderius at first drew back, but later his calm confidence and courage immediately confirmed his resolution.

"What do you say,—if I have courage? You shall soon see. And you shall see, too, what a lawyer-like defence I am able to improvise. I wager that if I put the case before them, they will give the verdict in our favor."

"Do so, I beseech you," said Lorand, soliciting his brother with humorously clasped hands.

"I shall do so."

"Well be quick: get your hat, and let us go."

Desiderius with determined steps went in search of his hat.

Czipra laughed after him. She saw how ridiculous it would be. He was going to calumniate the bridegroom before the bride. With what words she herself did not know: but she gathered from the gentlemen's talk that Gyáli had been driven from the company the night before for some flagrant dishonor. Since two days she too had detested that fellow.

Debts of Honor

Lorand meanwhile gazed after his brother with eyes flashing with a desire for vengeance.

Topándy grasped Lorand's hand.

"If I believed in cherubim, I should say: a persecuting angel had taken up his abode in you, to whisper that idea to you. Do you know, Desiderius is the very double of what your father was when he came home from the academy: the same face, figure, depth of voice, the same lightning fire in his eyes, and that same murderous frown, and you are now going to take that boy before Sárvölgyi that he may relate an awful story of a man who wished to murder a good friend in the most devilish manner, just as he did!"

"Hush! Desi of that knows not a word."

"So much the better. A living being, who does not suspect that to the man whom he is visiting, he is the most horrible phantom from the other world! The murdered father, risen up in the son! — It will make me acknowledge one of the ideas I have hitherto denied — the existence of hell."

Desiderius returned.

"Look at us, my dear Czipra," said Lorand to the girl, who was always fluttering around him: "are we handsome enough? Will the eyes of the beautiful rest upon us?"

"Go," answered Czipra, pushing Lorand in playful anger, "as if you didn't know yourselves! Rather take care you don't get lost there. Such handsome fellows are readily snapped up."

"No, Czipra, we shall return to you," said Lorand, pressing Czipra so tenderly to him, that Desiderius considered as superfluous any further questions as to why Lorand had brought him there. He approved his brother's choice: the girl was beautiful, natural, good-humored and, so it seemed, in love with him. What more could be required? — "Don't be afraid, Czipra; nobody's beautiful blue eyes shall detain us there."

"I was not afraid for your sakes of beautiful eyes," replied Czipra, "but of Mistress Boris's pies:—such pies cannot be got here."

Thereat all three laughed—finally Desiderius too, though he did not know what kind of mythological monster such a sadly bewitched cake might be, which came from Mistress Boris's hand.

Topándy embraced the two young fellows. He was sorry he could not accompany them, but begged Lorand notwithstanding to remain as long as he liked.

Czipra followed them to the door. Lorand there grasped her hand, and tenderly kissed it. The girl did not know whether to be ashamed or delighted.

Thrice did Lorand turn round, before they reached Sárvölgyi's home, to wave his hand to Czipra.

Desiderius did not require any further enlightenment on that point. He thought he understood all quite well.

Mistress Boris meanwhile had a fine job at her house.

"He was a fool who conceived the idea of ordering a banquet for an indefinite time:—not to know whether he, for whom one must wait, will come at one, at two, at three,—in the evening, or after midnight."

Twenty times she ran out to the door to see whether he was coming already or not. Every sound of carriage wheels, every dog-bark enticed her out into the road, from whence she returned each time more furious, pouring forth invectives over the spoiling of all her dishes.

"Perhaps that gypsy girl again! Devil take the gypsy girl! She is quite capable of giving this guest a breakfast there first, and then letting him go. It would be madness surely, seeing that the town gentleman is the fiancé of the young lady here: but the gypsy girl too has cursed bright eyes. Besides she is very cunning, capable of bewitching any man. The damned gypsy girl,—her spells make her cakes always rise beautifully, while mine wither away in the boiling fat—although they are made of the same flour, and the same yeast."

It would not have been good for any one of the domestics to show herself within sight of Mistress Borcsa[73] at that moment.

   [73] Boris.

"Well, my master has again burdened me with a guest who thinks the clock strikes midday in the evening. It was a pity he did not invite him for yesterday, in that case he might have turned up to-day. Why, I ought to begin cooking everything afresh.

"I may say, he is a fine bridegroom for a young lady, who lets people wait for him. If I were the bridegroom of such a beautiful young lady, I should come to dinner half a day earlier, not half a day later. There will be nice scenes, if he has his cooking ever done at home. But of course at Vienna that is not the case, everybody lives on restaurant fare. There one may dine at six in the afternoon. At any rate, what midday diners leave is served up again for the benefit of later comers:—thanks, very much."

Finally the last bark which Mistress Boris did not deign even to notice from the kitchen, heralded the approach of manly footsteps in the verandah: and when in answer to the bell Mistress Boris rushed to the door, to her great astonishment she beheld, not the gentleman from Vienna, but the one from across the way, with a strange young gentleman.

"May I speak with the master?" inquired Lorand of the fiery Amazon.

"Of course. He is within. Haven't you brought the gentleman from Vienna?"

"He will only come after dinner," said Lorand, who dared to jest even with Mistress Boris.

Then they went in, leaving Mistress Boris behind, the prey of doubt.

"Was it real or in jest? What do *they* want here? Why did they not bring him whom they took away? Will they remain here long?"

The whole party had gathered in the grand salon.

They too thought that the steps they heard brought the one they were expecting—and very impatiently too.

Gyáli had informed them he would take a carriage and return, as soon as he could escape from the revelry at Szolnok. Melanie and her mother were dressed in silk: on Melanie's wavy curls could be seen the traces of a mother's careful hand: and Madame Bálnokházy herself made a very impressive picture, while Sárvölgyi had put on his very best.

They must have prepared for a very great festival here to-day!

But when the door opened before the three figures that courteously hastened to greet the new-comer, and the two brothers stepped in, all three smiling faces turned to expressions of alarm.

"You still dare to approach me?"—that was Melanie's alarm.

"You are not dead yet?" inquired Madame Bálnokházy's look of Lorand.

"You have risen again?" was the question to be read in Sárvölgyi's fixed stare that settled on Desiderius' face.

"My brother, Desiderius,"—said Lorand in a tone of unembarrassed confidence, introducing his brother. "He heard from me of the ladies being here, so perhaps Mr. Sárvölgyi will pardon us, if, in accordance with my brother's request, we steal a few moments' visit."

"With pleasure: please sit down. I am very glad to see you," said Sárvölgyi, in a husky tone, as if some invisible hand were choking his throat.

"Desiderius has grown a big boy, has he not?" said Lorand, taking a seat between Madame Bálnokházy and Melanie, while Desiderius sat opposite Sárvölgyi, who could not take his eyes off the lad.

"Big and handsome," affirmed Madame Bálnokházy. "How small he was when he danced with Melanie!"

"And how jealous he was of certain persons!"

At these words three people hinted to Lorand not to continue, Madame Bálnokházy, Melanie and Desiderius. How indiscreet these country people are!

Desiderius found his task especially difficult, after such a beginning.

But Lorand was really in a good humor. The sight of his darling of yesterday, dressed in such magnificence to celebrate the day on which her poor wretched cast-off lover was to blow his brains out, roused such a joy in his heart that it was impossible not to show it in his words. So he continued:

"Yes, believe me: the lively scamp was actually jealous of me. He almost killed me—yet we are very true to our memories."

Desiderius could not comprehend what madness had come over his brother, that he wished to bring him and Melanie together into such a false position. Perhaps it would be good to start the matter at once and interrupt the conversation.

On Madame Bálnokházy's face could be read a certain contemptuous scorn, when she looked at Lorand, as if she would say: "Well, after all, prose has conquered the poetry of honor, a man may live after the day of his death, if he has only the phlegm necessary thereto. Flight is shameful but useful,—yet you are as good as killed for all that."

This scorn would soon be wiped away from that beautiful face.

"Mesdames," said Desiderius in cold tranquillity. "Beyond paying my respects, I have another reason which made it my duty to come here. I must explain why your solicitor has not returned to-day, and why he will not return for some time."

"Great Heavens! No misfortune has befallen him?" cried Madame Bálnokházy in nervous trepidation.

"On that point you may be quite reassured, Madame: he is hale and healthy; only a slight change in his plans has taken place: he is just now flying west instead of east."

"What can be the reason?"

"I am the cause, which drove him away, I must confess."

"You?" said Madame Bálnokházy, astonished.

"If you will allow me, and have the patience for it, I will go very far back in history to account for this peculiar climax."

Lorand remarked that Melanie was not much interested to hear what they were saying of Gyáli. She was indifferent to him: why, they were already affianced.

So he began to say pretty things to her: went into raptures about her beautiful curls, her blooming complexion, and various other things which it costs nothing to praise.

As long as he had been her lover, he had never told her how beautiful she was. She might have understood his meaning. Those whom we flatter we no longer love.

Desiderius continued the story he had begun.

"Just ten years have passed since they began to prosecute the young men of the Parliament in Pressburg on account of the publication of the Parliamentary journal. There was only one thing they could not find out, viz:—who it was that originally produced the first edition to be copied: at last one of his most intimate friends betrayed the young man in question."

"That is ancient history already, my dear boy," said Madame Bálnokházy in a tone of indifference.

"Yet its consequences have an influence even to this day; and I beg you kindly to listen to my story to the end, and then pass a verdict on it. You must know your men."

(What an innocent child Desiderius was! Why, he did not seem even to suspect that the man of whom he spoke was the designated son-in-law of Madame Bálnokházy.)

"The one, who was betrayed by his friend, was my brother Lorand, and the one who betrayed his friend, was Gyáli."

"That is not at all certain," said Madame. "In such cases appearances and passion often prove deceptive mirrors. It is possible that someone else betrayed Mr. Áronffy, perhaps some fickle woman, to whom he babbled of all his secrets and who handed it on to her ambitious husband as a means of supporting his own merits."

"I know positively that my assertion is correct," answered Desiderius, "for a magnanimous lady, who guarded my brother with her fairy power, hearing of this betrayal from her influential husband, informed Lorand thereof in a letter written by her own hand."

Madame Bálnokházy bit her lips. The undeserved compliment smote her to the heart. She was the magnanimous fairy, of whom Desiderius spoke, and that fickle woman of whom she had spoken herself. The barrister was a master of repartee.

Melanie, fortunately, did not hear this, for Lorand just then entertained her with a wonderful story: how that, curiously enough, when the young lady had been at Topándy's, the hyacinths had been covered with lovely clusters of fairy bells, and how, one week later, their place had been taken by ugly clusters of berries. How could flowers change so suddenly?

"Very well," said Madame Bálnokházy, "let us admit that when Gyáli and Áronffy were students together, the one played the traitor on the other. What happened then?"

"I only learned last night what really happened. That evening I was on a visit to Lorand, and found Gyáli there. They appeared to be joking. They playfully disputed as to who, at the farewell dance, was to be the partner of that very honorable lady, who may often be seen in your company. The two students disputed in my presence as to who was to dance with the 'aunt.'"

"Of course, as a piece of unusual good fortune."

"Naturally. As neither wished to give the other preference, they finally decided to entrust the verdict to lot; on the table was a small piece of paper, the only writing material to be found in Lorand's room after a careful rummaging, as all the rest had just been burned. This piece of lilac-colored paper was torn in two, and both wrote one name: these two pieces they put in a hat and called upon me to draw out one. I did so and read out Lorand's name."

"Do you intend to relate how your brother enjoyed himself at that dance?"

Melanie had not heard anything.

"I have no intention of saying a single word more about that day—and I shall at once leap over ten years. But I must hasten to explain that the drawing had nothing to do with dancing with the 'aunt' but was the lottery of an 'American duel' caused by a conflict between Gyáli and Lorand."

Desiderius did not remark how the coppery spots on Sárvölgyi's face swelled at the words "American duel," and then how they lost their color again.

"One moment, my dear boy," interrupted Madame Bálnokházy. "Before you continue: allow me to ask one question: is it customary to speak in society of duels that have not yet taken place?"

"Certainly, if one of the principals has by his cowardly conduct made the duel impossible."

"Cowardly conduct?" said Madame Bálnokházy, darting a piercing side glance at Lorand. "That applies to you."

But Lorand was just relating to Melanie how the day-before-yesterday, when the beautiful moonlight shone upon the piano, which had remained open as the young lady had left it, soft fairy voices began suddenly to rise from it. Though that was surely no spirit playing on the keys, but Czipra's tame white weasel that, hunting night moths, ran along them.

"Yes," said Desiderius in answer to the lady. "One of the principals who accepted the condition gave evidence of such conduct on that occasion as must shut him out from all honorable company. Gyáli wrote in forged writing on that ticket the name of Lorand instead of his own."

Madame Bálnokházy incredulously pursed her lips.

"How can you prove that?"

"I did not cast into the fire, as Gyáli bade me, the two tickets, but in their stead the dance programme I had brought with me, the two tickets I put away and have kept until to-day, suspecting that perhaps there might be some rather important reason for this calculating slyness."

"Pardon me; but a very serious charge is being raised against an absent person, who cannot defend himself, and to defend whom is therefore the duty of the next and nearest person, even at the price of great indulgence. Have you any proof, any authentic evidence, that either one of the tickets you have kept is forged?"

Madame Bálnokházy had gone to great extremes in doubting the faithfulness and truth-telling of a man,—but rather too far. She had to deal with a barrister.

"The similarity admits of no doubt, Madame. Since these two slips are nothing but two halves that fit together, of that same letter in which Lorand's good-hearted fairy informed him of Gyáli's treachery; on the opposite side of the slips is still to be seen the handwriting of that deeply honored lady: the date and watermark are still on them."

Madame's bosom heaved with anger. This youth of twenty-three had annihilated her just as calmly, as he would have burnt that piece of paper of which they were speaking.

Desiderius quietly produced his pocket-book and rummaged for the fatal slips of paper.

"Never mind. I believe it," panted Madame Bálnokházy, whose face in that moment was like a furious Medusa head. "I believe what you say. I have no doubts about it:" therewith she rose from her seat and turned to the window.

Desiderius too rose from his chair, seeing the sitting was interrupted, but could not resist the temptation of pouring out the overflowing bitterness of his heart before somebody; and, as Madame was displeased and Melanie was chatting with Lorand of trifles, he was obliged to address his words directly to his only hearer, to Sárvölgyi, who remained still sitting, like one enchanted, while his gaze rested ever upon Desiderius' face. This face, drunken with rage and terror, could not tear itself from the object of its fears.

"And this fellow has allowed his dearest friend to go through life for ten years haunted with the thought of death, has allowed him to hide himself in strangers' houses, avoiding his mother's embraces. It did not occur to him once to say 'Live on; don't persecute yourself; we were children, we have played together. I merely played a joke on you.'..."

Sárvölgyi turned livid with a deathly pallor.

"Sir, you are a Christian, who believes in God, and in those who are saints: tell me, is there any torture of hell that could be punishment enough for so ruining a youth?"

Sárvölgyi tremblingly strove to raise himself on his quivering hand. He thought his last hour had come.

"There is none!" answered Desiderius to himself. "This fellow kept his hatred till the last day, and when the final anniversary came, he actually sought out his victim to remind him of his awful obligation. Oh, sir, perhaps you do not know what a terrible fatality there is in this respect in our family? So died grandfather, so it was that our dearly loved father left us; so good, so noble-hearted, but who in a bitter moment, amidst the happiness of his family turned his hand against his own life. At night we stealthily took him out to burial. Without prayer, without blessing, we put him down into the crypt, where he filled the seventh place; and that night my grandmother, raving, cursed him who should occupy the eighth place in the row of blood-victims."

Sárvölgyi's face became convulsed like that of a galvanized corpse. Desiderius thought deep sympathy had so affected the righteous man and continued all the more passionately:

"That fellow, who knew it well, and who was acquainted with our family's unfortunate ill-luck, in cold blood led his friend to the eighth coffin, to the cursed coffin—with the words 'Lie down there in it!'"

Sárvölgyi's lips trembled as if he would cry "pity: say nothing more!"

"He went with him down to the gate of death, opened the dark door before him, and asked him banteringly 'is the pistol loaded?' and when Lorand took his place amid the revellers: bade him fulfil his obligation—the perjured hound called him to his obligation!"

Sárvölgyi, all pale, rose at this awful scene:—for all the world as if Lörincz Áronffy himself had come to relate the history of his own death to his murderer.

"Then I seized Lorand's arm with my one hand, and with the other held before the wretch's eyes the evidence of his cursed falseness. His evil conscience bade him fly. I reached him, seized his throat...."

Sárvölgyi in abject terror sank back in his chair, while Madame Bálnokházy, rushing from the window, passionately cried "and killed him?"

Desiderius, gazing haughtily at her, answered calmly: "No, I merely cast him out from the society of honorable men."

To Lorand it was a savage pleasure to look at those three faces, as Desiderius spoke. The dumb passion which inflamed Madame Bálnokházy's face, the convulsive terror on the features of the fatal adversary, strove with each other to fill his heart with a great delight.

And Melanie? What had she felt during this narration, which made such an ugly figure of the man to whom fate allotted her?

Lorand's eyes were intent upon her face too.

The young girl was not so transfixed by the subject of the tale as by the speaker. Desiderius in the heat of passion, was twice as handsome as he was otherwise. His every feature was lighted with noble passion. Who knows—perhaps the beautiful girl was thinking it would be no very pleasant future to be the bride of Gyáli after such a scandal! Perhaps there returned to her memory some fragments of those fair days at Pressburg, when she and Desiderius had sighed so often side by side. That boy had been very much in love with his beautiful cousin. He was more handsome and more spirited than his brother. Perhaps her thoughts were such. Who knows?

At any rate, it is certain that when Desiderius answered Madame's question with such calm contempt—"I cast him out, I did not kill him,"—on Melanie's face could be remarked a certain radiance, though not caused by delight that her fiancé's life had been spared.

Lorand remarked it, and hastened to spoil the smile.

"Certainly you would have killed him, Desi, had not your good angel, your dear Fanny, luckily for you, intervened, and grasped your arm, saying 'this hand is mine. You must not defile it.'"

The smile disappeared from Melanie's face.

"And now," said Desiderius, addressing his remarks directly to Sárvölgyi; "be my judge, sir. What had a man, who with such sly deception, with such cold mercilessness, desired to kill, to destroy, to induce a heart in which the same blood flows as in mine—to commit a crime against the living God, what, I ask, had such a man deserved from me? Have I not a right to drive that man from every place, where he dares to appear in the light of the sun, until I compel him to walk abroad at night when men do not see him, among strangers who do not know him;—to destroy him morally with just as little mercy as he displayed towards Lorand?—Would that be a crime?"

"Great Heavens! Something has happened to Mr. Sárvölgyi," cried Madame Bálnokházy suddenly.

And indeed Sárvölgyi was very pale, his limbs were almost powerless, but he did not faint. He put his hands behind him, lest they should remark how they trembled, and strove to smile.

"Sir," he said in a hesitating voice, which often refused to serve him: "although I have nothing to say against it, yet you have told your story at an unfortunate time and in an ill-chosen place:—this young lady is Mr. Gyáli's fiancée and to-day we had prepared for the wedding."

"I am heartily glad that I prevented it," said Desiderius, without being in the least disturbed at this discovery. "I think I am doing my relations a good service by staying them at the point where they would have fallen over a precipice."

"You are a master-hand at that," said Madame Bálnokházy with scornful bitterness. She remembered how he had done her a service by a similar intervention—just ten years ago. "Well, as you have succeeded so perfectly in rescuing us from the precipice, perhaps we may hope for the honor of your presence at the friendly conclusion of this spoiled matrimonial banquet?"

Madame Bálnokházy's wandering life had whetted her cynicism.

It was a direct hint for them to go.

"We are very much obliged for the kind invitation," replied Lorand courteously, paying her back in the same coin of sweetness, "but they are expecting us at home."

"Hearts too, which one may not trifle with," continued Desiderius.

"Then, of course, we should not think of stealing you away," continued Madame Bálnokházy, touched to the quick. "Kindly greet, in our names, dear Czipra and dear Fanny. We are very fond indeed of the good girls, and wish you much good fortune with them. The arms of Áronffy, too, find an explanation therein: the half-moon will in one case mean a horse-shoe, in the other a bread-roll. Adieu, dear Lorand! Adieu, dear Desi!"

Then arm-in-arm they departed and hurried home to Topándy's house.

Madame's last outburst had thrown Desiderius into an entirely good humor. That was the first thing about which he began to converse with Topándy. Madame Bálnokházy had congratulated the Áronffy arms on the possession of a "horse-shoe" and a "roll," a gypsy girl and a baker's daughter!

But Lorand did not laugh at it:—what a fathomless deep hatred that woman must treasure in her heart against him, that she could break out so! And was she not right that woman who had desired the young man to embrace her, and thus embracing her to rush on to the precipice, into shame and death, and damnation, if he could love really:—had she no right to scorn, him who had fled before the romantic crimes of passion and had allowed her to fall alone?

At dinner Desiderius related to Topándy what he had said at Sárvölgyi's. His face beamed like that of some young student who was glorying in his first duel.

But he could not understand the effect his narration had caused. Topándy's face became suddenly more determined, more serious; he gazed often at Lorand.

Once Desiderius too looked up at his brother, who was wiping his tear-stained eyes with his handkerchief.

"You are weeping?" inquired Desiderius.

"What are you thinking of? I was only wiping my brow. Continue your story."

When they rose from table Topándy called Lorand aside.

"This young fellow knows nothing of what I related to you?"

"Absolutely nothing."

"So he has not the slightest suspicion that in that moment he plunged the knife into the heart of his father's murderer?"

"No. Nor shall he ever know it. A double mission has been entrusted to us, to be happy and to wreak vengeance. Neither of us can undertake both at once. He has started to be happy, his heart is full of sweetness, he is innocent, unsuspicious, enthusiastic: let him be happy: God forbid his days should be poisoned by such agonizing thoughts as will not let me rest!—I am enough myself for revenge, embittered as I am from head to foot. The secret is known only to us, to grandmother and the Pharisee himself. We shall complete the reckoning without the aid of happy men."

CHAPTER XXIII

THE DAY OF GLADNESS

"Let us go back at once to your darling," said Lorand next morning to his brother. "My affair is already concluded."

Desiderius did not ask "how concluded?" but thought it easy to account for this speech. It could easily be concluded between Topándy and Lorand, as the former was the girl's adopted father: Lorand had only to disclose to him everything about which it had been his melancholy duty to keep silence until the day of the catastrophe, which he was awaiting, had arrived.

Nor could Desiderius suspect that the word "concluded" referred to the visit they had paid together to Sárvölgyi. How could he have imagined that Melanie, who had been introduced to him as Gyáli's fiancée, had one week before filled Lorand's whole soul with a holy light.

And that light had indeed been extinguished forever.

Even if they had not succeeded in murdering Lorand they had made a dead man of him, such a dead man as walks, throws himself into the affairs of the world, enjoys himself and laughs—who only knows himself the day of his death.

Desiderius ventured to ask "When?"

He always thought of Czipra.

Lorand answered lightly:

"When we return."

"Whence?"

"From your wedding."

"Why, you said yours must precede mine."

"You are again playing the advocate!" retorted Lorand. "I referred not to the execution, but to the arrangements. My banns have been called before yours; that was my desire. Now it is your business to carry your affair through before I do mine. Your affair of the heart can easily be concluded in three days."

"An excellent explanation! And your marriage requires longer preparations?"

"Much longer."

"What obstacle can Czipra present?"

"An obstacle which you know very well: Czipra is still—a heathen. Now the first requisite here for marriage is the birth-certificate. You know well that Topándy has hitherto brought the poor girl up in an uncivilized manner. I cannot present her to mother in this state. She must learn to know the principles of religion, and just so much of the alphabet as is necessary for a country lady—and you must realize that several weeks are necessary for that. That is what we must wait for."

Desiderius had to acknowledge that Lorand's excuse was well-grounded.

And perhaps Lorand was not jesting? Perhaps he thought the poor girl loved him with her whole soul, and would be happy to possess these fragments of a broken heart. Yet he had not told her anything. Czipra had seen him in desperation over that letter: as far as the faithful, loving girl was concerned, it would have been merely an insult, if the idol of her heart had offered her his hand the next moment, out of mere offended pride; and, while she offered him impassioned love, given her merely cold revenge in return.

This feeling of revenge must soften. Every impulse guided to the old state of things.

Meantime the marriage of Desiderius would be a good influence. He was marrying Fanny. The young couple would, during their honeymoon, visit Lankadomb: true love was an education in itself: and then—even cemeteries grow verdant in spring.

Debts of Honor

The two young men reached Szolnok punctually at noon.

And thence they returned home.

Home, sweet home! At home in a beloved mother's house. A man visits many gay places where people enjoy themselves: finds himself at times in glorious palaces; builds himself a nest, and rears a house of his own:—but even then some sweet enchantment overcomes his heart when he steps over the threshold of that quiet dwelling where a loving mother's guardian hand has protected every souvenir of his childhood,—so that he finds everything as he left it long ago, and sees and feels that, while he has lived through the changing events of a period in his life, that loving heart has still clung to that last moment, and that the intervening time has been but as the eternal remembrance of one hour spent within those walls.

There are his childhood's toys piled up; he would love to sit down once more among them, and play with them: there are the books that delighted his childhood's days; he would love to read them anew, and learn again what he had long forgotten, what was in those days such great knowledge.

Lorand spent a happy week at home, in the course of which Mrs. Fromm took Fanny back to Pressburg.

As Desiderius had asked for Fanny's hand, it was only proper that he should take his bride away from her parents' house.

One week later the whole Áronffy family started to fetch the bride; only Desiderius' mother remained at home.

In the little house in Prince's Avenue the same old faces all awaited them, only they were ten years older. Old Márton hastened, as erstwhile, to open the carriage door; only his moving crest was as white as that of a cockatoo. Father Fromm, too, was waiting at the door, but could no longer run to meet his guests, for his left arm and leg were paralyzed: he leaned upon a long bony young man, who had spent much pains in trying to twist into a moustache by the aid of cunning unguents the few hairs on his upper lip, that would not under any circumstances consent to grow. It was easy to recognize Henrik in the young fellow who would have loved so much to smile, only that cursed waxed moustache would not allow his mouth to open very far.

"Welcome, welcome," sounded from all sides. Father Fromm opened his arms to receive the grandmother: Henrik leaped on to Desiderius' neck, while old Márton slouched up to Lorand, and, nudging him with his elbows, said with a humorous smile, "Well, no harm came of it, you see."

"No, old fellow. And I have to thank this good stick for it," said Lorand, producing from under his coat Márton's walking stick, for which he had had made a beautiful silver handle in place of the previous dog's-foot.

The old fellow was beside himself with delight that they thought so much of his relics.

"Is it true," he asked, "that you fought two highwaymen with this stick? Master Desiderius wrote to say so."

"No, only one."

"And you knocked him down?"

"It was impossible for he ran away. Now I have done my walking, and give back the stick with thanks."

But it was not the silver handle that delighted Márton so. He took the returned stick into the shop, like some trophy, and related to the assistants, how Master Lorand had, with that alone, knocked down three highwaymen. He would not have surrendered that stick for a whole Mecklenburg full of every kind of cane.

Old Grandmother Fromm, too, was still alive and counted it a great triumph that she had just finished the hundredth pair of stockings for Fanny's trousseau.

And last, but not least, Fanny, even more beautiful, even more amiable! — as if she had not seen Desiderius and his grandmother for an eternity!

"Well, you will be our daughter!"

And they all loved Desiderius so.

"What a handsome man he has grown," complimented Grandmother Fromm.

"What a good fellow!"—remarked Mother Fromm.

"What a clever fellow! How learned!" was Father Fromm's encomium.

"And what a muscular rascal!" said Henrik, overcome with astonishment that another boy too had grown as large as he. "Do you remember how one evening you threw me on to the bed? How angry I was with you then!"

"Do you remember how the first evening you put away the cake for Henrik?" said grandmamma. "How you blushed then!"

"Do you remember," interrupted Father Fromm, "the first time you addressed me in German? How I laughed at you then!"

"Well, and do you remember me?" said Fanny playfully, putting her hand on her fiancé's arm.

"When first you kissed me here," retorted Desiderius, looking into her beaming eyes.

"How you feared me then!"

"Well, and do you remember," said the young fellow in a voice void of feeling, "when I stood resting against the doorpost, and you came to drag my secret out of me. How I loved you then!"

Lorand stepped up to them, and laying his hands on their shoulders, said with a sigh:

"Forgive me for standing so long in your path!"

At that everyone's eyes filled with tears, everyone knew why.

Father Fromm, deeply moved, exclaimed:

"How happy I am,—my God!" and then as if he considered his happiness too great, he turned to Henrik, "if only you were otherwise! but look, my dear boy: nothing has come of him! *fuit negligens.* If he too had learned, he would already be an *'archivarius!'* That is what I wanted to make of him. What a fine title! An *'archivarius!'* But what has become of him? An *'asinus!' Quantus asinus*! I ought to have made a baker of him. He did not wish to be other, the fool: the *'perversus homo.'* Now he is nothing but a *'pistor.'"*

At this grievous charge poor Henrik would have longed to sink into the earth for very shame, a longing which would have met with opposition, not only from the ground-floor inhabitants, but also from the assistants working in the underground cellars.

Lorand took Henrik's part.

"Never mind, Henrik. At any rate in both families there is a good-for-nothing who can do nothing except produce bread: I am the peasant, you the baker: I thresh the wheat, you bake bread of it: let the high and mighty feast on their pride."

Then the common good-humor of the high and mighty put a good tone on the conversation. Father Fromm actually made peace though slowly with fate, and agreed that it was just as well Henrik could continue his father's business. He might find some respite in the fact that at least his second child would become a "lady."

Desiderius had a joy in store for him in that he was to meet his erstwhile Rector,[74] who was to give away the bride. The old fellow had still the same military mien, the same harsh voice, and was still as sincerely fond of Desiderius and the two families as ever.

[74] The director of the school when he was educated at Pressburg.

Lorand was to be Desiderius' best man.

In this official position he was obliged to stand on the bridegroom's left, while the latter swore before the altar, to provide for the bride's happiness "till death us do part," receiving in trust a faithful hand which even in death would not loosen its hold on his. He was the first to praise the bride for repeating after the minister so courageously and clearly those words, at which the voices of girls are wont to tremble. He was the first to raise his glass to the happy couple's health: he opened the ball with the bride: and one day later, it was he who took her back on his arm to his mother's home, saying:

"Dear sister-in-law, step into the house from which your calm face has driven all signs of mourning: embrace her who awaits you—the good mother who has to-day for the first time exchanged her black gown for that blue one in which we knew her in days of happiness. Never has bride brought a richer dowry to a bridegroom's home, than you have to ours. God bless you for it."

And even Lorand did not know how much that hand which pressed his so gently had done for him.

It is the fate of such deeds to succeed and remain obscure.

"Let the children spend their happy honeymoon in the country," was the opinion of the elder lady. "They must grow accustomed to being their own masters, too."

But the idea met with the most strenuous opposition from Desiderius' mother and Fanny. The mother's prayers were so beautiful, the bride so irresistible, that the other two, the grandmother and Lorand, finally allowed themselves to be persuaded, and agreed that the mother should stay with Desiderius.

"But we two must leave," whispered grandmother to Lorand.

She had already noticed that Lorand's face was not fit to be present in that peaceful life.

His gaiety was only for others: a grandmother's eyes could not be deceived.

While the others were engaged with their own happiness, the old lady took Lorand's hand and, without a word of "whither," they went down together to the garden, to the stream flowing beside the garden: to the melancholy house built on the bank of the stream.

Debts of Honor

Ten years had passed and the creeper had again crawled over the crypt door: the green leaves covered the motto. The two juniper trees had bowed their green branches together over the cupola.

They stayed there, her head leaning on his bosom.

How much they must have said to one another, tacitly, without a single word! How they must have understood each other's unspoken thoughts!

Deep silence reigned around: but within, inside the closed, rusted, creeper-covered door, it seemed as if someone beckoned with invisible finger, saying to the elder boy, "one great debt is not yet paid."

One hour later they returned to the house, where they were welcomed by boisterous voices of noisy gladness—master and servant were all merry and rejoicing.

"I must hasten on my way," said Lorand to his mother.

"Whither?"

"Back to Lankadomb."

"You will bring me a new joy."

"Yes, a new joy for you, mother,—and for you, too," he said pressing his grandmother's hand.

She understood what that handclasp meant.

The murderer lived still.—The account was not yet balanced! Lorand kissed his happy relations. The old lady accompanied him to the carriage, where she kissed his forehead.

"Go."

And in that kiss there was the weight of a blessing that urged him to his difficult duty.

"Go—and wreak vengeance."

CHAPTER XXIV

THE MAD JEST

Let us leave the happy ones to rejoice.

Let us follow that other youth, in whom all that sweet strength for action, which might have brought a mutually-loving heart into the ecstasy of happiness, had changed into a bitter passion, capable of driving a mutually-hating soul to destruction.

It was evening when he reached Lankadomb.

Topándy was already very impatient. Czipra informed him she would not give Lorand even time to rest himself, but took him at once with her to the laboratory, where they had been wont to be together, to study alone the mysteries of mankind and nature.

The old fellow seemed to be in an extraordinarily good humor, which in his case was generally a sign of excitement.

"Well, my dear boy," he said, "I have succeeded in getting myself tangled up in a mess. I will explain it to you. I have always desired to make the acquaintance of the county prison by reason of some meritorious stupidity; so finally I have committed something which will aid my purpose."

"Indeed?"

"Yes, indeed:—for two years at least. Ha ha! I have perpetrated such a mad jest that I am myself entirely contented. Of course they will imprison me, but that does not matter."

"What have you done now, uncle?"

"Just listen, it is a long story. First I must begin by saying that Melanie is already married."

"So much the better."

"I only hope it is for her—for me it is. But it is the turning-point of my fate too: so just listen to the end, to all the little trifling incidents of the tale—as Mistress Boris related them to Czipra, and Czipra to me. They all belong to the complete picture."

"I am all ears," said Lorand, sitting down, and determining to show a very indifferent face when they related before him the tale of Melanie's marriage.

"Well, after you left here, they knowing nothing of your departure, Madame Bálnokházy said to her daughter: 'Just for mere obstinacy's sake you must marry Gyáli: let these men see how much we care for their fables!'—therewith she wrote a letter herself to Gyáli to come back immediately to Lankadomb, and show himself: they were awaiting him with open arms. He must not be afraid of the brothers Áronffy. He must look into their faces as behooved a man of dignity. To provide against any possible insults, he must protect himself with a couple of pocket-pistols: such things he must always carry in his pocket, to display beneath the nose of anyone who attempted to frighten him with his gigantic stature!—Gyáli shortly appeared in the village again, and very ostentatiously drove up and down before my window, driving the horses himself with the ladies sitting behind, as if he hoped to take the greatest revenge upon me in this way. I merely said: 'If you are satisfied with him, it is nothing to me.' It seems that in the world of to-day the ladies like the man, upon whom others have spat, whom others have insulted and kicked out!—they know all—well, I had no wish to quarrel with their taste.

"I determined just for that reason not to do anything mad. I would be clever. I would look down upon the world's madness with contemplative philosophy, and merely carry out the clever jest of annulling my previous will in which I had made Melanie my heiress, and which had been stored away in the county archive room, making another which I shall keep here at home, in which not a single mention is made of my niece.

"The wedding was solemnized with great pomp.

"Sárvölgyi did not complain of the expense incurred. He thought to revenge himself on me. He collected all the friends he could from the vicinity: I too received a lithographed invitation. Look at that!"

Topándy took the vellum from his pocket-book and handed it to Lorand.

Dear Mr. Topándy:

It will give me great pleasure if you and your nephew Lorand Áronffy will accept our invitation to the wedding of my daughter Melanie and Joseph Gyáli, at Mr. Sárvölgyi's house.

Emilia Bálnokházy.

"Keep half for yourself."

"Thanks: I don't want even the whole."

"Well, it just happened to be Sunday. Sárvölgyi chose that day, because it would cost so much less to array the village folk in holiday garb. He had the bells rung, so did the Vicar: every window and door was full of curious on-lookers. I too took my seat on the verandah to see the sight.

"The long line of carriages started. First the bridegroom with Sárvölgyi, after them the bride, dressed in a white lawn robe, and wearing, if I am not mistaken, many theatrical jewels."

Lorand interrupted impatiently:

"You evidently think, uncle, that I shall write all this for some fashion-paper, as you are telling me in such detail about the costumes."

"I have learned it from English novel-writers: if a man wants to convince his hearers that something is true history and no fable, he must describe externals in detail, that they may see what an eye-witness he was.—Well, I shall leave out all description of the horses' trappings.

"As the long convoy proceeded up the street, a carriage drawn by four horses clattered up from the opposite end, a county court official beside the coachman, behind, two gentlemen, one lean, the other thickset.

"When this equipage met the wedding procession, the lean gentleman stopped his carriage and called out to Sárvölgyi's coachman to bring his coach to a standstill.

"The lean man leaped down from his carriage, the stout man after him, the official following them, and stepped up to the bridegroom.

"'Are you Joseph Gyáli?' inquired the lean man, without any prefix.

"'I am,' he said, looking at the dust-covered man with angry hauteur, not comprehending by what right anyone could dare to stop him at such a time and to address him so curtly.

"But the lean man seized the door of the carriage and said to the bridegroom:

"'Well, sir, have you any soul?'

"Our dear friend could not comprehend what new form of greeting it was, to ask a man on the road whether he had a soul.

"But the lean man seemed to wish to know that at any cost.

"'Sir, have you any soul?'

"'What?'

"'Have you any soul, that you can lead an innocent maiden to the altar, in the position in which you are?'

"'Who are you? And how dare you to address me?'

"'I am Miklós Daruszegi, county court magistrate, and have come to arrest you, in consequence of a proclamation of the High Court of Justice in Vienna, which has sent us instructions to arrest you wherever you may be found on the charge of several forgeries and deceits, *in flagrante*, and not to accept bail!'

Debts of Honor

"'But, sir—!'

"'There is no chance for resistance. You knew already in Vienna to what charge you were liable, and you came directly to Hungary in the hope that if you could ally yourself with some propertied lady, your honorable person might be defended, thus practising fresh deceit against others. And now again I ask you, whether you have the soul to wish, on the prison's threshold, to drag an innocent maiden with you?'"

"Poor Melanie!"—whispered Lorand.

"Poor Melanie naturally fainted, and the poor P. C.'s widow was beside herself with rage: poor Sárvölgyi wept like a child: all the guests fled back to the house, and the bridegroom was compelled to descend from the bridal coach, and take his place in the magistrate's muddy chaise, still wearing his costume covered with decorations: they supplied him with a rug, it is true, to cover himself with, but the heron-plumed hat remained on his head for the public wonder.

"I truly sympathised with the poor creatures! Still it seems I have survived that pain too.—If only it had not happened in the street! Before the eyes of so many men! If I at least had not seen it! If only I might give a romantic version of the catastrophe. But such a prosaic ending! A bridegroom arrested for the forgery of documents at the church door!—His tragedy is surely over!"

"But according to that, Melanie did not become his wife?" said Lorand. "Melanie has not been married at all."

Topándy shook his head.

"You are an impatient audience, nephew. Still I shall not hurry the performance. You must wait till I send a glass of absinthe down my throat, for my stomach turns at the very thought of what I am about to relate."

And he was not joking: he looked among the many chemicals for the bottle bearing the label "absynthium," and drank a small glass of it. Then he poured one out for Lorand.

"You must drink too."

"I could not drink it, uncle," said Lorand, full of other thoughts.

"But drink this glass, I tell you: until you do I shall not continue. What I am going to say is strong poison, and this is the antidote."

So Lorand drank, that he might hear what happened.

"Well, my dear boy. You must dispense with the idea that Melanie is not a wife: Melanie two days ago married—Sárvölgyi!"

"Oh, that is only a jest!" exclaimed Lorand incredulously.

"Of course it is a jest: only a very mad one. Who could take such things seriously? Sárvölgyi was jesting when he said to Madame Bálnokházy: 'Madame, there is a scandal—your daughter is neither a miss nor a Mrs. She is burdened both by loss and contempt. You cannot appear any more before the world after such a scandal. I have a good idea: we are trying to agree now about a property; let us shake hands, and the bargain's made, the property and the price of purchase remain in the same hands.'—Madame Bálnokházy too was jesting when she said to her daughter: 'My dear Melanie, we have fallen up to our necks in the mire, we cannot be very particular about the hand that is to drag us out. Lorand will never come back again, Gyáli has deceived us; but only tit for tat,—for we deceived him with that tale of the regained property in which only one man believes,— honorable Sárvölgyi. If you accept his offer, you will be a lady of position, if not, you can come with me as a wandering actress. We can take our revenge upon them, for they hate Sárvölgyi too. And after all Sárvölgyi is a very pleasant fellow.'—And surely Melanie was jesting when two days later she said to the priest before the altar that in the whole world there was only one man whom she could deem worthy of her love, and he was Sárvölgyi.—I believe it was all a jest—but so it happened."

Lorand covered his face with his hands.

"A jest indeed, a fine jest fit to stir one's blood," Topándy angrily burst out. "That girl, whom I so loved, whom I treated as my child, who was to me an image of what they call womanly purity, throws herself away upon my most detested enemy, a loathsome corpse, whose body, soul, and spirit had already decayed. Why if she had returned broken-hearted to me, and said, 'I have erred,' I should have still received her with open arms: she should not thus have prostituted the feeling which I held for her.

"Oh, my friend, there is nothing more repulsive in this round world, than a woman who can make herself thus loathed."

Lorand's silence gave assent to this sentence.

"And now follows the madness I committed.

"I said: if you jest, let me jest too. My house was at that moment full of gay companions, who were helping me to curse. But what is the value of curses? A mad idea occurred to me. I said: 'If you are holding a marriage feast yonder, I shall hold one here.' You remember there was an old mangled-eared ass, used by the shepherd to carry the hides of slaughtered oxen, called by my servants, out of ridicule, Sárvölgyi. Then there was a beautiful thoroughbred colt, which Melanie chose betimes to bear her name. I dressed the ass and foal up as bridegroom and bride, one of the drunken revellers dressed as a 'monk' and at the same time that Sárvölgyi and Melanie went to their wedding, here, in my courtyard, I parodied the holy ceremony in the persons of those two animals."

Lorand was horror stricken.

"It was a mad idea: I acknowledge it," continued Topándy. "To ridicule religious ceremonies! That will cost me two years at least in the county prison: I shall not defend myself—I have deserved it. I shall put up with it. I knew it when I carried out this raving jest—I knew what the outcome would be. But if they had promised me all the good things that lie between the guardian of the Northern Dogstar and the emerald wings of the vine-dresser beetle, or if they had threatened me with all that exists down to the middle of the earth, down to hell, I should have done it, when once I had thought it out. I wanted a hellish revenge, and there it was. How hellish it was you may imagine from the fact that the jovial fellows at once sobered, disappeared from the house; and since then one or two have written to beg me not to betray their presence here on that occasion. I am only pleased you were not here then."

"And I am sorry I was not. Had I been, it would not have happened."

"Don't say that, my dear boy. Don't think too well of yourself. You don't know what you would have felt, had you seen pass before you in a carriage her whom we had idolized with him whom we detest so. It destroyed my reason. And even now I feel a terrible void in my soul. That girl occupied such a large place therein. I feel it is still more painful for me that I perpetrated such a trivial jest in her name, in her memory.—Still, it has happened and we cannot recall it. We have begun the campaign of hatred, and don't know ourselves where it will end. Now let us speak of other things. During my imprisonment you will take over the farm and remain here."

"Yes."

"But you have still another difficult matter to get through first."

"I know."

"Oh dear no. Why do you always wish to discover my thoughts? You cannot know of what I am thinking."

"Czipra...."

"That is not quite it. Though it did occur to me to ask how could I leave a young man and a young girl here all alone. Yet in that matter I have my own logic: the young man either has a heart or none at all. If he has a heart, he will either keep his distance from the girl, or, if he has loved her, he will not ask who her father and mother were or what her dowry is. He will estimate her at her own value for her own self—a faithful woman. If he has no heart, the girl must see to having more: she must defend herself. If neither has a heart,—well a daily occurrence will occur once more. Who has ever grieved over it? I have nothing to say in the matter. He who knows himself to be an animal, nothing more, is right: he who considers himself a higher being, a man, a noble man, is right too: and he who wishes to be an angel, is only vain. Whether you make the girl your mistress or your wife, is the affair of you two: it all depends which category of the physical world you desire to belong to. The one says, 'I, a male ass, wish to graze with you, a female-ass, on thistles;' or, 'I, a man, wish to be your god, woman, to care for you.' It is, as I say, a matter of taste and ideas. I entrust it to you. But I have matter for serious anxiety here. Have you not remarked that here, round Lankadomb, an enormous number of robberies take place?"

"Perhaps not more than elsewhere: only we do not know about the misfortunes of others."

"Oh, dear, no; our neighborhood is in reality the home of a far-reaching robber-band, whose dealings I have long followed with great attention. These marshes here around us afford excellent shelter to those who like to avoid the world."

"That is so everywhere. Fugitive servants, marauding shepherds, bandits, who visit country houses to ask a drink of wine, bacon and bread,—I have met them often enough: I gave them from my purse as much as I pleased, and they went on their way peacefully."

"Here we have to deal with quite a different lot. Czipra might know more about it, if she chose to speak. That tent-dwelling army, out of whose midst I took her to myself, is lurking around us, and is more malicious than report says. They conceal their deeds splendidly, they are very cunning and careful. They are not confined to human society, they can winter among the reeds, and so are more difficult to get at than the mounted highwaymen, who hasten to enjoy the goods they have purloined in the inns. They have never dared to attack me at home, for they know I am ready to receive them. Still, they have often indirectly laid me under obligation. They have often robbed Czipra, when she went anywhere alone. You were yourself a witness to one such event. I suspect that the robber-chief who strove with Czipra in the inn was Czipra's own father."

"Heavens! I wonder if that can be so."

"Czipra always closed their mouths with a couple of hundred florins, and then they remained quiet. Perhaps she threatened them in case they annoyed me. It may be that up to the present they have not molested us in order to please her. But it may be, too, that they have another reason for making Lankadomb their centre of operations. Do you remember that on the pistol you wrenched from that robber were engraved the arms of Sárvölgyi?"

"What are you hinting at, uncle?"

"I think Sárvölgyi is the chieftain of the whole highwayman-band."

"What brought you to that idea?"

"The fact that he is such a pious man. Still, let us not go into that now. The gist of the matter is, that I would like to relieve our district of this suspicious guest, before I begin my long visit."

"How?"

"We must burn up that old hay-rick, of which I have said so many times that it has inhabitants summer and winter."

"Do you think that will drive them from our neighborhood?"

"I am quite sure of it. This class is cowardly. They will soon turn out of any place where war is declared against them: they only dare to brawl as long as they find people are afraid of them: wolf-like they tear to pieces only those they find defenceless: but one wisp of burning straw will annihilate them. We must set the rick on fire."

"We could have done so already; but it is difficult to reach it, on account of the old peat-quarries."

"Which our dangerous neighbors have covered with wolf traps, so that one cannot approach the rick within rifle-shot."

"I often wished to go there, but you would not allow me."

"It would have been an unreasonable audacity. Those who dwell there could shoot down, from secure hiding-places, any who approached it, before the latter could do them any harm. I have a simpler plan: we two shall take our seats in the punt, row down the dyke, and when we come against the rick, we shall set it on fire with explosive bullets. The rick is mine, no longer rented: all whom it may concern must seek lodging elsewhere."

Lorand said it was a good plan: whatever Topándy desired he would agree to. He might declare war against the bandits, for all he cared.

That evening, guided by moonlight, they poled their way to the centre of the marsh: Lorand himself directed the shots, and was lucky enough to lodge his first shell in the side of the rick. Soon the dry mass of hay was flaming like a burning pyramid in the midst of the morass. The two besiegers had reached home long before the blazing rick had time to light up the district far. As they watched, all at once the flame scattered, exploding millions of sparks up to heaven, and the fragments of the burning rick were strewed on the water's surface by the wind. Surely hidden gunpowder had caused that explosion.

At that moment no one was at home in this barbarous dwelling. Not a single voice was heard during the burning, save the howling of the terrified wolves round about.

CHAPTER XXV

WHILE THE MUSIC SOUNDS

At Lankadomb the order of things had changed.

After the famous scandal, Topándy's dwelling was very quiet—no guest crossed its threshold: while at Sárvölgyi's house there was an entertainment every evening, sounds of music until dawn of day.

They wished to show that they were in a gay mood.

Sárvölgyi began to win fame among the gypsies. These wandering musicians began to reckon his house among one of their happy asylums, so that even the bands of neighboring towns came to frequent it, one handing on the news of it to the other.

The young wife loved amusement, and her husband was glad if he could humor her—perhaps he had other thoughts, too?

Sárvölgyi himself did not allow his course of life to be disturbed: after ten o'clock he regularly left the company, going first to devotions and these having been attended to, to sleep.

His spouse remained under the care of her mother—in very good hands.

And, after all, Sárvölgyi was no intolerable husband: he did not persecute his young wife with signs of tenderness or jealousy.

In reality he acted as one who merely wished, under the guise of marriage to save a victim, to free an innocent, calumniated, unfortunate girl in the most humane way from desperation.

It was a good deed,—friendship, nothing more.

Sárvölgyi's bedroom was separated from the rest of the dwelling house by a kind of corridor, bricked in, where the musicians were usually placed, for the obvious reason that the sun-burnt artists are passionately fond of chewing tobacco.

Debts of Honor

This mistaken arrangement was the cause of two evils: firstly, the master of the house, lying on his bed, could hear all night long the beautiful waltzes and mazurkas to which his wife was dancing; secondly, being obliged to pass through the gypsies on his way from the ball-room to his bedroom, he came in for so many expressions of gratitude on their part that his quiet retirement gave rise to a most striking uproar, disagreeable alike to himself, to his wife, and his guests.

He called the brown worthies to order often enough: "Don't express your gratitude, don't kiss my hand. I am not going away anywhere:" but they would not allow themselves to be cheated of their opportunity for grateful speeches.

One night in particular an old, one-eyed czimbalom-player, whose sole remaining eye was bound up—he had only joined the band that day—would not permit himself to be over-awed: he seized the master's hand, kissed every finger of it in turn, then every nail: "God recompense you for what you intend to give, multiply your family like the sparrows in the fields: may your life be like honey...."

"All right, foolish daddy," interrupted Sárvölgyi. "A truce to your blessings. Get you gone. Mistress Borcsa will give you a glass of wine as a reward."

But the gypsy would not yield: he hobbled after the master into his bedroom, opening the door vigorously, and thrusting in his shaggy head.

"But if God call from the world of shadows..."

"Go to hell: enough of your gratitude."

But the czimbalom-player merely closed the door from the inside and followed his righteous benefactor.

"Golden-winged angels in a wagon of diamonds...."

"Get out this moment!" cried Sárvölgyi, hastily looking for a stick to drive the flatterer out of his room.

But at that moment the gypsy sprang upon him like a panther, grasping his throat with one hand and placing a pointed knife against his chest with the other.

"Oh!"—panted the astonished Sárvölgyi. "Who are you? What do you want?"

"Who am I?" murmured the fiend in reply, looking like the panther when it has set its teeth in its victim's neck. "I am Kandur,[75] the mad Kandur. Have you ever seen a mad Kandur? That is what I am. Don't you know me now?"

[75] Tom-cat.

"What do you want?"

"What do I want? Your bones and your skin: your black blood. You highwayman! You robber!"

So saying, he tore the bandage from his eye: there was nothing amiss with that eye.

"Do you know me now, herdsman?"

It would have been in vain to scream. Outside the most uproarious music could be heard: no one would have heard the cry for help. Besides the assailed had another reason for holding his peace.

"Well, what do you want with me? What have I done to you? Why do you attack me?"

"What have you done?" said the gypsy, gnashing his teeth so that Sárvölgyi shivered—this gnashing of human teeth is a terrible sound. "What have you done? You ask that? Have you not robbed me? Eh?"

"I robbed you? Don't lose your senses. Let go of my throat. You see, I am in your hands anyhow. Talk sense. What has happened to you?"

"What has happened to me? Oh yes—act as if you had not seen that beautiful illumination the day before yesterday evening—that's right—when the rick was burned down, and then the gunpowder dispersed the fire, so that nothing but a black pit remained for mad Kandur."

"I saw it."

"That was your work," cried the fiend, raising high the flashing knife.

"Now, Kandur, have some sense. Why should *I* have set it on fire?"

"Because no one else could have known that my money was stored away there. Who else would have dreamed I had money, but you? You who always changed my bank-note into silver and gold, giving me one silver florin for a small bank-note, and one gold piece for a large one. How do I know what was the value of each? — You knew I collected money. You knew how I collected, and why — for I told you. My daughter is in a certain gentleman's house; they are making a fool of her there. They are bringing her up like a duchess, until they have plucked her blossoms, — and then they will throw her away like a wash-rag. I wished to buy her off! I had already a pot of silver and a milk-pail of gold. I wanted to take her away with me to Turkey, to Tartary, where heathens dwell; and she would be a real duchess, a gypsy duchess! I shall murder, rob, and break into houses until I have a pot full of silver, and a pail full of gold. The gypsy girl will want it as her dowry. I shall not leave her for you, you white-faced porcelain tribe! I shall take her away to some place where they will not say 'Away gypsy! off gypsy! Kiss my hand, eat carrion, gypsy, gypsy!' — Give me my money."

"Kandur."

"Don't gape, or tire your mouth. Give me a pot of silver, and a pail of gold."

"All right, Kandur, you shall get your money — a pot of silver and a pail of gold. But now let me have my say. It was not I who took your money, not I who set the rick on fire."

"Who then?"

"Why those people yonder."

"Topándy, and the young gentleman?"

"Certainly. The day before yesterday evening I saw them in a punt on the moat, starting for the morass, and I saw them when they returned again—the rick was then already burning. Each of them had a gun: but I did not hear a single shot, so they were not after game."

"The devil and all his hell-hounds destroy them!"

"Why, Kandur, your daughter was mad after that young gentleman—she certainly confessed to him that her father was collecting treasures: so the young gentleman took off daughter and money too—he will shortly return the empty pot."

"Then I shall kill him."

"What did you say, Kandur?"

"I shall kill him, even if he has a hundred souls. Long ago I promised him, when first we met. But now I wish to drink of his blood. Did you see whether the old mastiff too was there at the robbing?"

"Topándy? A plague upon my eyes, if I did not see him. There were two of them, they took no one with them, not even a dog: they rowed along here beside the gardens. I looked long after them, and waited till they should return. May every saint be merciless to me, if I don't speak the truth!"

"Then I shall murder both."

"But be careful: they go armed."

"What?—If I wish I can have a whole host. If I wish I can ravish the whole village in broad daylight. You do not yet know who Kandur is."

"I know well who you are, Kandur," said Sárvölgyi, carefully studying the robber's browned face. "Why we are old acquaintances. It is not you who are responsible for the deeds you have done, but society. Humankind rose up against you, you merely defended yourself as best you could. That is why I always took your part, Kandur."

"No nonsense for me now," interrupted the robber hastily. "I don't mind what I am. I am a highwayman. I like the name."

"You had no ignoble pretext for robbing,—but the saving of your daughter from the whirlpool of crime. The aim was a laudable one, Kandur: besides you were particular as to whom you fleeced."

"Don't try to save me—you'll have enough to do to save yourself soon in hell, before the devil's tribunal—you may lie his two eyes out, if you want. I have been a highwayman, have killed and robbed—even clergymen. I want to kill now, too."

"I shall pray for your soul."

"The devil! Man, do you think I care? Prayer is just about as potent with you as with me. Better give a pile of money to enable me to collect a band. My men must have money."

"All right, Kandur: don't be angry, Kandur:—you know I'm awfully fond of you. I have not persecuted you like others. I have always spoken gently to you and have always sheltered you from your persecutors. No one ever dared to look for you in my house."

"No more babbling—just give over the money."

"Very well, Kandur. Hold your cap."

Sárvölgyi stepped up to a very strong iron safe, and unfastening the locks one by one, raised its heavy door—placing the candle on a chair beside him.

The robber's eyes gleamed. Sufficient silver to fill many pots was piled up there.

"Which will you have? silver or bank-notes?"

"Silver," whispered the robber.

"Then hold your cap."

Kandur held his lamb-skin cap in his two hands like a pouch, and placed his knife between his teeth.

Sárvölgyi dived deeply into the silver pile with his hand, and when he drew it back, he held before the robber's nose a double-barrelled pistol, ready cocked.

It was a fine precaution—a pistol beautifully covered up by a heap of coins.

The robber staggered back, and forgot to withdraw the knife from his mouth. And so he stood before Sárvölgyi, a knife between his teeth, his eyes wide opened, and his two hands stretched before him in self-defence.

"You see," said Sárvölgyi calmly, "I might shoot you now, did I wish. You are entirely in my power. But see, I spoke the truth to you.—Hold your cap and take the money."

He put the pistol down beside him and took out a goodly pile of dollars.

"A plague upon your jesting eyes!" hissed the robber through the knife. "Why do you frighten a fellow? The darts of Heaven destroy you!"

He was still trembling, so frightened had he been.

The loaded weapon in another's hand had driven away all his courage.

The robber could only be audacious, not courageous.

"Hold your cap."

Sárvölgyi shovelled the heap of silver coins into the robber's cap.

"Now perhaps you can believe it is not fear that makes me confide in you?"

"A plague upon you. How you alarmed me!"

"Well, now collect your wits and listen to me."

Debts of Honor

The robber stuffed the money into his pockets and listened with contracted eyebrows.

"You may see it was not I who stole your money; for, had I done so, I should just now have planted two bullets in your carcass, one in your heart, the other in your skull. And I should have got one hundred gold pieces by it, that being the price on your head."

The robber smiled bashfully, like one who is flattered. He took it as a compliment that the county had put a price of one hundred gold pieces on his head.

"You may be quite sure that it was not I, but those folks yonder, who took away your money."

"The highwaymen!"

"You are right—highwaymen:—worse even than that. Atheists! The earth will be purified if they are wiped out. He who kills them is doing as just an action as the man that shoots a wolf or a hawk."

"True, true;" Kandur nodded assent.

"This rogue who stole away your daughter laid a snare for another innocent creature. He must have two, one for his right hand, the other for his left. And when the persecuted innocent girl escaped from the deceiver to my house and became my wife, those folks yonder swore deadly revenge against me. Because I rescued an innocent soul from the cave of crime, they thrice wished to slay me. Once they poured poison into my drinking-well. Fortunately the horses drank of the water first and all fell sick from it. Then they drove mad dogs out in the streets, when I was walking there, to tear me to pieces. They sent me letters, which, had I opened them, would have gone off in my hands and blown me to pieces. These malicious fellows wish to kill me."

"I understand."

"That young stripling thinks that if he succeeds he can carry off my wife too, so as to have her for his mistress one day, Czipra, your daughter, the next."

Debts of Honor

"You make my anger boil within me!"

"They acknowledge neither God nor law. They do as they please. When did you last see your daughter?"

"Two weeks ago."

"Did you not see how worn she is? That cursed fellow has enchanted her and is spoiling her."

"I'll spoil his head!"

"What will you do with him?"

Kandur showed, with the knife in his hand, what he would do—bury that in his heart and twist it round therein.

"How will you get at him? He has always a gun in the daytime: he acts as if he were going a-shooting. At night the castle is strongly locked, and they are always on the lookout for an attack,—they too are audacious fellows."

"Just leave it to me. Don't have any fears. What Kandur undertakes is well executed. Crick, crick: that's how I shall break both the fellows' necks."

"You are a clever rascal. You showed that in your way of getting at me! You may do the same there, by dressing your men as fiddlers and clarinet-players."

"Oh ho! Don't think of it. Kandur doesn't play the same joke twice. I shall find the man I want."

"I've still something to say. It would be good if you could have them under control before they die."

"I know—make them confess where they have put my money which they stole?"

"Don't begin with that. Supposing they will not confess?"

"Have no fears on that score. I know how to drive screws under finger-nails, to strap up heads, so that a man would even confess to treasures hidden in his father's coffin."

"Listen to me. Do what I say. Don't try long to trace your stolen money: it's not much—a couple of thousand florins. If you don't find it, I shall give you as much—as much as you can carry in your knapsack. You can, however, find something else there."

"What?"

"A letter, sealed with five black seals."

"A letter? with five black seals?"

"And to prevent them making a fool of you, and blinding you with some other letter which you cannot read, note the arms on the respective seals. On the first is a fish-tailed mermaid, holding a half-moon in her hand—those are the Áronffy arms:—on the second a stork, three ears of corn in its talons—those are the High Sheriff's arms: on the third a semi-circle, from which a unicorn is proceeding,—those are the Nyárády arms; the fourth is a crown in a hand holding a sword—those are the lawyer's arms. The fifth, which must be in the middle, bears Topándy's arms,—a crowned snake."

The robber reckoned after him on his fingers:

"Mermaid with half moon—stork with ears of corn—a half circle with unicorn—crown with sword-hand—snake with crown. I shall not forget. And what do you want the letter for?"

"That too I shall explain to you, that you may see into the innermost depths of my thoughts and may judge how seriously I long to see the completion of that which I have entrusted to you. That letter is Topándy's latest will. While my wife was living with him, Topándy, believing she would wed his nephew, left his fortune to his niece and her future husband, and handed it in to the county court to be guarded. But when his niece became my wife, he wrote a new will, and had all those, whose arms I have mentioned, sign it; then he sealed it but did not send it to the court like the former one; he kept it here to make the jest all the greater, thinking we stand by the former will. Then, the latter will comes to light, making void the former—and excluding my wife from all."

"Aha! I see now what a clever fellow you are!"

"Well, could that five-sealed letter come into my hands, and old Topándy die by chance, without being able to write another will—well, you know what that little paper might be worth in my hands?"

"Of course. Castle, property, everything. All that would fall to you—the old will would give it you. I understand: I see—now I know what a wise fellow you are!"

"Do you believe now that if you come to me with that letter...."

The robber bent nearer confidingly, and whispered in his ear:

"And with the news that your neighbors died suddenly and could not write another."

"Then you need have no fear as to how much money you will get in place of what they stole. You may go off with your daughter to Tartary, where no one will prosecute you."

"Excellent—couldn't be better. Leave the rest to me. Two days later Kandur will have no need to indulge in such work."

Then he began to count on his fingers, as if he were reckoning to himself.

"Well, in the first place, I get money—in the second, I have my revenge—in the third, I take away Czipra,—in the fourth, I shall have my fill of human blood,—in the fifth, I get money again.—It shall be done."

The two shook hands on the bargain. The robber left by the same door through which he had entered; Sárvölgyi went to bed, like one who has done his business well; and in the corridor the gypsies still played the newest waltz, which Melanie and Madame Bálnokházy were enjoying with flushed faces amidst the gay assembly.

CHAPTER XXVI

THE ENCHANTMENT OF LOVE

How many secrets there are under the sun, awaiting discovery!

Books have been written about the superstitions of nations long since passed away: men of science have collected the enchantments of people from all quarters of the globe: yet of one thing they have not spoken yet: of that unending myth, which lives unceasingly and is born again in woman's heart and in the heated atmosphere of love.

Sweet are the enchantments of love!

"If I drink unseen from thy glass, and thou dost drain it after me:— thou drinkest love therefrom, and shalt pine for me, darling, as I have pined for thee.

"If at night I awake in dreams of thee and turn my pillow under my head: thou too wilt have as sweet dreams of me, as I of thee, my darling.

"If I bind my ring to a lock of thy hair thou hast given me, and cast the same into a glass, as often as it beats against the side of the glass, so many years wilt thou love me, darling.

"If I can sew a lock of my hair into the edge of thy linen garment, thy heart will pine for me, as often as thou puttest the same on, my darling.

"If, in thinking of thee, I pricked my finger, thou wert then faithless to me, darling.

"If the door opens of itself, thou wert then thinking of me, and thy sigh opened the door, my darling.

"If a star shoots in the sky, and I suddenly utter thy name as it shoots, thou must then at once think of me, darling.

"If my ear tingles, I hear news of thee: if my cheeks burn, thou art speaking of me, my darling.

"If my scissors fall down and remain upright, I shall see thee soon, darling.

"If the candle runs down upon me, then thou dost love another, my darling.

"If my ring turns upon my finger, then thou wilt be the cause of my death, darling."

In every object, in every thought lives the mythology of love, like the old-world deities with which poets personified grass, wood, stream, ocean and sky.

The petals of the flowers speak of it, ask whether he loves or not: the birds of song on the house-tops: everything converses of love: and what maiden is there who does not believe what they say?

Poor maidens!

If they but knew how little men deserved that the world of prose should receive its polytheism of love from them!

Poor Czipra!

What a slave she was to her master!

Her slavery was greater than that of the Creole maiden whose every limb grows tired in the service of her master:—every thought of hers served her lord.

From morn till even, nothing but hope, envy, tender flattery, trembling anxiety, the ecstasy of delight, the bitterness of resignation, the burning ravings of passion, and cold despair, striving unceasingly with each other, interchanging, gaining new sustenance from every word, every look of the youth she worshipped.

And then from twilight till dawn ever the same struggle, even in dreams.

"If I were thy dog, you would not treat me so."

That is what she once said to Lorand.

And why? Perhaps because he passed her without so much as shaking hands with her.

And at another time:

"Were I in Heaven, I could not be happier."

Perhaps a fleeting embrace had made her happy again.

How little is enough to bring happiness or sorrow to poor maidens.

One day an old gypsy woman came by chance into the courtyard.

In the country it is not the custom to drive away these poor vagrants: they receive corn, and scraps of meat: they must live, too.

Then they tell fortunes. Who would not wish to have his fortune so cheaply.

And the gypsy woman's deceitful eye very soon finds out whose fortune to tell, and how to tell it.

But Czipra was not glad to see her.

She was annoyed at the idea that the woman might recognize her by her red-brown complexion, and her burning black eyes, and might betray her origin before the servants. She tried to escape notice.

But the gypsy woman did remark the beautiful girl and addressed her as "my lady."

"I kiss your dear little feet, my lady."

"My lady? Don't you see I am a servant, and cook in the kitchen: my sleeves are tucked up and I wear an apron."

"But surely not. A serving maid does not hold her head so upright and cannot show her anger so. If your ladyship frowns on me I feel like hiding in the corner, just to escape from the anger in your eyes."

"Well if you know so much, you must also know that I am married, fool!"

The gypsy woman slyly winked.

"I am no fool: my eyes are not bad. I know the wild dove from the tame. You are no married woman, young lady: you are still a maiden. I have looked into the eyes of many girls and women: I know which is which. A girl's eye lurks beneath the eyelids, as if she were looking always out of an ambuscade, as if she were always afraid somebody would notice her. A woman's eye always flashes as if she were looking for somebody. When a girl says in jest 'I am a married woman,' she blushes: if she were a woman, she would smile. You are certainly still unmarried, young lady."

Czipra was annoyed at having opened a conversation with her. She felt that her face was really burning. She hastened to the open fireplace, driving the servant away that she might put her burning face down to the flaming fire.

The gypsy woman became more obtrusive, seeing she had put the girl to confusion. She sidled up to her.

"I see more, beautiful young lady. The girl that blushes quickly has much sorrow and many desires. Your ladyship has joy and sorrow too."

"Oh, away with you!" exclaimed Czipra hastily.

It is not so easy to get rid of a gypsy woman, once she has firmly planted her foot.

"Yet I know a very good remedy for that."

"I have already told you to be off."

"Which will make the bridegroom as tame as a lamb that always runs after its mistress."

"I don't want your remedies."

"It is no potion I am talking of, merely an enchantment."

"Throw her out!" Czipra commanded the servants.

"You won't throw me out, girls: rather listen to what I say. Which of you would like to know what you must do to enchant the young fellows so that even if every particle of them were full of falsity, they could not deceive you in their affection. Well, Susie: I see you're laughing at it. And you, Kati? Why, I saw your Joseph speaking to the bailiff's daughter at the fence: this spell would do him no harm."

All the grinning serving-maids, instead of rescuing Czipra from the woman, only assisted the latter in her siege. They surrounded her and even cut off Czipra's way, waiting curiously for what the gypsy would say.

"It is a harmless remedy, and costs nothing."

The gypsy woman drew nearer to Czipra.

"When at midnight the nightingale sings below your window, take notice on what branch it sat. Go out bare-footed, break down that branch, set it in a flower-pot, put it in your window, sprinkle it with water from your mouth: before the branch droops, your lover will return, and will never leave you again."

The girls laughed loudly at the gypsy woman's enchantment.

The woman held her hand out before Czipra in cringing supplication.

"Dear, beautiful young lady, scorn not to reward me with something for the blessing of God."

Czipra's pocket was always full of all kinds of small coins, of all values, according to the custom of those days—when one man had to be paid in coppers, another in silver. Czipra filled her hand and began to search among the mass for the smallest copper, a kreutzer,[76] as the correct alms for a beggar.

[76] One-half of a penny.

"Golden lady," the gypsy woman thanked her. "I have just such a girl at home for sale, not so beautiful as you, but just as tall. She too has a bridegroom, who will take her off as soon as he can."

Czipra now began to choose from the silver coins.

"But he cannot take her, for we have not money enough to pay the priest."

Czipra picked out the largest of the silver coins and gave it to the gypsy woman.

The latter blessed her for it. "May God reward you with a handsome bridegroom, true in love till death!"

Then she shuffled on her way from the house.

Czipra reflectingly hummed to herself the refrain:

> "A gypsy woman was my mother."

And Czipra meditated.

How prettily thought speaks! If only the tongue could utter all the dumb soul speaks to itself!

"Why art thou what thou art?

"Whether another's or mine, if only I had never seen thee!

"Either love me in return, or do not ask me to love thee at all.

"Be either cold or warm, but not lukewarm.

"If in passing me, thou didst neither look at me, nor turn away, that would be good too: if sitting beside me thou shouldst draw me to thee, thou wouldst make me happy:—thou comest, smilest into mine eyes, graspest my hand, speakest tenderly to me, and then passest by.

"A hundred times I think that, if thou dost not address me, I shall address thee: if thou dost not ask me, I shall look into thine eyes, and shall ask thee:

"'Dost thou love me?'

"If thou lovest, love truly.

"Why, I do not ask thee to bring down the moon from the heavens to me: merely, to pluck the rose from the branch.

"If thou pluckest it, thou canst tear it, and scatter its leaves upon the earth, thou must not wear it in thy hat, and answer with blushes, if they ask thee who gave it thee. Thou canst destroy it and tear it. A gypsy girl gave it.

"If thou lovest, why dost thou not love truly? If thou dost not love me, why dost thou follow me?

"If thou knewest thou didst not love me, why didst thou decoy me into thy net?

"He has cast a spell upon me: yet I would be of the race of witches.

"I know nothing. I am no wizard, my eye has no power.

"If I address him once, I kill him and myself.

"Or perhaps only myself.

"And shall I not speak?"

The poor girl's heart was full of reverie, but her eyes, her mouth, and her hand were busy with domestic work: she did not sit to gaze at the stars, to mourn over her instrument: she looked to her work, and they said "she is an enthusiastic housekeeper."

"Good day, Czipra."

She had even observed that Lorand was approaching her from behind, when she was whipping out cream in the corridor, and he greeted her very tenderly.

She expected him at least to stop as long as at other times to ask what she was cooking; and she would have answered with another question:

"Tell me now, what do you like?"

But he did not even stop: he had come upon her quite by chance, and as he could not avoid her, uttered a mere "good day:" then passed by. He was looking for Topándy.

Debts of Honor

Topándy was waiting for him in his room and was busy reading a letter he had just opened.

"Well, my boy," he said, handing Lorand the letter, "That is the overture of the opera."

Lorand took the letter, which began: "I offer my respects to Mr. ——"

"This is a summons?"

"You may see from the greeting. The High Sheriff informs me that to-morrow morning he will be here to hold the legal inquiry: you must give orders to the servants for to-morrow."

"Sir, you still continue to take it as a joke."

"And a curious joke too. How well I shall sweep the streets! Ha, ha!"

"Ah!"

"In chains too. I always mocked my swine-herd, who for a year and a half wore out the county court's chains. Ever since he walks with a shambling step, as if one leg was always trying to avoid knocking the other with the chain. Now we can both laugh at each other."

"It would be good to engage a lawyer."

"It will certainly be better to send a sucking pig to the gaoler. Against such pricks, my boy, there is no kicking. This is like a cold bath: if a man enters slowly, bit by bit, his teeth chatter: if he springs in at once, it is even pleasant. Let us talk of more serious matters."

"I just came because I wish to speak to my uncle about a very serious matter."

"Well, out with it."

"I intend to marry Czipra."

Topándy looked long into the young fellow's face, and then said coldly,

"Why will you marry her?"

"Because she is an honest, good girl."

Topándy shook his head.

"That is not sufficient reason for marrying her."

"And is faithful to me. I owe her many debts of gratitude. When I was ill, no sister could have nursed me more tenderly: if I was sad, her sorrow exceeded my own."

"That is not sufficient reason, either."

"And because I am raised above the prejudices of the world."

"Aha! magnanimity! Liberal ostentation? That is not sufficient reason either for taking Czipra to wife. The neighboring Count took his housekeeper to wife, just in order that people might speak of him: you have not even the merit of originality. Still not sufficient reason for marrying her."

"I shall take her to wife, because I love her...."

Topándy immediately softened: his usual strain of sarcastic scorn gave way to a gentler impulse.

"That's another thing. That is the only reason that can justify your marriage with her. How long have you loved her?"

"I cannot count the days. I was always pleased to see her: I always knew I loved her like a good sister. The other I worshipped as an angel: and as soon as she ceased to be an angel for me, as a mere woman I felt none of the former fire towards her: nothing remained, not even smoke nor ashes. But this girl, whose every foible I know, whose beauty was enhanced by no reverie, whom I only saw as she really is,—I love her now, as a faithful woman, who repays love in true coin: and I shall marry her—not out of gratitude, but because she has filled my heart."

"If that is all you want, you will find that. What shall you do first?"

"I shall first write to my mother, and tell her I have found this rough diamond whom she must accept as her daughter: then I shall take

Czipra to her, and she shall stay there until she is baptized and I take her away again."

"I am very thankful that you will take all the burden of this ceremony off my shoulders. What must be done by priests, do without my seeing it. When shall you tell Czipra?"

"As soon as mother's answer comes back."

"And if your mother opposes the marriage?"

"I shall answer for that."

"Still it is possible. She may have other aims for you. What should you do then?"

"Then?" said Lorand reflectively: after a long pause he added: "Poor mother has had so much sorrow on my account."

"I know that."

"She has pardoned me all."

"She loves you better than her other son."

"And I love her better than I loved my father."

"That is a hard saying."

"But if she said 'You must give up forever either this girl or me,' I would answer her, and my heart would break, 'Mother, tear me from your heart, but I shall go with my wife.'"

Topándy offered his hand to Lorand.

"That was well said."

"But I have no anxiety about it. Mountebank pride never found a place in our family: we have sought for happiness, not for vain connections, and Czipra belongs to those girls whom women love even better than men. I have a good friend at home, my brother, and my dear sister-in-law will use her influence in my favor."

"And you have an advocate elsewhere, in one who, despite all his godlessness, has a man's feelings, and will say: 'The girl has no name; here is mine, let her take that.'"

Topándy did not try to prevent Lorand from kissing his hand.

Poor Czipra! Why did she not hear this?

CHAPTER XXVII

WHEN THE NIGHTINGALE SINGS

The night following upon this day was a sleepless one for Czipra.

Every door of the castle was already closed: it was Lorand's custom to look for himself and see that the bolts were firmly fastened. Then he would knock at Czipra's door and bid her good-night; Czipra reciprocated the good wish, and Lorand turned into his room. The last creaking door was silent.

"Good night! Good night! But who gives the good night?"

Every day Czipra felt more strongly what an interminable void can exist in a heart which lacks—God.

If it sorrows, to whom shall it complain?—if it has aspirations to whom can it pray? if terrors threaten it, to whom shall it appeal for help and courage? if in despair, from whom shall it ask hope?

When the heavy beating of her heart prevents a poor girl from closing her eyes, she tosses sleeplessly where she lies, agonised with unknown suspicions, and there is no one before her mind, from whom she can ask, "Lord, is this a presentiment of my approaching death, or my approaching health? What annoys, what terrifies, what allures, what fills my heart with a sweet thrill? Oh, Lord, be with me."

The poor neglected girl only felt this, but could not express it.

She knelt on her bed, clasped her hands on her breast, raised her face, and collected every thought of her heart—how ought one to pray? What may be that word, which should bring God nearer? What sayings, what enchantments could bring the Great Being, the all-powerful, down from the heavens? What philosophy was that, which all men concealed from one another and only spoke of to each other in secret, in the form of letters, which opened to erring humanity the road leading to the home of an invisible being? How did it begin? How end? What an awful heart-agony, not to know how to pray,—just to kneel so with a heart full of crying aspirations, and dumb lips! How weak the voice of a sobbing sigh, how terribly far the starry heavens—who could hear there?

Yet there is One who hears!

And there is One who notes the unexpressed prayer of the silent suppliant, One who hears the unuttered words.

Poor girl! She did not imagine that this feeling, this exaltation, was prayer—not the words, not the sermon, not addresses, not the amens. He who sees into hearts—reads from hearts, does not estimate the elegance of words.

In the same hour that the suffering girl knelt thus dumbly before the Lord of all happiness, that man whom she had worshipped in her heart so long, whom she must worship forever, was sitting just as sleeplessly beside his writing-table, separated from her only by two walls, and was thinking and writing about her, and often wiped his eyes that filled betimes with tears.

He was writing to his mother about his engagement.

About the poor gypsy girl.

In the dim light of the beautiful starry night twelve horsemen were following in each others' tracks among the reeds of the morass.

Kandur was leading them.

Each man had a gun on his shoulder, a pistol in his girdle.

Along the winding road the mare Farao, treading lightly, led them: she too seemed to hasten, and sometimes broke through the reeds, making a short cut, as if she too were goaded on by some thirst for vengeance.

Among the willows, wills-o'-the-wisps were dancing.

Debts of Honor

They surrounded the horsemen, and followed their movements. Kandur smote at them with his lash.

"On the return journey we shall be two more!" he muttered between his teeth.

When they reached the lair there was merely a black stubbled ground left where the hay-rick stood before.

In all directions shapeless burnt masses lay about.

These were the ruins of the highwaymen's palace.

And the tears flow from their eyes, as they see their haunt thus destroyed.

All twelve had reached the burnt dwelling.

"See what the robbers have made of it," said Kandur to his comrades. "They have stolen all we had collected, the riches we were to take with us to another land, and then they have set the dwelling on fire. They came here in a boat: they found out the way to our palace. We shall now return the visit. Are you all here?"

"Yes," muttered the comrades. "We are all here."

"Dismount. Now for the punts."

The robbers dismounted.

"No need to tether the horses, they cannot get away anywhere. One man may remain here to guard them. Who wishes to stay?"

All were silent.

"Some one must guard the horses, lest the wolves attack them while we are away."

To which an old robber answered:

"Then you should have brought a herd-boy with you, for we didn't come here to guard horses."

"Very well, mate, I only wished to know whether anyone of us would like to remain behind. Whether anyone's 'sandal-strap was unloosed.' Does each one know his own business? Come up one by one, and let me tell each one his duty once more. Kanyó and Fosztó."[77]

[77] Pilferer.

Two of the men stepped forward.

"You two will guard the two doors of the servants' quarter when we arrive. Death to him who tries to escape by door or window."

"We know."

"Csutor[78] and Disznós.[79] you will be in ambush before the hunting-box, and anyone who attempts to come out to the rescue, must be killed."

[78] Nightshade.

[79] Swinish.

"Very well."

"Bogrács![80] You will occupy the street-door, and if any peasant dares to approach you must shoot him: you alone are sufficient to keep peasants off."

[80] Kettle.

"Quite sufficient!" said the robber with great self-reliance.

"Korvé[81] and Pofók.[81] You must take your stand opposite the first verandah, near the well, and if anyone wishes to escape by the first door, fire at him. But don't waste powder.—You others, Vasgyúró,[82] Hentes,[83] Piócza,[84] Agyaras,[85] will come with me through the garden, and will stay behind in the bushes until I give the sign. If I whistle once, that's for you. If I can get in quietly, by craft, without being obliged to fire a shot, that will be the best. I have planned the way. I think it will succeed. So three will come with me, one will remain in the doorway. Have the halters ready, to throw upon his neck, drag him to the ground and bind him. The black-bearded strong man must be dealt with suddenly, with the butt of your gun on his head, if not otherwise. But we must take the old man alive, for we shall make him confess."

[81] Blub-cheeked.

[82] Bully.

[83] Butcher.

[84] Leech.

[85] Wild-boar.

"Just leave him to me," said a fellow with a pox-pitted face, in a tone of entire confidence.

"I shall be there too," continued Kandur: "and if we cannot enter the castle stealthily, if some one should make a noise, if those within wake up, then the first whistle is for you four: two come with me to break open the garden door. Have you got the 'jimmies'?"

"Yes," said a robber, displaying the crowbars.

"Piócza, and Agyaras, your business is to answer any fire of people from the windows.—If I whistle twice, that means that something's up, then you must run from all sides to help me. If I cannot break open the door, or if those robbers defend themselves well, set the roof on fire over their heads and give them a dose of singeing. That will do just as well. Don't forget the tarred hay."

"Ha ha! The gentlemen will be warm."

"Well Pofók, perhaps you're cold? You'll soon get warm. Hither with the canteen. Let's drink a little Dutch courage first. Begin. Hentes. A long draught of brandy is, you know, good before a feast."

The tin went round and returned to Kandur almost empty.

"Look, I have hardly left you any," said the last drinker in a tone of apologetic modesty.

"To-day I don't drink brandy. The private must drink that he may be blind when he receives orders, but the general must not drink, that he may see to give orders. I shall drink something else when it is all over. Now look to the masking."

They understood what that meant.

Each one took off his sheepskin jacket, reversed it and put it on again. Then dipping their hands in the strewn ashes, they blackened their faces, making themselves unrecognizable.

Only Kandur did not mask himself.

"Let them recognize me. And anyone who does not recognize me, shall learn from my own lips, 'I am Kandur, the mad Kandur, who will drink thy blood, and tear out thy entrails. Know who I am!' How I shall look into their eyes! How I shall gnash upon them with my teeth, when they are bound. How tenderly I shall say to the young gentleman: 'Well, my boy, my gypsy child, were you in the garden? Did you see a wolf? Were you afraid of it? Shoo! Shoo!'"[86]

[86] A favorite child-verse in Hungary.

Farao was impatiently pawing the scorched grass.

"You too are looking for what is no more, Farao," the robber said, patting his horse's neck. "Don't grieve. To-morrow you shall stand up to your knees in provender, and then you shall carry your master on your back. Don't grieve, Farao."

The robbers had completed their disguises.

"Now take up the boats."

Hidden among the reeds lay two skiffs, light affairs, each cut out of a piece of tree trunk: just such as would hold two men, and such as two men could carry on their shoulders over dry ground.

The robber-band put the skiffs into the water and started one after the other on their way; they went down until they reached the stream leading to the great dyke, by which they could punt down to the park of Lankadomb, just where the shooting-box was.

It was about midnight when they reached it.

On the right of Lankadomb the dogs were baying restlessly, but the hounds of the castle watchman did not answer them. They were sleeping. Some vagrant gypsy woman had fed them well that evening on poisoned swine-flesh.

The robbers reached the castle courtyard noiselessly, unnoticed, and each one at once took the place allotted to him, as Kandur had directed.

The silence of deep sleep reigned in the house.

When everyone was in his place, Kandur crept on his stomach among the bushes, which formed a grove under Czipra's window that looked on to the garden, and putting an acacia leaf into his mouth, began to imitate the song of the nightingale.

It was an artistic masterpiece which the wild son of the plains had, with the aid of a leaf, stolen from the mouth of the sweetest of song-birds.

All those fairy warblings, those plaintive challenging tones, those enchanting trills, which no one has ever written down, he could imitate so faithfully, so naturally, that he deceived even his lurking comrades.

"Cursed bird," they muttered, "it too has turned to whistling."

Czipra was sleeping peacefully.

That invisible hand, which she had sought, had closed her eyes and sent sweet dreams to her heart. Perhaps, had she been able to sleep that sleep through undisturbed, she would have awakened to a happy day.

The nightingale was warbling under her window.

The nightingale! The song-bird of love! Why was it entrusted with singing at night when every other bird is sitting on its nest, and hiding its head under its wing. Who had sent it, saying, "Rise and announce that love is always waking?"

Who had entrusted it to awake the sleepers?

Why, even the popular song says:

> "Sleep is better far than love
> For sleep is tranquillity;
> Love is anguish of the heart."

Fly away, bird of song!

Czipra tried to sleep again. The bird's song did not allow her.

She rose, leaned upon her elbows and continued to listen.

And there came back to her mind that old gypsy woman's enchantment,—the enchantment of love.

"At midnight—the nightingale ... barefooted—... plant it in a flower-pot ... before it droops, thy lover will return, and will never leave thee."

Ah! who would walk in the open at night?

The nightingale continued:

"Go out bare-footed and tear down the branch."

No, no. How ridiculous it would be! If somebody should see her, and tell others, they would laugh at her for her pains.

The nightingale began its song anew.

Malicious bird, that will not allow sleep!

Yet how easy it would be to try: a little branch in a flower-pot. Who could know what it was? A girl's innocent jest, with which she does harm to no one. Love's childish enchantment.

It would be easy to attempt it.

And if it were true? If there were something in it? How often people say, "this or that woman has given her husband something to make him love her so truly, and not even see her faults?" If it were true?

How often people wondered, how two people could love each other? With what did they enchant each other? If it were true?

Suppose there were spirits that could be captured with a talisman, which would do all one bade them?

Czipra involuntarily shuddered: she did not know why, but her whole body trembled and shivered.

"No, not so," she said to herself. "If he does not give heart for heart,—mine must not deceive him. If he cannot love me because I deserve it, he must not love me for my spells. If he does not love, he must not despise me. Away, bird of song, I do not want thee."

Then she drew the coverlet over her head and turned to the wall. But sleep did not return again: the trembling did not pass: and the singing bird in the bushes did not hold his peace.

It had come right under the window; it sang, "Come, come."

Sometimes it seemed as if the song of the nightingale contained the words "Czipra, Czipra, Czipra!"

The warm mist of passion swept away the maiden's reason.

Her heart beat so, it almost burst her bosom, and her every limb trembled.

She was no longer mistress of her mind.

She left her bed, and therewith left that magic circle which the inspiration of the Lord forms around those who fly to Him for protection, and which guards them so well from all apparitions of the lower world.

"Go bare-footed!"

Why it was only a few steps from the door to the bushes.

Who could see her? What could happen in so short a time?

It was merely the satisfaction of an innocent desire.

It was no deed of darkness.

Every nerve was trembling.

She was merely going to break a little branch, and yet she felt as if she was about to commit the most heinous crime, for which she needed the shield of a sleepless night.

She opened the door very quietly so that it should not creak.

Lorand was sleeping in the room vis-à-vis: perhaps he might hear something.

She darted with bare feet before Lorand's door, she carefully undid the bolt of the door leading into the garden and turned the key with such precaution that it did not make a sound.

Noiselessly she opened the door and peered out.

It was a quiet night of reveries: the stars, as is their wont when seen through falling dew, were changing their colors, flashing green and red.

The nightingale was now cooing in the bushes, as it does when it has found its mate.

Czipra looked around her. It was a deep slumbering night: no one could see her now.

Yet she drew her linen garment closer round her, and was ashamed to show her bare feet to the starry night.

Ah! it would last only a minute.

The grass was warm and soft, wet with dew as far as the bushes: no sharp pebble would hurt her feet, no cracking stick betray her footsteps.

She stepped out into the open, and left the door ajar behind her.

She trembled so, she feared she would fall, and looked around her: for all the world like someone bent on thieving.

She crept quietly towards the bushes.

The nightingale was warbling there in the thickest part.

She must pierce farther in, must quietly put the leaves aside, to see on which branch the bird was singing.

She could not see.

Again she listened: the warbling lured her further.

It must be near to her: it was warbling there, perhaps she could grasp it with her hand.

But as she bent the bough, a fierce figure sprang up before her and grasped the hand she had stretched out.

CHAPTER XXVIII

THE NIGHT-STRUGGLE

The dark figure, which seized Czipra's hand so suddenly, stared with a blood-thirsty grin into his victim's face, whose every limb shuddered with terror at her assailant.

"What do you want?" panted the girl in a choking, scarcely audible voice.

"What do I want?" he hissed in answer. "I want to cut your gander's throat, you goose! Do you want a nightingale?"

Then he whistled a shrill whistle.

His mates leaped out suddenly from their ambush at the sound of the whistle.

At that moment Czipra recovered her self control in sheer despair: she suddenly tore her hand from the robber's grasp, and in three bounds, like a terrified deer, reached the threshold of the door she had left open.

But the wolf had followed in her tracks and reached her at the door. The girl had no time to close it in his face.

"Don't whine!" hissed Kandur, seizing the girl's arm with one hand, with the other attempting to close her mouth.

But terror had made Czipra frantic: tearing down the robber's hand from her mouth, she pushed him back from the door, and with shrill cries awoke the echoes of the night.

"Lorand, help! Robbers!"

"Silence, you dog, or I'll stab you!" thundered the robber, pointing a knife at the girl's breast.

The knife did not frighten Czipra: as she struggled unceasingly and desperately with the robber, she cried "Lorand! Lorand! Murder! Help!"

"Damn you!" exclaimed the robber thrusting his knife into the maiden's bosom.

Czipra suddenly seized the knife with her two hands.

At that moment Lorand appeared beside her.

At the first cry he had rushed from his room and, unarmed, hastened to Czipra's aid.

The girl was still struggling with the robber, holding him back, by sheer force, from entering the door.

Lorand sprang towards her, and dealt the intruder such a blow with his fist in the face, that two of his teeth were broken.

Two shots rang out, followed by a heavy fall and a cry of cursing.

Topándy had fired from the window and one of the four robbers fell on his face mortally wounded, while another, badly hit, floundered and collapsed near the corridor.

The two shots, the noise behind his back, and the unexpected blow confused Kandur; he retreated from the door, leaving his knife in Czipra's hand.

Lorand quickly utilized this opportunity to close the door, fasten the chain, and draw the bolt.

The next moment the robbers' vehement attack could be heard, as they fell upon the door with crowbars.

"Come, let us get away," said Lorand, taking Czipra's hand.

The girl faintly answered.

"Oh! I cannot walk. I am fainting."

Debts of Honor

"Are you wounded?" asked Lorand, alarmed. It was dark, he could not see.

The girl fell against the wall.

Lorand at once took her in his arms and carried her into his room.

The lamp was still burning: he had just finished his letters.

He laid the wounded girl upon his bed.

He was terrified to see her covered with blood.

"Are you badly wounded?"

"Oh, no," said the girl: "see, the knife only went in so deep."

And she displayed the robber's knife, showing on the blade how far it had penetrated.

Lorand clasped his hands in despair.

"Here is a kerchief, press it on the wound to prevent the blood flowing."

"Go, go!" panted the girl. "Look after your own safety. They want to kill you. They want to murder you."

"Aha! let the wretches come! I shall face them without running!" said Lorand, whose only care was for Czipra: he quickly tried to stem the flow of blood from the wound in the girl's breast with a handkerchief. "Lie quiet. Put your head here. Here, here, not so high. Is it very painful?"

On the girl's neck was a chain made of hair: this was in the way, so he wished to tear it off.

"No, no, don't touch it," panted the girl, "that must remain there as long as I live. Go, get a weapon, and defend yourself."

The blows of the crowbars redoubled in force, and the bullets that broke through the closed windows dislodged the plaster from the walls; shot followed shot.

Lorand had no other care than to see if the wounded girl's pillows were well arranged.

"Lorand," said the girl breathlessly. "Leave me. They are numerous. Escape. Put the lamp out, and when everything is dark—then leave me alone."

Certainly it would be good to extinguish the lamp, because the robbers were aiming into that room on account of it.

"Lorand! Where are you? Lorand," Topándy's voice sounded in the corridor.

At that sound Lorand began to realize the danger that threatened the whole household.

"Come and take your gun!" said the old man standing in the doorway. His face was just as contemptuous as ever. There was not the least trace of excitement, fright or anger upon it.

Lorand rose from his kneeling posture beside the bed.

"Don't waste time putting your boots on!" bawled the old fellow. "Our guests are come. We must meet them. Where is Czipra? She can load our weapons while we fire."

"Czipra cannot, for she is wounded."

Topándy then discovered for the first time that Czipra was lying there.

"A shot?" he asked of Lorand.

"A knife thrust."

"Only a knife thrust? That will heal. Czipra can stand that, can't you, my child? We'll soon repay the wretches. Remain here, Czipra, quietly, and don't move. We two will manage it. Bring your weapon and ammunition, Lorand. Bring the lamp out into the corridor. Here they can spy directly upon us. Luckily the brigands are not used to handle guns; they only waste powder."

"But can we leave Czipra here alone?" asked Lorand anxiously.

Czipra clasped her hands and looked at him.

"Go," she panted. "Go away: if you don't I shall get up from here and look out for myself."

"Don't be afraid. They cannot come here," said Topándy; then, lifting the lamp from the table himself, and taking Lorand's hand, he drew him out from the room.

In the corridor they halted to decide on a plan of action.

"The villains are still numerous," said Topándy: "yet I've accounted for two of them already. I have been round the rooms, and see that every exit is barred. They cannot enter, for the doors have been made just for such people, and the windows are protected by bolts and shutters. I have eight charges myself: even if they break in, before anyone can come this far, there will be no one left.—But something else may happen. If the wretches see we are defending ourselves well they will set the house on fire over us and so compel us to rush into the open. Then the advantage is theirs. So your business is to take a double-barrelled gun and ascend to the roof. My butler and the cook have hidden themselves away and I cannot entice them out: if they were here I should send one of them with you."

The robbers were beating the door angrily with their crowbars.

"In a moment!" exclaimed Topándy jokingly.—"The rogues seem to be impatient."

"And what shall I do on the roof?" asked Lorand.

"Wait patiently! I shall tell you in good time. No Turk is chasing you.—You go up and make your exit upon the roof by means of the attic window: then you crawl round on all fours along the gutter, without trying to shoot: leave them to pound upon all four doors. I shall join in the serenade, when necessary. But if you see they are beginning to strike lights and set straw on fire, you must put a stop to it. The gutter will defend you against their fire, they cannot see you, but when they start a blaze, you can accurately aim at each one. That is what I wanted to say."

"Very well," said Lorand, taking his cartridges from his gun-case.

"You'd better use shot instead of bullets," remarked Topándy. "It's easier to hit with shot when one is shooting in the dark, especially in the case of a large company. A little *sang froid*, my boy—you know: all of life is a play."

Lorand grasped the old man's hand and hurried up to the garret.

There in the dark he could only feel his way. For a long time he wandered aimlessly about, striking matches to discover his whereabouts, until he came upon the attic window, which he raised with his head and so came out on the roof.

Then he slid down softly on his stomach as far as the gutter.

Below him the ball was in progress. The thunder of crowbars, the cracking of panels, the strong blows dealt to the tune of oaths; fresh oaths, thunder, pole-axe blows upon the wall. The robbers, unable to break in the doors, were trying to dislodge their posts.

And in the distance no noise, no sign of help. The cowardly neighbors, shutting themselves in, were crouching in their own houses: nor could one blame unarmed men for not coming to the rescue. A gun is a terrible menace.

Silence reigned in the servants' hall. They too dared not come out. Courage is not for poor men.

In the whole courtyard there were but two men who had stout hearts in their bosoms.

The third courageous heart was that of a girl, who lay wounded.

As he thought of this, Lorand became the victim of an excited passion. He felt his head swimming: he felt that he could not remain there, for sooner or later he must leap down.

Leap down!

An idea occurred to him. A difficult feat, but once thought out, it could be accomplished.

He scrambled up the roof again: cut away one of those long dry ropes which in the garrets of many houses stretch from one rafter to another, tied to one end of it the weight of an old clock lying idle in the attic, and returned again to the roof.

Not far from the house there stood an old sycamore tree: one of its spreading branches bent so near to the house that Lorand could certainly reach it by a cast of the rope. The lead-weighted rope, like a lasso, swung over and around the branch and fastened itself on it firmly.

Lorand looped the other end of the rope round a rafter.

Then, throwing his gun over his shoulder, and seizing the rope with both his hands, he leaned his whole weight on it, to see if it would hold.

When he was convinced that the rope would bear his weight, he began to clamber over from the roof to the sycamore tree, suspended in the air, on the slender rope.

Those below could not see him as they were under the verandah, nor could they notice the noise because of their own efforts: the little disturbance caused by the shaking of a branch and the dropping of a figure from the tree was drowned by the shaking of doors, and the discharge of firearms.

Lorand reached the ground without mishap.

The sycamore tree stood at a corner of the castle, about thirty paces from the besieged door.

Lorand could not see the robbers from this position: the northern side of the verandah was overgrown with creepers which covered the windows.

He must get nearer to them.

The bushes under Czipra's window offered him a suitable position, being about ten paces from the door, which was plainly visible from them.

Lorand cocked both triggers, and started alone with one gun against the whole robber-band.

When he reached the bushes he could see the rascals well.

They were four in number.

Two were trying the effect of the "jimmy" on the heavy iron-bound door, while a third, the wounded one, though he could no longer stand, still took part in the siege, notwithstanding his wounds. He put the barrel of his gun into the breaches made and fired over and over, so as to prevent the people inside from defending the door.

Sometimes single shots answered him from within, but without hitting anybody or anything.

The fourth robber, crowbar in hand, was striving to break down the door-supports. That was Vasgyúró.

On the other side of the courtyard Lorand saw two armed figures keeping guard over the servants' hall. It was six to one.

And there were still more than that altogether.

The door was very shaky already: the hinges were breaking. Lorand thought he heard his name called from within.

"Now, all together," thundered the robbers in self-encouragement, exerting all their united force on the crowbars. "More force! More!"

Lorand calmly raised his gun to his shoulder and fired twice among them in quick succession.

No cry of pain followed the two shots—merely the thud of two heavy bodies. They were so thoroughly killed, they had no time to complain.

The one in whose hands the crowbar remained dropped it behind him, as he darted away.

The man who had been previously wounded began to cry for assistance.

"Don't shout," exclaimed the fifth robber. "You'll alarm the others."

Then putting two fingers in his mouth he whistled shrilly twice.

Lorand saw that at this double whistle the two robbers running hastily came in his direction, while the din that arose on the farther side of the castle informed him of an attack from that side too. So he was between three fires.

He did not lose his presence of mind.

Before the new-comers arrived he had just time to load both barrels:—the bushes hid him from anyone who might even stand face to face, so that he could take no sure aim.

Haste, care and courage!

Lorand had often read stories of famous lion-hunters, but had been unable to believe them: unable to imagine how a lonely man in a wild waste, far from every human aid, defended only by a bush, could be courageous enough to cover the oldest male among a group of lions seeking their prey, and at a distance of ten paces fire into his heart. Not to hit his heart meant death to the hunter. But he is sure he will succeed, and sure, too, that the whole group will flee, once his victim has fallen.

What presence of mind was required for that daring deed! What a strong heart, what a cool hand!

Now in this awful moment Lorand knew that all this was possible. A man feels the extent of his manliness, left all to himself in the midst of danger.

He too was hunting, matched against the most dangerous of all beasts of prey—the beasts called "men."

Two he had already laid low. He had found his mark as well as the lion-hunter had found his.

He heard steps of the animals he was hunting approaching his ambuscade on two sides: and the leader of all stood there under cover, leaning against a pillar of the verandah, ready to spring, ten paces away. He had only two charges, with which he had to defend himself against attack from three sides.

Dangerous sport!

One of the robbers who hurried from the servants' hall disappeared among the trees in the garden, while the other remained behind.

Lorand quietly aimed at the first: he had to aim low for fear of firing above him in the dark.

It was well that he had followed his uncle's advice to use shot instead of bullets. The shot lamed both the robber's legs: he fell in his flight and stumbled among the bushes.

The one who followed was alarmed, and standing in the distance fired in Lorand's direction.

Lorand, after his shot, immediately fell on his knees: and it was very lucky he did so, for in the next moment Kandur discharged both his barrels from beside the pillar, and the aim was true, as Lorand discovered from the fact that the bullets dislodged leaves just above his head, that came fluttering down upon him.

Then he turned to the third side.

There had come from that direction at the call of the whistle Korvé, Pofók, and Bogrács, who had been guarding the street-door and the other exit from the castle.

At the moment they turned into the garden their comrade Fosztó, seeing Kanyó fall, stood still and fired his double-barrelled gun and pistols in the direction of Lorand's hiding-place. It was quite natural they should think some aid had arrived from the shooting-box, for the bullets whistled just over their heads: so they began to fire back: Fosztó, alarmed, and not understanding this turn of affairs, fled.

Old Kandur's hoarse voice could not attract their attention amidst the random firing. He cried furiously: "Don't shoot at one another, you asses!"

They did not understand, perhaps did not hear at all in the confusion.

Lorand hastened to enlighten them.

Taking aim at the three villains, who were firing wildly into the night, he sent his second charge into their midst from the bushes, whence they least expected it.

This shot had a final effect. Perhaps several were wounded, one at any rate reeled badly, and the other two took to flight: then, finding their comrade could not keep up with them, they picked him up and dragged him along, disappearing in a moment in the thickest part of the park.

Only the old lion remained behind, alone, old Kandur, the robber, burning with rage. He caught a glimpse of Lorand's face by the flash of the second discharge, recognized in him the man he sought, whom he hated, whose blood he thirsted after: that foe, whom he remembered with curses, whom he had promised to tear to pieces, to torture to death, who was here again in his way, and had with his unaided power broken up the whole opposing army, for all the world like the archangel himself.

Kandur knew well he must not allow him time to load again.

It was not a moment for shooting:—but for a pitched battle, hand to hand.

Nor did the robber load his weapon: he rushed unarmed from his ambuscade as he saw Lorand standing before him, and threw himself in foaming passion upon the youth.

Lorand saw that here, among the bushes, he had no further use for his gun, so he threw it away, and received his foe unarmed.

Now it was face to face!

As they clutched each other their eyes met.

"You devil!" muttered Kandur, gnashing his teeth; "you have stolen my gold, and my girl. Now I shall repay you."

Lorand now knew that the robber was Czipra's father.

He had tried to murder his own daughter.

This idea excited such rage in Lorand's heart that he brought the robber to his knees with one wrench.

But the other was soon on his feet again.

"Oho! You are strong too? You gentlemen live well: you have strength. The ox is also strong, and yet the wolf pulls him down."

And with renewed passion he threw himself on Lorand.

But Lorand did not allow him to come close enough to grasp his wrist. He was a practised wrestler, and was able to keep his opponent an arm's length away.

"So you won't let me come near you? You won't let me kiss you, eh? Won't let me bite out a little piece of your beautiful face?"

The wild creature stretched out his neck in his effort to get at Lorand.

The struggle was desperate. Lorand was aided by the freshness of his youthful strength, his *sang froid*, and practised skill: the robber's strength was redoubled by passion, his muscles were tough, and his attacks impetuous, unexpected, and surprising like those of some savage beast.

Neither uttered a sound. Lorand did not call for help, thinking his cries might bring the robbers back: and Kandur was afraid the house party might come out.

Or perhaps neither thought of any such thing: each was occupied with the idea of overthrowing his opponent with his own hand.

Kandur merely muttered through his teeth, though his passion did not deter his devilish humor. Lorand did not say a single word.

The place was ill-adapted for such a struggle.

Amid the hindering bushes they stumbled hither and thither; they could not move freely, nor could they turn much, each one fearing that to turn would be fatal.

"Come, come away," muttered Kandur, dragging Lorand away from the bushes. "Come onto the grass."

Lorand agreed.

They passed out into the open.

There the robber madly threw himself upon Lorand again.

He tried no more to throw him, but to drag him after him, with all his might.

Lorand did not understand what his foe wished.

Always further, further:—

Lorand twice threw him, but the robber clung to him and scrambled up again, dragging him always further away.

Suddenly Lorand perceived what his opponent's intention was.

A few weeks previously he had told his uncle that a steward's house was required: and Topándy had dug a lime-pit in the garden, where it would not be in the way. Only yesterday they had filled it to the brim with lime.

The robber wished to drag Lorand with him into it.

The young fellow planted his feet firmly and held back with all his might.

Kandur's eyes flashed with the stress of passion, when he saw in his opponent's terrified face that he knew what his intention was.

"Well, how do you like the dance, young gentleman? This will be the wedding-dance now! The bridegroom with the bride—together into the lime-pit. Come, come with me! There in the slacked lime the skin will leave our bodies: I shall put on yours, you mine: how pretty we two shall be!"

Debts of Honor

The robber laughed.

Lorand gathered all his strength to resist the mad attempt.

Kandur suddenly caught Lorand's right arm with both of his, clung to him like a leech, and with a devilish smile said, "Come now, come along!"—and drew Lorand nearer, nearer to the edge of the pit. A couple of blows which Lorand dealt with his disengaged fist upon his skull were unnoticed: it was as hard as iron.

They had reached the edge of the pit.

Then Lorand suddenly put his left arm round the robber's waist, raised him in the air, then screwing him round his right arm, flung him over his head.

This acrobatic feat required such an effort that he himself fell on his back—but it succeeded.

The robber, feeling himself in the air, lost his head, and left hold of Lorand's arm for a moment, with the intention of gripping his hair; in that moment he was thrown off and fell alone into the lime-pit.

Lorand leaped up at once from the ground and, tired out, leaned against the trunk of a tree, searching for his opponent everywhere, and not finding him.

A minute later from amidst the white lime-mud there rose an awful figure which clambered out on the opposite side of the pit, and with a yell of pain rushed away into the courtyard and out into the street.

Lorand, exhausted and half dazed, listened to that beast-like howl gradually diminishing in the distance.

CHAPTER XXIX

THE SPIDER IN THE CORNER

That day about noon the old gypsy woman who told Czipra her fortune had shuffled into Sárvölgyi's courtyard, and finding the master out on the terrace, thanked him that he did not set his dogs upon her—did not tear her to pieces.

"I wish you a very good day, sir, and every blessing that is on earth or in Heaven."

Mistress Borcsa looked out from the kitchen.

"Well, it's just lucky you didn't wish what is in hell! And what is in the water! Gypsy, don't leave us a blessing without fish to go with it, for fish is wanted here twice a week."

"Don't listen to Mistress Boris' jokes."

"Good day, my daughter," said the master gently.

"Well he actually calls the ragged gypsy woman 'my daughter,'" grumbled the old housekeeper. "Blood is thicker than water."

"Well, what have you brought, Marcsa?"

"Csicsa sent to say he will come with his twelve musicians this evening: he begs you to pay him in advance as the musicians must hire a conveyance—then," she continued, dropping her voice to a tone of jesting flattery,—"a little suckling pig for supper, if possible."

"Very well, Marcsa," said Sárvölgyi, with polite gentility. "Everything shall be in order. Come here towards evening. You shall get payment and sucking pig too."

Yet this overflowing magnanimity was not at all in conformity with the well-established habits of the devotee. Close-fisted niggardliness displayed itself in his every feature and warred against this unnatural outbreak.

The gypsy woman kissed his hand and thanked him. But Mistress Boris saw the moment had arrived for a ministerial process against this abuse of royal prerogative; so she came out from the kitchen, a pan in one hand, a cooking-spoon in the other.

She began her invective with the following Magyar *"quousque tandem!"*

"The devil take your insatiable stomachs! When were they ever full? When did I ever hear you say 'I've eaten well, I'm satisfied!' I don't know what has come over the master, that, ever since he became a married man, he has nothing better to do with his income than to stuff gypsies with it!"

"Don't listen to her, Marcsa," said the pious man softly, "that's a way she has. Come this evening, and you shall have your sucking pig."

"Sucking pig!" exclaimed Mistress Boris. "I should like to know where they'll find a sucking pig hereabouts. As if all those the two sows had littered were not already devoured!"

"There is one left," said Sárvölgyi coolly, "one that is continually in the way all over the place."

"Yes, but that one I shall not give," protested Mistress Boris. "I shan't give it up for all the gypsies in the world. My little tame sucking pig which I brought up on milk and breadcrumbs. They shan't touch that. I won't give up that!"

"It is enough if I give it," said Sárvölgyi, harshly.

"What, you will make a present of it? Didn't you present me with it in its young days, when it was the size of a fist? And now you want to take it back?"

"Don't make a noise. I'll give you two of the same size in place of it."

"I don't want any larger one, or any other one: I am no trader. I want my own sucking pig; I won't give it up for a whole herd,—the little one I brought up myself on milk and bread-crumbs! It is so accustomed to me now that it always answers my call, and pulls at my apron: it plays with me. As clever, as a child, for all the world as if it were no pig at all, but a human being."

Mistress Borcsa burst into tears. She always had her pet animals, after the fashion of old servants, who, being on good terms with nobody in the world, tame some hen or other animal set aside for eating purposes, and defend its life cleverly and craftily; not allowing it to be killed; until finally the merciless master passes the sentence that the favorite too must be killed. How they weep then! The poor, old maid-servants cannot touch a morsel of it.

"Stop whining, Borcsa!" roared Sárvölgyi, frowning. "You will do what I order. The pig must be caught and given to Marcsa."

The pig, unsuspicious of danger, was wandering about in the courtyard.

"Well, *I* shall not catch it," whimpered Mistress Boris.

"Marcsa'll do that."

The gypsy woman did not wait to be told a second time: but, at once taking a basket off her arms, squatted down and began to shake the basket, uttering some such enticing words as *"Pocza, poczo, net, net!"*

Nor was Mistress Borcsa idle: as soon as she remarked this device, she commenced the counteracting spell. "Shoo! Shoo!"—and with her pan and cooking-spoon she tried to frighten her *protégé* away from the vicinity of the castle, despite the stamping protests of Sárvölgyi, who saw open rebellion in this disregard for his commands.

Then the two old women commenced to drive the pig up and down the yard, the one enticing, the other "shooing," and creating a delightful uproar.

But, such is the ingratitude of adopted pigs! The foolish animal, instead of listening to its benefactor's words and flying for protection among the beds of spinach, greedily answered to the call of the charmer, and with ears upright trotted towards the basket to discover what might be in it.

The gypsy woman caught its hind legs.

Mistress Borcsa screamed, Marcsa grunted, and the pig squealed loudest of all.

"Kill it at once to stop its cries!" cried Sárvölgyi. "What a horrible noise over a pig!"

"Don't kill it! Don't make it squeal while I am listening," exclaimed Borcsa in a terrified passion: then she ran back into the kitchen, and stopped her ears lest she should hear them killing her favorite pig.

She came out again as soon as the squeals of her *protégé* had ceased, and with uncontrollable fury took up a position before Sárvölgyi. The gypsy woman smilingly pointed to the murdered innocent.

Mistress Borcsa then said in a panting rage to Sárvölgyi:

"Miser who gives one day, and takes back—a curse upon such as you!"

"Zounds! good-for-nothing!" bawled the righteous fellow. "How dare you say such a thing to me?"

"From to-day I am no longer your servant," said the old woman, trembling with passion. "Here is the cooking-spoon, here the pan: cook your own dinner, for your wife knows less about it than you do. My husband lives in the neighboring village: I left him in his young days because he beat me twice a day; now I shall go back to the honest fellow, even if he beat me thrice a day."

Mistress Borcsa was in reality not jesting, and to prove it she at once gathered up her bed, brought out her trunks, piled all her possessions onto a barrow, and wheeled them out without saying so much as "good bye."

Sárvölgyi tried to prevent this wholesale rebellion forcibly by seizing Mistress Borcsa's arm to hold her back.

"You shall remain here: you cannot go away. You are engaged for a whole year. You will not get a kreutzer if you go away."

Debts of Honor

But Mistress Borcsa proved that she was in earnest, as she forcibly tore her arm from Sárvölgyi's grasp.

"I don't want your money," she said, wheeling her barrow further. "What you wish to keep back from my salary may remain for the master's—coffin-nails."

"What, you cursed witch!" exclaimed Sárvölgyi. "What did you dare to say to me?"

Mistress Borcsa was already outside the gate. She thrust her head in again, and said:

"I made a mistake. I ought to have said that the money you keep from me may remain—to buy a rope."

Sárvölgyi, enraged, ran to his room to fetch a stick, but before he came out with it, Mistress Borcsa was already wheeling her vehicle far away on the other side of the street, and it would not have been fitting for a gentleman to scamper after her before the eyes of the whole village, and to commence a combat of doubtful issue in the middle of the street with the irritated Amazon.

The nearest village was not far from Lankadomb; yet before she reached it, Mistress Borcsa's soul was brimming over with wrath.

Every man would consider it beneath his dignity to submit tamely to such a dishonor.

As she reached the village of her birth, she made straight for the courtyard of her former husband's house.

Old Kólya recognized his wife as she came up trundling the squeaking barrow, and wondering thrust his head out at the kitchen door.

"Is that you, Boris?"

"It is: you might see, if you had eyes."

"You've come back?"

Instead of replying Mistress Boris bawled to her husband.

"Take one end of this trunk and help me to drag it in. Take hold now. Do you think I came here to admire your finely curled moustache?"

"Well, why else did you come, Boris?" said the old man very phlegmatically, without so much as taking his hand from behind his back.

"You want to quarrel with me again, I see; well, let's be over with it quickly: take a stick and beat me, then let us talk sense."

At this Kólya took pity on his wife and helped her to drag the trunk in.

"I am no longer such a quarreller, Boris," he answered. "Ever since I became a man with a responsible position I have never annoyed anyone. I am a watchman."

"So much the better: if you are an official, I can at any rate tell you what trouble brought me here."

"So it was only trouble drove you here?"

"Certainly. They robbed and stole from me. They have taken away my yellow-flowered calico kerchief, a red 'Home-sweet-Home' handkerchief, which I had intended for you, a silver-crossed string of beads, twelve dollars, ten gold pieces, twenty-two silver buttons, four pairs of silver buckles, and a scolloped-eared, pi-bald, eight-week-old pig...."

"Whew!" exclaimed Kólya as he heard of so much loss. "This is a pretty business. Well, who stole them?"

"No one else than the cursed gypsy woman Marcsa, who lives here in this village."

"We shall call her to account as soon as she appears."

"Naturally. She went there while I was weeding in the garden; she prowled about and stole."

"Well I'll soon have her by the ears, only let her come here."

Debts of Honor

Not a word of the whole story of the theft was true: but Mistress Boris reasoned as follows:

"You must come here first, gypsy woman, with that scolloped-eared pig: if they find it in your possession, they will put you in jail, and ask you what you did with the rest. Whether your innocence is proved or not, the pig-joint will in the meanwhile become uneatable, and won't come into your stomachs. You may say you got it as a present,—no one will believe you, and the magistrate will not order such a gentleman as Sárvölgyi to come here and witness in your favor."

Kólya allowed himself to be made a participant in his wife's anger, and went at once to inform the servants of the magistrate, who was sitting in the village.

Towards evening Kólya, in ambush at the end of the village, spied the gypsy woman as she came sauntering by Lankadomb, carrying on her arm a large basket as if it were some great weight.

Kólya said nothing to her, he merely let her pass before him, and followed her on the other side of the street, until she reached the middle of the market-place, where many loiterers sauntered and listened to the tales of his wife.

"Halt, Marcsa!" cried Kólya, standing in the gypsy woman's way.

"What do you want?" she asked, shrugging her shoulders.

"What have you in your basket?"

"What should I have? A pig which you shall not taste, is in it."

"Of course. Has not the pig scolloped ears?"

"Suppose it has?"

"You speak lightly. Let me look at the pig."

"Well look—then go blind. Have you never seen such an animal? Have a look at it."

The gypsy woman uncovered the basket, in which lay the unhappy victim, reposing on its stomach, its scolloped ears still standing up straight.

A crowd began to collect round the disputants.

Mistress Boris burst in among them.

"There it is! That was my pig!"

"As much as the shadow of the Turkish Sultan's horse was yours. Off with you: don't look at it so hard, else you will be bewitched by it and your child will be like it."

The loiterers began to laugh at that; they were always ready to laugh at any rough jest.

The laughter enraged Kólya: he seized the much-discussed pig's hind legs and before the gypsy woman could prevent him, had torn it out of the basket.

But the pig was heavier than such animals are wont to be at that age, so that Kólya bumped the noble creature's nose against the ground.

As he did so a dollar rolled out of the pig's mouth.

"Oho!—the thalers are here too!"

At these words the gypsy woman took up her basket and began to run away. When they seized her, she scratched and bit, and tried her best to escape, till finally they bound her hands behind her.

Kólya was beside himself with astonishment.

There was quite a heap of silver money sewn into that pig. Loads of silver.

Mistress Boris herself did not understand it.

This must be reported to the magistrate.

Kólya, accompanied by a large crowd, conducted Marcsa to the magistrate's house, where the clerks, pending that official's arrival, took the accused in charge, and shut her up in a dark cell, which had only one narrow window looking out on the henyard.

When the magistrate returned towards midnight, only the vacant cell was there without the gypsy woman. She had been able to creep out through the narrow opening, and had gone off.

The magistrate, when he saw the *"corpus delicti,"* was himself of the opinion that the pig was in reality Mistress Boris's property, while the money that had been hidden in its inside must have come also from Sárvölgyi's house. There might be some great robbery in progress yonder. He immediately gave orders for three mounted constables to start off for Lankadomb; he ordered a carriage for himself, and a few minutes after the departure of the constables, was on his way in their tracks with his solicitor and servant.

The spider was already sitting in its web.

As night fell, Sárvölgyi hastened the ladies off to bed, for they were going to leave for Pest and so had to wake early.

When all was quiet in the house, he himself went round the yard and locked the doors: then he closed the door of each room separately.

Finally he piled his arms on his table—two guns, two pistols, and a hunting-knife.

He was loath to believe the old gossip. Suppose Kandur should, in the course of his feast of blood be whetted for more slaughter, and wish to slice up betrayer after betrayed?

In the presence of twelve robbers, he could not even trust an ally.

The night watchman had already called "Eleven."

Sárvölgyi was sitting beside his window.

The windows were protected on the street side by iron shutters, with a round slit in the middle, through which one could look out into the street.

Sárvölgyi opened the casements in order to hear better, and awaited the events to which the night should give birth.

It was a still warm evening towards the end of spring.

All nature seemed to sleep; no leaf moved in the warm night air: only at times could be heard a faint sound, as if wood and field had shuddered in their dreams, and a long-drawn sigh had rustled the tops of the poplars, dying away in the reed-forest.

Then, suddenly, the hounds all along the village began to bay and howl.

The bark of a hound is generally a soothing sound; but when the vigilant house-guard has an uneasy feeling, and changes his bark to a long whining howl, it inspires disquietude and anxiety.

Only the spider in the web rejoiced at the sound of danger! They were coming!

The hounds' uproar lasted long: but finally it too ceased; and there followed the dreamy, quiet night, undisturbed by even a breath of wind.

Only the nightingales sang, those sweet fanciful songsters of the night, far and near in the garden bushes.

Sárvölgyi listened long—but not to the nightingale's song. What next would happen?

Then the stillness of the night was broken by an awful cry as when a girl in the depth of night meets her enemy face to face.

A minute later again that cry—still more horrible, more anguished. As if a knife had been thrust into the maiden's breast.

Then two shots resounded:—and a volley of oaths.

All these midnight sounds came from above Topándy's castle.

Then a sound of heavy firing, varied by noisy oaths. The spider in the web started. The web had been disturbed. The stealthy attack had not succeeded.

Yet they were many—they could surely overcome two. The peasants did not dare to aid where bullets whistled.

Then the firing died away: other sounds were heard: blows of crowbars on the heavy door: the thunder of the pole-axe on the stone wall, here and there a single shot, the flash of which could not be seen in the night. Certainly they were firing in at doors and out through windows. That was why no flash could be seen.

But how long it lasted! A whole eternity before they could deal with those two men! From the roots of Sárvölgyi's sparse hair hot beads of sweat were dripping down.

Not in yet? Why cannot they break in the door?

Suddenly the light of two brilliant flashes illuminated the night for a moment: then two deafening reports, that could be produced only by a weapon of heavy calibre. So easy to pick out the dull thunder roar from those other crackling splutterings that followed at once.

What was that? Could they be fighting in the open? Could they have come out into the courtyard? Could they have received aid from some unexpected quarter?

The crack of fire-arms lasted a few minutes longer. Twice again could be heard that particular roar, and then all was quiet again.

Were they done for already?

For a long time no sound, far or near.

Sárvölgyi looked and listened in restless impatience. He wished to pierce the night with his eyes, he wished to hear voices through this numbing stillness. He put his ear to the opening in the iron shutter.

Some one knocked at the shutter from without.

Startled, he looked out.

The old gypsy woman was there: creeping along beside the wall she had come this far unnoticed.

"Sárvölgyi," said the woman in a loud whisper: "Sárvölgyi, do you hear? They have seized the money: the magistrate has it. Take care!"

Then she disappeared as noiselessly as she had come.

In a moment the sweat on Sárvölgyi's body turned to ice. His teeth chattered from fever.

What the gypsy woman had said was, for him, the terror of death.

The most evident proof was in the hands of the law: before the awful deed had been accomplished, the hand that directed it had been betrayed.

And perhaps the terrible butchery was now in its last stage. They were torturing the victims! Pouring upon them the hellish vengeance of wounded wild beasts! Tearing them limb from limb! Looking with their hands that dripped with blood among the documents for the letter with five seals.

Already all was betrayed! Fever shook his every limb. Why that great stillness outside? What secret could this monstrous night hide that it kept such silence as this?

Suddenly the silence was broken by a wild creature's howl.

No it was no animal. Only a man could howl so, when agony had changed him to a mad beast, who in the fury of his pain had forgotten human voice.

The noise sounded first in the distance, beyond the garden of the castle, but presently approached, and a figure of horror ran howling down the street.

A figure of horror indeed!

A man, white from head to foot.

All his clothes, every finger of his hand, was white: every hair of his head, his beard, moustache, his whole face was white, glistening, shining white, and as he ran he left white footsteps behind him.

Was it a spirit?

The horror rushed up to Sárvölgyi's door, rattling the latch and in a voice of raving anger began to howl as he shook the door.

"Let me in! Let me in! I am dying!"

Sárvölgyi's face, in his agony of terror, became like that of a damned soul.

That was Kandur's voice! That was Kandur's figure. But so white!

Perhaps the naked soul of one on the way to hell?

The horrible figure thundered continuously at the door and cried:

"Let me in! Give me to drink! I am burning! Bathe me in oil! Help me to undress! I am dying! I am in hell! Help! Drag me out of it!"

All through the street they could hear his cries.

Then the damned soul began to curse, and beat the door with his fist, because they would not open to him.

"A plague upon you, cursed accomplice. You shut me out and won't let me in? Thrust me into the tanpit of hell and leave me there? My skin is peeling off! I am going blind! An ulcer upon your soul!"

The writhing figure tore off his clothes, which burned his limbs like a shirt of Nessus, and while so doing the hidden silver coins he had received from Sárvölgyi fell to the ground.

"Devil take you, money and all!" he shouted, dashing the coins against the door. "Here's your cursed money! Pick it up!"

Then he staggered on, leaning against the railing and howling in pain:

"Help! Help! A fortune for a glass of water! Only let me live until I can drag that fellow with me! Help, man, help!"

A deathly numbness possessed Sárvölgyi. If that figure of horror were no "spirit," he must hasten to make him so. He would betray all. That was the greatest danger. He must not live.

He could not see him from the window. Perhaps if he opened the shutters, he could fire at him. He was a highwayman: who could call Sárvölgyi to account for shooting him? He had done it in self-defence.

If only his hands would not tremble so! It was impossible to hit him with a pistol except by placing the barrel to his forehead.

Should he go out to him?

Who would dare to go out to meet that demon face to face? Could the spider leave its web?

While he hesitated, while he struggled to measure the distance from door to window and back, a new sound was heard in the street: — three horsemen came trotting up from the end of the village, and in them Sárvölgyi recognized, from their uniforms, the country police.

Then the bell began to ring, and the peasants came out of their doors, armed with pitchforks and clubs: noisy crowds collected. In their midst were one or two bound figures whom they drove forward with blows: they had seized the robbers.

The battle was irremediably lost. The chief criminal saw the toils closing in on him but had no time to make his escape.

CHAPTER XXX

I BELIEVE....!

Day was dawning.

Topándy had not left Czipra since she had been wounded. He sat alone beside her bed.

Servants and domestics had other things to do now: they were standing before the magistrate, face to face with the captured robbers. The magisterial inquiry demanded the presence of them all.

Topándy was alone with the wounded girl.

"Where is Lorand?" whispered Czipra.

"He drove over to the neighboring village to bring a doctor for you."

"No harm has come to him?"

"You might have heard his voice through the window, when all was over. He could not come in, because the door was closed. His first care was to bring a surgeon for you."

The girl sighed.

"If he comes too late...."

"Don't fret about that. Your wound is not fatal; only be calm."

"I know better," said the girl in a flush of fever. "I feel that I shall not live."

"Don't worry, Czipra, you will get better," said Topándy, taking the girl's hand.

And then the girl locked her five fingers in those of Topándy, so that they were clasped like two hands in prayer.

"Sir, I know I am standing on the brink of the grave. I have now grasped your hand. I have clasped it, as people at prayer are wont to clasp their hands. Can you let me go down to the grave without teaching me one prayer. This night the murderer's knife has pierced my heart to liberate yours. Does not my heart deserve the accomplishment of its last wish? Does not that God, who this night has liberated us both, me from life, you from death, deserve our thanks?"

Topándy was moved. He said:

"Repeat after me."

And he said to her the Lord's Prayer.

The girl devoutly and between gasps repeated it after him.

How beautiful it is! What great words those are!

First she repeated it after him, then again said it over, sentence by sentence, asking "what does this or that phrase mean?" "Why do we say 'our Father?' What is meant by 'Thy Kingdom?' Will he forgive us our trespasses, if we forgive them that trespass against us? Will he deliver us from every evil? What power there is in that 'Amen!'"— Then a third time she repeated it alone before Topándy, without a single omission.

"Now I feel easier," she said, her face beaming with happiness.

The atheist turned aside and wept.

The shutters let in the rays of the sun through the holes the bullets had made.

"Is that sunset?" whispered the girl.

"No, my child, it is sunrise."

"I thought it was evening already."

Topándy opened one shutter that Czipra might see the morning light of the sun.

Then he returned to the sick girl, whose face burned with fever.

"Lorand will be here immediately," he assured her gently.

"I shall soon be far away," sighed the girl with burning lips.

It seemed so long till Lorand returned!

The girl asked no more questions about him: but she was alert at the opening of every door or rattling of carriages in the street, and each time became utterly despondent, when it was not he after all.

How late he was!

Yet Lorand had come as quickly as four fleet-footed steeds could gallop.

Fever made the girl's imagination more irritable.

"If some misfortune should befall him on the way? If he should meet the defeated robbers? If he should be upset on one of the rickety bridges?"

Pictures of horror followed each other in quick succession in her feverish brain. She trembled for Lorand.

Then it occurred to her that he could defend himself against terrors. Why, he knew how to pray.

She clasped her hands across her breast and closed her eyes.

As she said "Amen" to herself she heard the rattling of wheels in the courtyard, and then the well-known steps approaching along the corridor.

What a relief that was!

She felt that her prayer had been heard. How happy are those who believe in it!

The door opened and the youth she worshipped stepped in, hastening to her bed and taking her hand.

"You see, I was lucky: I found him on the road. That is a good sign."

Czipra smiled.

Her eyes seemed to ask him, "Nothing has happened to you?"

The surgeon examined the wound, bandaged it and told the girl to be quiet, not to move or talk much.

"Is there any hope?" asked Lorand in a whisper.

"God and nature may help."

The doctor had to leave to look after the wounded robbers. Lorand and his uncle remained beside Czipra.

Lorand sat on the side of her bed and held her hand in his. The doctor had brought some cooling draught for her, which he gave the sufferer himself.

How Czipra blessed the knife that had given her that wound!

She alone knew how far it had penetrated.

The others thought such a narrow little wound was not enough to cut a life in two.

Topándy was writing a letter on Lorand's writing-table: and when asked "to whom?" he said "To the priest."

Yet he was not wont to correspond with such.

Czipra thought this too was all on her account.

Why, she had not yet been christened.

What a mysterious house it was, the door of which was now to open before her!

Perhaps a whole palace, in the brilliant rooms of which the eye was blinded, as it looked down them?

Soon steps were heard again outside. Perhaps the clergyman was coming.

She was mistaken.

In the new-comer she recognized a figure she had seen long before—Mr. Buczkay, the lawyer.

Despite the customary roundness of that official's face, there were traces of pity on it, pity for the young girl, victim of so dreadful a crime.

He called Topándy aside and began to whisper to him.

Czipra could not hear what they were saying: but a look which the two men cast in her direction, betrayed to her the subject of their discourse.

The judges were here and were putting the law into force upon the guilty.—They were examining into the events, from beginning to end.—They must know all.—They had taken the depositions of the others already: now it was her turn.—They would come with their documents, and ask her "Where did you walk? Why did you leave your room at night? Why did you open the house-door? Whom were you looking for outside in the garden?"

What could she answer to those terrible questions?

Should she burden her conscience with lies, before the eyes of God whom she would call as a witness from Heaven, and to whom she would raise her supplicating hands for pity, when the day of reckoning came?

Or should she confess all?

Should she tell how she had loved him: how mad she was: how she started in search of a charm, with which she wished to overcome the heart of her darling?

She could not confess that! Rather the last drop of blood from her heart, than that secret.

Or should she maintain an obdurate silence? That, however, would create suspicion that she, the robber's daughter, had opened the door for her robber father, and had plotted with workers of wickedness.

What a desperate situation!

And then again it occurred to her that she too could defend herself against terrors: she knew now how to pray. So she took refuge in the sanctuary of the Great Lord, and, embracing the pillars of his throne, prayed, and prayed, and prayed.

Scarce a quarter of an hour after the lawyer's departure, some one else came.

It was Michael Daruszegi, the magistrate.

The girl trembled as she saw him. The confessor had come!

Topándy sprang up from his seat and went to meet him.

Czipra plainly heard what he said in a subdued voice.

"The doctor has forbidden her to speak: in her present condition you cannot cross-question her."

Czipra breathed freely again. He was defending her!

"In any case I can answer for her, for I was present from the very beginning," said Lorand to the magistrate. "Czipra heard the noise in the garden, and was daring enough, as was her wont, to go out and see what was the matter. At the door she met the robber face to face: she barred his way, and immediately cried out for me: then she struggled with him until I came to her help."

How pleased Czipra was at that explanation, all the more because she saw by Lorand's face that he really believed it.

"I have no more questions to ask the young lady," said Daruszegi. "This matter is really over in any case."

"Over?" asked Topándy astonished.

"Yes, over: explained, judged, and executed."

"How?"

"The robber chief, Kandur, before he died in agony, made such serious and perfectly consistent confessions as, combined with other circumstances, compromised your neighbor in the greatest measure."

"Sárvölgyi?" inquired Topándy with glistening eyes.

"Yes.—So far indeed that I was compelled to extend the magisterial inquiry to his person too. I started with my colleague to find him. We found the two ladies in a state of the greatest consternation. They came before us, and expressed their deep anxiety at not finding Sárvölgyi anywhere in the house: they had discovered his room open and unoccupied. His bedroom we did indeed find empty, his weapons were laid out on the table, the key of his money-chest was left in it, and the door of the room open.—What could have become of him?—We wanted to enter the door of the dining-room opposite. It was locked. The ladies declared that room was generally locked. The key was inside in the lock. That room has two other doors, one opening on to the kitchen, one on to the verandah. We looked at them too. In both cases the key was inside, in the lock. Some one must be in the room! I called upon the person within, in the name of the law to open the door to us. No answer came. I repeated the command, but the door was not opened: so I was compelled to have it finally broken open by force; and when the sunlight burst through into the dark room, what horrible sight do you think met our startled gaze? The lord of the house was hanging there above the table in the place of the chandelier: the chair under his feet that he had kicked away proved that he had taken his own life...."

Topándy at these words raised his hands in ecstasy above his head.

"There is a God of justice in Heaven! He has smitten him with his own hand."

Then he clasped his hands together with emotion and slipped towards the head of Czipra's bed.

"Come, my child, say: 'I believe in God'—I shall say it first."

The doctor had not forbidden that.

Czipra devoutly waited for the words of wonder.

What a great, what a comforting world of thoughts.

A God who is a Father, a mother who is a maiden. A God who will be man for man's sake, and who suffered at man's hands, who died and rose again promises true justice, forgiveness for sins, resurrection, life eternal!

"What is that life eternal?"

If only some one could have answered!

The atheist was kneeling down beside the girl's bed when the priest arrived.

He did not rise, was not embarrassed at his presence.

"See, reverend sir, here is a neophyte, waiting for the baptismal water: I have just taught her the 'credo.'"

The girl gave him a look full of gratitude. What happiness glittered in those eyes of ecstasy!

"Who will be the god-parents?" asked the clergyman.

"One, the magistrate,—if he will be so kind: the other, I."

Czipra looked appealingly, first at Topándy, then at Lorand.

Topándy understood the unspoken question.

"Lorand cannot be. In a few minutes you shall know why."

The minister performed the ceremony with that briefness which consideration for a wounded person required.

When it was over, Topándy shook hands with the minister.

"If my hand has sinned at times against yours, I now ask your pardon."

"The debt has been paid by that clasp of your hand," said the priest.

"Your hand must now pronounce a blessing on us."

"Willingly."

"I do not ask it for myself: I await my punishment: I am going before my judge and shall not murmur against him. I want the blessing for those whom I love. This young fellow yesterday asked of me this maiden's hand. They have long loved each other, and deserve each other's love:—give them the blessing of faith, father. Do you agree, Czipra?"

The poor girl covered her burning face with her two hands, and, when Lorand stepped towards her and took her hand, began to sob violently.

"Don't you love me? Will you not be my wife?"

Czipra turned her head on one side.

"Ah, you are merely jesting with me. You want to tease, to ridicule a wretched creature who is nothing but a gypsy girl."

Lorand drew the girl's hand to his heart when she accused him of jesting with her. Something within told him the girl had a right to believe that, and the thought wrung his heart.

"How could you misunderstand me? Do you think I would play a jest upon you—and now?"

Topándy interrupted kindly.

"How could I jest with God now, when I am preparing to enter his presence?"

"How could I jest with your heart?" said Lorand.

"And with a dying girl," panted Czipra.

"No, no, you will not die, you will get well again, and we shall be happy."

"You say that now when I am dying," said the girl with sad reproach. "You tell me the whole beautiful world is thine, now, when of that world I shall have nothing but the clod of earth, which you will throw upon me."

"No, my child," said Topándy, "Lorand asked your hand of me yesterday evening, and was only awaiting his mother's approval to tell you yourself his feelings towards you."

A quick flash of joy darted over the girl's face, and then it darkened again.

"Why, I know," she said brushing aside her tangled curls from her face, "I know your intentions are good. You are doing with me what people do with sick children. 'Get well! We'll buy you beautiful clothes, golden toys, we'll take you to places of amusement, for journeys—we shall be good-humored—will never annoy you:—only get well.' You want to give the poor girl pleasure, to make her better, I thank you for that too."

"You will not believe me," said Lorand, "but you will believe the minister's word. See last night I wrote a letter to mother about you: it lies sealed on my writing-table. Reverend sir, be so kind as to open and read it before her. She will believe you if you tell her we are not cajoling her."

The minister opened the letter, while Czipra, holding Lorand's hand, listened with rapt attention to the words that were read:

"My Dear Mother:

"After the many sorrows and pains I have continuously caused throughout my life to the tenderest of mothers' hearts, to-day I can send you news of joy.

"I am about to marry.

"I am taking to wife one who has loved me as a poor, nameless, homeless youth, for myself alone, and whom I love for her faithful heart, her soul pure as tried gold, still better than she loves me.

"My darling has neither rank nor wealth: her parents were gypsies.

"I shall not laud her to you in poetic phrases: these I do not understand. I can only feel, but not express my feelings.

Debts of Honor

"No other letter of recommendation can be required of you, save that I love her.

"Our love has hitherto only caused both of us pain: now I desire happiness for both of us.

"Your blessing will make the cup of this happiness full.

"You are good. You love me, you rejoice in my joy.

"You know me. You know what lessons life has taught me.

"You know that Fate always ordained wisely and providentially for me.

"No miracle is needed to make you, my mother, the best of mothers, who love me so, and are calm and peaceful in God, clasp together those hands of blessing which from my earliest days you have never taken off my head.

"Include in your prayer, beside my name, the name of my faithful darling, Czipra, too.

"I believe in your blessing as in every word of my religion, as in the forgiveness of sins, as in the world to come.

"But if you are not what God made you,—quiet and loving, a mother always ready to give her blessing with the halo of eternal love round your brow,—if you are cold, quick to anger, a woman of vengeance, proud of the coronet of a family blazon, one who wishes herself to rule Fate, and if the curses of such a merciless lady burden the girl whom I love, then so much the worse, I shall take her to wife with her dowry of curses—for I love her.

"... God intercede between our hearts.

"Your loving son,

"Lorand."

As the minister read, Czipra at each sentence pressed Lorand's hand closer to her heart. She could neither speak nor weep: it was more than her spirit could bear. Every line, every phrase opened a Paradise before her, full of gladness of the other world: her soul's idol loved her: loved her for love's sake: loved her for herself: loved her because she made him happy: raised her to his own level: was not ashamed of her wretched origin: could understand a heart's sensitiveness: commended her name to his mother's prayers: and was ready to maintain his love amidst his mother's curses.

A heart cannot bear such glory!

She did not care about anything now: about her wound: about life, or death: she felt only that glow of health which coursed through every sinew of her body and possessed every thought of her soul.

"I believe!" she said in rapture, rising where she lay: and in those words was everything: everything in which people are wont to believe, from the love of God to the love of man.

She did not care about anything now. She had no thought for men's eyes or men's words: but, as she uttered these words, she fell suddenly on Lorand's neck, drew him with the force of delight to her heart, and covered him with her kisses.

The wound reopened in her breast, and as the girl's kisses covered the face of the man she loved, her blood covered his bosom.

Each time her impassioned lips kissed him, a fresh gush of blood spurted from that faithful heart, which had always been filled with thoughts of him only, which had beat only for him, which had, to save him, received the murderer's knife:—the poor "green-robed" faithful girl.

And as she pressed her last kiss upon the lips of her darling, ... she knew already what was the meaning of eternity....

CHAPTER XXXI

THE BRIDAL FEAST

"Poor Czipra! I thought you would bury us all, and now it is I that must give you that one clod of earth the only gift you asked from the whole beautiful world."

Topándy himself saw after the sad arrangements.

Lorand could not speak: he was beside himself with grief.

He merely said he would like to have his darling embalmed and to take her to his family property, there to bury her.

This wish of his must be fulfilled.

It would be a sad surprise for his mother, to whom Topándy only the day before had written that her son was bringing home a new daughter-in-law.

When Lorand had asked Topándy for Czipra's hand, he immediately wrote to Mrs. Áronffy, thinking that what Lorand himself wrote to his mother would be in a proud strain. He anticipated his nephew's letter, told his mother quietly and restrainedly in order that Lorand's letter might be no surprise to her.

Now he must write again to her, telling that the bride was coming, and the family vault must be ready for her reception.

And curiously Topándy felt no pain in his heart as he thought over it.

"Death is after all the best solution of life!"

He did not shed a single tear upon the letter he wrote: he sealed it and looked for a servant to despatch it.

But other thoughts occupied him.

He sought the magistrate.

"My dear sir, when do you want to lock me up?"

"When you like, sir."

"Would you not take me to gaol immediately?"

"With pleasure, sir."

"How many years have they given me?"

"Only two."

"I expected more. Well, then I can take this letter myself into the town."

"Will Mr. Áronffy remain here?"

"No. He will take his dead love home to the country. I have asked the doctor to embalm her, and I have a lead casket which I prepared for myself with the intention of continuing my opposition to the ordinance of God within it: now I have no need of it. I will lend it to Czipra. That is her dowry."

An hour later he went in search of Lorand, who was still guarding his dead darling. The magistrate was there too.

"My dear sir," he said to the officer. "I am not going to the gaol now."

"Not yet?" inquired Daruszegi. "Very well."

"Not now, nor at any other time. A greater master has given me orders—in a different direction."

They began to look at him in astonishment.

His face was much paler than usual: but still that good-humored irony and light-hearted smile was there.

"Lorand, my boy, there will be two funerals here."

"Who is the second dead person?" asked Daruszegi.

"I am."

Then he drew from his breast his left hand which he had hitherto held thrust in his coat.

"An hour ago I wrote a letter to your mother. As I was sealing it the hot wax dripped onto my nail, and see how my hand has blackened since."

The tips of his left hand were blue and swollen.

"The doctor, quickly," cried Daruszegi to his servant.

"Never mind. It is already unnecessary," said Topándy, falling languidly into an arm-chair. "In two hours it is over. I cannot live more than two hours. In twenty minutes this swelling will reach my shoulder, and the way from thence to the heart is short."

The doctor, who hastened to appear, confirmed Topándy's opinion.

"There is nothing to be done," he said.

Lorand, horror-stricken, hastened to take care of his uncle: the old fellow embraced the neck of the youth kneeling beside him.

"You philosopher, you were right after all, you see. There is One who takes thought for two-legged featherless animals too. If I had known,—'Knock and it shall be opened unto you:' I should long have knocked at the door and cried, 'O Lord, let me in!'"

Topándy would not allow himself to be undressed and put to bed.

"Draw my chair beside Czipra. Let me learn from her how a dead man must behave. My death will not be so fine as hers: I shall not breathe my soul into the soul of my loved one: yet I shall be a gay travelling-companion."

Pain interrupted his words.

When it ceased, he laughed at himself.

"How a foolish mass of flesh protests! It will not allow itself to be overlorded. Yet we were only guests here! 'Animula, vagula, blandula. Hospes comesque corporis. Quae nunc adibis loca? Frigidula, palidula, undula! Nec, ut soles, dabis jocos.' Certainly you will be 'extra *dominium'* immediately. And my lord Stomach, his Grace, and my lord Heart, his Excellency, and my lord Head, his Royal Highness all must resign office."

The doctor declared he must be suffering terrible agony all the time he was jesting and laughing; and he laughed when other people would have gnashed their teeth and cried aloud.

"We have disputed often, Lorand," said the old man, always in a fainter voice, "about that German savant who asserted that the inhabitants of other planets are much nobler men than we here on earth. If he asks what has become of me, tell him I have advanced. I have gone to a planet where there are no peasants: barons clean earls' boots. Don't laugh at me, I beg, if I am talking foolishly.—But death dictates very curious verses."

The hand-grasp with which he greeted Lorand, proved that it was his last.

After that his hand drooped, his eyes languished, his face became ever more and more yellow.

Once again he raised his eyes.

They met Lorand's gaze.

He wished to smile: in a whisper, straining desperately he said:

"Immediately now ... I shall know—what is—in the foggy spots of the Northern Dog-star:—and in the eyeless worm's——entrails."

Then, suddenly, with a forced final spasmodic effort, he seized the arms of his chair, and rose, lifted up his right arm, and turned to the magistrate.

"Sir," he cried in a strong full-toned voice, "I have appealed."

He fell back in the arm-chair.

Some minutes later every wrinkle disappeared from his face, it became as smooth as marble, and calm, as those of dead persons are wont to be.

Lorand was standing there with clasped hands between his two dear dead ones.

On the morrow at dawn Lorand rose for his journey and stepped into the cart with a closed lead coffin. So he took home his dead bride.

The second letter which Topándy had written to his mother, the sealing of which had sealed his own fate, had not been posted, and could not have prepared them for his coming.

At home they had received only the first letter.

When that letter of good tidings arrived it caused feelings of intoxicated delight and triumph throughout the whole house.

After all they loved him still best of all. He was the favorite child of his mother and grandmother. No word of Desiderius is required for his heart was already united to his darling: and good Fanny was doubly happy in the idea that she would not be the only happy woman in the house.

With what joy they awaited him!

Could he ever have doubted that the one he loved would be loved by all?—no need to speak of her virtues: everybody knew them: all he need say was "I love her."

It was certainly very well he did not send his mother that letter, in which he had written of Czipra and requested his mother's blessing:—well that he had not wounded the dearest mother's heart with those final words—"but if you curse her whom I love—"

Curse her whom he loves!

Why should they do so? That letter brought a holiday to the house. They arranged the country dwelling afresh: Desiderius took up his residence in the town, handing over to his elder brother his birthright.

The eldest lady put off her mourning. Lorand's bride must not see anything that could recall sad thoughts. Everything sad was buried under the earth.

Desiderius could relate so much that was pleasant of the gypsy girl: Lorand's letters during the past ten years of silence always spoke of the poor despised diamond, whose faithful attachment had been the sunny side of Lorand's life. They read the bundles of letters again and again: it was a study for the two mothers. Where Lorand had been giving merely a passing hint, they could make great explanations, all pointing to Czipra.

Providence had ordered it so!

After the first meeting in the inn, it had all been ordained that Lorand should save Czipra from the murderer's knife, in order to be happy with her later.

... Why the gypsy girl was happy already.

Topándy's letter informed them that, immediately after the despatch of the letter, Lorand would wed Czipra, and they would come home together to the house of his parents.

So the day was known, they might even reckon the hour when they would arrive.

Desiderius remained in town to await Lorand. He promised to bring them out, however late they came, even in the night.

The ladies waited up until midnight. They waited outside under the verandah. It was a beautiful warm moonlit night.

The good grandmother, embracing Fanny's shoulder, related to her how many, many years ago they had waited one night for the two brothers to come, but that was a very awful night, and the waiting was very sorrowful. The wind howled among the acacias, clouds chased each other across the sky, hounds howled in the village, a hay-wain rattled in at the gate—and in it was hidden the coffin.— And the populace was very suspicious: they thought the ice would break its bounds, if a dead man were taken over it.

But now it was quite a different world. The air was still, not a breath of air: man and beast sleeps, only those are awake who await a bride.

How different the weather!

Then, all at once, a wain had stood at the gate: the servants hastened to open it.

A hay-wain now rattled in at the gate, as it did then.

And after the wain, on foot, the two brothers, hand in hand.

The women rushed to meet them, Lorand was the first whom everyone embraced and kissed.

"And your wife?" asked every lip.

Lorand pointed speechlessly to the wain, and could not tell them.

Desiderius answered in his place.

"We have brought his wife here in her coffin."

CHAPTER XXXII

WHEN WE HAD GROWN OLD

Seventeen years have passed since Lorand returned home again.

What old people we have become since then!

Besides, seventeen years is a long time:—and seventeen heavy years!

I have rarely seen people grow old so slowly as did our contemporaries.

We live in a time when we sigh with relief as each day passes by—only because it is now over! And we will not believe that what comes after it will bring still worse days.

We descend continuously further and further down, in faith, in hope, in charity towards one another: our wealth is dissipated, our spirits languish, our strength decays, our united life falls into disunion: it is not indifference, but "ennui" with which we look at the events of the days.

One year to the day, after poor Czipra's death Lorand went with his musket on his shoulder to a certain entertainment where death may be had for the asking.

I shall not recall the fame of those who are gone—why should I? Very few know of it.

Lorand was a good soldier.

That he would have been in any case, he had naturally every attribute required for it: heroic courage, athletic strength, hot blood, a soul that never shrank. War would in any case have been a delight for him:—and in his present state of mind!

Broken-hearted and crushed, his first love contemptuously trampling him in the dust, his second murdered in the fervor of her passion, his soul weighed with the load of melancholia, and that grievous fate which bore down and overshadowed his family:

always haunted by that terrible foreboding that, sooner or later, he must still find his way to that eighth resting-place, that empty niche.

When the wars began his lustreless spirit burst into brilliance. When he put on his uniform, he came to me, and, grasping my hand, said with flashing eyes:

"I am bargaining in the market where a man may barter his worn-out life at a profit of a hundred per cent."

Yet he did not barter his.

Rumor talked of his boldness, people sang of his heroic deeds, he received fame and wreaths, only he could not find what he sought: a glorious death.

Of the regiment which he joined, in the end only a tenth part remained. He was among those who were not even wounded.

Yet how many bullets had swept over his head!

How he looked for those whistling heralds of death, how he waited for the approach of those whirring missiles to whom the transportation of a man to another world in a moment is nothing! They knew him well already and did not annoy him.

These buzzing bees of the battlefield, like the real bees, whir past the ear of him who walks undaunted among them, and sting him who fears them.

Once a bullet pierced his helmet.

How often I heard him say:

"Why not an inch lower?"

Finally, in one battle a piece of an exploded shell maimed his arm, and when he fell from his horse, disabled by a sword-cut, a Cossack pierced him through with his lance.

Yet even that did not kill him.

Debts of Honor

For weeks he lay unconscious in the public hospital, under a tent, until I came to fetch him home. Fanny nursed him. He recovered.

When he was better again, the war was over.

How many times I heard him say:

"What bad people you are, for loving me so! What a bad turn you did me, when you brought me away from the scene of battle, brother! How merciless you were Fanny, to watch beside me! What a vain task it was on your part to keep me alive! How angry I am with you: what detestable people you are!—just for loving me so!"

Yet we still loved him.

And then we grew old peacefully.

We buried kind grandmother, and then dear mother too: we remained alone together, and never parted.

Lorand always lived with us: as long as we lived in town he did not leave the house sometimes for weeks together.

The new order of things compelled me to give up the career which father had held to be the most brilliant aim of life. I threw over my yearning for diplomacy, and went to the plough.

I became a good husbandman.

I am that still.

Then too Lorand remained with us.

His was no longer a life, merely a counting of days.

It was piteous to know it and to see him.

A strapping figure, whose calling was to be a hero!

A warm heart, that might have been a paradise on earth to some woman!

A refined, fiery temperament that might have been the leading spirit of some country.

Debts of Honor

Who quietly without love or happiness, faded leaf by leaf and did not await anything from the morrow.

Yet he feared the coming days.

Often he chided me for wanting to brick up the door of that lonely building there beside the brook.

Lest my children should ask, "what can dwell within it?" Lest they try to discover the meaning of that hidden inscription as I had tried in my childish days.

Lorand did not agree with the idea.

"There is still one lodging vacant in it."

And that was a horror to us all.

To him, to us too.

Every evening we parted as if saying a last adieu.

Nothing in life gave him pleasure. He took part in nothing which interested other men. He did not play cards, or drink wine: he was ever sober and of unchanging mood. He read nothing but mathematical books. I could never persuade him to take a newspaper in his hand.

"The whole history of the world is one lie."

Every day, winter and summer, early in the morning, before anyone had risen, he walked out to the cemetery, to where Czipra lay "under the perfumed herb-roots:" spent some minutes there and then returned, bringing in summer a blade of living grass, in winter of dried grass from her grave.

He had a diary, in which nought was written, except the date: and pinned underneath, in place of writing, was the dry blade of grass.

The history of a life contained in thousands of grass-blades, each blade representing a day.

Could there be a sadder book?

The only things that interested him, were fruit trees and bees.

Animals and plants do not deceive him who loves them.

The whole day long he guarded his trees and his saplings, and waged war against the insects: and all day long he learned the philosophy of life from those grand constitutional monarchists, the bees.

There are many men, particularly to-day, in our country, who know how to kill time: Lorand merely struggled with time, and every day as it passed was a defeat for him.

He never went shooting, he said it was not good for him to take a loaded gun in his hand.

At night one of my children always slept in his room.

"I am afraid of myself," he confessed to me.

He was afraid of himself and of that quiet house, down there beside the brook.

"I would love to sleep there under the perfumed herb-roots."

A life wasted!

One beautiful summer afternoon my little son rushed to me with the news that his uncle Lorand was lying on the floor in the middle of the room, and would not rise.

With the worst suspicions, I hastened to his side.

When I entered his room, he was lying, not on the floor, but on the bed.

He lay face downward on the bed.

"What is the matter?" I asked, taking his hand.

"Nothing at all:—only I am dying slowly."

"Great heavens! What have you done?"

"Don't be alarmed. It was not my hand."

"Then what is the matter?"

"A bee-sting. Laugh at me—I shall die from it."

In the morning he had said that robber bees had attacked his hives, and he was going to destroy them. A strange bee had stung him on the temple.

"But not there ... not there ..." he panted, breathing feverishly: "not into the eighth resting-place—out yonder under the perfumed herb-roots. There let us lie in the dust one beside the other. Brick up that door. Good night."

Then he closed his eyes and never opened them again.

Before I could call Fanny to his side he was dead.

The valiant hero who had struggled single-handed against whole troops, the man of iron whom neither the sword nor the lance could kill, in ten minutes perished from the prick of a tiny little insect.

God moves among us!

When the last moment of temptation had come, when weariness of life was about to arm his hand with the curse of his forefathers, He had sent the very tiniest of his flying minions, and had carried him up on the wings of a bee to the place where the happy ones dwell.

And we are still growing older: who knows how long it will last?

FINIS

Lightning Source UK Ltd.
Milton Keynes UK
UKHW010818210223
417383UK00001B/41